2084

a novel

2084

a novel

Chris Durer

www.ivyhousebooks.com

PUBLISHED BY IVY HOUSE PUBLISHING GROUP
5122 Bur Oak Circle, Raleigh, NC 27612
United States of America
919-782-0281
www.ivyhousebooks.com

ISBN: 1-57197-471-7
Library of Congress Control Number: 2006929915

Printed in the United States of America

For Jennifer and Andrew

book
one

Chapter 1

Fun and Games

Siegfried La Rochelle's heart beat faster and faster upon hearing faint footsteps on the floor above, and he at once flattened himself against the heavy curtains obscuring the etageres filled with priceless statuettes of the gods and heroes of medieval Japan. Was it the guards, the devoted safety-keepers of the imperial household, or handpicked equerries protecting the honor and virtue of Princess Sayko? He could not tell. But the faint sound ceased as abruptly as it had become audible, and now all was reassuringly quiet in the residential quarters at the imperial palace in Tokyo, occupied by the sovereign's grandchildren. Siegfried advanced several steps, doing his best to make very little or no noise at all and aiming at Sayko's bedroom, fourth door to the right. He was about to turn the doorknob when a scantily dressed figure flashed by him, halted in her tracks, turned round, and stuck out her tongue at him.

"You're late, Siegie. I've been waiting for ages . . . heartless you . . . and me pining away. Shame on you!"

Her reproaches, carefully nurtured, strove for the highest histrionic effect, and he placed a finger across her lips. Once inside the bedroom he spoke gently and patiently. "Sayko, we said midnight, and it's barely quarter to. I'm not late."

"Liar!" she cried. "Liar, we agreed on eleven, not midnight. You're totally wrong, and I'm totally right, as I usually am." She again stuck out her tongue.

"If you say so," he whispered lovingly, "if you say so." He put his arms around her.

Much later into the night, her chin resting comfortably on his hairy chest, she began mercilessly firing questions at him, demanding prompt and exhaustive answers.

"I've been noticing for some time," she began petulantly, "that you bestow much more attention on my left breast than on the right one. When you kiss and fondle my breasts—I am using the plural figuratively, it's always the left breast, never the right one. And yet both my breasts are equally attractive. You discriminate, and I am told by my tutors the disgraceful age of discrimination is far behind us. Or are you perhaps a lefty, a communist? I expect an explanation right now, Siegie, right this very minute. No excuses!"

"Impossible," he wailed, "quite impossible!" He began to kiss her mouth with mounting passion and then kiss and caress every inch of her body, ardently, ceaselessly.

"You want it again, don't you?" she muttered, licking and touching him. "You're a stud, I'll say this for you, and . . . and this is not unwelcome."

It was not until the yellow rays of dawn began to break into the bedroom through the rare silver drapes that Sayko found her words again.

"You keep telling me you love me . . ."

"I do, Sayko. I do love you and you must believe me."

"What about your wife? Do you love her too?"

"Not in the way I love you. Millie and I are held together by a bond of mutual trust, understanding, friendship."

"Ooh, la la. But you sleep together?"

"Yes, but when we make love, which is once in a blue moon, I think of you, of you exclusively."

"Siegie, I want you to stop sleeping with your wife. Lord knows I've put up with this highly unnatural arrangement long enough, but there are limits. From now on, you'll have only one wife—Princess Sayko, granddaughter of the emperor of Japan and the president of the United States, when he, the emperor, stands on American soil. I won't be lied to, and I won't brook unfaithfulness on my husband's part. Are we agreed?"

"Yes," Siegfried uttered, hastily looking away. His hands and mouth were glued to her body in a long-lasting impassioned caress and soon he was lying on top of her. They were united once more. They were one.

The bedroom was now bathed in morning light, and Siegfried touched Sayko's cheek.

"I have to be going, duty calls."

"Of course," she readily assented. "And I have the family breakfast and then my tutors. One of them bores the lights out of me."

He smiled. "Masters are not always popular with their disciples. Still . . ." He left the sentence unfinished.

As they were dressing he again cautioned her not to talk freely outside the confines of her bedroom, and at a low voice even in there.

"We can be easily overheard, and I worry about all those ADCs, secretaries, and hangers-on who are continually in attendance. I don't want them to latch on."

"Don't worry, Siegie. They have strict orders not to listen to what members of the imperial family are saying, and they take their duties seriously."

He waved a hand. "And your brother whose bedroom is next to yours?"

"Set your mind at ease about Takahito—Prince Mikasa to the wide world. He's my friend; he'd never repeat to others what he heard."

"Does he know about us?"

"Probably, he's put two and two together. He's a bright lad."

"How old is he?"

"Fourteen and at loggerheads with his tutors."

"Why?"

"Well, he has no respect for traditional learning; he likes supercomputers and ultra-modern gadgets. But that's not all. Takahito is an anti-monarchist. He believes the Japanese monarchy should be abolished and power vested in the president elected by a direct popular vote. He has little use for the American-style electoral college."

"My, my."

"Father is in a perpetual huff with Takahito, and Grandfather, the emperor, sees red."

"But your brother can be trusted?"

Sayko nodded vigorously. "When shall I see you?"

Siegfried reflected for a moment. "Tonight I am the guest of honor at the dinner given by the Japanese Foreign Ministry, and tomorrow I shall be knee-deep in discussions with your members of parliament. The day after tomorrow, Thursday."

"When are you returning to D.C.?"

"Friday night."

"So I shan't see you for another two weeks?"

"Duty calls," he said lamely.

"Before you disappear in the next ten seconds I want you to tell me again that you love me, and no one else, and I want the truth. I won't settle for anything less than the truth."

"I love you, Sayko. You and no one else," he murmured, holding her very close.

"You'd better," she gasped, smothering his face with kisses. "Hurry before the change of the guard. And remember you have only one wife—me—and you shall know no other woman but her."

"How could I not remember," he answered with ferocious self-confidence, opening the door and blowing her a kiss.

/   /   /

The empress of Japan cast a lovingly exploratory glance at Princess Sayko, who stood respectfully ten feet away, her hands locked.

"Sit down, child."

"Thank you, Grandmother."

"Well now," the empress went on in a warm confiding tone of voice, which nevertheless failed to conceal a sharp edge underneath. "We are all rather proud of you, Sayko."

"Thank you, Grandmother."

"The emperor read very carefully the latest reports from your tutors, and I can tell you, child, they make happy reading."

"I have tried, Grandmother."

"Of course you have, Sayko, and proof of the pudding is in the eating. Nowadays even the emperor has been won over to the idea that the children of the imperial family ought to receive professional education, and this includes girls."

"We are moving with the times, and girls are as important as boys. If a man is entitled to a career, be he prince or pauper, so is every single woman. To think otherwise, Grandmother, would be a crime."

The empress's hands floated briefly in the air, the fingers bending, unbending, then shooting forth with extraordinary precision as if observing an arcane rite.

"Quite, quite," she agreed with a touch of impatience. "We are on the same page." Then she consulted typed sheets of paper in her hand.

"You are very good in math and calculus, in physics and chemistry, the only wrinkle in your tutors' report being a less than enthusiastic attitude toward literature. 'A blasé view of your country's and the world's literary masterpieces,' as Dr. Satsuma put it."

"Oh, Grandmother, if you only knew . . . if you only knew," Sayko raised and spread her hands in a gesture of mock despair, "how all this literary crap bores me. It bores me stiff."

The empress smiled indulgently. "I can hardly speak as a devotee of classical literature. Still, what kind of a professional woman do you want to be?"

"CEO in a real big business, dealing with billions of yen or dollars, merging gigantic companies and creating new ones, laying down new financial policies for our planet."

"Excellent! Your parents and your grandparents are duly impressed."

But Sayko did not receive this assurance buoyantly. She curled up on the floor by her grandmother's feet, desperately clinging to her legs, submissively laying her head on the grandmother's knees. She was quietly sobbing.

"What is it, child?" the empress asked, her voice ringing with emotion. "Tell me all about it. I am more than half-certain this concerns the affairs of the heart."

"Yes, yes, but I don't know if I should tell you, Grandmother." The granddaughter's sobs were no longer quiet.

"Listen to me, Sayko. I am a very old woman who has lived a rich and adventurous life. Nothing you can tell me will shock or offend me. Furthermore, what you say to me will be *entre nous*." Noticing the innocent, nonplussed look on her granddaughter's fair visage, she added quickly, "It will be our secret. No one else will know."

Sayko was one foot out of the gloomy regions, but she was still tongue-tied.

"It's Siegfried, isn't it?" the grandmother asked gently. "Siegfried La Rochelle?"

"How did you know? How could you know, Grandmother?"

"Well, there were signs, unmistakable signs."

"Do you think the others know about us?"

"I doubt it. I'd say your parents and your grandfather are totally ignorant of your love affair with the American National Security Advisor, and so are probably your various uncles, aunts, cousins, and the rest of the imperial household. You have covered your tracks well."

"I wonder about Takahito, though."

"You are not my granddaughter for nothing," the empress put in with a knowing smile. "Yes, I'd lay the odds twenty-to-one he knows all there is to know. He's a smart little so-and-so, the tutors' and the professors' nightmare."

"I was afraid of that."

"But he won't babble about it. I've watched you together. You are pals, no? Takahito betraying you is most unlikely, I'd say. If there is a danger it may come from some officious ADC or secretary trying to ingratiate himself with the emperor or the crown prince."

The empress paused and hugged her granddaughter.

"And now you've gotten to unburden yourself. Why the tears? Doesn't Siegfried love you anymore? Has there been one lovers' quarrel too many?"

Her hands cupped around the brooch clasped to the top edge of her pantyhose and her immobile posture an enormous badge of respect for her grandmother whose every word she avidly took in and assimilated, Sayko gradually found her own words. With aplomb she told of her relationship with Siegfried, of their first meeting five months before when she knew she had been smitten, of his understanding and concern for her, of their precious meetings when she was discovering for the first time the full range of carnal fulfillment, of their scintillating conversations, of their mutual love. She was so happy with him, and he gave every appearance of being happy with her.

"Then what in heavens is the matter," her grandmother shot at her, looking stern and forbidding, "and why were you crying?"

"It's so difficult to put into words, Grandmother, so infernally difficult."

"Try to," the grandmother advised severely. "The gods gave us the power of speech and we should use it, all of us except the politicians."

"It's all right when Siegie is with me, but when he is away I am beset by gnawing doubts whether he really loves me. And then there is that wife of his, the Kentucky bitch. I am madly jealous. I wake up in the middle of the night, and I see my Siegie and that Millicent bitch in bed together. It's horrible, truly horrible."

"She's Siegfried's wedded wife."

"Siegie belongs to me and to me alone. I am his true wife, Grandmother. No other woman has the right. No other woman is allowed to touch him." Sayko was looking daggers.

The empress let her eyes wander over the tapestries adorning the walls depicting uniquely heroic moments in Japanese history. "They are a little overdone, don't you think so?" When Sayko was silent she clapped her hands. "Please bring a large glass of very cold lemonade for Princess Sayko," she told her servant.

While the princess was reluctantly sipping the drink, the empress assumed a regal mien.

"Just now you spoke like a goose, child. Get it through your youthful head that nowadays there are no exclusive rights to anything in this world. Perhaps in the very distant past exclusive rights actually existed, but I rather doubt it. Today all of us are symbiotically connected—we share things; we work toward the same goals; we depend on one another. No one can claim anything exclusively for oneself, and the sooner you grasp that, young lady, the better."

"I extracted a promise from Siegie that from now on he won't have anything to do with Millie. She'll have to live in perpetual chastity. I, Princess Sayko, am Siegfried La Rochelle's only wife. Sexual act outside marriage is adultery, and I know that my Siegie will never stoop so low."

The empress was flabbergasted and asked Sayko to repeat what she had just said. Hearing her fears confirmed she was hard put in restraining her anger.

"You little goose . . . you half-witted little imp! I want you to listen very carefully."

"Of course, Grandmother."

"Don't breathe another word to Siegfried about his wife—Millicent is her name, I believe."

"That's right . . . Millicent Kirby La Rochelle, Kirby being her maiden name."

"I am aware of it, Sayko. You are not speaking to one of your moronic cousins," the empress let out with fury.

"You won't breathe another word about Millicent. The subject is closed. After a while Siegfried will understand you were overwrought and you didn't have the slightest understanding of what you were saying. He will forgive you."

"Is there anything to forgive, Grandmother?"

"I am trying to save your relationship with Dr. La Rochelle, or do you want it to be broken, irretrievably broken?"

"No, no, I don't. Of course I don't; I love him. I simply thought—" Sayko cried with passion.

But the empress was still furious and cut her short. "Then you will do what I advise. I want it to be clearly understood."

Sayko nodded awkwardly, pouting. "You sound as if you hated me." She uttered the words haltingly, looking away, utterly miserable.

"Child, you're very close to my heart. Come here and give granny a hug." The empress' fury had all but exhausted itself. She held her granddaughter lovingly in her arms, telling her that she hated interfering in other people's lives, be they family or friends, and only felt compelled to do so when a person dear to her was making an absolute ass of herself or himself, as her granddaughter had done a short while ago by demanding God knows what from her married lover.

"I only tried to follow the voice of probity and the highest ideals within me," Sayko said quietly but with firmness.

"Of course, child, I understand your motives, but you have to bear in mind that a successful and rewarding life is made up of compromises. By the way, Sayko, refresh my memory. How old are you?"

"I am fifteen, Grandmother."

"I thought you were a little older, but no matter. You are very lucky to have found such a devoted lover at such an early age. I have reason to believe yours is a happy union."

"Yes, except for . . . "

"Tut, child, Millicent is no threat. She is not trying to take Siegfried away from you. Banish her from your thoughts, forget she exists. Savor every moment of your life with your beloved. This is what counts. The rest is dross."

"I think I am beginning to understand what you're saying, Grandmother."

"Clever girl," the empress let fall gently in an undertone, and then she added more stridently, "and no offense to your ideals."

"I'd like to talk to you more often, the way we are talking now, Grandmother. I really would like that."

"The door is always open." The empress smiled affectionately, cryptically.

"I am all ears, Your Majesty," Sayko recited with all due formality, bowing low.

"What, what?" the empress queried.

"It is my firm belief Your Majesty would like to lay something open."

"Just a passing thought, Sayko. Let me say again how happy I am you have found love with a man who merits respect, a man of such knowledge, such brilliant accomplishments, not that these are in any way prerequisites for a happy union."

Sayko retreated a few steps and stood there quite still, intensely observing her grandmother.

"I find it puzzling," the empress began, "that someone like Siegfried La Rochelle could be a great lover, a lover at all." She paused and a rapid glance flying at Sayko convinced her that her granddaughter would not break her silence come what may. She continued airily, "We all know what a brilliant mind the gods have given to La Rochelle. His is a brain as huge as the Ausci Kembun Roken crater, if not greater, and the dual republic/monarchy plan is a stroke of genius. But love? I wonder at times whether La Rochelle has a penis at all, let alone whether he knows how to use it."

"Grandmother!"

"And whether the two of you are not spending long nights drafting a new constitution for Amernipp."

"Grandmother! If I lie, let the gods strike me dead. Siegie is a wonderful lover. He was my first and will remain my only one."

The empress patted Sayko on the cheek. "You are a princess of blood and my granddaughter. I believe you. Life can be stranger than fiction."

Sayko warmly embraced her grandmother and kissed her hand.

"I wish you both many years of happiness. Mine was short-lived, lasting barely three years," the empress said in a flat voice. "I see myself in you. May you fare better."

As her granddaughter was watching her expectantly, she went on, "I was a little older than you, but not much, when I met the love of my life. He was a sailor, an officer in the Royal Canadian Navy, and he came to Tokyo with his admiral on some high-power nonsense. We first caught sight of each other in the gardens of the imperial palace. Our eyes met and we knew at once we were meant for each other. Quentin was his name, and he was a few years younger than your Siegfried. Those three years of happiness would've been envied by the gods! Like you, I was a virgin when I met him, and like you I tasted for the first time the extraordinary joy and ecstasy of physical fulfillment. Quentin was not only a superlative lover, he was also well educated and highly accomplished, sensitive, witty, a brilliant conversationalist.

"Above all, he understood me—he understood my mind and my body. We spent hours upon hours discussing all kinds of subjects, ranging from the divinely intricate structure of the plum blossom and the wild rose to the latest theories of personality integration, which held a particular fascination for Quentin. Enraptured, we listened to music, Occidental and Oriental, we challenged each other to paint more striking watercolors, damned what we had done, quarreled, made up, and started anew with the rising or the setting sun.

"In bed we invariably spoke French—Quentin was fluent in it, and so am I, of course. In truth we were both incorrigible Francophiles, me more than him, because I still consider the rise of British English in the last three centuries and of American English in the last century as a means of international communication with the concomitant neglect of the French language to be a deplorable lapse, a sure sign of the decline of culture in this world. An Englishman or an American will tell you that his language is the richest among the Indo-European tongues. Bah! Perhaps so, but it is also uncrystallized, unpolished, and highly imprecise because of its quaint and chaotic syntax and grammar. If you want to rant indiscriminately about everything under the sun, by all means employ English. But if you want to focus on a particular subject and do justice to it with the maximum of conciseness and precision, turn to French."

The empress's disquisition on languages left Sayko indifferent. But something she had broached earlier made the young lady's cheeks burn.

"So Quentin was artistic?" she asked, exhilarated.

"Highly artistic," the empress replied, gazing nostalgically into space.

"Siegie has no taste for art or music or for literature for that matter," Sayko announced flatly.

"You should help him develop a taste, child."

"Easier said than done. Politics is his province, and he's a genius at it. We talk a great deal, of course, about the people he meets, his work, the new projects he's embarking on, and he listens to my comments. I help him in his work. He calls me his sounding board."

"A-ha."

"But there's no room for art or music, no room and no time. Siegie enjoys good food, and being in bed with me, of course. This is the first priority. After a good meal he opts for an expensive cigar, and I light it for him."

"Excellent."

But Sayko was unwilling to bare her soul.

The handsome figure of Quentin, who had given so much happiness to her grandmother whose intimate life story she had heard for the first time, hardly believing her ears, impressed itself upon her mind. Vicariously she felt very close to the graceful lover, closer still to her grandmother, and a new world was opening before her—a world of those she loved and trusted whose innermost feelings she was beginning to share and of whose experiences she partook of to the fullest. Sayko had never really suffered from loneliness—her parents, grandparents, her sisters, her brother, and of late the towering persona of Siegfried, had provided companionship and diversion—but now she enjoyed a new bond with her grandmother and, through her, with others she had never met. It was like lifting the curtain and stepping into a chamber full of people where she would be at once initiated into the realm of intimacy with them. Empathy, longing, curiosity were pounding in her breast, and she felt she now understood the others, her family and friends, as never before. She was crossing her fingers praying that they too might understand her as never before.

"What happened to Mr. Quentin?" Sayko asked, coming out of her sympathetic trance.

The empress looked pained.

"He drowned, went down with the ship," she said very quietly. "In those days there were still quantities of old tubs about. We had them, and so did the Canadians and the Americans. Not shipshape by any means. On the way from Japan to San Francisco, somewhere in the middle of the Pacific, Quentin's ship the *Charlton* sprang a leak and then explosions unaccountably followed. Quentin managed to get everyone out—he was in command—but was himself trapped in the engine room. He went down. He died as befits an officer and a gentleman." Hastily the empress wiped off a tear. "I wish he'd been less brave and less punctilious."

"Did anyone take his place, Grandmother?"

"No one, child. No one could take Quentin's place. Yes, I have had other lovers since, but they were not in the same league. Quentin will always stand out." The empress's watchful eye followed Sayko, shifting her body weight from foot to foot. "I had my three years of happiness. I hope you'll have many, many more."

"Thank you, Grandmother."

"Remember, Sayko, women in our position do not marry for love. Our marriages are arranged; they are dynastic unions; they follow protocol. Pray to the immortal gods that the man you are destined to marry does not evoke in you unmitigated repugnance. I have seen it once too often. And in the meantime try to steal as much happiness for yourself as you can."

Sayko respectfully bowed her head.

"Talking about Quentin, he was under pressure to marry two years into our liaison, and he did marry. Daughter of a family his parents knew well, cementing the friendship of the two clans, and so on."

"I am devastated, Grandmother. You must've been hurt beyond belief. How did you survive?"

"It didn't make the slightest difference. If anything our love and passion grew as a result. Marriage seldom interferes with a grand love affair."

"I have to think this one through," Sayko remarked modestly.

"You do it, child. And now I really have to be going." Her laughter reverberated far and wide. "Come, give old granny a kiss."

Chapter 2

The Sweat of Power

Siegfried La Rochelle slid his body backward to the limit while reclining his custom-made swivel armchair. Mounted on noiseless wheels and equipped with a telephone, dictaphone, and a TV screen, its seat was fashioned out of ostrich feathers pressed into ovoid silk pillows—softness and comfort unparalleled. But at a light touch of the button just under the left elbow rest, sheets of finest morocco darted ingeniously upward from all sides, enveloping the seat and giving it traction. La Rochelle could plummet into the pliant lap of luxury, doze or recharge his batteries caressed by the silk pillows, or he could gallivant on his buttocks forward and backward as he pleased, à la vache, prone, or straining upward in search of new ideas. He believed in absolute comfort, and his office was strewn with magazines and ads vaunting new gadgets, new pieces of furniture, new cars, and helicopters calculated to give unheard of ease and pleasure. He considered the heavily equipped ambulatory swivel armchair satisfactory—it allowed him to flit from one computer or tape-container to the next in his capacious office without straining a single muscle. But recently an invention not exactly novel but presently more and more widely applied in many walks of life caught his eye. Machines of all sorts could be activated by brainwaves alone, the tactile being as much in demand as an ill-smelling sock. Siegfried promised himself that the old faithful, which had wheeled him around for more than a year now, would soon be replaced by a new model reading his brain and acting accordingly.

New science, new technology could be fascinating, and of course it heightened the coziness and joy of life.

"So you've cheated the jetlag of its true desserts, Mr. National Security Advisor!" a blatantly Bostonian voice boomed behind his back.

"Ah, Tim." La Rochelle hoisted himself up a little seeing his senior assistant Timothy Hysart looming expectantly.

"Actually there's no jetlag these days. I board Air Force II long before it takes off and immediately go to bed. My sleep is uninterrupted until we land in D.C. Couldn't ask for anything better."

"While you were in Tokyo, sir, things have been happening at the ranch."

"Nothing vexing, I trust."

"I'd like to bring you up-to-date when you're ready for it, and you can decide."

"Now is as good a time as any, Tim." La Rochelle yawned theatrically in anticipation. "We'll call it a preprandial fix," he added, laughing. "Pull up a chair."

In an even voice Tim reported on a recent wave of anti-Americanism and anti-Amernippism in South America, where Brazil and Argentina, backing each other as never before, strove for the leadership of the continent and demanded a warmer place in the sun for all countries south of Panama. He explained the new realignments in Africa, which had been consummated only two days before, whereby Nigeria and the Sudan broke off their longstanding alliance, the former reaching out covetously to the Republic of South Africa, and the latter forging a new friendship with Egypt and Libya, the surrounding countries dealing as best they could with the resulting shock waves.

He reported on yet another inflammatory speech the president of the French Republic, Jacques Merdeacac, made the day before, this time in Berlin. He again called on all of Europe to unite and stand up against Amernipp, the only superpower defiling the planet. "The rhetoric was fiercer than at any at time in the past," Tim recounted, consulting his notes. "He called Amernipp a rank obscenity and urged all European nations to build a counterweight to us. There should be several centers of power in the world—he practically shouted himself hoarse in the Sportpalast—and Europe, with its long tradition of statecraft and intellectual maturity, should be one of them. The world mustn't be ruled by ignorant Yanks and bloodthirsty Japs. Usual Merdeacac tirade, but much longer this time."

"Anything else?" La Rochelle inquired.

Tim gave him the latest information on the nearly hopeless struggle against a severe recession in Russia, which seemed to be growing more severe with every hour, and on the unexpected cabinet changes in China. "Yesterday I called Duncan Dobrovy at the CIA and asked for his evaluation of all these events. I told him I spoke for you."

La Rochelle nodded approvingly. "You did the right thing."

"Mr. Dobrovy kept me on the scrambler for a good hour, and he's sending us further material."

"Good, have the digests on my desk first thing Monday morning. Some of it may have to be brought up at the next NSC meeting, which is—"

"In nine days."

"Thank you, Tim." La Rochelle leaned back, and his eye shot across the empty space all the way to a distant wall partly hidden by a partition.

"Do my eyes deceive me?" he queried, pleased as punch.

"They do not. I found the last four etchings of the set at a rare books dealer in New York City. You now have all twelve of them. The reception of the Huguenots in Brandenburg in the year 1687."

"They look marvelous," La Rochelle gasped, examining the four additions carefully with the help of opera glasses. "I can't thank you enough, Tim."

"Your pedigree is now immortalized and open to universal admiration."

"I am not certain whether my ancestors were in this particular bunch, but if not, they arrived in Brandenburg shortly thereafter, a couple or so years later at the most. I am very grateful."

"You're very welcome, sir. . . . There's something else, though, I'd like to bring up."

"Anything, Tim." The National Security Advisor was still in the best of moods.

"While you were away, the Secretary of State called five times. He wanted to speak to you urgently. I guess nowadays no one tells him anything. He didn't even know you were in Japan. I tried to be as courteous as possible, but he's hurt, deeply hurt."

A wrinkle formed on La Rochelle's brow and immediately disappeared.

"Roger Williamson should've gotten used to the idea by now that he's a figurehead only." He spoke brusquely. "Surely it must've dawned on him he has no authority over anything anymore, if he ever had any. Besides, the man is a pushover, unfit to conduct anybody's foreign policy, least of all the foreign policy of the only real superpower."

"I wonder why we go on with that rigmarole?"

"You know it as well as I do, Tim. During the last general election Roger's name was useful to us. He helped us to garner votes. We let him keep the title."

"Yes, I know," Tim said very quietly. Then he added with greater force, "The president visited Yosemite National Park while you were making polite noises in Tokyo."

"And?"

"He was enthusiastically welcomed wherever he went. He spoke to the rangers and dozens of visitors and shook hands right, left, and center. Even the blasé paparazzi were impressed. The people looked to him as though he were the one who could solve all their problems. And he looks so young for his age. Young and trim."

La Rochelle shrugged ostentatiously. "Those navy boys know how to husband their tender years. We'll have to put Jack Woods on the road more often. Let him shake every hand in Amernipp that wiggles his way. Good PR, very wholesome."

"He too has been cheated out of his office," Tim spoke very softly.

"You're not serious, are you, boy?" La Rochelle was doing his best to laugh Tim's statement off, and his cascading laughter was disarming.

"Is there anything you'd like me to do this afternoon?" the senior assistant asked very earnestly.

"No, carry on with your daily duties."

"Will you be staying long this afternoon?"

"Hardly. I'm having a late lunch with Phineas Léger and then straight home. Millie is holding a reception for her family, you know the Kentucky branch, and I've been warned not to be late, or else. It's a colorful and motley crowd, chicken and peanuts farmers, military types, and others, including some who operate illegal stills and manage to stay one foot ahead of the sheriff and the feds."

Tim's laughter clanged, impish and provoking.

"I'm bound to say, Dr. La Rochelle, that you married into a real American family, American to the marrow of its bones."

"Enjoy your Saturday night, Mr. Timothy Hysart," La Rochelle laughed back. "Enjoy, enjoy, enjoy!"

Then, as if a thought had struck him, his eyes were riveted again upon his senior assistant.

"Did you ever get those messages your father left for you last week while you were out of the office? He said the matter was urgent. Someone from the typing pool was going to give them to you personally."

"Yes, I got them," Tim answered, betraying every sign of disgust. "Everything my father says is always of earthshaking importance and crucial to the preservation of the human race."

"I don't mean to pry . . . but you're not in any kind of trouble?"

"At times I wish I were, but no." Tim laughed sardonically. "With every passing week my sire moves closer and closer to being no more than a lackey in the service of one Huston, Chief Justice of Amernipp. He'd started off as Uncle Tom, graduated in double time to the office of principal ass-kisser, and now he is on the way to new laurels—singled out to stick his tongue up Huston's asshole whenever the justice feels the urge and tickling his balls."

"My, my," La Rochelle sighed resignedly.

"My old man worships Huston, who in turn puts him to good use. It is a travesty of the moral order of the world, yet the lowdown flunky remains one of the best-known and influential African-American ministers in the country. He drums up support for Huston among black clergy, and the Church of the Holy Tabernacle where Father officiates is one of the oldest black churches in this part of the country. Huston gets a lot of mileage from father's servility. No doubt about it."

As Tim went on talking a reddish hue was breaking out and superimposing itself on his entire very light-darkish face. The reddishness was aggressive, surging, and the light-dark smudges were soon overrun by a mass of scarlet brooking no opposition and subjugating the entire field. Presently Tim was standing upright, his arms stretched downward along his torso and thighs, his countenance pulsating red, tiny drops of perspiration dotting it and the neck.

"I am sorry," La Rochelle let fall. "I didn't realize I touched the nerve."

"That's all right," Tim laughed off the remark. "But you can see Father is not my favorite topic of conversation."

"Sorry again," La Rochelle intoned self-effacingly. "But I have to ask you one more question, as a friend."

"Shoot."

"If your equation holds water, what does your father get in return?"

"The usual. Support, protection, pork. He's currently serving on all kinds of ecclesiastical and political committees, has easy access to the media controlled by Huston, and is tickled pink watching himself become a household name in governmental circles."

"I see."

"I am sure you do, better than most. And for crying out loud, don't tell me this is the way of the world. Because it isn't."

As if touched by a magic wand La Rochelle was now exuding kiloliters of bonhomie and blinking merrily. His busy hands were drawing asymmetrical figures in the air that Tim understood to be his boss's good wishes and a temporary farewell. He acted on cue as the National Security Advisor, now blessed with all the wise composure of the Buddha, let out in a stage whisper, "And I'll my silence keep."

After Tim had left, La Rochelle wheeled himself to where the etchings of the Huguenots being welcomed in the Prussian town of Brandenburg shortly after the revocation of the Edict of Nantes were hanging and examined them through a magnifying glass. He concluded that the last four of the twelve-part set, so ingeniously located by his senior assistant, were decidedly of higher artistic quality than the preceding ones. The drawing in them was surer and more exact, the figures in front better characterized and differentiated, the sense of solemn occasion more strikingly captured. It was the same German artist, of course, who executed the entire set (allegedly in the year 1869), but La Rochelle wondered whether the last four etchings were not in fact completed later, much later perhaps, long after the artist had gone through his apprenticeship. Next La Rochelle wheeled himself back to his largest desk—he claimed three private desks of varying size in his office—and gazed entranced at the etchings through opera glasses. Then he fell into a reverie.

La Rochelle had been born in Germany of Huguenot stock. His family, according to oral tradition, emigrated from Clermont-Ferrand to the town of Brandenburg shortly after the eventful year of 1685. But there were no documents to validate this claim because the Huguenot records were consumed in great fires that devastated Brandenburg first in 1841 and then in 1887, much of the town being also razed to the ground by the advancing Soviet armies in 1945. As for Clermont-Ferrand, no records could be found of a Huguenot family by the name of La Rochelle having ever lived there at any time, not a conclusive piece of evidence since historians insisted that Huguenot records in many parts of France before and after 1685 had been periodically tampered with by royal agents and many of them destroyed. Paying absolutely no attention to those irritating historical blanks and misdeeds, La Rochelle always maintained that his family, of pure Huguenot stock, had emigrated from Clermont-Ferrand in France to the town of Brandenburg in Prussia shortly after the revocation of the Edict of Nantes.

As a teenager, Siegfried La Rochelle emigrated to the United States with his parents and a younger brother, and once the family settled in New York City he enrolled in George Washington High School, where he did extremely well. After graduation he attended City College of New York and shortly thereafter joined as a sophomore the 2059 class at Harvard, where he was a star undergraduate and graduate student in the departments of history and government. His doctoral dissertation *D-Day, Yalta, and Beyond* was much praised, and when it was published in book form it was at once pronounced the most significant exploration of the far-reaching consequences of the events in the final stages of World War II, offering brilliant new analyses and revamping the heretofore blindly accepted historiography.

Other books followed, on the Cold War of the 1950s, on the balance of power under the Eisenhower and Kennedy administrations, on the political potentialities of China and Japan in the fast-changing world. Each of them was dubbed a revelation, a genius-like disquisition into foreign relations. In 2070, at the tender age of thirty, La Rochelle was already a tenured full professor at Harvard University, holding a permanent joint appointment in the departments of history and of government, and he was already dabbling in politics.

The 2070s were the last decade when the traditional two-party system still existed in the United States, and La Rochelle joined the Republicans, acting as advisor on foreign policy to two Republican presidents. In 2081, when through a set of maneuvers and rigged referenda the two-party system was abolished and one party, the Church and State Party (C&S for short), came to dominate the American political forum, La Rochelle supported its leaders, and as a reward was given a free hand in conducting the foreign policy of the United States. With iron determination he set about translating into reality the ideas that had been germinating in his mind already in the early seventies when he was still a Harvard professor, and later while acting as foreign policy advisor.

The world of the 2070s and '80s was vastly different from what it had been twenty or even ten years earlier. The prolonged recessions that had affected most of the globe with the exception of the United States and Japan had isolated those two countries as the only real superpowers, and they were invested with economic and industrial might so staggering as to reduce the rest of the world to virtual insignificance. It was true that what had once been called the Third World made giant steps forward, raising the standard of living and developing myriad industries. But that enormous segment of the world, sadly torn by political instability and internecine conflicts, could hardly compete with the United States or with Japan. South America was still a hotbed of endless revolutions and insurrections where the populace, given to jingoistic outcries, was avidly awaiting Men on Horseback, such men regularly presenting themselves and regularly falling short of expectation. The dream of European unity had never been realized.

Nobly conceived toward the end of the twentieth century, the future united Europe was hailed as a superpower destined to overshadow other superpowers, incorporating as it did the most civilized parts of the globe as the world's athenaeum, as well as its guardian armed to the teeth. But the dozens of countries, which with a varying degree of enthusiasm were promoting the cause of unity, could agree about precious little, and some of the smaller ones resented the domineering posture of the larger ones, who saw themselves as natural leaders. Though the multiplicity of trade and monetary agreements, of pacts and treaties between individual European nations would have filled a goodly part of the Great Wall of China, Europe was decidedly disunited and no match either for the United States or Japan.

Meanwhile Britain, nominally part of the European bloc, was living modestly, her worldwide ambitions laid to rest, drawing at times closer to the countries of the former commonwealth, and at others to the Continental powers as her commercial interests dictated. Russia was perennially occupied by grave economic problems, one slump followed by another and little in between, and China, potentially the greatest power on the face of this planet, was still at pains reconciling socialist ideology with capitalistic private enterprise under the aegis of social justice. China's energy was directed at alleviating the economic problems of its immense population and at modernizing the country, not at flexing its muscles before the world. Its foreign policy was pragmatic and economically oriented, and there was wide agreement that the realization of its prodigious potential lay in the not too distant future. However for the time being the two super-engines in the world were the United States and Japan, both shining examples of enlightened capitalism, highly industrialized, and boasting of a dynamic economy able to withstand temporary reverses. This was the world picture in the mid-seventies when La Rochelle, a political animal, was first getting his feet wet. A student of realpolitik, his ambition had been from the very start to make the United States infinitely more powerful than ever before and thus guarantee its supremacy on the world stage for centuries to come.

He strongly believed in alliances, in building common fronts against potential enemies and rivals, thus creating new balances of power advantageous to the United States, and he believed even more strongly in flexibility in conducting foreign policy. But much as he admired the achievements of some secretaries of state of the preceding century, especially those of Dean Acheson, he also realized that something more than multiple alliances with partners weaker than the United States was needed now to perpetuate American standing in the changing world. Here the key concept was union, and there was only one country in the world with which it would be wise for the United States to unite. That country was Japan. La Rochelle was fully aware of the enormity of the problem given the history and origins of the United States and the history and origins of Japan. But old beliefs and prejudices had to be put in mothballs. It was the future that mattered, and the new country born of a union of the two most powerful nations in the world would remain immune to political quicksand, to unexpectedly emerging menaces, and to new configurations of world power. The new country would be what Rome under Augustus was to the ancient world.

La Rochelle began modestly by airing his views to a handful of receptive colleagues and later progressed to a full-fledged campaign of persuasion, waving the banner of national security and raising the specter of America standing deserted and alone in the wicked world. In 2080 he finally convinced the President, the Administration, and the Congress, and in 2081, through a series of highly dramatic appearances on Japanese soil, he won the emperor, the government, and the parliament over to his cause, being at one time carried high by a jubilant crowd in the streets of Tokyo and at another very nearly torn to pieces in the very same streets and rescued in the nick of time by a passing SWAT team sent on another assignment.

In 2082 the union and the birth of a new country, Amernipp, was at last consummated, and it was given two national holidays, the Fourth of July and the birthday of the reigning emperor, which fell on October 17. Both were enthusiastically celebrated in the American and the Japanese part of the new country. Standing on the soil that earlier had been Japan, the American president became at once the emperor of Japan while retaining the status of president, and standing on the soil which earlier had been the U.S.A. the emperor immediately became the president, retaining the title of the Japanese emperor. La Rochelle thought that the simultaneous presence of two emperors or of two presidents would strengthen the union, and in this effort he was widely supported.

Every citizen of what was earlier the United States of America became a citizen of Amernipp, and every citizen of what was earlier the Empire of Japan became a citizen of Amernipp. The United States of America as a sovereign country was dissolved and so was the Empire of Japan as a sovereign country. In their place arose Amernipp, composed of the former United States and of the former Empire of Japan, now indissolubly united into a new sovereign state. The Japanese part of Amernipp, named Eastern Amernipp, or the Eastern Province, retained its old political structure, entailing the continued existence of the legislative, executive, and judicial branches of government with all the rights and powers thereof, and so did the American part of Amernipp, now named Western Amernipp or the Western Province. Moreover each part of Amernipp, American and Japanese, retained its own national constitution.

However, from that point on, the foreign policy of the new country was conducted by a specially created department composed in equal numbers of former members of the governmental structure of the United States and the Empire of Japan, and the same department was entrusted with external security of the country as a whole. Numerous trade provisions, bylaws, and ordinances drafted by experts were added to the instrument of the union so that its citizens might have a clear notion of their new rights and privileges in a variety of situations. Amernipp was given a new overwhelmingly ambitious economic policy, carefully fashioned to protect and advance the interests of its two geographically separate parts, and a succession of what came to be known as "brotherly commissions" set to work cementing the new national identity of the citizens and forging multiple bonds between them in the work-oriented and private spheres.

Marriage between those born and bred, or simply residing, in the North American province of the state, and those in the East Asian archipelago was encouraged, and the Herculean task of creating one educational system on primary, middle, and high school levels for the country as a whole had begun. An essential provision in the instrument of the union was the establishment of bilingualism in Amernipp on the official level, so that all official documents relating to national, regional, or local affairs would appear both in English and Japanese, both languages enjoying the same official status, concomitant to it being intensive training of civil servants in Japanese or English, so that they would show competency in the usage of both primary languages of the country. Casting its net wide, the instrument of the union also took decisive steps to promote learning of Japanese in the North American Province, and of English in the East Asian Province of the state so that as years went by more and more Amernippians would have a working command of both English and Japanese, the goal of a more widespread bilingualism within this great and unique nation being not far away.

La Rochelle came out of his reverie and effortlessly reminded himself that in less than a month Amernipp would celebrate its second anniversary, the Fourth of July festivities promising to be a lively occasion to be followed by the other national holiday on October 17, according to all predictions an equally animated one. He was immensely proud of his achievement. Amernipp had been brought to life by his efforts, he had been the chief architect of this unique union, and he well remembered that the notion of it succeeding had been formerly laughed at and laughed out of court. Still, in the teeth of its detractors the Union from the outset proved to be a towering national and international success. The standard of living in both provinces rose dramatically, new industrial and technological techniques were being developed at breakneck speed, Amernippian goods outclassed and undersold foreign goods on the world market, and near-full employment kept the country stable and in a self-congratulatory mood. In the olden days the United States and Japan had been the political and military superpowers—now Amernipp was the only giant superpower left, a new Rome in the abject and cowed world. As a senior official at the British Embassy in Washington, where La Rochelle was known to repair now and then in search of quality scotch, put it while handing him the precious brew, "Sig, now nobody, but nobody will want to muck about with you. But, chummy, you take care!"

Effortlessly, La Rochelle's thoughts shifted in another direction. Two weeks before he met at an official reception in Washington the confidential secretary to the assistant attorney general of Amernipp, a ravishing beauty, a divorcee in her early thirties, vibrating with pent-up sexual energy. She was a knockout. Benny Kretchuar, assistant attorney general, an elderly widower and an old friend, was invariably accompanied at official functions by his confidential secretary by whose judgment he set high store. La Rochelle had made discreet inquiries and had found out that after her divorce the lady had been briefly involved with the ambassador of a friendly country and then with a judge on the Appeals Court. He felt he was hopelessly under her spell. "What is her last name?" he murmured to himself, snapping his fingers impatiently. "What's her name?" But try hard as he did, all he could recall was her first name, the enchanting name of Edith. He was already refining his strategy of bumping into her accidentally on purpose under auspicious circumstances.

Sexual fulfillment had stood high on La Rochelle's list of priorities ever since puberty, but in his teens and early twenties it competed with two other passions—soccer, which dated back to his childhood in Germany, and later baseball. He married while still in his mid-twenties, and the marriage was not a success. Dorothea too was an immigrant from Germany, of Huguenot stock, and she took her religion seriously. She belonged to the old and new Huguenot associations in the United States and insisted on Siegfried remaining in the Huguenot fold. He demurred. As a newly dubbed American citizen, already achieving academic and political distinction, he saw the Huguenot legacy and all the mumbo jumbo that went with it as fetters barring him from being fully integrated in American society and reaching the fullest degree of Americanization. Besides, Dorothea had no stomach for flamboyant social life, which Siegfried adored and which drew him closer and closer to the world of the powerful and to that of celebrities. She preferred staying at home with their two sons and spending her leisure hours in the company of close friends with German Huguenot roots.

An even greater impediment to a happy marriage was Siegfried's roving eye, to which Dorothea reacted with ready wrath, lacing her tirades with meticulously chosen verses from the Holy Writ. The marital union of the two had its better and worse weeks and months, yet it was continuously on the brink. Still it dragged on for eight long years, dispensing unhappiness to the two principals and their resigned offspring. When divorce finally took place, it gave both Siegfried and Dorothea a new lease on life. He was already a figure of importance and made the best of it. She retreated into her religious enclave, devoting herself to the welfare of her sons, of whom she had custody, with the father enjoying liberal visitation rights.

It was at this time that Siegfried became a man about town, a swinger being photographed whenever an opportunity presented itself with one gorgeous movie star or another, and finding his way to hosts of bedrooms where society and other women eagerly welcomed him. Washington was abuzz with stories of Siegfried's passionate friendships with attractive, highly placed women and of his magnetic charm, which compelled the opposite sex to pursue him as if there were nothing more important in their lives. Washington argued about the reasons for the fascination he evoked and settled nothing. But one confession coming from a woman who had known Siegfried well and over a long period of time was like the tinkle of a bell calling everyone to order. "He listens," the lady affirmed. "He listens to us talking about ourselves, and few men are capable of it. He listens, and he never hurries things."

Siegfried's colorfully advertised bachelorhood lasted barely two years when those claiming to be in the know made much noise about his alleged desire to settle down into an unruffled, well-regulated marriage. The story was first confirmed and then denied, Siegfried himself refusing to breathe a word on the subject. But the omens were falling into place. Several names were bandied about, a wealthy socialite, progeny of an ambassadorial family, whose two ex-husbands ranked high in the business world; a vivacious artist whose watercolors delighted the aesthetically-inclined Washingtonians; an operatic singer with uncles and cousins in the Senate and the House of Representatives, and two other well-connected ladies.

Rumors continued to circulate, but the banns astonished a great many. Siegfried was marrying one Millicent Kirby of Kentucky, a lady in her middle thirties, the widow of a hydrological engineer and daughter of a part owner of a well-known food chain. Some of Siegfried's friends opined that he had chosen a down-to-earth woman who would keep him in line, while others intimated this was the last and final step in his Americanization, the reaching out to rural America, to what was quintessentially American.

Siegfried evaded the probing questions, and by all accounts the marriage had been a happy one, Millie taking little interest in his work but always ready to attend official receptions, galas, and public entertainment of all sorts, enjoying them hugely and invariably feeling out of place. She had a sharp tongue and a very direct way of expressing herself which did not grate Siegfried in the least. She became known to the official and fashionable Washingtonians as that Kentucky virago who did not mince her words and put her foot down, her opening salvo to her husband in the presence of many others at a White House reception shortly after their wedding being, "If I ever find you with another woman, why, Siegfried, I'll chop your nuts off and feed them to the hogs, and that's God's truth."

Siegfried glanced at his wristwatch. Soon it would be time to meet Phineas. He had worked out everything down to the smallest detail for the meeting with the divine Edith, and he reminded himself that later in the day he would be calling Sayko in Tokyo to wish her a happy week.

Chapter 3

The Cross and the Scimitar

The succession of momentous events that imposed itself on the United States at the start of the 2060s tore apart the age-honored fabric of political life and transformed the country beyond the wildest nightmares of earlier Americans. The prelude to and the first link in this gloomy chain of circumstances was the rise of militant Islam in 2060, bent on the conquest of the infidel world and conversion of those who valued their lives to the religion of Prophet Mohammed. The teeming movement had been sparked by a new wave of terrorist activity reminiscent of the opening years of the twenty-first century, but more intensely determined and assaulting practically all the countries of the West. Soon coordinated terrorism took on the mantle of a jihad, expanding to different parts of the globe.

First came the attempted invasion of Turkey, that unforgivable traitor among the traitors, gallantly fought off by the heroic Turkish army and the heroic civilian population. But the Mahdis in Iran and Iraq passionately preached to the Muslim world and went on preaching.

Following in the footsteps of Tariq the Berber fourteen centuries earlier, the fanatical Arab armies advanced from the Middle East along the Mediterranean coast, swelling their ranks by the hour, and at Gibraltar crossed into Spain, routing the opposing forces in a matter of weeks and subjecting the entire country to the Muslim yoke. Simultaneously two great armadas, assisted by hundreds of planes, sailed from North Africa landing in Albania in the Balkans and in Taranto in

Italy, respectively, and swiftly advanced northward. The military leaders of Islam believed in highly coordinated action and in scoring maximum effect.

As their patrols were crossing the city limits of Bari in Italy and gaining more and more ground in Montenegro, two large Iraqi submarines filled with a company of highly trained special troops were moving noiselessly to the English coast north of the Thames, and disembarked near Wheathampstead, thus retracing the movements of Julius Caesar in 54 B.C. Their objective was to blow up as many buildings and bridges as they could and in London plant hundreds of dirty bombs and engage for the period of six hours in indiscriminate carnage before returning to the submarines. They were only partly successful. As if forewarned by the good fairy, British commandoes turned up when least expected, thwarting the enemy's designs. Hand-to-hand combat raged, and the streets of London were strewn with shattered corpses. A mere handful of invaders returned to the assembly point, only to see their submarines blown out of the water.

Simultaneously, the most ambitious part of the holy war was in progress. Two ultra-modern passenger planes with Red Cross markings and equipped with all the necessary passwords and codes, flying out of Geneva, were at present forty miles off Long Island. Each carried two twenty-megaton nuclear bombs. Once inland one of them was to turn south and head for Washington D.C. and the other fly straight to the heart of New York City. Ostensibly they carried top Red Cross officials for an urgent meeting with top American officials, but in reality their passengers consisted of a squad of heavily armed paratroopers in each plane kept in reserve if the bombs failed to explode. The idle chatter of the paratroopers was suddenly interrupted as the planes burst into flames, and the deafening explosion spurred on two enormous mushroom clouds shooting up at a split second interval from the level of thirty thousand feet. The major inside the top secret cabin at Andrews Air Force Base had his eyes glued to the monitor.

"Bull's-eye, number one and number two," he said more to himself than to anyone else. "Send the code word to Washington. What is it this time, Sergeant?"

"Well, actually, this time and for this particular operation the code word is 'cherry'"

"I'll be damned," the major said. Then he drew himself up. "I don't care what anybody says, Larry, I'm going out for a drink."

"Do you mind if I tag along, sir?" the sergeant asked, brushing his moustache.

The major heard himself say, "Be my guest, Sergeant."

/   /   /

The expulsion of the bellicose Islam from the continent of Europe was another matter. From the Rock of Gibraltar to the Pyrenees the scimitar reigned triumphant. The Spaniards have a long tradition of fighting doggedly against the invaders of their native land, but in this instance they stopped short of armed resistance. Whether fearing wholesale reprisals, or reluctant to condemn their young men and women to the life of permanent insurgents and to continued danger, or for other reasons, Spain as a whole sought an accommodation with the new rulers. Besides, their sovereignty was not excessively harsh or cruel. For the most part they considered Spain a province of the Islamic Empire, albeit an unfaithful one, but a province nevertheless. True, most of the inhabitants were now Christians, but Islam was tolerant and the new masters guaranteed religious freedom. Spanish exchequer carried the heavy burden of lodging, feeding, and recompensing the Muslim troops, and additional taxation was hastily introduced. But ordinary Spaniards were allowed to go about their business in peace, incidents of violence were rare, schools and universities maintained their ancient autonomy, cultural life flourished, and the press was virtually free provided it did not advocate or encourage rebellion.

In the second year of occupation the Spanish people experienced a change of heart, and a new mentality was born. It was widely believed that peace, peace at any price, was preferable to turmoil, however noble its goals. Law and order guaranteed personal safety and a large measure of personal freedom so long as the realities of remaining a country occupied and governed by foreigners were recognized. In certain intellectual circles a philosophical foundation was being forged for a broader accommodation with the new regime, and it had the support of the majority of the people. This new orientation curtly relegated to the wastepaper basket most of the traditional ideas surrounding statehood and national sovereignty as well as beliefs, sanctified by Spanish history, of duty toward the mother country and of sacrifices every Spaniard should be prepared to make for her sake—all these ideas and beliefs interpenetrating, modifying and qualifying one another, and with every living breath creating, recreating, and creating anew a national consciousness. In their place the distinguished intellectuals posited the prospect of unhampered individual and societal development, a search for better social cohesion, for a better family structure, for better utilization of human intelligence and of natural resources, not in a national context but in a non-national, secular one largely determined by scientific data and an up-to-date teleology. As a distinguished representative of the movement put it, "Our task is to demythologize man, demythologize society, demythologize human existence itself, and this can only be done by tearing off from what confronts us and casting away the thoughtless incrustations which kings and princes, national assemblies and patriotic rallies, and, yes, Catholic priests and theologians implanted there." Soon the movement came to be known as "new humanism," and its adherents, "the new humanists," refused to sup with the devil for the good of their irrefutable data and their altruistic convictions.

But in the opposite corner stood a slim band of old and young incorrigibles who greeted the humanists with prolonged jeers and preached that total annihilation was preferable to a life lived in a society that was part zoo and part test tube. Their opponents comforted themselves with the thought that they, the Incorrigibles, were but a tiny minority and that very few gave them as much as a thought.

Elsewhere on the continent of Europe the face of Islam showed a more frightening aspect. In the Balkans their savage armies swept like a tornado from Tirana to the Swiss border, pillaging, burning towns and villages to the ground, and massacring whoever stood in their way. At first their commanders announced all they wanted was to avenge their fellow Muslims slaughtered in these parts earlier in the century, but soon carnage became indiscriminate, and one bloodbath followed another. The Muslims never established a civilian administration anywhere in the Balkans, as they had done in Spain where it worked closely with the Spanish authorities, and the whole Balkan Peninsula was under continual martial law, which in practice meant that roving bands of Muslims armed to the teeth could do what they pleased. Everywhere chaos reigned. The countries of the peninsula asked NATO and the

United Nations for assistance, but these organizations refused to commit troops to tame the aggressor. Instead they advised the distressed peoples of the Balkans to reach whatever accommodation they could with the followers of Prophet Mohammed and resign themselves to fate.

In Italy the situation was just as bad, if not worse. From the very outset the Mahdis and the Islamic military leaders had viewed Italy as a handmaiden of the Great Satan. They were loath to disregard her zealous compliance with American interests at the beginning of the century during the invasion of Iraq and later. Moreover, Italy was for them in every sense the forefront of the Western world, that world which they hated and wanted to bring down no matter what the cost, no matter what the sacrifice. The new masters ransacked Italian treasury, packed off thousands of men to concentration camps, and declared war on Italian intelligentsia, doing their best to reduce the whole country to the level of an enormous forced labor camp where only those exercising their brawn like Stakhanovites deserved consideration.

The enslavement of the Italian people was barbaric and humiliating in the extreme, and at first protests were organized, raids on military installations mounted, and numerous acts of sabotage engaged in. But the Muslims had apparently learned the art of quelling a restive population from the Nazis. Death penalty was summarily meted out, property confiscated with the stroke of the pen, and for every dead Islamic soldier twenty Italians, more often than not drawn from the professional classes, faced immediate execution. While quislings did their dirty work, brave Italians gave their lives for what many believed to be a lost cause. Things were going from bad to worse and still the United Nations and NATO did nothing. But the Mohammedans were regrouping and practically retching in anticipation. After more than a year and half of the occupation of Spain, Italy, and the Balkans, the swaggering armies converged on Milano and held there revels and victory parades several days running. In the United States and Britain this was widely interpreted as a respite preparatory to the invasion of France or Germany, or both.

But the Mohammedans surprised everyone. Assembling their large armies at the three principal ports of entry from Italy into Switzerland, they easily overpowered the border guards and rushed across the peaceful Helvetian landscape. In a matter of days the country was overrun and held in the Islamic grip. The Swiss were so astounded that they had no time to feel indignant or offended. "What's happened to Swiss neutrality, an article of faith in the modern world and immensely benefiting the whole world for centuries?" they asked in despair. The Muslims wasted no words or time. Their financial experts, flown posthaste from the Middle East, went to work ransacking the national treasury and appropriating the funds and money certificates in all Swiss banks. If the deposits were shared by Swiss and foreign banking houses, hostages were immediately taken and orders given to return the balance to Switzerland within twenty-four hours. Non-compliance sealed the fate of the hostages, who were hanged one by one in public squares, and very soon all orders issued by the invading force, financial and otherwise, were scrupulously obeyed.

There were, of course, protests, and delegations of leading citizens called repeatedly on the Muslim commander-in-chief. The meetings led nowhere. Still the Swiss would not desist. They were quick to remind their new masters that only six months before the president of Switzerland, eager to emphasize his country's centuries-old pledge of neutrality, had made a goodwill tour of the Islamic world—a decidedly triumphant one, as his aides had assured him. Over the course of that tour he had visited not only large cities like Baghdad, Tehran, Cairo, Kabul, and Beirut, but a quantity of small towns and villages, forging new bonds between ordinary Helvetians and ordinary Arabs including school children in both parts of the world. Hundreds of Swiss teachers were training young Islamic minds in all subjects, not forgetting the political lessons of the Swiss Confederation, which had taught the world so much and could teach it even more.

When confronted by such a barrage of self-righteousness the Muslim commander in chief, a rough diamond at best, invariably belched in the faces of his interlocutors and told them in a queer mixture of French and German that he didn't give two hoots for the lessons of Swiss history and the pledges of Swiss neutrality. He asserted that the Muslim world needed cash, and as Switzerland was a very wealthy country it would be fleeced and squeezed to the last franc, this being the only thing that mattered. Furthermore, the much-touted Swiss neutrality was hogwash anyway because the Swiss sided with the Great Satan when it suited them and had to be punished! Finally he said that he was sick and tired of all those cute Swiss stories of "Heidi this" and

"Heidi that" and of "William Tell and the goddamn apple" and assorted others, and that he didn't give a damn about Swiss legends and the Swiss Family Robinson and the rest, having heard it all ad nauseum during his diplomatic posting in Bern years before, and that the sole things Swiss he cared for were Swiss apple strudel and Swiss cheeses and that the rest of the confounded Helvetiana could go to hell. As he had important matters to attend to, he asked the delegation to depart from his office, and told them if they refused he'd have them shot.

The nine months of merciless Islamic occupation that the Swiss nation endured were not leading to anything better as time went on, and almost two and half years had passed since the fanatical armies had crossed the Straits of Gibraltar and landed in Italy and the Balkans. The West had not responded. The United Nations and NATO had not come to the rescue. Still, public opinion in the United States, Canada, and Britain, in the countries of Eastern Europe, in Japan, Australia, and New Zealand was becoming more and more vocal, clamoring for the liberation of the enslaved nations.

In the United States in particular demonstrations outside the White House, in Times Square, in big cities, and on select college campuses were growing more intense and militant. At Harvard a doctoral candidate of high promise by the name of Siegfried La Rochelle was watching the events very closely, already making notes on how American foreign policy could be improved and how in the future the Western world could be made immune from Islamic and other attacks.

Then fate intervened. Shortly before the invasion of Switzerland very large sums of private money—mostly from the United States, but also from Canada, Great Britain, and other English-speaking countries—amounting to billions of dollars had been temporarily deposited in Swiss banks under reciprocal agreements. As the Mohammedan troops were overturning border signs, several brainy bank officials guessing what to expect transferred electronically very large sums of money from Switzerland to Denmark and Sweden, including the American deposits and those from other English-speaking countries. So clever was the ruse that for a long time the finance teams from the Middle East could not get to the bottom of it, and Islamic authorities were left with the discouraging thought that much less money was actually in the possession of the major Swiss banks than they had expected. But one day the secret was out, and the Islamic *gauleiters* demanded prompt electronic return of the funds from Copenhagen and Stockholm to Zürich and Geneva. The Danes and the Swedes refused, invoking international law and declaring that present-day Switzerland to be no longer a free agent but occupied territory in the clutches of a criminal foreign power.

The Mohammedans threatened to invade Denmark and Sweden and applied the sternest measures against the Swiss. At this point blood rose and a bone crackled in the highly complex organism of Western society. The bulk of the transferred billions belonged to mammoth corporations, but some of it was the property of small investors risking their life savings, and everyone stood to lose if the Muslim barbarians were not stopped in their tracks. For once Wall Street and Main Street joined hands, not superficially and for appearances' sake as they had done so often in times past, but with unswerving commitment and a grim determination. Something like a spontaneous national movement swept the country. Deposits in Switzerland were a routine move calculated to benefit corporate America and individual America and no one blamed the American banks. But everyone blamed the rogue Islamic states, their criminal methods and ways.

The Republican administration responded to the people's demands, and the president addressed the nation on all TV channels promising swift retaliatory action. In the next forty-eight hours American, Canadian, and British bombers dropped an unheard-of quantity of high explosives on Islamic military installations in the Middle East and elsewhere and followed it with precision bombing in Spain, Italy, and the Balkans. Three days later advance units of the Allied Expeditionary Force were parachuted into Spanish Morocco, encountering scant resistance, and the following day they crossed into Spain. Fighting was fierce as the Allies advanced eastward and northward, but now the Spaniards rose in revolt, forming their own battalions and charging the enemy. They also resorted to every imaginable manner of sabotage, crippling and demoralizing the Mohammedans. Seven days later, even before the ink was dry on multiple international covenants, a gigantic coalition was born, encompassing twenty-one countries and pledged to the expulsion of the invaders from Europe, defeating them on their home ground and stamping out once and for all the danger of a jihad. American, Canadian, and British troops—nobly supported by Swedish, Norwegian, and Danish contingents, by ones from the Czech and

Slovak republics, from Romania and Hungary, Austria, and Poland, the Ukraine and Belorussia, Lithuania, Latvia, Estonia, and Greece—landed in overpowering numbers in Sicily and at Genoa, at Trieste and Delvine.

In the American contingent Second Lieutenant Siegfried La Rochelle, fresh from ROTC, impatiently waited for combat and was soon to be decorated and mentioned in dispatches. Australia and New Zealand had accomplished the impossible: they had transported entire armies by air to Gibraltar and the boot of Italy at a day's notice, and Japan had put a division of its new citizen army, democratic in spirit yet hearkening back to the warlike code of the samurai, at the disposal of the coalition. Highly trained troops poured in from South Korea, and combined forces of Dutch and Israeli paratroopers were dropped outside Bern, Zürich, Geneva, and Lansanne to start the counteroffensive on Swiss soil.

Only France, Germany, and Russia abstained, secretly hoping for a Muslim victory and the eventual strangulation of the Great Satan and his minions. France, moreover, offered asylum to all Muslim troops crossing her borders in flight, in the words of her president, "to those heroes who defended civilization against the encroaches of Western barbarians." The coalition, it was noted by friend and foe alike, was the work of the United States and its allies, and the United Nations and NATO played no part in it.

In fact already in the late 2050s and more noticeably in the early '60s the United Nations was becoming no more than a debating society with no teeth, passing resolutions, expressing indignation, calling the culpable countries to order, and indulging in endless discussions without being able to prevent or punish a single instance of rank aggression or international misconduct. To be sure, successive secretaries general of this once powerful organization flew to all parts of the globe to confer with national and opposition leaders, always under klieg lights, and later presented reports that no one read. In the general assembly the unfailing response to a new topic introduced for consideration was a call for further study, the assumption being that the present degree of knowledge of any new topic by the delegates was hopelessly inadequate and that votes could not be counted. But when additional study or studies were completed the skeptics were still far from being satisfied, and they demanded another study or studies of the not-so-new topic, thus eliminating it from the arena of possible action. For reasons that no one could cogently explain, the skeptics and the procrastinators in the general assembly were usually in the majority, though the size of this majority varied from session to session in accordance with the hidden laws that once again were a cipher. The security council was constantly divided and constantly wrangling. The reforms that had increased its composition and that were later rescinded to be followed by new reforms did not create anything even remotely resembling a parliamentary spirit, and there was much discontent in that highly select body whose origins were multiple and apparently multiplying. France in particular was stirring the embers, but Germany and Russia were not too far behind.

For all practical purposes the security council of the United Nations as a tribunal safeguarding the rights of nations and punishing the violations of these rights was dead in the water. Still it held regular meetings and provided a forum for ventilating issues deemed worthy of its attention. As several embittered wits in different countries put it, "We are so much in love with ancient forms that we have given up any interest in the essence these forms are designed to enclose. We have lost all sense of proportion. We have become a race of nostalgic perverts and disoriented dreamers."

As for NATO, since the collapse of the communist empire it had lost much of its luster. Its leaders banked on the return of this empire with a vengeance, and when it did not happen they began to view their immense organization as having lost its *raison d'être*. They had once been after big game, and later as the decades of the twenty-first century rolled on they were continually confronted by petty tasks, quarrels between insignificant countries about trivial matters that could have been settled easily by a justice-of-the-peace or a police chief. When the Islamic Holy War broke out NATO was incredulous of it posing a serious threat to any European country. The North Atlantic Treaty Organization had been caught napping, and eventually the United States government decided it would rather do without the egregiously prestigious and antiquated war machine with its grand headquarters in Brussels.

The initiative to liberate Spain, Italy, and the Balkans came from the United States, but from the outset this country was supported by other English-speaking countries, and thereafter by practically all of Europe, with notable exceptions. The coalition set about its task methodically, expecting no quick and easy victories, but in reality the Muslim forces everywhere did not show the same spunk as before in the heyday of their fanatical advancement. Early in the campaign the West attained absolute superiority in the air, and the disintegrating enemy was strafed night and day. Entire regiments surrendered, with thousands of enlisted men claiming they had been pressed into military service against their conscience and asking only to be returned to their homes. Concurrently the revitalized and emboldened partisans in occupied territory, freshly armed and resupplied, harassed the foe, and no quarter was given.

Few Mohammedan soldiers managed to escape into France as the coalition had constructed enormous POW camps at the foot of the Pyrenees in Spain and in Italy and Switzerland in the regions adjoining the French border. They hunted down what was left of the regular Muslim army, the marauders and the deserters. In the Balkans the camps were situated along the length and width of the peninsula. All of them were closely guarded. Because of the atrocities committed wherever the Mohammedan boot touched the ground, the coalition refused to differentiate between captured officers and men. All were herded into the same camps and subjected to the same stern disciplinary rules including many hours of heavy manual labor each day. Disquieting reports reached the outside world of kangaroo courts held in these camps and of wild acts of violence and revenge perpetrated. But the coalition refused to interfere. Here and there pockets of Muslim resistance could still be spotted, but the coalition's campaign of liberation was winding down to a close. It lasted six months.

By Christmas of 2064 the enemy was either dead or in POW camps, only a handful having successfully escaped in makeshift boats to North Africa. Christmas of that year was celebrated in Spain, Italy, Switzerland, and all the countries of the Balkans as no other Christmas in living memory. In solemn ceremonies Te Deums were sung in cathedrals and churches filled to capacity and for days there was dancing in the streets. Even before the fighting stopped Swiss embassies in the countries of the coalition were receiving urgent messages asking for an armistice. "The war is now over," the messages read, "and we give you our solemn promise that Islamic forces will not attack the West again.

Let's have peace, peace for centuries to come." But the coalition was incredulous of these promises born of dire necessity.

In the meantime there were things to be settled in the liberated countries. Once national governments were restored and civil administration brought back to life, the coalition handed all the POWs, millions of them, over in perpetuity to the countries concerned, appointing these countries sole judges and arbiters of their fate with undisputed authority over the duration of their imprisonment, the manner of their treatment, and all other matters pertaining thereto. In Spain, Italy, Switzerland, and the Balkans special tribunals were at once created to try the collaborators. While upholding the spirit and the letter of the law, these tribunals showed no mercy. As for the former POWs, now unhappy wards of the state, the great majority were destined to live out their lives in the countries where they were captured, condemned to perpetual hard labor. Repatriation was never an option. Death of natural causes and suicide were high, and reports of appalling conditions under which the prisoners lived, particularly in the Balkans and in Italy, reached Western countries. The International Red Cross and various humanitarian organizations studied the matter, but in the end very little was done to improve prison conditions.

Soon members of the coalition turned their eyes to the Middle East, the hotbed of Muslim fanaticism and the hub of military planning. All Muslim countries had taken part in the holy war against the West but some more actively than the others. The undisputed leaders were Iraq, Iran, and Syria, but Afghanistan, Egypt, Saudi Arabia, and Libya stood in the forefront. On the other hand, Tunisia, Algiers, and Morocco provided for the most part only logistical support, while Yemen, Jordan, and Lebanon did as little as possible, officially proud to be counted as combatants, but behind closed doors trying every trick in the book to wash their hands of the entire experience. It was in Iraq and preeminently in Baghdad that plots had been hatched, strategies formulated, bold military strokes recommended and finalized. Iraq continued to be the head of Islam and Baghdad its hateful never-sleeping brain. Thence orders were dispatched to the other parts of the Mohammedan world, and when urgent councils were to be held the new satraps and sheiks congregated in the fair city on the Tigris.

Members of the coalition promptly decided that utter defeat and swift reoccupation of Iraq were their first priority. "Knock Iraq out of the game, that twisted command post, and the rest of the Mohammedan Empire will fall to the ground like an overripe plum off a withered branch," shouted the generals, and the politicians nodded their assent. The President of the United States approved the invasion, and the Congress declared it legitimate and in the best interest of the country. Few voices of dissent were raised, and other countries followed suit.

Early in 2065 the coalition mounted an attack against Iraq from three sides: from bases in Israel, from Turkey, and from the Persian Gulf. Fierce fighting raged but the outcome was never in doubt, and the coalition's superiority in ground troops, in air support, and at sea was overwhelming. In this second phase of the war against the barbaric Islam, First Lieutenant Siegfried La Rochelle again performed famously, this time as a tank commander. Within four weeks the Mohammedan forces were routed and Iraq occupied. Two months later after weak and haphazard resistance, occupation extended to all the other combatant countries. When the hostilities had ceased the coalition addressed itself to the arduous task of converting former foes to peace-loving neutrals or, better still, fledgling friends. Democratic elections were held and governments formed renouncing wars of aggression against the West and against their neighbors. Huge subsidies, mostly from the United States, revived the bankrupt economies, and slowly the face of Islam changed. The occupation lasted for five years, and the last coalition troops left just before the end of 2069. At this juncture there was peace everywhere on earth, and the Middle East was inching toward better life for all under a democratic aegis.

While the peoples of the world were smugly congratulating themselves on the final dousing of the main trouble spot whence lethal flames had once shot forth spelling panic far and wide, and while sociologists and political scientists in all countries were calling for more effective governmental structures, profound cultural changes were at work, principally in the United States but also in other English-speaking countries. They had first been noticed in the early 60s, and they gathered momentum as the decade progressed. A mighty religious awakening shook the American people, comparable in scope and intensity to the Great Awakening of the 1730s and '40s.

The fuse setting in motion this strapping movement was a novel and extremely earnest evangelicalism kneading practically all the churches and religious communities in the United States to heights formerly unknown. No new religion was founded and no new messiah stood on the world stage. Instead each existing church was reinvigorated beyond its pastor's wildest dreams, in each of them revivalistic zeal placed church dogma and church law far above secular laws, with ministers and priests pontificating ad infinitum and ad nauseam on the subject of the church alone being able to point to the right path for men and women to follow and sanctifying the individual with beliefs and obligations making him or her worthy of being called a child of God.

Episcopalians and Lutherans, Presbyterians and Baptists, Mormons and fundamentalists of every conceivable stripe all danced to the same merry tune. Roman Catholics went one better. Histrionically alert, their jig of joy drew now and then from the mystical contemplations of Ignatius of Loyola but kinetically it was modeled on tap dancing. As an instrument of anti-secularism it was bewitching, far surpassing the most emotively charged artifacts of counter-reformation. It won thousands of converts to the Roman cause. A belief gained ground that good citizenship, social responsibilities, ethics, and morality all emanated from the church and ended there. In this all-consuming wave of religiosity there was no room for secular institutions, secular principles, for anything secular, in fact. Whatever was not sanctioned by a Christian church was deemed worthless and ready to be tossed away onto the garbage pile.

Nor was Jewry left behind. In synagogues across the United States hundreds of rabbis, their breasts swelling with passion, preached a new faith. They called it "Judaism reborn." Whether Orthodox, Conservative, or Reformed, they feverishly taught that observance of the Law was not enough. It must be zealous, full-hearted observance in the course of which the exalted standards of the Jewish faith were lived through and relived with every pore of one's body, with every beat of one's heart. "Feeling is all," they shouted to the multitude, and the multitude responded, clamorously doing their bidding. In Jewish communities no less than in Christian ones there promptly grew an apathy about the state and what it stood for, its laws and institutions, its values, its educational policies and administrative patterns, and it was followed by a resounding censure of all of them. The clerics saw the state as a dump filled with the dregs of a played-out civilization, and soon more extreme views were advanced. It was asserted more and more frequently that it was only the church or the synagogue that had the right to regulate human lives individually and collectively and that the state's stamp of approval was not only meaningless but contrary to God's law. And violation of God's law invited a terrible punishment.

The revivalistic flame burned also in places of worship outside the Judeo-Christian tradition, in mosques, in Buddhist and Shinto temples, among the followers of Confucius, and in other lesser known congregations tracing their pedigree to remote places and continents. Yes, the flamed burned there too, but not as fervently. Americans of one or the other of these persuasions were more levelheaded, less likely to be enslaved by frantic emotion and more reluctant than their Christian and Judaic brethren to erase centuries of Western civilization for an exotic pipe dream. Cold-shouldered and not infrequently taken to task, they were called "primitives" by the nobs of the mainstream.

Chapter 4

The Pale Shadow

In the early 2070s rising religious fervor began to corrode American political institutions. To be sure general elections were held every four years, and members of the House of Representatives were duly elected every two years, and U.S. senators every six years, as of yore. But progressively the elected officials enjoyed less and less power and less and less authority. The old-fashioned hustings were retained and enthusiastically engaged in, adorned by the candidates' speeches, debates and all the fuss and commotion associated with the American elective process. But visibly these hustings were becoming no more than sporting events, like contests of nationally prominent football or baseball teams where rooting crowds boisterously favored one team or the other. Nine out of ten voters knew that the elected or reelected congressman or senator would be a figurehead and no more. And the same net of deception was being cast over the presidency. More and more and unmistakably the real power came to rest in the hands of clerics representing the gamut of Christian churches and Jewish temples, who used the machinery of the legislative, executive, and judicial branches of the government but were not answerable to them.

The president still appointed members of his cabinet, but these members had as much authority as parking attendants catering to drivers pooh-poohing regulations and staunchly refusing to pay parking fees. New secretaries of departments, officials in everything but name, were emerging from the shadows, and they and no one else held the reins of power. The United States was ceasing to be a democracy and was fast becoming an oligarchy and a theocracy. As a well-placed and very perceptive foreign commentator put it, "Today the United States is a somnambulistic nation. The Americans march behind their real leaders shoulder to shoulder like a bunch of zombies still paying histrionic lip service to the forms of old, to what had substance once and to what they truly loved. Such dissociation of personality on a national scale had been unknown in world history and in the annals of clinical psychology. It came to pass in one of the most advanced countries in the world. I wonder," the commentator wound up by saying, "whether this is not the starkest danger facing postmodern man."

The rise to power of Everett Huston reflected the new ethos of the Great Republic and served as a corrective to those who were not amenable to the winds of change. Born to poverty on a small farm in North Carolina, young Ev, together with his three elder brothers and four sisters, was brought up on the word of the Lord. His stern father, sometime a lay preacher, saw to it that Christian faith and the example of the Savior permeated every nook and cranny of his family's life, and a lengthy Bible reading, followed by an equally lengthy meditation, was the highlight of every single day. Quicker and more ambitious than his brothers, Ev aspired from a very early age to be an evangelist, and when at the age of fourteen he attended a revival in Charlotte at which a famous evangelist preached, his mind was made up once and for all. While still in high school he helped the pastor at his Baptist church in Charlotte in a variety of ways, and even before he graduated he tried his hand at preaching before small rural congregations. He was well received wherever he went, and before long the word spread that young Ev, or Preacher Ev, was as good as he looked and with his upright freckled face, his mane of light-brown hair falling over his cheeks and neck, and standing trim and firm at six feet, four inches, he looked like every mother's dream for her daughter.

Doing odd jobs after graduation and then trying his hand at carpentry and door-to-door selling to help the family, Ev went on preaching and his reputation grew. Two years later he won a scholarship to the Alabama Bible Institute and after a year transferred to Casibian College in Nebraska, a much-touted Baptist institution accepting with open arms students from all Christian denominations. He majored in history and political science, and in four years graduated magna cum laude.

He also met a girl, Bonnie Leckstrum, whose parents had been Christian missionaries in South America. Ev and Bonnie were married a week after graduation on the same day that he became an ordained minister. They moved to Georgia and later to South Carolina where Ev tended to his flock and Bonnie proved to be a highly efficient and extremely helpful minister's wife. By now Ev was frequently invited to preach at revivals not only in the South but in the entire Midwest, and the papers took note of his fiery preaching style as he jabbed a point home with his index finger.

The five years Ev and Bonnie and their two toddling children spent in Georgia and South Carolina were the time to remember. Ev had an uncanny talent of awakening in large crowds and small a desire to commit their lives to Jesus Christ. With one voice new converts made it clear this desire had come from within, from their own psyches, from their own souls. They staunchly denied that the evangelist had persuaded them to embrace the Savior making promises true or false. They asserted the step they had taken was of their own volition and Everett Huston, who habitually opened revivals with the words from John, "I am the way and the truth and the life," and stressed again and again "the new birth" wholeheartedly concurred.

One day while in the bosom of his family Ev dropped a bombshell. He informed Bonnie that he was taking a sabbatical from the ministry. He would enroll in a law school, since law was a stepping-stone to politics, and he had set his mind on entering politics, though he would always treasure his evangelical and revivalistic heritage. Bonnie was at first flabbergasted, then furious and beside herself. For a time she entertained the idea that her husband had cracked up and insisted on his seeing not only the family physician but also a "specialist" downtown. When the two of them pronounced Ev sane beyond the shadow of a doubt and not even suffering from a mild case of dejection, she was again beside herself. Everett was in holy orders; every month he enabled thousands of strangers to find their way to Christ. His was the noblest profession on the face of the earth, and besides the two of them made such a wonderful team and their life was the good life! Why fall down headlong into the gutter—because she was convinced the world of politics was the gutter, where every depravity was freely indulged in and redeeming features were as rare as robins on a snowy night! Why, why, why? Hard as he tried Everett could not make a cogent case for his decision—to Bonnie at least. Still arguing, they took their abode in Virginia where Everett enrolled in a law school while Bonnie started work in the offices of Crusade for Christ, a mammoth evangelical enterprise. They separated for a while, were reunited, separated again, and again joined forces but when at the end of three years Everett was getting his DJ degree, he and Bonnie went their separate ways, the only matter worth considering was whether they would opt for a speedy divorce or for an indeterminate separation, each of them half-hoping for a change of heart in the other. In the end they opted for the for-mer.

While getting his feet wet as a junior associate at a law firm on the outskirts of Macon, Everett devoted every free moment to his political agenda. He became a devoted member of the Republican Party, and in the general election of 2072 he greatly helped in the election of Republican candidates not only around Macon but statewide. After the Republican victory he was rewarded by being elected state judge, prac-tically unopposed and winning by a wide margin. Four years later he entered the state assembly and with evangelistic fervor castigated pub-lic and private vices. He made new friends, founded the Coalition for Clean Living, and made no secret of his deep suspicion of what he dubbed secularism on the rampage, targeting any enterprise large or small from a village sweepstakes to interstate highway construction from which the fine hand of a church or temple had been absent.

The presidential election of 2076 was the last one in which the winning candidate, a Democrat, made a spirited attempt to preserve the country within its historical and cultural legacy. Julia Hernandez was a no-nonsense man. He firmly believed in the separation of church and state, in the rule of law, and in carrying out his duties as chief executive in the manner spelled out in Article II of the United States Constitution. No less firmly did he believe in the two-party system, in the separation of power, in the trial of all crimes by jury except in cases of impeachment, in all the provisions of the Bill of Rights, in popular sovereignty and limited government. Hernandez was a feisty fighter, but on his watch the chinks and crevices in the national edifice the Founding Fathers had so carefully molded broke out relentlessly and soon threatened to mar it beyond recognition.

Everett, now the kingmaker in the Carolinas, hammered his point home again and again that President Hernandez ought to be impeached for having violated the Constitution of the United States. But this course of action proved far less popular than had been expected. Infinitely more euphoria was created by a rapid emergence of new organizations committed to strengthening the role of religion in all walks of life: "Sacred Partnership," "Coalition to Abolish Separation of Church and State," "Christ Triumphant at Last," "The New Yeshiva and What It Can Do for You," "The Torah Society," and a host of similar ones, all of them leaving no stone unturned in the pursuit of their sacred cause.

As the weeks and months of 2076 fleeted by, Everett came to the realization that to turn the country inside out and achieve total victory need not entail capturing the legislative, executive, and judicial branches of the government. Such a plan, praiseworthy though it appeared, called for a long haul, and the outcome remained problematic at best. It was more politic to create alternatives to the government, counter-forces luring citizens away from the discredited and moribund corridors where power had once dwelt to the radiant workshops and smithies of the new society. Everett and his friends were right. The host of religious clubs and associations that sprang up like mushrooms after April showers created constituencies far stronger than the traditional ones still putting their faith in the existing government. Congressmen and congresswomen were persuaded to vote for measures strengthening the power of religion in every walk of life and ignoring the separation of church and state. In more than twenty states new assemblies had been formed challenging the authority of state legislatures and the U.S. Congress and proclaiming themselves duly elected legislative bodies.

Their number grew and in Washington President Hernandez fought a losing battle against his own cabinet, where the majority urged him to resign. He refused but from that moment on he became more and more powerless and his hands were tied. As the last resort he went to the country, patiently explaining in a succession of TV appearances how the newly risen sinister forces, hiding behind the shield of religion, were tearing up the Constitution and perverting American democracy.

The country's reaction to this direct appeal was mixed, and while some expressed a vivid sympathy for the president personally, a tiny minority among them going the full mile to pep him up, the majority wanted him either to start being fully accommodating or else to step down. A coup de grâce was administered to the president when his last

fireside chat was cancelled by the networks without a word of explanation minutes before it was due to begin.

Still, Julia Hernandez hung on, making the best of a rotten situation. By the fall of 2079, American political institutions were fast
becoming a pale shadow of what they once had been. Everett Huston
had been appointed to the United States Supreme Court by the previous president, and through a perfectly normal and expected succession
of deaths and retirements he now came to occupy the glorious office of
Chief Justice of the United States. More than that, he was the real ruler
of the country. In all national matters, be they administrative or legal,
federal, or emanating from individual states, his authority was supreme
and his voice decisive. He was ably assisted by three handpicked dignitaries who could have been his intellectual and spiritual clones, so faithfully close did they stand to him in general orientation, judgments
rendered, and philosophy of life: Phineas Léger, son of Yale, a brilliant
and highly sophisticated journalist and writer who, two decades earlier,
had founded *National Forum*, a right-wing religiously-oriented monthly whose editorials written by the founder paved the way for the Great
Awakening and helped to shake the republic to its very foundations.
Léger, an accomplished pianist and fluent in French, Italian, and
Spanish, was the overseer of the press, of education, of the channels of
communication between the new masters and the people, a polished
spokesman for and explicator of the policies of the new establishment.
Refined and witty, he was a justly acclaimed raconteur who knew the
power of the word, spoken and written, and was master of both. Everett
held him in high esteem; Homily Grister, a Southerner like his leader
and a Harvard MD, a tight-lipped and all-noticing chastener of vice—
public and private—in its multiple manifestations, and an eager
redeemer of those who were mending their evil ways. Taciturn Homily
certainly was, but now and then the Southern gift of the gab would
break through and, coupled with his loathing of everything that was not
virginal and decorous, would cascade into prolonged ranting that first
thrilled and then exasperated the audience. Homily's beat was the moral
welfare of the American nation, which had to be protected from the
rowdies and snakes in the grass by all means overt and covert available
to man.

He also made an excellent policeman. Everett looked upon Homily
as his alter ego.

The third member of the triumvirate, which carried out every single wish of Chief Justice to a tee, Ganymede Pillows, appeared at first sight modest and withdrawn and much younger than his biological age. Enthusing over baseball and football, about which he wrote for the daily papers, he spent much time in locker rooms and around the field. This, as many insisted, gave him that unmistakable clean-cut look that no passage of time could ravage. He was the cupbearer and the new all-American Peter Pan, a constant reminder to all and sundry of the irreplaceable values of adolescence without which American culture would be just another fake. But Ganymede was also a serious researcher and the author of highly prized books on economics. He had an uncanny knack for keeping his ear to the ground along Wall Street and Main Street and making sense of reams of economic statistics like no other. The area the Savior of the Country—the name by which Everett Huston was more and more frequently identified—had demarcated for his youthful-looking protégé was the economic life of the United States, pure and simple, with some religious duties added. Employment, which Ganymede kept near the full mark, labor disputes, economic growth and ways thereof, exports and imports, labor laws, the touchy subject of mergers of mammoth corporations, and a new place in the sun for small businesses, all these came under the aegis of the sports enthusiast and locker room frequenter who did not smoke, tasted nothing more potent than ginger ale, and was a living incarnation of the maxim "early to bed, early to rise."

When the associates and friends of Chief Justice pointed out that for all his economic savvy Ganymede projected the image of a college sophomore in love with himself and on the loose, such an image far from sitting well with the country at large, Everett would cast a long look far above the interlocutors' heads and sound off with the conviction of a rabbit judge, "It takes all kind to build a dam." But secretly he was highly gratified with his brainy coadjutor, who had all the answers even though at times short pants suited him better than long ones. Moreover, as discriminating news watchers were quick to notice, even though Ganymede's youthfulness was what first caught the eye the man practiced the ruses and the self-elevating guile of a seasoned politician. At roundtable discussions on and off TV he usually managed to be the last one to speak, making it plain he was not just another discussant but the ultimate voice of truth. Others might tackle this or that aspect of the topic and express their personal views but he, Ganymede Pillows, taking cognizance of all the aspects of the matter, offered the authoritative judgment, the way things really were. Others blithely flitted around a topic, but he, Ganymede Pillows, always spoke *ex cathedra*. Those who did not like him maintained he had missed his allotted time in history and should have been a medieval pope.

Everett Huston sat in Heaven pulling strings, and his three deputies on earth, Phin, Hom, and Gan, did a yeoman's job. As for the foreign policy of the United States, he left it entirely in the hands of Siegfried La Rochelle. At first he had misgivings, resulting mostly from his scathing disparagement of La Rochelle's private life. "Why, he's a shameless woman chaser, a sex maniac!" he hollered in the faces of his confidants. "A sex mill. He has no place in our New Jerusalem of faith and virtue." In due course, however, Huston came to understand La Rochelle's genius in diplomacy and politics and the services he had rendered to the state. He would praise La Rochelle's public successes and hold his tongue on the subject of his character. When. in early 2082, the foundation was being laid for the National Security Advisor's greatest coup, the union of the United States and Japan under the name of Amernipp, Chief Justice's support was speedy and unqualified. And he brought scores of others round.

In 2079, as the decade was fast drawing to a close, Everett Huston was almost sixty, but he looked much older and worn out. Gone were the agility and nimbleness of his younger years, and gone too were the buoyancy and joy of life. His face was thickly lined with furrows and wrinkles, moles of hardened yellow skin dotted his forehead, cheeks, and jaw, and deep dark rings encircled his heavy, drooping eyelids. His eyes had lost their luster, and the life that oozed out of his entire person was cheerless, wrapped around the banner of sacred duty that dispensed with levity and profane delights. His goal was the goal of the Prophets, his purpose the purpose of the Apostles, and as his spirit now resided in a super-terrestrial sphere, it judged its fellow man according to the super-terrestrial laws of the Almighty.

Several years after he and Bonnie had separated Everett remarried, this time to an older woman, twice widowed whose mature and stable personality offered the prospect of a well-regulated family life. But this was not what happened. Everett soon discovered that Donna had a veritable aversion to sex, which she considered vulgar and dehumanizing and that she had nothing but scorn for the emotional warmth that a man and a woman might share and give each other. There remained, of course, a well-regulated family life, the two of them partaking of punctually served meals, entertaining and going out as per schedule, and passing the allotted time in reading and conversation. But it was a cold regimen, and it grew colder with each passing day. As for the matters of the bed, Donna informed her husband that of course she would fulfill her wifely duties, hoping at the same time that those duties would be infrequent and of short duration. Everett's temper was getting the best of him, his fuse—always short—was getting shorter, and in social circles he was building for himself a reputation as a grouch. His temper did not improve when he began finding sexual gratification outside of marriage, and a pattern of anger and frustration set in that he was unable to shake off.

He still had stupendous reservoirs of energy that he was putting to good use day after day, and as time went on he was winning new victories for religion, extending its frontiers to places previously untrodden. One day in late spring of 2079 a thought struck him as he was balancing in his head the relative obligations of church and state: why not have just one political party representing both church and state, with the former always getting the upper hand? "Why not?" he muttered to himself. "This will put the last nail in the coffin of that godless and crazy experiment worked up by a bunch of atheistic shysters in Philly in the year of our Lord 1787, the year which will live in infamy. Why not?" Everett confided in his closest associates and made common cause with Phineas Léger, Homily Grister, and Ganymede Pillows. They all concurred, Siegfried La Rochelle being pointedly excluded from deliberations on the grounds of this really not counting as his cup of tea and in addition threatening to distract him from his groundbreaking diplomatic labors.

Once a decision was reached events moved with breakneck speed. In the early days of October a new political party was created, the Church and State Party—C&S for short—and all the other political parties within the borders of the United States were abolished and outlawed, including of course the Democratic and Republican parties, effective April 15, 2080, with time being allowed to the disappearing political organisms to liquidate their affairs and make plans for the future. Many stalwart members of the two major parties and of lesser ones joined C&S, and beginning in that year the one-party system became entrenched in the United States of America. In all local elections and in the general election held in November of 2080 only C&S candidates were allowed to compete, and in the antecedent state primaries and caucuses the same law was upheld. With the advent of 2080 much winnowing went on at the national and state levels, the eager and uncompromising religionists getting rid of their more moderate brethren and sisters in the House of Representatives, in the senate, around the White House, and within the confines of the Supreme Court or securing the support of others who promised compliance with their own zealotry.

The presidential candidate, the one and only in the 2080 general election, was honest Jack Woods, a decent and accommodating ex-naval officer and a former Democratic governor who had lost much sleep over exchanging one political party for another. But in the end he was willing to serve as chief executive under strangely anomalous conditions realizing he would be no more than Chief Justice's messenger boy but consoling himself with the thought that here and there he might do some good, especially when no one was looking, and keep the red, white, and blue as little tarnished as possible. Years later President Woods was hailed as the first member of the American Underground poised against the tyranny the country was duped into, the first freedom fighter in the long annals of freedom fighters who put their lives on the line for what the USA stood for. He had begun modestly, matching every new trick of Huston's with a trick of his own, biding his time and keeping his powder dry.

One change in the composition of the houses of Congress, of the executive and the judicial branches of government stood out prominently after 2080 general election: it was the prevalence of the men and women of the cloth in all elected and appointed offices. Ministers of all Protestant denominations without exception, Roman Catholic priests of the ancient and more progressive dispensation and rabbis of every conceivable stripe were much in evidence. Here and there a divine of another faith could be seen in the legislative chambers or in the executive offices, his or her demeanor betraying that painful sense of isolation that comes from being part of a puny minority, an ayatollah, a Buddhist monk and teacher, and others, all of them equally ignored. After the 2080 general election four-fifths of congresspersons were ordained clerics in church or temple, and ninety-five U.S. senators were men and women of God. Putting his outstanding oratorical gifts to the test and emphasizing the importance of his holy office, Everett Huston had been encouraging clerics to enter the political arena. It was now their arena after centuries of imbecilic and criminal secular reign, and the new and sole party had successfully merged church and state in an innovative manner; the state was wholly subordinated to the church and a new political, social, and cultural unit emerged. The old schism had been healed and Americans could again, after the lapse of five centuries, call themselves children of God.

Everett was pleased as punch with the turn of events of the past twenty years. First a great spiritual awakening that showed conclusively American grit and the direction in which American spirit was tending; then creation of a mighty religious edifice conceived of as a counter-force to existing political institutions from which God's grace had been shamefully spirited away; and finally the taking over of American society and of American life as such by the divine spirit embodied in those fearless souls who marched beside him in the Great Crusade. "We are one foot in the New Jerusalem," he told friends as he was enjoying a brief respite after the resounding victory of November 2080. They urged him to take a long vacation, recharge his batteries, husband his strength, but he refused. "There is still so much to do," he told them, "and God can't be kept waiting."

The powers of his mind soon began converging on his next, and perhaps his final, goal. "Every vice, every blemish, every imperfection must be stamped out in America. All of us must be pure, guiltless, fault-less!" he cried, straining his vocal chords to the utmost as worried friends gathered round him. He was made to sit down, given a soft refreshing drink and a physician was sent for. But he could not be restrained. Piercing all those who wished him well with a bitter zealous stare, he inveighed against godlessness and immorality in a voice that would bring down the walls of Jericho.

"We have to stamp out vice, all vice!" he wound up. And he added on a quieter note, taking them into his confidence, "There is no other way. There is simply no other way."

Chapter 5

The Hole

Carved out of a sliver of northern Montana east of Havre and northwest of Glasgow, and to the north of southern Saskatchewan just below Cypress Hills lay a four hundred-acre camp popularly called "The Hole" even though its official name was the Retention Center for Unrehabilitable, RCU for short. But practically everyone including government officials, guards, and inmates at the center called it by its popular name "The Hole," and very few, if any, ever resorted to its authorized designation. Work on it had begun early in 2081 and was completed in June of 2082, only weeks before the celebration of the union of the United States and Japan and the creation of Amernipp, an immensely powerful new country, became a fait accompli on the Fourth of July and captured everyone's attention. Nevertheless the opening of The Hole was also a grand affair, complete with bands blaring, singers bellowing, and enough speeches to fill a bulky manual of rhetoric. President Woods, the emperor of Japan, and the prime minister of Canada officiated, the first on the last leg of his term of office, and the third a lusty opponent of everything The Hole stood for but sufficiently placated to be invited in. Despite the trio's solemn appearance and the surrounding pomp and circumstance the spectators knew full well this was Everett's show, that he was the prime mover and shaker of the enterprise, and they gave him credit for stepping graciously aside for ceremonial reasons.

Why Chief Justice insisted on tearing a patch of land from the bowels of Canada for his pet project was never fully explained, though Phineas Léger, his most vocal apologist, painted in vivid colors in the editorials of *National Forum* his chief's demonstrable affection for the Canadian nation and his unswerving desire to bring it round to the path of glowing religious faith and righteousness. In the United States and later in Amernipp the reaction to these editorials was very mixed, and in Canada they were laughed out of court. But Chief Justice did not lose any sleep over it. He had made up his mind early in the game. Wrenching the reins of American foreign policy from the hands of Siegfried La Rochelle, he had spoken directly to the Canadian government becoming his own National Security Advisor and his own Secretary of State. He had made an offer of equal partnership, ensuring a place in the detention center for all Canadians who could not be rehabilitated, but their government had demurred. He had made further concessions that were promptly rejected. His blood was up and he sent an ultimatum to the Prime Minister stressing that construction on the sight previously chosen and involving both the U.S. and the Canadian territory would begin soon whether he, the Prime Minister, liked it or not, and in the latter case stern measures would be taken.

"What stern measures?" the PM wired back, telling his cabinet there was no doubt at all the United States of America was ruled by a madman. Chief Justice did not mince words and wired in return that in the struggle to eliminate all vice from American soil much was permitted and that the accepted canons of diplomacy and international relations would have to be suspended. Canada was given forty-eight hours to decide whether she would take advantage of the very real benefits that would accrue to her in handling deviants and perverts or not. If not, the United States would go it alone, and in any event the designated area in Saskatchewan would remain under American control. Opposition on the part of the Canadian government would result in American sanctions, and again Chief Justice did not mince words: for starters air bombardment would be deployed against two large Canadian cities, and he would then be curious to find out whether Canadians came back to their senses or not. La Rochelle at once protested Huston's adventure in realpolitik and was dismissed with scorn.

"Barricade yourself inside a large university library for a month,

Siegfried. You can do least harm in there!" Everett shouted, waving the hapless National Security Advisor out of his office. Determined not to lose face, Canadian parliament met in two consecutive all-night sessions and did its duty. But it soon became apparent that the options were stringently limited and uneven. The fiercest xenophobic hawks had as little stomach for seeing city streets strewn with dead bodies as the liberals and the internationalists, and Prime Minister was telling the nation that the government had the responsibility to prevent wholesale slaughter and in fulfilling this responsibility national honor would not be compromised. Most Canadians agreed, many bottling up their discontent against Big Brother and saving it for another day. America's northern neighbor stared hard facts right in the face and managed to rake up a smile. PM sent a message to Chief Justice acceding to his demands but refusing to dispatch a single Canadian citizen to The Hole as an inmate, and an uneasy truce was reestablished between the two great North American nations.

/   /   /

Under Everett Huston's watchful eye Americans, and later citizens of Amernipp, domiciled in what used to be the United States of America were given every opportunity to find their way back to grace if they had strayed from it. The State was providing highly qualified help in the persons of psychiatrists and psychologists, nurses, counselors, theologians, and holy men. Huston's goal was twofold: a healthy wholesome society functioning in accordance with the law of God and a society rid of every vestige of vice, which also was God's command. The first was a medical, psychological, and theological problem, the second a criminal one. Huston's vision of the world as God had ordained it was free of any anomaly or deviation from the grand salubrious design that was God's gift to the world and that was fully understandable to every God-fearing man and woman. In this design symmetry and order reigned, rules of conduct were absolute and eternal, and no gray areas marred God's handiwork.

Unfortunately there were many violators who ran the gamut of human faithlessness and perversity: homosexuals, lesbians, those born with fewer or more than five fingers on each hand, the colorblind, the tone deaf, the deaf, the mute, those born with a physical deformity of one kind or another, those suffering from dyslexia, those suffering from speech impediments, the left-handed, and the ambidextrous, these last rousing Huston's ire as no other rank of offenders and being branded by him miscreants brought to life when the Almighty's back was turned. Still, all of them without exception had to be helped and brought back to the path of righteousness. But if the cure administered with all the assiduity and devotion possible aborted, they had to be quarantined and cast out of the New Jerusalem into The Hole, for this was the will of God.

In the elaborate theological-medical establishment charged with bringing lost souls back to the fold one simple rule reigned supreme and exacted obedience in every instance: to become rehabilitated the patient stands in dire need of God's grace but must also show ardorous desire to rejoin the life of holy normalcy. The first was infinitely more important than the second, which nevertheless could not be underestimated. It was the simultaneous fulfillment of both conditions that brought about the best results. Nevertheless in the curative process, which in some cases stretched over long periods of time, the religious and theological ingredient carried more weight than the medical one. Relatively few homosexuals, male or female, turned over a new heterosexual leaf, and there were no cases of colorblind or tone-deaf patients being able to distinguish between colors or gaining a new sensitivity in noticing differences in musical pitch even though the second condition, arduous desire to rejoin life of normalcy, had been fulfilled to the letter.

Huston had a ready explanation for these apparent failures, which in reality were not failures at all but veiled manifestations of divine intent, and this became the second rule of the theological-medical establishment. Every human being, Chief Justice proclaimed, carried within himself or herself a burden of guilt, and this burden was one of the following three: manifest guilt, resulting from a deliberate transgression by the sinner, of which the sinner was fully aware, prompt punishment following; secondly, revealed guilt, which sprung from a transgression committed very early in one's life and on occasion buried so deeply in the individual's subconscious that it had to be extracted with the help of therapy and psychoanalysis and then made evident to the offender; and thirdly, deductible guilt, which was not apparent at first and could only be grasped when placed with God's help in the context of His infinite goodness and His unceasing desire to see before Him His own inimitable creation in all its glory, a world free of vice, defect, blemish, or imperfection.

To the first category, that of manifest guilt, belonged homosexuals, lesbians, those guilty of any other sexual deviation, child molesters, sodomites, and the sexually promiscuous—lotharios of one kind or another, wife-and-husband swappers, sexual predators, and all others whose libido, savory or unsavory, quashed all else in their nervous and physiological system. All of them had violated God's law, and their guilt was manifest, but the Almighty was merciful and no stone was left unturned to tear them away from vice and lead them to God's shining house of normalcy. Everett Zacharias Huston, his entire person bursting with energy, did not tire of repeating again and again that every transgressor deserved a second birth.

Revealed guilt presented a more complex problem that, Huston and his cohorts concurred, called for particularly subtle handling. Under this umbrella were gathered those suffering from dyslexia and speech impediments, the left-handed, the ambidextrous, and others with very weak eyesight, or eyes that would not focus. Their treatment, combining imprecations for God's grace and the patients' arduous desire to be cured, bore mixed results. In many instances treatment was lengthened by months, and a search for divine grace was buttressed by collective orisons of hundreds of government workers shepherded to places of worship and asked to give their best. Still, results were often disappointing. There was a heart-rending case of a young woman of spotless reputation and high religious character sadly afflicted with dyslexia whose complete cure, Huston asserted again and again, was merely a matter of time. She was beyond the shadow of a doubt one of those rare creatures who were very dear to God, and God would never turn His countenance away from her. But for some unexplained reason the holy men and the theologians could do little for the young woman, and with time her disorder grew worse, not better. Huston racked his brains again and again and asked for divine guidance, but he was unable to provide a satisfactory explanation.

As it turned out, at the eleventh hour Phineas Léger came to the rescue. In a lengthy article in *National Forum* he argued with breathtaking dexterity that God's ways were often mysterious and mortal transgressors who know Him in so shallow a fashion and understand his design so imperfectly could aspire to no more than a whiff of His true intentions. As for the young woman in question, Léger went on, it was more than likely that her life had not been as blameless as it was made out to be and that a stain (or stains) of culpability darkened it at one time or other, be they invisible to mortal eyes. Only the Almighty in all His infinite wisdom and perspicacity can detect spots on the human escutcheon, spots we would rather forget, we being human, all too human.

The third burden of guilt, deductible guilt, appeared at first to present an insoluble problem to the Keepers of Zion but proved instead to be a cinch. With one mighty stroke Huston cut the Gordian Knot and all was light. Under scrutiny here were the colorblind, the tone-deaf, the deaf, the mute, and those born deformed or disfigured. Accusing newly born babes of having committed heinous crimes for which terrible punishment was inflicted on them may have struck many as an all-time hyperbole, but Huston knew precisely what he was after and, following in the footsteps of his mercurial apologist, built a watertight case.

"Our knowledge of the ways of God is so infinitely limited," he proclaimed with disarming candor, "that what for Him is wisdom and equity is at best for us a dark passage leading nowhere. There are countless areas and levels of human culpability, and some of them go as far back as the prenatal state. Concurrently culpability and the attendant punishment are not restricted by the here and now. It is very probable that many of us are branded with the guilt of our ancestors who lived more than nine generations ago and that we endure the attendant punishment both for their sake and for ours. Our disjointed and fragmented sense of time creates barriers everywhere and adds to our execrable myopia. But for the Almighty time is a continuum, unbroken, uninterrupted, and uniting past, present, and future as one. Do not jeer, son of man, at the apparent injustice when seemingly innocent babies are born with genetic defects of all sorts, some of them so repulsive and horrible as to drive men of little faith to blasphemy or worse. For God sees the whole, and space and time are but sham categories of silly minds. Submit, Tom, Dick, and Harry, for your submission will be the first step on the way to the palace of wisdom and grace and cast doubt out of your heart that guilt deductible is not living proof of God's eternal mercy and love."

The manly efforts to bring all sinners back to the sacred fold continued unabated, but when everything had been tried and failed the government saw no other option but to condemn the unrehabilitable to incarceration for life without possibility of parole within the confines of The Hole. Many had not been fired by sufficient zeal to reform, and it was patent that in many cases God had not bestowed His grace. The inmates were now adjudged as being beyond redemption, and no further attempts were made to cure them. They were the damned, but they were allowed to live out their lives without governmental interference and they were inducted into a variety of highly organized working details, thus defraying expense of shelter and board. They were lodged in accordance with the nature of their offenses: all the homosexuals together, all the lesbians together, all the color-blind inmates together, all those suffering from dyslexia together, and so on down the line. The inmates suffering from birth defects were subdivided by sex, age, and the gravity of the defect, and so were those suffering from physical deformities, the most serious and repugnant cases being classed together and the lesser ones in carefully arranged groups, each quartered separately.

The inmates enjoyed a certain amount of freedom, elected their barracks chiefs and spokespersons carrying their complaints to the administration, but their incoming and outgoing correspondence was rigorously censored; in addition there were frequent unscheduled inspections of personal belongings, and magazines and books in the library were chosen with a stern eye on respectability and moral values, as were the weekly movie showings and accessible TV programs. This being the case, dating back to the day when the first levy of unrepentant lawbreakers marched under the enormous arch bearing euphoric greetings to all newcomers, the premises became a veritable hotbed of illegal traffic in magazines, books, videos, and many other kinds of contraband which would make the administration's hair stand on end. Sooner than expected several keen entrepreneurial minds took the measure of the field—minds that under different circumstances could well have achieved fame and fortune. Constricted by fate they never realized their dreams.

The drab rectangular buildings of The Hole had the solid appearance of prisons, army barracks, or low-rent housing estates. Dull and gray, devoid of even the simplest ornaments, they stood guard as monuments of functionality, but not of the 2080s, rather of the time a half-century or more earlier, hapless throwbacks to the ugliness of prior generations. When the project of building The Hole had first been publicized numerous architects submitted prospectuses, among them several favoring structures epitomizing not only the welter of the inmates' conflicting beliefs, hopes, and aspirations but also the outside world's varied response to them, initiating an architectural dialogue between the jailed and the jailor. This new style, which came into vogue in the eighties and which came to be known as reconstruction, or social reconstruction, depending upon the weight assigned to social issues in it, generated many advocates in the all-important matter of The Hole. But Huston, fearing that all this architectural gimmickry would exculpate the lawbreaker and pillory the God-fearing minister, put his foot down. The architecture of The Hole would be of the plainest, the dullest, the most lifeless imaginable. And the last thing in the world he wanted was the buildings making any kind of statement, implicit, explicit, or tongue-in-cheek. The goddamned buildings ought to be mute eyesores, nothing more.

The instructions of Chief Justice of the United States were carried out to the letter, but there was some disagreement with respect to the general layout of The Hole. Different planners had different ideas about the use of space: width of intersecting streets, width of footpaths, width and length of sidewalks. As slide rules were being consulted and figures compared, a junior member of the team rummaging in the archives came upon yellow and much-thumbed pages containing blueprints of Nazi concentration camps of the 1930s and '40s. He was much struck by their judicious use of space and brought a stack of them to Huston. Chief Justice was elated. Here was a workmanlike employment of available space, economical and realistic, by guys who obviously kept both feet on the ground. Moreover, as layouts went, Nazi concentration camps and The Hole were not so drastically dissimilar. Here, Chief Justice became convinced, was a paradigm to follow, and after further consultation Buchenwald was selected as the model for his new camp, where chaff meticulously separated from grain was given half a lease on life and an expectation of early death. When La Rochelle heard about the use to which the Buchenwald blueprint was being put he hit the ceiling. He barged into Huston's office and threw his hard earned diplomatic savvy to the winds.

Huston watched him in silence, his teeth clenched, balancing a paperweight in his hand and aiming it at the National Security Advisor. "You're nothing but shit in a three thousand dollar business suit," he scowled. "Do you hear, nothing but shit!"

"And you're a loony from the word go," La Rochelle countered, picking up his own paperweight from a nearby table and taking aim.

"I'll get you first!" Huston shouted.

"No, you'll miss, and I'll smash your brains, or what's left of them. I want you to apologize." La Rochelle went on throwing the paper-weight up and catching it.

"Apologize?" Huston uttered the word in utter bafflement. "Apologize?"

"Captain Siegfried La Rochelle will depart and leave scum like you behind as soon as an apology is offered."

"Never, you Kraut bastard! Never!"

"You leave me little choice." National Security Advisor held the paperweight up to the light and began to move very slowly toward the door.

"Leave that thing behind!" Chief Justice shouted, angered to the limit. "This is theft, and in this country we send thieves to prison."

"It will be handy when the time comes and the blow will fall when you least expect it." Holding the precious paperweight with both hands like a gift from the gods, Siegfried made a leisurely exit.

/   /   /

As the decade of the seventies was drawing to a close and that of the eighties was due to begin in a matter of months, grave changes were taking place in the administration of justice in the United States, and they remained in force when in 2082 the country became the Western Province of Amernipp. The entire judiciary was affected. Rights of the accused, rules of evidence, trial by jury, examination of witnesses, and other hallmarks of the American legal system, which for centuries had proclaimed its wisdom and impartiality, were thrown overboard one by one like unusable rusty tools to keep the ship afloat. The procedure most commonly adopted in criminal and civil cases alike was the ordeal—which Huston preferred to call the "judgment of God." Ordeals by fire or water were the favorites. The defendant was bound and laid in a wooden shack that was set on fire. If he or she managed to extricate himself or herself from the fastening ropes and somehow escape to safety the verdict of not guilty was pronounced. But if the defendant perished in the flames it was proof incontrovertible of his or her guilt. Haystacks, parts of abandoned buildings, ditches half-filled with dry branches and sawdust were also used for this purpose, and those found guilty greatly exceeded in numbers the happy innocents.

Ordeal by water was even more popular in certain areas where a multiplicity of streams and brooks crisscrossed the country. Wisconsin, Michigan, and the Ozarks led the pack. The defendant was tied to a heavy log and placed against the current with his or her mouth barely above water. If he or she survived the onslaught of the waves, all was well. If not, Chief Justice would unctuously announce that God had punished yet another sinner. Lakes and ocean shores provided welcome venues for ordeals, and numerous devices were employed, God's own tools of trade: slowly sinking rafts, boards weighted down with heavy metal, high tide overrunning the immobilized prisoner, giving him or her only that much time to live and not a second more, and various others.

The Potomac became a superbly attended location where God's justice was handed down. Crowds booed or cheered, roared praise or insults as desolate defendants down to their last breath made a stand and willed not to give up but go on fighting. Not infrequently black commodious limousines brought to the bank politicians who stood close to the throne, high officials and dignitaries among them, or begowned figures whose dark attire was in stark contrast to the motley multicolored crowd. These were justices of the Supreme Court of the United States and later of the Western Province of Amernipp. More than once all nine of them stood on the bank, Everett Zacharias Huston prominently in front, seeing for themselves how the judicial process was being unraveled. They put many onlookers in mind of the superannuated gunfighters of the Old West in B movies, no longer ruling the land with the barrel of their guns, old men standing conceited in the bar hiring others to draw. In the country where the winds of change blew as never before there were no judicial reviews and no appeals. Many cases were resolved on purely political grounds before they came to trial, and the judiciary patted itself on the back citing indisputable speed with which dockets were emptied and cases settled once and for all. The days of uncertainty and interminable delays were long over. Adroitness and efficiency were the order of the day, and American jurisprudence had taken a giant step forward.

book
two

Chapter 1

This Happy Breed of Men . . .
This Little World . . .

Encircling the continental United States from the banks of the Missouri River to the Pacific Ocean and from 2082 on bearing the name of Western Amernipp, lies a broad tract of land containing some twelve states, which is called the American West. It covers more than a hundred thousand square miles and stretches from the extreme northern tip of Montana and North Dakota all the way down to the golden sands of New Mexico, stopping short of the malodorous plains of Texas, and from the corn fields of eastern Nebraska through the mining settlements of Colorado, the pastures of Wyoming, and the potato farms of Idaho to the shores of Oregon and Washington.

But the vast expanse of the American West is not an issue at hand. It is the character of its people, which even in the eighth decade of the twenty-first century, after generations of pressing everyone into the same mold and making a virtue of obliterating whatever dissimilarities might exist between Tom, Dick, and Harry, Jean, Joan, and Susan, still breathes out its own distinct spirit. It is not that the men and women of the American West are inspired by higher moral values and ideals than the other Americans—no, sir. Or that their intelligence is keener and their brains more inventive than those of their compatriots—no again. Rather it is that many of them, no matter what their station in life, have managed to preserve a little more of that inner independence that centuries before was rightly considered to be a distinctive feature of the American character as opposed to the European character. Now in the eighth decade of the new century their marked independence of mind made them less amenable than their numerous countrymen hailing from other parts of the American land to be bamboozled or imposed upon. Though the West closed ranks with other parts of the country when it came to the creation of Church and State Party, the abolishment of the two-party system, and the ratification of the far-reaching theocratic reforms, they did it without enthusiasm.

Already in the late seventies Huston put his finger on the problem and confided in his cronies. "Those guys in Wyoming, Nebraska, Idaho, and so on listen to me with half an ear," he remonstrated indignantly. "I wish someone had taught them to take orders. They are just a rabble, undisciplined." Listening to the Savior of the Country with half an ear, playing all kinds of delaying games, asking embarrassing questions, the electorate of the western states refused to join a sleepwalking nation led by a holy man whom the Almighty had chosen above all others. On a rainy evening sometime in the fall of 2082 a guy in a bar in Nebraska who had just put his tools away was trying to figure out to himself what face to put forward in those baffling days.

"Bide your time, and keep your powder dry," he spoke out to himself, but other men in the bar heard him and took a fancy to it. Soon the phrase was sputtered all over the West and became a watchword, with Farmer Jenkins wishing Rancher Scott a safe trip home and sounding off close to his ear, "Bide your time, and keep your powder dry," tens of thousands of Westerners doing just the same. The patriots had used their own watchwords in the 1770s when the redcoats were overrunning the colonies, and the patriots of the 2080s swore up and down their watchword was just as important as those in circulation more than three hundred years ago. Furthermore, anything that was said now in the West had as much weight, if not more, than what had passed between the interested parties in times gone by, at Bunker Hill, while crossing the Delaware, at Trenton, Princeton, and at the two battles of Bermis Heights.

Cells of discontent and dissension had existed in several western states since the seventies, but the acknowledged nucleus of opposition to American theocracy with Huston at its head lay in Cheyenne, Wyoming, and was directed by one man. Nathan Chadwick, scion of an old Wyoming family who had settled in the vicinity of what later became the city of Cheyenne before the completion of Union Pacific and long before the land became U.S. territory. Nathan's roots were in Cheyenne, and his people had been the pioneers on the sword and the distaff side, his father and grandfather being local sheriffs and his mother and two grandmothers schoolteachers. Growing up in Cheyenne in the thirties and forties, Nathan took to the spoken and written word like a duck to water, earning his living after graduating from high school as a TV announcer for several networks in succession and then as a reporter and assistant editor for several Wyoming newspapers one after the other. But the political itch erased all other ambitions in him, and in 2064 the thirty-year old TV personality and a seasoned newspaperman, looking much younger than his age, took his seat in the state assembly as a moderate and progressive Republican with full backing of the state Republican organization. He stayed in the Assembly for ten years fighting for industrial expansion and commercial growth in his state but invariably supporting multiple job training programs and bills to strengthen education, which came from across the aisle. He knew he was being groomed for higher office, both the congressional and a senatorial seat falling vacant in 2076, and he was patted on the back and told to get ready.

But to no one's surprise the country was undergoing a revolting change, and what was once the birthright of every American was trampled underfoot. At the end of the 2074 session in Cheyenne he resigned his seat, refusing to run for the U.S. House of Representatives in 2076 as a Republican, the last general election in which the two major parties still competed. He saw the writing on the wall and knew that soon there would be one party only, with Huston's religiously inspired stranglehold on the American nation tight and unrelenting. Something had to be done to defend the Constitution of the United States, and seeking an elective office, Nathan was convinced, was not the right way.

In the same year he founded the Center for Democratic West with headquarters in Cheyenne, a nationwide organization committed to the defense of the principles of 1776 and 1787 and to the exposure and punishment of those committing high treason. Both liberals and conservatives from the four corners of the land rallied round him, and he threw down the gauntlet before Huston and his gang. At first Nathan's policy had been straight as an arrow. It aimed at a speedy return to the two-party system, separation of church and state, free elections, and preservation and defense of the U.S. Constitution. By the spring of

2083 he moved farther left to an unabashed libertarian and anarchist position, finding no virtue in government as such no matter how constituted, and advocating civil disobedience, a passive resistance to the government's edicts.

In newspaper articles and in pamphlets, on the radio and on TV, at rallies and town meetings, Nathan Chadwick boldly called the government evil and unnecessary, any government be it federal or regional, because by its very presence it violated and did its best to stamp out the freedom to which every human being was entitled and with it the inalienable resources of human individuality. As for the idea of social contract allegedly binding the state and the people, the former offering protection to the latter and governing in a manner respectful of natural rights, it was so much hooey. The government, any government, was a tyrant and nothing more. Nathan urged his listeners not to pay taxes because they had no control over how taxed money would be spent; he urged them to disobey all laws and regulations that limited their freedom and when indicted to go to court and show spunk. He declared again and again the only natural and defensible social unit was the family. The state, or any part or branch thereof, was cancer on the body of the American nation and later on the body of Western Amernipp, and he strongly advised each family to fly its own flag. He recommended that the individual family or a group of families make voluntary ad hoc arrangements with the authorities in times of need and that the relationship between the two be always voluntary and limited to the resolution of a specific issue or issues.

Nathan was jailed twice, for two months the first time and then for six, even though he did not advocate violent resistance. But he was a thorn in the side of Huston's government, and Chief Justice made a point of identifying him by name in his speeches and memoranda, painting a not easily forgettable picture of the virulent and treacherous length to which this confounded cowboy would go. Since obstacles were constantly put in Nathan's way—searches, seizures, restraining orders—before his public appearances, and so on and so forth, some members of the administration put their trust in his leaving the country voluntarily with no intention of returning. But their trust turned to ashes. With great ceremony Nathan told the audience of the administration's wishful thinking and then assured them categorically that going into exile was farthest from his mind. He knew where his duty lay, the captain does not abandon ship sinking though it may be. And besides, he added grinning from ear to ear, he could not be permanently severed from Wyoming, "This happy breed of men . . . this little world . . ." and more particularly from Cheyenne, where he was born and bred.

As a last resort the head of state dispatched a personal emissary to the leader of the opposition who, conforming as he did to all the precepts of courtesy and decorum, nevertheless pressed Nathan with vigor to leave the country for good and settle down in some alluring spot, Switzerland, or Rio de Janeiro, or one of those tiny sparsely populated islands still left in the Pacific where a reflective man would not be distracted by shrieks of postmodern supercomputers, the gritting choppers ceaselessly floating overhead, and the clang and clatter of the ever-updated, ever-advancing technology. Furthermore, the emissary went on waxing more and more matey with every passing word, moving Nathan Chadwick lock, stock, and barrel to a foreign location all impedimenta included would be executed at the government's expense—papers, files, books, articles of clothing, furniture, and cars being handled with delicacy befitting museum exhibits. It would be the most carefully arranged moving operation in recent history. Chief Justice had heard, the emissary continued, of the recent marital divisions within the Chadwick family and the consequent separation of Mr. and Mrs. Chadwick. He was of course sending his most sincere commiserations but remained in hopes that these divisions would soon be healed. When this happened Mrs. Chadwick, their daughter, and all their belongings would be promptly transported with all due care to wherever Mr. Chadwick resided, unless of course young Agnes had elected beforehand to travel with her father. Nathan listened patiently to the emissary's lengthy argument, whose fine-chiseled head and countenance faithfully registered his pride at having been charged with the commission of importance.

"Please thank Chief Justice for his concern and for putting the resources of the government at my disposal. However, I cannot accept his offer, and I will not leave this land. I have a duty to discharge, and this duty is to return the country to the American form of government shored up by institutions and practices sanctioned by the Constitution of the United States. I very much doubt whether Chief Justice has ever had even an inkling of what our constitution signifies."

"Have you taken leave of your senses? I can't tell him that. Haven't you heard of what happens to the messenger who brings unwelcome news? Just think for a moment."

"Tell him word for word what I said." Nathan was raising his voice. "And if you don't, I promise I will. I have no stomach for playing games."

The two men parted on a note of icy politeness, and the hapless emissary repeated verbatim to his boss what Nathan had said, not forgetting the very last remark, and the boss took note and never forgot it. Nor did he ever forgive Nathan for having made it.

Multitudes in the West and elsewhere took exception to some of the things Nathan called upon them to do, and the notion of Dad and Mom and their two kiddies sporting a flag of their own and their neighbors to the right and left each sporting a flag of their own too and so ad infinitum until there were more individual family flags in each American town than there were rooters for the favorite team in a championship game, all this struck many as just a tad heavy-handed. Objections were also raised to some of Nathan's other proposals faithfully embodying his libertarian and anarchistic convictions, and they were flung in his face, accompanied by cautionary phrases like, "Nat, let's keep a steady hand," "Nat, there ain't no need to tickle the lion's throat," "Nat, let's keep our feet on the ground," and similar ones that made for lively exchanges. But one day early in 2083 Nathan had heard as much censure of his specific proposals as he could stand, and as a town meeting was winding down he made a dramatic announcement.

"It is clear to me that you good people don't give a skunk's bald ass for what I am advocating, which is for the common good and is meant to lift us from the gutter to which the present administration has shoved us. And it is clear to me that you good people don't give any part of the skunk's anatomy, bald or hairy, for the improvements I want to institute, and furthermore that you have no further use for me. And as I still look upon our western states as a free country I say unto you you'll have your wish this very minute for I am closing down Center for Democratic West, and I betake myself out of your lives and your memories and will follow a different line, but where that line leads is none of your goddamn business." He was pressing papers into an undersized briefcase and forcing an enormous cowboy hat onto his head when pandemonium broke out. Many voices rose simultaneously, and Nathan could not distinguish between them and understand anything they were shouting though the purport was crystal clear: they wanted him to stay on the job and go about his duties as before, and they wanted Center for Democratic West to stay open and carry on without interruption. They wouldn't settle for less. It had been a long, hard day and Nathan's patience was wearing thin. "Good-bye, folks, and find yourselves another whipping boy," he roared, pulling a succession of faces.

"You will reconsider, Nat. You will reconsider!" two self-appointed spokesmen for the crowd sounded off.

"Never!" he thundered at them. "Never!" He made ready to go, but solicitous supporters crowded round him as if nothing had happened. "Nat, go home and have a nice cup of jasmine tea. It will do wonders for you," a clergyman's wife said. "How I wish Linda were here looking after you. You gotta take care of that short fuse of yours, Nat."

"No one is worse off because of a little friendly criticism," a man said.

"You call it friendly criticism—friendly criticism?" Nathan cried out, exasperated. Other advice followed, and he finally departed gazing at them sternly while they smiled and waved amicably. Two days later he reconsidered and things went back to normal. A well attended policy meeting at the Center for Democratic West took place where new ground was cut, new ideas aired, old alliances cemented anew.

The marriage of Nathan and Linda had been a stormy one from the outset. Celebrated while he was still in the Wyoming legislature, it united two people very much in love, sharing similar interests, and animated by the same political goals. Linda's family also had roots in Wyoming, and she was employed as a highly trained nurse and x-ray technician. There was something unmistakable but difficult to pin down when the two were together, which provoked friends and strangers alike to say that they belonged to each other, that they were joined by an invisible thread of fate, that they were kindred spirits. Nathan had sustained a head injury when he had fallen off a swing at the age of seven, and improperly diagnosed, then plainly misdiagnosed, and later inadequately treated, the injury had left a deep mark. Nathan's quick and resourceful mind functioned flawlessly and at its normal high speed, but what brought it down dangerously close to the breaking point at uneven intervals were those shadowy specters rising from the very depths of human personality, the four horsemen of the subconscious mind: distrust, anger, hatred, and sleeplessness. Especially after periods of pro-longed and intensive work Nathan would experience bouts of depression and wrath or attacks of persecution mania followed by deeply rooted suspicion and hatred of those closest to him. Then, when the first three horsemen had ridden far away, the fourth one would hold him captive, and feverish debilitating insomnia set in. These attacks did not take place frequently—often four or five weeks or more would pass in tranquility—but they always returned and they always combined. Soon after the wedding Linda realized that her husband was suffering from a medical problem and that her own behavior, backed by love and under-standing, as it was, had no impact on his condition.

On his wife's advice Nathan was examined by specialists, under-went batteries of tests, and was handed different diagnoses recom-mending different treatments, some suggesting surgery and some not, and different forms of medication. Linda consulted MDs whom she knew and trusted, and she and Nathan decided upon the treatment rec-ommended by a young but already eminent specialist with an impres-sive track record. Against Nathan's expectation the treatment was successful and five unperturbed years followed. Their daughter Agnes, who was unfortunately an epileptic, was born and doctors could do very little to chase her illness away. Years went by, but in the summer of 2082, days before the two countries merged and the new state of Amernipp was created, Nathan's symptoms returned with a vengeance. Linda nursed him through the haunted days, and she was soon at the end of her tether. Now the attacks were much more frequent than before, and Nathan was hospitalized. A week later he was back at home claiming he was infinitely better. He was not. After another relapse and seeing how run down Linda was, he suggested that she ought to stay with her family for the time being. She refused. Another dismal and exhausting month ensued. Finally Linda made arrangements to have a male nurse live on the premises to cope with the attacks while attend-ing to Nathan in every other way. This was not crowned with success as Nathan vented his rage and hatred on her and not on the nurse. Finally Linda decided to move for the duration to Sheridan, Wyoming, where her brother lived with his family, but remain in close contact with Nathan and be always at his beck and call.

By mutual consent Agnes, who was now nine, would live for three months with her mother, then for three months with her father, then again with her mother and then with her father following an alternating schedule. She promptly declared the idea rotten to the core since as soon as she made friends at one place and school she was uprooted and then uprooted again and again. She expostulated with each parent asking them to tie a real knot but to no avail, and she spoke to both of them like a Dutch aunt. They listened attentively, her father kissing her on the forehead and her mother wiping off a tear. The alternating schedule remained in force, but now Linda would often visit Nathan in Cheyenne and stay with him for days and he would often be her houseguest in Sheridan.

There was only one commitment of Nathan's that Linda turned away from, his passion for Romantic opera. He would listen for hours to the recordings of *Manon Lescaut, Tosca, La Boheme, Carmen, Tristan und Isolde,* play excerpts on the piano and sing the arias, *Manon Lescaut* being his favorite.

"How can you stand that sentimental twaddle?" Linda would ask. "These are not real people, just marionettes cranked up to spout out hours of mawkish drivel. They are sick." But Nathan would not be dissuaded. It was his escape hatch to a world so different from the sordid world of politics, and when he was not working the house was filled with musical crescendos of operatic passion and love. Nathan left behind in his Cheyenne home folders full of notes, texts of lectures delivered or to be delivered, of articles and letters to editors. Years later his collected papers were deposited at the Nathan Holman Chadwick Library in Cheyenne, Wyoming, pride of the state and of Amernipp, and a mecca for thousands of scholars, sympathizers, and eager beavers from all over the world. Among his writings were the following:

> Some of you have asked me why I call for family banners, why I urge each family to fly its own flag. The answer is simple. The state has lost all viability to be an even-handed partner in a social contract. The state spells tyranny where the principles of the Founding Fathers are daily trampled underfoot. Old Glory is no longer Old Glory of times past. It is abused and misrepresented as a symbol of treachery perpetrated on the souls of all Americans, an emblem of madness and injustice. Everett Huston and his administration wave it in high places and soil it with every breath in their bodies. Let us take Old

Glory out of harm's way and put it in a safe place until a dawn of freedom breaks again and then unfurl it in all its majesty. And while we toil for the new dawn let every family flag bearing the designs and colors of this or any other individual family be both a family coat of arms and mystically a microcosm of the American nation, for our nation is made up of a myriad of families, each of them an epitome of the whole. The Founding Fathers held the family in high regard, and let us join hands with them across the quicksand of centuries. Today let each family bear their flag with pride, for in doing so we honor our country and salute the Founding Fathers.

(From notes for a lecture to be delivered in Omaha on May 2, 2083.)

Sanctity of the family flag. . . . Until better days come along we shall continue having hundreds of thousands of national flags, each of them as important as the next, a family and a national emblem rolled into one. But a family flag is more than a festive banner. It is also a call to action. As we raise it on the pole, or brandish it, it constantly reminds us of our obligations toward other members of the family, be they spouse or child, one parent or the other, brother or sister. Mystically the flag sends a signal that our comportment leaves much to be desired, that our anger is baseless, our understanding of others shallow, our self-righteousness bordering on the criminal, our ambition lacking even an iota of divine approval, bulldozing others out of our way. The flag tells us to be better. It speaks to us in the words of St. Paul and those who have taken his words to heart: Martin Luther, Phillipp Melanchton, Jean Chauvin. The family flag is like a moral barometer, and those of us endowed with keen eyesight can see it shrinking when we transgress and expand when we earn our moral keep. When we put Old Glory back on display maybe we ought to retain the family flag for it can do us a great deal of good, the national flag notwithstanding.

(From notes for a symposium on government held in Boise on February 26, 2083.)

In these troubled times the words of Henry David Thoreau take on a new and awesome meaning: "That government is best which governs not at all." One can hardly imagine a situation more conducive to universal harmony and happiness than one in which the present government with Chief Justice Everett Zacharias Huston at its head would simply abdicate all its powers, do nothing, and govern not at all. But this is the longest shot of all. The government will remain at the helm, and one vicious scheme will be followed by another and another. Under these conditions civil disobedience becomes more than a tool to temper the government's tyrannical folly. It proudly takes the seat of honor in the chamber of our intellect and resolve. It is our most precious resolution, the best of ourselves given freely to our country and our fellow citizens. To eschew it or practice it halfheartedly would blow our status as rational human beings to smithereens. Yet let us bear in mind two thoughts: first, civil disobedience must always remain civil—passive or active, it must never degenerate into violence or hysteria. The other side habitually employs every dirty trick in the book, every disreputable method and stratagem to whip us into shameful conformity and obedience. Are we to totter into the gutter with our enemies? I say no, and no again! Let us be brave and resourceful and not miss a wink on their smudgy infamous faces. Yet let us watch them with the eye of a hawk; let us walk ahead of them and maintain our dignity.

Secondly, our acts of civil disobedience should be whenever possible collective and not individual. Here out in the West we have always bestowed more attention on individuals than on the masses, and a loner quick on the draw has been our hero for centuries. Let him forever ride down the mountain and catch bad guys. The succeeding decades changed our society from one made up of individuals to one made up of organizations, and in the last resort the latter are more powerful than the former. When the IRS plays havoc with your taxes, march into court not alone but with fifty co-defendants. When you put finishing touches on a peaceful demonstration make certain that so many businesses and associations of one kind or another are represented that you can't rightly see the end of the col-

umn. And when you jump up and down hollering that the new law or regulation violates your rights as a citizen, see to it that not you alone, but a hundred men good and true standing right behind you, bear witness. Don't go it alone, 'cause these are not the times for going it alone. Bide your time and keep your powder dry.
(Notes for a conference on civil disobedience held in Sioux Falls on November 15, 2083.)

Anywhere one turns nowadays one hears fantastic stories of West Amernipp entering in the very near future the paradisiacal spheres. It is not clear whether this is God's reward to the people of our country for leading blameless lives or whether something else is at stake. Will everyone be transported to heaven, all sins forgiven, or will only certain sections of the population be singled out? And I wonder how this union of mortals and the Almighty will be executed. Are we going to fly in an enormous spaceship from our humble shores past the stratosphere to heights unimagined to be welcomed by angels wearing their Sunday best, mooring our ship and conducting us with all due ceremony into the presence of our Heavenly Father, and will it be then or a tad later that this union will be consummated? Or will the powers that be decree some other, infinitely more mystical manner for our sanctification? Are we going to be wholly or only in part dematerialized, and if the latter applies can one reasonably expect that a poker game could be worked in as we listen to the blast of golden trumpets, stuff our mouths with *pâté de foi gras*, and are ennobled by the bearded presence of the Almighty? And what about sex? Are we to retain our sexual instincts and desires, and will those who played the field here on earth be able to play it in heaven, limitless spaces in those sublime regions affording an ample opportunity for all kinds of razzle-dazzle? Or will this transformation of our sinful selves into goodness and holiness beyond compare be accomplished by some novel and entirely original method to which the Almighty alone is privy, something on the order of the instantaneous fusion of our corporeal identities with the Godhead whereby the former is totally absorbed by the latter, though I still think our dirty toes should be sticking out from under the spotless heavenly vestments to remind the Almighty where we came from. I am sure as I stand here members of the audience are itching to find out what other thoughts I have on the subject and to articulate their own thoughts on the very same subject, and we'll find time for both at question time.

(Excerpt from a lecture entitled "Whither Now Western Amernipp?" delivered before the Evangelical Society of New Mexico, at Albuquerque on December 10, 2083.)

Chapter 2

All Men Are Equal but
Some Are More Equal than Others;
The Scribe and the Schoolmarm

Other profound changes had affected the country beginning in the late seventies, gaining momentum early in the following decade. Free press, as the term had been understood through centuries of American history, underwent curious innovations of meaning. Sensors, sensitive electronic instruments registering when touched the subject and the desired way of it being treated, were installed in every community and in large cities in shopping centers and principal plazas. Readers determined what should be printed in newspapers and how each topic should be handled simply by touching the sensors, which read their minds. Newspapers were ordered to print what the majority demanded and in the manner it demanded, and the majority rule was most of the time observed, except when popular demand collided with a government policy that overrode the electorate's wishes and predilections. Otherwise censorship of the press and of the media was rigorous and continuous, and there was no way of getting around it.

Many journalists left what had been their chosen profession and migrated to other occupations—ones not depending on the power of the written or spoken word, since the multifarious world of publishing and the glittering world of advertising were also under governmental thumb. Editorial offices began to be filled with glib, unprincipled hacks ready to write anything they were commanded to write, and in media and publishing houses only those who toed the line were assured of permanent employment. Grants and subsidies of all sorts were readily available to writers, journalists, and members of the media who were willing to eulogize religion, any religion, and those who did were handsomely rewarded and invited to the receptions Everett Huston held at even intervals for "the kindred spirits," as he called them. The plight of higher education went hand in hand with that of the press, and both underscored drastic changes in American society, tearing it asunder as never before and pitting one side against the other.

Already in the late seventies the American nation began to fall into two distinct but very uneven and diverse camps. In the first stood the bulk of the population, some ninety-five percent of it, the vast masses of ordinary folks, the toilers and breadwinners, the various layers of the salt of the earth, those living very quietly and those barely vegetating, whose road to distinction and eminence was often blocked by their inferior status, and who were progressively denied the right to use their brains and assume positions of leadership. To be sure, there was some social and economic mobility among those vast masses, individuals striking it rich in business or climbing the religious ladder, but these were rare exceptions. Principally these teeming masses constituted an enormous blue-collar and white-collar workforce, living in security and taking advantage of full employment, which the United States of America and later Western Amernipp enjoyed. They were the helots of the twenty-first century, of the computerized age where ill-trained men and women carried out menial tasks, leaving the thinking and planning to supercomputers and their betters.

Opposed to them in every respect stood a much smaller camp of highly educated, highly trained individuals who exercised full power and control. At the outset of the nation being bisected and unevenly divided, they and their predecessors had been handpicked by Huston and his lieutenants, but later more sophisticated methods were used to perpetuate the new ruling class. Theoretically, between the ages of eleven and fourteen every child was to be exposed to a battery of tests measuring his or her IQ, aptitude, and potential with the view of determining the child's future education and place in society. But in practice a high percentage of children drawn from the workforce never presented themselves for testing, and the majority of those who did tested poorly. The new leaders came almost exclusively from the newly formed managerial class, and they in turn did what they could to secure a privileged position for their children. In 2080 Huston commandeered the great and famous American universities exclusively for the education of the new managerial class, and a year later he rescinded his own order in disgust. The administration and faculty at Harvard, Yale, Princeton, Berkeley, University of Chicago, and at other well-known institutions of higher education raised such a rumpus about his educational policies, the selection and eligibility of incoming students, and the endlessly promulgated matter of academic freedom that Huston had a mind to close all those overbearing bailiwicks down or better still shoot every living professor and administrator and the dead ones too just to be absolutely certain. As always, Berkeley led the pack. In the end he relented, and the deepening chasm between the two classes of society, the leaders and the followers, spawned two distinct educational systems and a nickname for the members of each class.

In January of 2082, still suffering from the effects of what he called the criminal obtuseness of those overeducated SOBs, Huston created the High Governmental Institute in charge of the nurture and education of the progeny of the managerial ruling class from kindergarten through graduate school, popularly called High Gov, and the Low Governmental Institute, popularly called Low Gov, which busied itself with whatever upbringing and training was offered to the offspring of the workforce. The contrasts between the two educational systems were staggering. The highgovies, as they came to be called, received the best possible education from grade school on, designed to develop their intellectual talents to the fullest, learning European, Asian, and African languages, analyzing the business and governmental structures of industriously highly developed nations, and tirelessly parsing the uses and possibilities of the sciences. Some of the most brilliant minds from Amernipp and abroad were lured to the new universities functioning under the aegis of the High Governmental Institute.

These new universities were placed in carefully selected locations as far away as possible from the history-ennobled quads of the famous institutions of learning, which, with the stroke of the pen, were converted to lunatic asylums, Huston, scowling to all and sundry and entertaining high hopes that the former occupants of those institutions would stay on the hallowed grounds, in a new capacity, of course—in a new capacity to be sure. Though by now he had absolutely no stomach to travel, Chief Justice nevertheless flew to Berkeley and with his own hands tore down Sather Gate, being assisted by mechanized cohorts and gracing the occasion with a speech, which unfortunately could neither be broadcast nor printed because of its unusual candor and diction.

Education meted out under the auspices of the Low Governmental Institute was meager and sketchy; it was mostly vocational and religious and ended in eighth grade. There were no colleges or universities for lowgovies. In the few years spanning the time spent in traditional grade and junior high schools, boys and girls were taught rudiments of knowledge and basic skills needed in various forms of manual and clerical work. What was instilled into them once they set foot in the classroom was faith and religious values, unqualified obedience to the government, and veneration for the Savior of the Country, Everett Zacharias Huston. The authorities expressly forbade any improvements in the curricula designed for the lowgovies. Huston made the point again and again that the workforce should not be well educated in the intellectual sense. This, he insisted, would only lead to discontent and "God knows what else." The country depended on those brawny and paper-shuffling battalions for basic services, for industrial expansion, for the maintenance of a new lifestyle which descended like grace itself upon this nation chosen by God after centuries of blunders and disasters."

Ill-trained and left deliberately ignorant, the masses of the workforce, some ninety-five percent of the population, were nevertheless the basis on which the entire country rested. Their lives were secure—employment being steady and uninterrupted, medical services at hand, and the prospect of a continuously well regulated existence constantly dangled before their eyes—these were the advantages, and they easily outweighed whatever disadvantages lowgovies could dream up.

The sacred duty of every family within the workforce, as of every other family, of course, was to stamp out vice both at home and abroad. This was God's command, and those who obeyed were promptly rewarded. Informing on one's neighbors and charging them with practicing vice in one form or another became already in 2081 something of a national pastime, and it grew inordinately in the next three years. The most commonly reported offenses were adultery, fornication, prostitution, drunkenness, and loose talk making light of the government, of one church or another, and of the person of Chief Justice Huston. In most cases the word of the informer carried much more weight than that of the defendant, and rules of evidence were applied cavalierly and subjectively. Those whom fortune favored were able to cut a deal with the informer through bribery or by undertaking to do him or her an important favor, a promise it would be most unwise to break. Usually the judge was privy to what was going on and so were the attorneys; and since such deals were the order of the day they were given a fancy name, *iustitia post facto*, which found its way to the legal vocabulary and textbooks. Justices of the Supreme Court pronounced *iustitia post facto* a significant contribution to American jurisprudence, and countless members of the legal profession followed suit.

Yet all was not well in that vast reservoir of down-to-earth humanity where ambition was held in check while zealous religious faith, pursuit of virtue, and detestation of vice acted like a three-pronged magnetic needle of a divine compass which, Huston declared with pride, never missed the mark. All was not well. In the fall of 2082, when the memories of the signing of the union between the United States of America and the Empire of Japan on July Fourth of that year were still fresh in people's minds, lowgovies in half a dozen cities took to the streets demanding higher wages, shorter working hours, better educational opportunities for their children, better opportunities for continued education for themselves, better public libraries, and a bite at the cultural and political apple that lay within easy reach of highgovies but not within theirs. For eight days the helots rebelled, taking police officers and several members of regional governments hostage, holding public meetings in parks and stadiums where their grievances were detailed and canvassed before large sympathetic crowds, and penning an open letter to the government. In all this time destruction of property was minimal and there was no loss of life. But the government refused to take the lowgovies' complaints seriously. Huston promised the appointment of a commission to investigate their working and living conditions and their educational status, but few believed that such a body would ever come into being. Privately Huston vented his rage against the overeducated SOBs whom he blamed for inciting honest men and women to rebellion and perverting their minds. As a sop to protesters he allocated a little more money to public libraries in the districts where the majority of the population was made up of lowgovies and beefed up their cultural programs. Clearly this was not enough, and discontent seethed and rankled in the minds of the masses as they went about their business. Petitions were sent again to the government, and during the winter and early spring marches were organized, protesters carrying banners condemning all forms of discrimination and demanding far-reaching reforms.

In those days the country was like an enormous fuse already lit, the fire inching at an inexorable pace toward the explosive charge, the only question being when, when would the fire reach the charge? It reached it on April 1, 2084, and the explosion shook the nation. A rebellion against the government broke out in forty states and six hundred communities. An unspecified number of highgovies joined their downtrodden comrades, and what was happening clearly brought to the fore national all-American character. A friend told Huston, "Mind how you handle it, this may be the writing on the wall." But Chief Justice did not take these words to heart. This time frenzy ran amok, and the first two days of the rebellion claimed twenty-two dead and over two hundred wounded. As days rolled by the number of casualties rose dramatically, and it was obvious that the rebellion was carefully planned and coordinated. Lowgovies and their allies were no longer demanding an end to discrimination and speedy reforms that would really change the shape of things. They boldly called for a national referendum to determine whether an entirely new government and an entirely new governmental structure would not serve the country better. In the meantime they took more hostages, burnt more official buildings, and appointed summary courts to try those government officials, both high and low, whose conduct had been inexcusable and cruel. A handful of prisoners were hanged and scores sentenced to life imprisonment.

Huston gathered his principal lieutenants and asked for their counsel. Phineas Léger advised moderation. He urged his boss to visit the troubled areas, agree to what the workers wanted, and talk to as many of them as possible, preferably on a one-to-one basis. "Our best bet is to diffuse the situation and you, Everett, must crisscross the land, shake hands, make speeches, and present yourself wherever you go as everyone's friend who is here in their midst to resolve the situation that is hurting everyone. There's still a vast reservoir of goodwill and respect toward you in the country. Use it; ride on the crest of the wave."

Homily Grister dismissed Phineas's advice as the gutless babble of an armchair strategist. "One doesn't negotiate with traitors¡" he shrieked. "Send the National Guard, send the Army and the Marines. If we have to build detention camps for thousands upon thousands of those miscreants, so be it! They've broken the law and they have to be punished. There's no other way. If you give in, they'll march on Washington next. Break their backs while we still have the power and the means, and show no mercy."

Uncharacteristically, Ganymede Pillows had no original strategy to recommend. "Yes, order should be restored, and yes the rebels should be brought to book." Having said this he began to waffle, advocating stern measures one minute and conciliatory ones the next, opening the door for negotiations, closing it, and then opening it again. "Much can be said on both sides," he ended by saying. Huston's other advisors and confidants ran the gamut of options from dropping nuclear bombs on faithless insurgents to inviting all of them to Washington for a fancy shindig during which high government officials would fraternize with humble lowgovies and press for new channels of communication and understanding.

Toward the end of the session Royster McCallum, a close associate of Chief Justice, formerly a professor of philosophy, offered what he dubbed "both a summation and an explication." He was true to his word, gracefully reviewing one side of the argument, positing the the-sis, and then with the magic expression of, "on the other hand," mov-ing to the antithesis, an attempt at synthesis being invariably absent. This went on for a long time, and Huston convincingly demonstrated his capacity for patience. At long last he raised his hand and stopped McCallum in mid-sentence. "I want to thank one and all for his and her suggestions," he announced in high tones, looking daggers at each of them. They muttered, "Thank you, Chief Justice," and were gone.

Huston's manner of dealing with the rebellion was haphazard and often self-contradictory, but order was slowly being imposed and the violence had run its course. He used both the National Guard and the regular Army for patrolling city streets and large tracts of land yet stopped short of arresting thousands of former rebels now moving freely and uneasily about. Even the alleged ringleaders were not put in custody and everyone was told to go back to work and resume the old schedule and routine. There was no pardon or amnesty for those who had rebelled, but neither was there any punishment imposed upon them and no threat of future punishment was voiced. Some of Huston's associates credited him with extraordinary adroitness in weathering the crisis. He waved their encomia aside and told them he had been moving one step at a time, trying to stay in the middle whenever possible and a master plan was farthest from his mind. He added pointedly that they, the governments and their supporters that is, had neither fallen into the abyss, nor had they climbed to the top of the mountain. They stood precisely where they had stood before the rebellion, on square one, and this by itself was an outstanding achievement.

Few had feared that those living under the protection of the High Governmental Institute, the highgovies, could ever be a source of trouble. But fate can be fickle when she is least expected to be. The highgovies were the untitled aristocracy of Western Amernipp. They had their own country clubs to which no outsider could gain access, their own schools, their own holiday resorts and retirement homes. Above the main entrance of their churches hung wide silk ribbons on which inscriptions were stamped in oversize capitals: THIS CONGREGATION ALLOWS ONLY THE HIGHGOVIES TO ATTEND THE SERVICE; INTERLOPERS WILL BE ESCORTED OUT BY SECURITY GUARDS. Highgovies received high salaries and enjoyed numerous fringe benefits, low-interest loans to purchase expensive homes, substantial discounts on overseas travel, and patronage of specially selected stores from which lowgovies were banned where high quality goods from groceries to automobiles and airplanes could be bought on easy terms. They usually resided in particular parts of towns and cities, which soon became exclusive, allowing only their peers to take abode there. They socialized amongst themselves, taking good care to keep outsiders at arm's length, and they intermarried to the fanfare of golden trumpets, champagne, and *pâté de foi gras*.

They resembled the highly privileged class in the Soviet Union after the Second World War, composed of eminent party officials, high government functionaries, select scientists, and top members of the armed forces, cut off from the populace in every imaginable way, a state within the state, an empire of their own within the vast Soviet Empire. Like their Soviet counterparts a hundred and forty years earlier, highgovies were the managers, the planners, the leaders, and the masters lording over the masses and perpetuating their rule from one year to the next.

At the outset of the 2080s, when American society was being broken up into two unequal segments and reconstituted, the prerequisite for being counted a member of the High Governmental Institute and wearing its badge of honor was fervent religious faith, the acceptance of the law of God as superior to any other law, and the placing of the house of worship above secular institutions no matter how exalted. Huston liked to call the early highgovies the saints—his saints—mystically rubbing shoulders with the religious paragons of ages past. Yet in the intervening years cracks began to appear in the noble monument of faith and love of God unbounded. Successive rumors and strictures about the highgovies' mounting secular and self-indulging lifestyle and their shady business practices were largely ignored or swept under the rug because they were for the most part anonymous and so shocking as to instill into the reviewing bodies doubts about their veracity. Besides, no one wanted to upset Everett, whose confidence in the legions of his saints was boundless.

But in late summer of 2083 a lengthy report was placed on Homily Grister's desk detailing in a most explicit manner, with evidence given under oath and affidavits attached, of numerous cases of gross immorality, rank dishonesty, falling church attendance beneath the threshold of decency, monetary exploitation of the lowgovies by the highgovies, and of other religious and ethical transgressions in no less than twenty-two communities spread over ten states where a sizeable part of the population bore allegiance to the High Governmental Institute. Homily in his capacity as the guardian of public morality at once scheduled a meeting with his two close colleagues, Phineas Léger and Ganymede Pillows. As the three of them waded through the report and scrupulously examined the evidence, they were floored. Unless this was a litany of scurrilous inventions, slanderous and libelous, which they doubted, what they were poring over was an account of every sexual perversion under the sun, of moral decay so shameless and deeply rooted as to be unredeemable, of disappearance of business ethics and common decency that made humiliating mockery of any claim that Western Amernipp was a God-fearing, law-abiding country. Prostitution, wife-swapping, rampant adultery, group sex practiced by numerous couples in luxury hotels rented for the purpose, use of controlled substances, prolonged drinking bouts, and other sins of the flesh were among the least serious violations of the law allegedly perpetrated. What made Grister's and his friends' hair stand on end were stories of brutalization of lowgovie servants by their highgovie masters, including locking them up in basements and cellars of their houses and starving them for days on end, flogging them and administering other forms of corporal punishment for inattention and minor offenses, wholesale fraud through banks and financial centers, illegal transportation of children of both sexes from the South Sea Islands and South America to Western Amernipp for the purpose of sexual gratification and prostitution, and what Grister, Léger, and Pillows found particularly revolting, continued undermining of the authority of any given church or synagogue, non-participation in its rituals and services, a dour fist thrust in the faces of ministers, priests, and rabbis where there should have been hosannas, genuflection, and Bible-reading galore.

Individual portions of the report were signed by former lowgovie servants employed by highgovies, by other lowgovies who went under-cover to obtain the needed proof, and by several highgovies who, horrified by what they saw was happening, closed ranks with the lowgovies, putting their careers on the line. Léger, Grister, and Pillows re-interviewed the witnesses, checked and re-checked all the accusations made, and took written statements from those named as law-breakers in a wide variety of violations. After a lengthy investigative and corroborative process they reached the unanimous conclusion that all the charges in the report were true, and the black picture painted of numerous criminals in high places was correct to a tee.

Chief Justice has been ailing, and his three friends were loath to break the news to him lest he suffer a stroke or worse. Instead they dispatched confidential emissaries to the ten states and twenty-two communities with direct orders to impress upon everyone named in the indictment that this sort of lowdown conduct would come to an end immediately and not a minute later. The emissaries were received with icy politeness by the nobs who listened patiently, denied any misconduct, and once left alone laughed up their sleeves. They reckoned they had nothing to fear. Their admonitory commission carried out, the emissaries reported to the executive trio and told each of them in no uncertain terms that the nobs were neither repentant nor on the way to moral regeneration, and if the government wanted results it should indict and not play Boy Scout games. But this would alert Everett to the painful facts, and the trio would not take the chance. Resorting to what they thought was an intelligent and opportune compromise, they dispatched the emissaries once more to the same parties with similar instructions, avoiding as before even a hint of legal sanctions. The results were again disappointing, and after a few more weeks of paper shuffling and reshuffling the file containing the record of the alleged misdeeds of the aristos of Western Amernipp was closed for eternity. Huston was beginning to feel better, and his doctors were telling him he was on the mend. Phin, Hom, and Gan, the tricky streak past them, turned their hearts and minds to fresh woods and pastures new.

Chapter 3

The Loveseat and the Chapel

Two new police departments were installed in the country in the late 2070s, their powers and jurisdiction being more closely defined in January of 2080—the Sex Police, known popularly as SP, and the Faith Police, answering to the popular name of FP. Members of both these divisions considered themselves vastly superior to all the other departments within law enforcement. Homicide boys might be putting cuffs on brutal murderers and the fraud squad was fighting a malignant cancer on the body of society, but SP and FP were the guardians of the flesh and the spirit respectively; they were the Almighty's special envoys charged with the awesome responsibility of enforcing His law in this valley of sin which now and then became the valley of redemption. Besides, they were Chief Justice's protégés, his blue-eyed boys and girls, his special and irreplaceable battalions. Four years running he had attended graduation at the S and F Academy—cadets of the two departments shared the same academy though their curricula were widely different—delivering stirring graduation addresses and reminding others that God's eyes were upon those young men and women who had sworn to stamp out vice and protect faith, God's own faith, at the risk of their lives.

Sex Police had the right to enter anyone's home at any hour of the day or night, and their favorite time of entry was between three and five A.M. As a rule they headed straight for the bedroom, subjecting the suddenly awakened couple to a lengthy third degree, and ordering them to hand over their marriage manifest, a detailed list with dates of kisses, cuddles, and caresses—no matter how chaste, and of the actual acts of love. The marriage manifest, called in the streets "the dirties," was a public book, periodically signed by examining MDs and at all times subject to scrutiny by the Sex Police, magistrates, and higher authorities. Beginning in the late seventies and more rigorously with the advent of the eighties, sexual practices in the great republic and soon thereafter in Western Amernipp had been allowed for the purpose of procreation only. Otherwise sex was banned. "The dirties" of married couples were scrupulously examined to ascertain whether the listed or unlisted occasions of intimacy between spouses resulted in pregnancies or not. If not, there was indisputable evidence of criminal misconduct, punishable by a fine for the first time round, a tripled fine for the second offense, and imprisonment for the third. All forms of contraception, for men and women, including the pill, were banned and even though they were readily available on the black market their possession constituted violation of the law and was severely punished.

When squads of SP raided the homes of single people, whether men or women, sophisticated medical and other methods were used to find out whether suspects in question had had sex in the previous twelve or twenty-four hours. When a nightly raid on a home occupied by a single tenant led to the discovery of a guest or guests on the premises, suspicions mounted and an arrest could be imminent. If the guest or guests were not of the same gender as the tenant, suspicions of foul play were at once raised and the worst could follow; if they were of the same gender, charges of homosexuality or lesbianism could be leveled at once and they were difficult to refute. Since *habeas corpus*, Miranda ruling, search and arrest warrants, and other forms of protection of the individual from self-asserting governmental authority no longer carried the slightest weight, brutalization and victimization of prospective suspects were the order of the day, their incarceration arbitrary with or without a shred of evidence, its duration set at the whim of the jailors.

As Huston advanced in years he came to regard sexual practices more and more as satanic forms of degeneracy and sexuality itself as a fatal flaw that played havoc with men's and women's lives. Sexuality slouched out of the original sin that for millennia weakened human reason and will. It was both the ultimate punishment inflicted by the

Almighty on the human species and His constant reminder that the species He had created was imperfect, yet capable of breaking through the boundaries of sin and taking its rightful place in His house light years away from the moral gutters of planet earth.

All over the country sublimation centers, sub-cens for short, sprung up like mushrooms. There, highly qualified staffs of doctors, nurses, and theologians taught young and old alike how to channel sexual urges into more productive and godly outlets. The results of this painstaking therapy varied: failures were often swept under the rug, enabling the government to save face, and success stories were endlessly trumpeted in the press and in the media, with one slight disadvantage—few gave them any credence. What captured the popular imagination were morbid tales of the utter inefficacy of this type of therapy, of unmitigated botchery of its methods laced with black humor.

One story continually made the rounds about a young man of impeccable credentials and high moral character pronounced cured after a lengthy stay at a sublimation center, his thoughts and feelings presumed to be roaming the highest spheres of religion and spirituality, being arrested by a local sheriff one hour after his release for attempted rape. Another popular tale focused on a girl, also highly thought of, from whose mind and body any tinge of sexual desire had been removed by psychoanalytic and theological surgery, leaving a sublimation center with a summa cum laude certificate in her hand yet before sundown joining a striptease club and in her off-duty hours laboring devotedly as a streetwalker. Still the government persevered and with the assistance of blue ribbon committees opened new sublimation centers and hired more men and women of the cloth, more practicing theologians, more MDs and nurses to combat the horrifying evils of sex.

Concurrently another scheme was put into operation: Huston had pronounced artificial insemination vastly preferable to natural insemination and in nationwide telecasts urged the electorate to adopt the former. Semen could be obtained expeditiously enough without any contact between a man and a woman—thus practically eliminating sexual pleasure—and then artificially implanted. This was another important step on the way to making Western Amernipp more holy and placing it closer to God. Another malign form of vice would be eliminated. The Almighty was applauding His children as they were clearing yet another hurdle barring them from the state of grace absolute and exhorted them not to slacken till they stamped out all the remaining pockets of vice. Art-Ins condos—no one could rightly say why this particular name was selected—were far from being popular and the numbers of those seeking their services pitifully low. But the government sped up its campaign of holy propaganda and asked all religious denominations to lend a hand. Most of them did. Homily Grister was the federal commissioner of Sex Police, and he was also the executive director of all sublimation centers, art-ins condos, and any other offices or services created ad hoc and lying within the purview of his guardianship of public and private morals. Grister told friends that being commissioner of Sex Police and director of the centers and condos gave him more satisfaction than any other office he had held in the past or might hold in the future because he knew with absolute certainty he was doing God's work.

Faith Police, which was headed by Ganymede Pillows, was expected by many to work in tandem with Sex Police, the two being the opposite sides of the same coin. In practice just the opposite happened. Faith Police was considered by its commissioner infinitely superior to its loudmouthed neighbor in the Headquarters Building. Its business was with faith, religion, matters of the spirit, not with copulation and varieties of oral sex. Members of this gallant band, who never slept and labored devotedly under his leadership, touched the very vestments swathing the figure of the Almighty. The thugs who put other folks' dirty linen out for everyone to see barely rose above the gutter where their foes and victims were rotting. Any comparison of the two law-enforcing divisions, however broad, was off base at best and the arguments shoring up each of them in turn multiplied. In actuality the rift within the ranks of the boys and girls in blue helped the suspects and future internees. They could claim that guilty though they might be of sexual peccadilloes, their religious faith remained intact and their religious observances exemplary. Or conversely, though they may have temporarily lapsed in religious devotion, their sex life, or rather the absence of it, was blameless and set a high example.

Although the breakdown in communication and much else placed the SP and FP at loggerheads, their methods remained almost identical. In squads of five or six the FP would barge into a home, usually in the late afternoon or early evening, after the children had returned from school and their bedtime was at least a couple of hours away, browbeatingly order the whole family into the living room or the kitchen, and start the interrogation. They wanted to know all about their attendance at the church, synagogue, mosque, or other place of worship, the extent of their participation in the religious life of the community, the financial commitments they had made in the sacred cause, and whether these were scrupulously honored.

The children, no matter what their age, were asked detailed questions about the history of their religion, and when they could not answer them to FP's satisfaction the blame was laid squarely on the parents' shoulders. The parents themselves were grilled in a hundred different ways: whether they read religious journals and if not, why not; whether they attended religious meetings and belonged to religious clubs; whether they associated with truly religious people, whether they were bringing their children up in the true spirit of their faith and according to the commands of Chief Justice, and countless others.

A home decorated with religious symbols, displaying pictures of the elders, prophets, and leaders of this particular denomination and of other denominations similar to it usually created a positive impression on the interrogators; the full-size official portrait of Chief Justice wearing all the regalia hanging in a prominent place in the house was worth more than the flaming protestations of innocence. When everything else had been accounted for a question on which the world hung was fired at the family, "Do you have knowledge of persons who neglect their religious obligations, who speak ill of religion, or whose outlook is markedly secular and who put their children's souls in jeopardy? If so, it is your bounden duty to denounce them." Those who denounced no one were viewed with extreme suspicion, usually taken to the station and interrogated further. Those who pointed a finger at a friend, neighbor, or a total stranger gained a reprieve until the next time round and were sometimes rewarded.

Faith Police followed the same procedure when confronting single persons, young or old, living by themselves or in the company of friends or companions. Young people in general, except those he had handpicked himself, rankled Chief Justice, and he held places where they were found in large numbers—colleges, universities, sports clubs and associations of one kind or another—to be hotbeds of irreligion and discontent. Not unexpectedly senior citizens did not elude the eye of the hawk either, and he warned the God-fearing citizenry about the machinations of suave elderly gentlemen pretending to be pillars of society yet muttering high treason with every breath, and, worse still, about Machiavellian schemes of little old ladies, all of them looking exactly like first cousins of Jane Marple and so unbelievably deft at bridge but in reality raising the ghost of Mata Hari, ruthless agents with license to kill, their knitting needles and scissors held ready to silence the opposition. In the end the inevitable question always came up, "Do you have knowledge of persons who neglect . . ." and so on, and the answers to it created an unbridgeable gulf between the highs and the lows of humanity. Mindful of his sacred duty at all times, Chief Justice of Western Amernipp cherished the belief that all men, women, and children were guilty until proven innocent.

In transforming the United States of America into a theocracy and in carrying out fundamental social and political reforms, Huston and his band of saints enjoyed the support of most Protestant churches, of the Roman Catholic Church, of he Jewish establishments, and of congregations falling outside the Judeo-Christian tradition—Muslims, Buddhists, and others. But non-Christian congregations offered support that was at best lukewarm, and at times it turned into passive resistance. Such obstructionism was duly noted, but because its adherents were relatively few in number, no action was taken. This disposition of religious alliances persisted after 2082, the year when the United States of America became the Western Province of Amernipp, but with two notable exceptions. The Society of Friends refused to accede to Huston's demands, and its members overnight became the Fighting Quakers. The secretary of the American Society of Friends Service Committee blasted the new theocracy as the unholy alliance of rats and vermin and called on Friends in other countries to come to his aid. The aid came promptly in bucketfuls. Emboldened, the secretary laid the record of Huston's misrule before the executive board at an extraordinary international meeting of the society and before the International Court of Justice at The Hague. Infuriated, Huston threatened to throw the secretary in the slammer for eternity but was advised to relent and bide his time. An uneasy truce intervened.

Within the Roman Catholic Church veneration of Huston was prevalent, and his merciless policy of stamping out vice in its myriad forms was lauded. Several Roman Catholic clerics opined that Huston's theocratic state was the most important event in the history of the world since the crucifixion of Jesus Christ, and masses of communicants of other churches heartily concurred. After a spell of inaction Chief Justice was back in the saddle, but there was a fly in the ointment. Its name was the Order of Preachers. Heirs to devotion, humility, preaching and teaching skills and to the wisdom of Saint Dominic, the friars of the order bearing his name would not be bamboozled by yet another charlatan who also happened to be a criminal. They refused to kiss the tainted rod and they stood firm. In the course of a tempestuous colloquy the provincial of the order, himself a convert to Roman Catholicism and a distinguished scholar, told Chief Justice to his face that his pact was with the devil and that he ought to be harried out of the land. Insults from both sides followed, and Huston flew into a rage. But the Dominicans stuck to their breviaries, and the Savior of the Country was again advised that the time was unpropitious for a frontal, or any other, attack against the insolent friars. An uneasy truce between the two was the order of the day.

Still there was a good deal Huston could feel gratified about. On the Protestant side of the fence, the Presbyterians and the Baptists, the Lutherans, the Episcopalians, and the Churches of Christ all marched to his drummer. Only the Methodists made polite noises of dissent, but they were so polite as to be totally ignored. An especially valuable supporter was the president of the Church of Jesus Christ of Latter Day Saints, who was blessed with daily revelations from the Almighty urging him to join forces with Huston against common enemies. Huston did everything that was humanly possible to cultivate the newly forged friendship, and he was amply rewarded. Within the Roman fold he could count on the unqualified support of several archbishops and bishops and on the good will of several orders, including the Jesuits, who as a rule knew what he was going to do before he knew it himself.

In addition, he made an important friend in Rome. Alexander IX, the newly elected pontiff of the Roman Catholic Church, born just outside Valencia under the name of Raoul Borgia, was a vigorous man in his late forties harboring Napoleonic ambitions for the institution he headed. As a youth he was the star of the local soccer team and excelled in other sports. He was handsome, extremely popular, made friends easily, and was inordinately fond of girls. And girls were inordinately fond of him.

Everyone predicted he would enter the army where a splendid career awaited him. But Raoul demurred. The age of Spanish conquests was long past and pacifying the Basques, maintaining public order when police forces were shorthanded, or being led blindfolded with NATO partners onto some ill-planned peacekeeping adventure were hardly his idea of military glory. He surprised everyone by entering the seminary, where he did very well. Once ordained he was snatched up by a bishop to be his principal secretary, and two years later joined the staff of an influential archbishop as secretary and advisor. He performed meritorious work in the ticklish area of ecumenicalism, stood guard when overly liberal reformers were pounding at the gate, put the finances of the archbishopric in the black, and chaired innumerable national and international committees. He had the knack of swiftly earning the respect of friend and foe alike and his boss was duly grateful. When he suggested that Raoul might consider spending a couple of years in Rome being attached to the Curia, the young prelate readily agreed.

In Rome, Raoul was soon singled out as a very brainy diplomat and administrator who stayed the middle course and was endowed with considerable social talents. When he stepped again on Spanish soil two years later the young bishop Raoul Borgia was assigned first to Sevilla and later to Madrid. Two years later, with the affectionate support of his patron, the archbishop, he was elevated to the same rank, and four years later he received the red hat. He was already pegged by many as a comer, the future pope, and he devoted much time to cultivating the right friends.

When in 2082 the aged and universally respected pontiff of the Roman Catholic Church finally succumbed to dogging ill health, Raoul was immediately put forth as a very serious contender. In Spain most churchgoers were delighted at the prospect of a Spanish pope after more years of regrettable exclusion than they cared to count. And abroad the support for the Clever Boots of a Spaniard mounted. He was elected not on the first ballot but soon thereafter, with the support of some conservatives and some liberals from a wide range of countries, including African and Asian cardinals. Few expected him to assume the official name of Alexander IX and link it to one of his Spanish predecessors Alexander VI, another Borgia, but he did just that.

The new pope at once set to work revitalizing channels of international communication, streamlining papal administration, and extending the powers of the Church as far as he could. It was only when he at last sat on the throne of St. Peter that Raoul Borgia felt at liberty to speak frankly on subjects that had previously commanded silence. He wholeheartedly approved of theocratic governments and gave high marks to "the grim Yankee," one Everett Zacharias Huston, who had turned the secular establishment on its head. Over the centuries persistent encroachments of secularism very nearly emasculated the Catholic Church and the enemy had been continually at the gate. Raoul dreamt of leading the papal armies against the enemies of the Church, as Cesare Borgia had done, extending the borders of Vatican City north, south, east, and west, as far as Tuscany in the north, and Campania in the south, and farther perhaps, and in due course annexing all of Italy. The Republic of Italy, that joke of a secular democratic state and an insult to the Catholic Church, would cease to exist, and in its place would rise the enlarged Catholic State answerable to God and not to parliaments and politicos. He, Pope Alexander IX, would be the head of this state and he would rule not democratically—the word roused in him unspeakable disgust—but autocratically, in the manner of the great Spanish kings.

Raoul put final touches to his plans but could do little to translate them into reality, and he waited for the opportune moment. In the interim he armed Swiss Guards with automatic weapons and issued a number of executive orders demanding that the Catholic Church be always referred to by word of mouth and in print with the utmost respect. Then he turned his prodigious energy and talents to making the Church of Rome populous as never before, wealthy as never before, and powerful as never before. Conversion Corps was created at the Vatican, attracting young men and women from many nations whose orders were to convert the populace in Asian and African countries to Catholicism and make sure they remained within the Church. In the eyes of Raoul Borgia and the managers of Conversion Corps the end justified the means, and when the goal was eternal salvation all other goals lapsed into insignificance. The youthful missionaries whose breasts were swelling with idealistic notions were told point-blank that the Curia's prime duty was to count noses, and if conversion could be facilitated by bribery, blackmail, or some other unorthodox means they should have no qualms of conscience.

Concurrently another scheme was put into effect—sending squads of highly educated laymen with advanced degrees in psychology and social studies to northern Europe, North America, Australia, New Zealand, and South Africa to wean the middle and upper layers of society off Protestantism and guide them to the true faith. The scheme was being executed by the Jesuit order and codenamed Black Rose. Raoul set great store by conversion but, mindful of swelling the ranks of the faithful by every possible means, he also led a campaign for large families, the larger the better. Under his direct supervision the Curia created numerous financial awards and issued certificates of merit to parents with more than three children, offering substantial financial assistance in case of hardship. Raoul's avowed goal, to be attained by peaceful means, was Catholicism triumphantly reigning as the sole religion on the face of this earth, with all other religious persuasions having been eliminated in one way or another. Looking at sheer numbers this was only possible if the highly populated countries of the Orient—China, India, Pakistan, Indonesia, Japan, Korea—embraced the true doctrine, and some of the sharpest brains within the Curia were already burning the midnight oil to find a *modus vivendi* between materialistic political philosophies and Catholicism.

Raoul inherited from his predecessors well-filled coffers and an economy that was sound, smoothly running, and profitable. Setting his sights high, he made a vow to double the wealth of the Church and put some of the shrewdest businessmen in Italy to work, ordering them not to leave a stone unturned. As a result the Vatican's financial structure was revamped from the ground floor up, a string of new businesses purchased and many an old one sold for a pittance, daring stock exchange policies adopted, appeals to donors redoubled, levies and taxes raised. Raoul kept a watchful eye on the sacks of gold, one reason being his unseasonably poor relations with the Italian government and the eventual necessity of buying off members of the government to avoid rupture or worse.

As for enhancing the political power of the Church, Raoul very much regretted his inability to engage in open warfare and make Vatican City the hub of a mighty Catholic Empire feared in the chanceries all over the world. He was counting on the corrosion of democratic governments in Europe and in parts of the English-speaking world that would usher in dictatorial leaders admired and not jeered at by the electorate. In such a plight the Catholic Church, putting her best foot forward, could come to power by popular demand—in Italy but also in other countries. What had happened in the former United States of America, now known by the slightly ridiculous name of Western Amernipp—he chuckled—was a movable scenario for the future, and Raoul watched what went on there, not missing a single detail. He felt he had a stake in the comings and goings of that faraway land. It was like seeing a preview of what fate decreed would happen very soon there on native ground and maybe on the other side of the mountain too. But for the present his hands were tied.

The pontiff's theological credo was simple, and there was no room in it for baffling complexities, hesitation, or uncertainty. Courageously, he would air his views often, usually in a direct and succinct manner. The Catholic Church was the only true church, having been given to man by God Himself. It was sanctified by Jesus Christ, and its commands were God's commands. Catholics born in the Church and converts to Catholicism were because of this very fact assured of salvation. They did not have to earn it or distinguish themselves in any way. Their birthright was their passport to heaven. Admittedly, if a Catholic committed a succession of heinous crimes this right could be deferred pending penance and God's forgiveness. But in the normal course of events the lines of demarcation were clearly drawn. The millions born before the time of the Savior and ignorant of His teachings would end up in limbo, not a makeshift hell by any means but a painless and tranquil abode, albeit not permeated with the presence of the Almighty.

As for the other churches in Christendom, particularly Protestant churches, the pontiff's views were equally firm. He compared them to fallen angels and counseled that no mercy should be shown to them. If a Protestant converted to Catholicism he or she would be accepted, after a probationary period of course, as a full-fledged Catholic. But those who remained faithful to their heretical sects faced nearly insurmountable obstacles. The road to salvation was open to them only if they performed extraordinary deeds glorifying God and defending the Church. Otherwise they would always be branded by God as traitors, the lowest of the lowest. As a last resort, the pontiff stressed the point again and again, it was the sense of belonging that counted. Only by passing through the portals of the Catholic Church and manifesting total obedience to Her rules could one be elevated onto the path of salvation. The pontiff wanted this simple truth to be engraved in the minds of all his listeners. As for matters of morality and ethics, he refused to be a hanging judge. Human foibles were regrettable, but they held no sway over the noble labor of enriching and strengthening the Church. The much publicized revelations of sexual molestation of children by Catholic priests at the outset of the twenty-first century did disservice to many of those found guilty and to others who gave of themselves in the service of Mother Church. The pontiff stretched out his long arm with the index finger uplifted. "Always remember that private morality has very little to do with the essence of Catholic religion."

Huston and Borgia had corresponded and had conversed by phone ever since the former had risen to eminence, but they did not meet until the fall of 2083 when both decided that a personal encounter would be useful. Geneva was selected as the rendezvous to which they proceeded under assumed names, checking into the same luxury hotel. They took long walks along the lake, reviewing a multiplicity of topics, and they lunched and dined together at exclusive restaurants, repairing afterwards to the one's or the other's suite for drinks and general conversation. In the lobby and in town they both wore disguises—Borgia a black Vandyke, sideburns wide as a church door, and eyebrows that rose and spread like a peacock's upper tail, Huston an ostentatious flaming red wig and oversized red mustache to boot. Huston was six-foot-four, and Borgia barely six feet tall. On their promenades he did not want to appear shorter than his Protestant companion and wore elevator shoes. He sported a sombrero and Huston a diminutive brown derby. No one recognized them.

Borgia understood that even though the theocratic government of Western Amernipp considered all religions equal and worthy of highest praise, it was Protestant Christianity, that painful oxymoron, that had an edge on all other churches. And he understood it was expected of Huston, as the real ruler of Western Amernipp, still a preponderantly Protestant country, and the most famous Protestant theologian alive to pile praise on Protestantism at the expense of its traditional enemy, the Catholic Church. He recognized the realities of the situation, and he was not in the least offended.

For his part Huston expected Borgia's official position to be hyped up now and then by diatribes against the Protestant establishment. After

all, the pontiff of the Roman Catholic Church had obligations to fulfill and masses of the faithful to nurture and placate. If it were otherwise
Huston would suspect a super-plot of satanic proportions standing
everything on its head and boding a catastrophe at the end of the tun-
nel, a total collapse of the established order. But he was pleased at the
way things stood and encouragingly patted the younger man on the
back. Everything was in order.

In fact a sense of freemasonry had sprung up between the two clerics, and they drew enjoyment from each other's company. They told
barroom jokes, fumed over the brainlessness of many of their subordinates, and laughed their heads off at the pious proposals put forth by
their respective offices that would have led to disaster had they not been
rescinded at the eleventh hour. On a deeper level the two respected and
admired each other. Borgia was immensely impressed by the transformation of the most powerful and diverse country in the world into a
religiously governed entity, leaving far behind its deplorable and ungod-
ly democratic heritage, and Huston gave the pontiff high marks for
putting the Vatican's finances in order, reforming the Church and bringing it to the point where it commanded fear and respect among nations
as never before since the ebb of the Middle Ages.

The common denominator in their respective orientations was the
unswerving belief that a religion, a church, a community bound by
divine law, was all about power and expansion and not about faith in
God and morality. Once a church had abrogated her temporal dynam-
ics, once it had abandoned her rightful ambition to double or triple the
body of her communicants and push the boundaries of her earthly
power to limits yet unknown, it began to die, like a wounded calf
deserted in a snowstorm on a frozen prairie. For Huston and Borgia the
spiritual and the temporal spheres were so inextricably joined as to be
indistinguishable, the spiritual inspiring the temporal and becoming
one with it, and the temporal nurturing the spiritual every inch of the
way and effecting its own unbreakable union. Despite the easily notice-
able differences between the two men, they were brothers-in-arms. The
five-day sojourn in Geneva passed very fast for each of them, and on
the way to the airport they ranted about staying longer together. But
this was impossible. Each had urgent business to attend to and duty
came first. As they shook hands before disappearing down the con-
course, regular future meetings were on both their lips. As for the onc

that was ending, the only way to describe it was "an unqualified success." They had finally met in person; they took the measure of each other; they cemented their friendship.

Upon returning to the Vatican, Borgia turned to his pet project, which was still in its infancy. For many years he had idolized Francisco Franco as the man of destiny appointed by Almighty God to lead the Spanish people from the valley of sin and despair to the gardens of godliness and grace. He had been watching successive generations of historians, revisionist, post-revisionist, and others, raising the reputation of El Caudillo in certain respects and lowering it in others, missing the mark and playing intricate in-games of which only pedagogues were capable. There was, of course, a corpus of historiography that placed Franco at the apex of humanity, albeit not a bulky one. But this was not enough! Secular historians fiddling with sources and evidence, self-assertive and consumed by the plaguing ambition to earn respect and reward from their peers, were not enough. Only canonization could repair this rank iniquity. Only by investing El Caudillo with the insignia of sainthood and placing him in the long tier of Catholic saints could proper encomium be bestowed upon him; and this time encomium would come from God Himself, and not from shifty professors feverishly toting up their bank accounts.

Before flying to Geneva, Borgia had broached the matter to a small circle of advisors and confidants and had been taken aback by their negative reception. Next he canvassed senior members of the Curia and received the same disheartening responses. On both occasions suggestions were put forth to honor Generalissimo Franco with a papal title or devise some other means of perpetuating his glorious accomplishments; anything within reason, but not another word about canonization! Sitting in his study Borgia again reviewed the situation and picked up the threads he had left behind. Pussyfooting at this point would be tantamount to the admission of defeat, and he could not countenance defeat. He remained in meditation for an hour, then summoned his confidential secretary and ordered an extraordinary meeting of the entire College of Cardinals—no absences permitted—two days hence. At the meeting he presented his case at some length, dwelling on the allegiance and loyalty the future Saint Francisco always bore to the Catholic faith and on his many policies and individual acts that shored up the Church and sanctified the Catholic doctrine. He adduced testimonials and judgments from Franco's contemporaries, priests and laymen alike, and from his apologists in the twentieth and twenty-first centuries. He ended on a spirited note, eliciting candid comments from the cardinals and telling them how highly he valued their advice.

Almost at once he was shocked by what he heard. Not a single red hat stood behind him and the swelling diapason of the College's commentary ranged from obstinate indifference to open hostility and brutally registered scorn for the former head of the Spanish state. A very aged Spanish cardinal, who has been on the list of retirees for a dozen years or so and who according to Borgia should have been put out to pasture years before, stood up with difficulty and, brandishing his heavy walking stick, snarled at the Holy Father, "You want to make Franco a saint of the Church? Well, let me tell you he has as much right to be canonized as Genghis Khan." A storm of applause followed the words of the very aged cardinal and abruptly lapsed into jeering laughter. Borgia listened to several other opinions, bowed, and ceremoniously thanked members of the college for their constructive contributions. The meeting over, he took pains to shake as many hands as he could and helped the very aged cardinal out of the conference chamber and into the hall where two young priests took charge.

Back in his study Borgia let his hair down. He confided in his secretary that he was mortally disappointed but realized that starting the canonization process for Francisco Franco in the present climate of opinion would lead nowhere. Another avenue would have to be explored, and his brain was already spinning full tilt. He was not a quitter, and it was God's will that the savior of Spain be honored posthumously in an exalted and unique way. Borgia shut himself up in the Vatican Library for two weeks, and with the exception of his academic assistant, who in normal times advised him about scholarly matters, saw no one. When he emerged from seclusion a roguish smile adorned his face, and he sent for his Secretary of State and other high functionaries of the Curia. He announced to them that, after poring over ancient rules and laws of the Church for days on end, he had discovered one giving the Pope the authority to raise a meritorious Catholic decedent to the rank of cardinal, such decedent being named according to canon law the "roving cardinal," his vote to be exercised in any election at the discretion of the Pope.

"Consequently," Borgia continued with glee, "Francisco Franco is now and will remain a cardinal and a prince of the Catholic Church." Those assembled listened to him in stony silence.

/   /   /

Immediately after his return to Washington, Huston concentrated on several urgent matters, one of them being a personal oath of allegiance pledged to him as Chief Justice by the armed forces of Western Amernipp. The new oath would supplant the current one in existence since July 4, 2082, whereby all the branches of the service simply pledged allegiance to the state. Phineas Léger, Homily Grister, and Ganymede Pillows all supported the measure, and the first of them argued eloquently in *National Forum* that the emerging political culture of Amernipp put high premiums on the personalization of the national leadership, thus creating a stronger bond between it and the electorate. Critics of the measure compared it to the German army's personal oath of allegiance to Adolf Hitler exacted before the outbreak of the Second World War. Huston read what the critics said and, casting his mind many years back to the time when he was taking history courses, concluded that the German army had fought bravely and well in the Second World War and that Hitler was a dandy leader. The new oath was administered as scheduled five days before Christmas of 2083.

/   /   /

Several blocks away from the Supreme Court, where Huston continued to maintain his headquarters, Simon Hertzfeld, Chief Rabbi of Western Amernipp, was playing host to Joe Pitkin, a young rabbi from Cleveland. The young man was troubled and he looked it.

"It's beyond me how you could even think of making this shady deal, Dr. Hertzfeld. You of all people. You know I've always held you in high esteem," he began for the third time.

Hertzfeld gave every indication of his unwillingness to answer the questions, but the young man persisted.

"Why, why? I have the right to know."

"Joe, you were my best student at the seminary, and I always credited you with keen intelligence and understanding of the circumstances surrounding the rabbinate and our Jewish communities."

A faint smile flickered across Joe's frozen countenance.

"Flattery will get you nowhere, sir. I want the goods, not complimentary speeches."

"So be it," Hertzfeld answered quietly. "Have you read the papers in the last few days? Has anything caught your attention?"

Joe shrugged his shoulders and said nothing.

"There were anti-Semitic outbursts in several large cities. Stores owned by Jews were smashed, and in three instances the owners held at gunpoint until the police arrived."

"Isolated incidents," Joe snapped. "I refuse to read more into it. Now and then Mormons are manhandled, as well as Catholics. It all depends what part of town you live in."

"I wish I could agree with you, Joe," Hertzfeld said sadly. "I wish I could. This was plain violence, and unlike protests against other denominations, anti-Semitic protests are invariably violent, and they are getting worse. More and more damage to property, a rising threat to human life."

"Assuming what you say is true, and I have my doubts, what is your solution?"

Hertzfeld adjusted his pince-nez. "When we read about pogroms in history books or consult the written and certified accounts of eyewitnesses and victims of those terrible massacres that took place in the olden times in Russia, Poland, and other countries, we are usually struck by the same MO. Pogroms are started by a handful of Gentiles who bear the Jews a grudge, but violence spreads like wildfire and soon everybody's hands are covered in blood. When the soldiers arrive, they do nothing to stop the mayhem. Just the reverse; they join in the fray. Our pogroms that will surely come to pass will have a different MO. Perhaps they will be less bestial, though I doubt it, but involving though they may the bulk of the population of a town or community, aid and comfort from the authorities will be forthcoming. In the highly disciplined society of Western Amernipp unauthorized violence is strictly forbidden. Still I wanted to make sure, and I wanted to hammer the nail right in."

"So what happened, Chief Rabbi?"

"Several weeks ago I got a call from Huston. He asked me to come and see him on a matter of some delicacy."

"Wow," Joe enunciated derisively. "The plot thickens."

"I told Huston about the new wave of anti-Semitism, and he appeared genuinely upset. He said the government would be most obliged if it could receive a little more information about the training of rabbis, the work of our rabbinical councils, and related matters—all this to ensure fairness and equity on the highest level."

"Isn't this information conveyed routinely to the high priest whose dog tags read something . . . something Pillows?"

"Yes, it is, but Huston wanted something a little more confidential and from an insider's perspective."

"And you obliged, sir?"

"I asked him to send advisors to the synagogues and to the rabbinate to help us look after the flock and interpret the law."

"Why?"

"Because he would've done it anyway, and by preempting him, so to speak, I scored a point. I vented my fears about imminent anti-Semitic violence, and I painted what I thought was a horrifying picture. He at once promised full governmental support to our people, protection of our holy places, compensation to the victims, all kinds of security measures."

"Can his word be trusted?"

"In this situation, yes. He is probably under pressure to keep tighter reins on the Jewish establishment. Remember when the new regime came to power we Jews fell between the cracks. Protestants and Catholics commanded its undivided attention, and we were largely left to our own devices. Thank God for that. But now they want us to cut the distance."

"So you . . . ?"

"Yes, Joe, I supped with the devil for the good of the church, and I'd do it again."

"Those thugs of Huston's, advisors as you call them, know as much about our religion as the man in the moon."

"It doesn't matter. They are in place to shore up Huston's standing vis-à-vis his potential rivals. They won't interfere with our work."

"Are you all that sure?"

"I don't want to see Jewish blood spilt, not a single drop if I can help it. I don't want pogroms. I don't want another holocaust."

"Aren't you exaggerating just a tad?"

"No, I am not. This was a very small price to pay. And even if I over-shot here and there the sacrifice was well worth it."

Joe leaned back in his seat and was lost in reflection, the combative partner in the dialogue nailing new colors to the mast. When he spoke at last it was in gentler tones. "How long, d'you think, this insane regime will last?"

Hertzfeld spread his hands.

"I don't know. Nothing would give me more satisfaction than to tell you the day is near. But I can't. There are too many imponderables."

"Many of our young people are spoiling to storm the Bastille now, men and women alike. I hear it all the time at meetings and outside the temple."

"This would be a grievous mistake and a bloodbath would follow. No! We must have patience."

"Someone has to fire the first shot, Chief Rabbi. Why not us? Or are you in favor of the old motto: 'Let others die so we can serve Mammon'?"

"No, I am not. The moment is not yet ripe for a revolution, but the moment will come."

"It's all well and good for you to make those terribly sensible state-ments. Huston ought to give you a medal." Hertzfeld cast a resolute sideways glace and fell silent, and Joe added immediately, "I'm sorry, that last remark was unnecessary to say the least."

"That's all right. No harm done. You see, Joe, all that nonsense the new messiahs and apostles have saddled us with gave rise to a shocking side effect: all kinds of primitive savage forces locked up in the human psyche are let loose, and they are not tamed and partly refined as they were in a free society. We are held in the vise of holiness and perfection, and I am given to understand that very soon we shall embark on a mys-tical journey to become one with the Godhead. But in the meantime the savagery within us will force the cork out and tumble upon the world with unheard of passion. Yes, I fear violence, for it will be savage, heretofore unknown violence, and its victims will be legion, our peo-ple more than the Christians, the Muslims, and the sons and daughters of other religions, for when everything else fails they will fall on the old slogan, 'Blame the Jew.' Yes, Joe, I fear the savage violence which is just around the corner."

"All the more reason to man the barricades now—today—not the day after tomorrow."

"The time is not yet ripe."

"When, for heaven's sake, will it be ripe?"

"We shall know when the time comes. We shall all know," Hertzfeld said quietly, laying a hand on Joe's shoulder.

Chapter 4

The Royals and the Sansculottes

"I didn't realize things had gone that far," the empress said beckoning to Princess Sayko to sit down. "Has Takahito really taken leave of his senses? And when did that nonsense first see the light of day? You've always been close to your brother, and presumably he confided in you. Well, what do you have to say for yourself, young lady?" The empress sounded prosecutorial, and her tiny green eyes, usually ceaselessly flitting this way and that, came to rest with finality on the agitated face of the granddaughter. "Well?" she repeated, at pains to quench her fury. "Well?"

Sayko jumped off her stool and, bending forward histrionically before the empress, threw her arms high up in the air in a sacerdotal gesture as if she were playing the part of a high priest in amateur theatricals.

"Grandmother, you have to take my word," she gasped out, her arms still shooting up and in all directions. "Takahito didn't confide in me, but even if he had it would've been very bad form—" She stopped abruptly and spread her arms imploringly. "Very bad form."

"I want to get to the bottom of it." The empress's tones were a tad less stern.

"Takahito is a good boy!" Sayko cried out with passion. "A very good boy, but he fell among thieves."

"Go on, child."

"He's been a liberal and an anti-monarchist for several years now, but of late his views became much more extreme. It's not his fault and . . ."

"Remind me, how old is that good boy of yours?" the empress interrupted with verve.

"He's going on seventeen, and things got worse when he came under the influence of Tarako Lepra."

"That common criminal who wants to abolish monarchy in our country and put all the members of the imperial family to the sword—with one exception of course, his precious snitch and sidekick, one Prince Mikasa of unhappy memory."

"Takahito is a good boy, Grandmother." Sayko's words were ringing with conviction.

"It's one thing to entertain political views however execrable, but it's quite another to try to put them into practice by violent and criminal means. I thought that Tarako Lepra person was still in jail."

"He's out on parole, Grandmother."

"This only goes to show that our legal system is beyond redemption. On the other hand our security police is up to scratch. I understand that person, whose name I don't even wish to pronounce, is under constant surveillance, and that's how they got to your brother. He's attending their meetings; he's one of them. The commissioner handed the emperor a confidential report, and I don't have to tell you how your grandfather reacted. You should be able to guess, and guess right."

"Takahito is a good boy," Sayko repeated doggedly. "Hotheaded perhaps and impressionable, but his heart is in the right place."

"Your defense of Prince Mikasa does you credit. This is how it ought to be. As for his heart being in the right place, well, I have grave doubts. The plan, as I understand it, is to make Eastern Amernipp a republic with an elected president and so on, by peaceful means if possible; but if not by mounting a revolution and of course heads will roll. Your precious brother may already have been given the enviable commission of escorting members of the imperial family to the guillotine or some other instrument of death, in order of precedence, to be sure. The emperor first and so on, you being a little ways behind unless of course you collaborate and are spared."

"Grandmother, those are ghastly thoughts."

"No more ghastly than the conspiracy Takahito is part of. The commissioner told us the traitors meet in those filthy places by the docks and pose as longshoremen. But we know better, don't we?"

"It's a short-lived lapse. Takahito's been tricked. He's too trusting, and he is a good boy."

"Good boy or bad boy, he has to regain his senses. So far the matter has been kept secret. Only the emperor, myself, and a handful of others know that the future emperor of Japan is ready to lend a hand to what may be the bloodiest revolution of all. And if you tell me one more time that Takahito is a good boy, child, I won't be able to control myself."

Sayko stooped over her grandmother and kissed her on the cheek. "This is for my favorite granny."

"You told me once," the empress began partly mollified, "that Takahito holds your friend in high regard."

"My friend?"

"Yes, your friend, your lover, the mighty National Security Advisor of Western Amernipp."

"My husband. You should've called him by his proper name."

A peal of sardonic laughter and then another sounded so overwhelming as to reduce Sayko to painful silence.

"Stop behaving like a goose, girl, and for once stare facts in the face. Yes, facts!"

"Siegie and I think of ourselves—"

The empress cut her short. "Siegfried La Rochelle is not your husband. He has a wife in Washington D.C., and her name is Millicent, I believe. Yes, Millie Kirby La Rochelle, and she is the most outspoken figure in Washington since the late lamented Ulysses S. Grant. These are facts, dear, and facts must be recognized for what they are. The sooner you come down to earth from whatever cloud you are floating on the better for you. Well?"

"Indeed, Grandmother. Takahito thinks the world of Siegie. He admires his intellect and his extraordinary diplomatic talents. His mind may have been temporarily seduced by Tarako Lepra, but I'll wager all my worldly possessions that his respect for Dr. La Rochelle has not diminished a jot."

"Good. Then you'll have to ask your friend to come to Tokyo as soon as possible and have a very serious talk with your brother."

"Will Takahito agree to it?"

"It is your job to see to it that he does. I am trying to save my grandson's hide, or whatever else about his person merits to be saved. And in the long run I may be on the way to saving all our lives. Noblesse oblige."

"Grandmother," Sayko whispered, tiptoeing toward the empress, "Siegie and I think of ourselves as a married couple, and now and then our fondest wish turns into reality, reality for us I mean, reality that has ceased to be a mere dream. How can I forget about Millie, the Kentucky bitch? She's constantly on my mind. But . . . but . . ."

"Careful about confusing the two. Careful, my child."

Princess Sayko drew herself up and then bowed ceremoniously to the empress of Japan.

"Your Majesty may rest assured that Prince Mikasa will wait upon the National Security Advisor of Western Amernipp upon his arrival in Eastern Amernipp and that the two will discuss very frankly an important affair of state."

/   /   /

Siegfried La Rochelle took another sip of the drink his Japanese hosts had especially prepared for him and which in its own inimitable way joined the Orient and the Occident within the few cubic inches of a large whisky glass. The basic ingredients of the "La Rochelle mix" as the drink was promptly named, were bourbon and several skinny ice cubes. Then a measure of sake was added, a dash of vermouth and carefully selected herbs gathered—the hosts insisted—at Japanese holy sites. A level spoon of brown sugar completed the imbibatory ritual, and the potion was ready for consumption. La Rochelle had tasted it twice before, and he soon grew extremely fond of it. The La Rochelle mix gave one the best of both worlds, and it offered something novel, not just two entities joined together but an entirely new creation transcending its separate parts, just as Amernipp was much more than merely a union of the United States and Japan—a long-awaited nation that drew its strength from the ancient wisdom of two great cultures and then blended them so that a new culture arose far superior to its diverse constituent parts. La Rochelle felt in his breast pocket for the recipe that the prime minister of Eastern Amernipp had presented him with, delivering a speech appropriate for the occasion.

He and Prince Mikasa were sitting on deck chairs in a secluded part of the imperial gardens next to a sparsely visited summerhouse and discretely watched over by the Secret Service. When La Rochelle had heard Sayko's lengthy account of Mikasa's initiation into the antimonarchist revolutionary conspiracy, punctuated by her comments and explanations, suggestions, and predictions he could hardly credit his ears. He had always viewed the prince as a genteel, rather refined youngster more at home at the yachting club and at fashionable parties than in the smoke-filled rooms of political levelers who would stop at nothing. Carefully placing the glass in the middle of a rickety table, he turned his eyes again on Princess Sayko's younger brother, and he saw what he had so often seen in the past: an American preppie smartly dressed, a languid expression on his face, an air of unobtrusive superiority about him, a young man who did not have to insist on his exalted position because he took it for granted as the most natural thing in the world, and the world knew it.

"Your liberal leanings are not an issue, Prince Mikasa, nor is your association with socialist and communist groups and with what one can only call the dregs of society. You have not yet reached your seventeenth birthday, but you have already been bitten by the radical bug and the discriminating ones among us cry out 'Good show!' The great poet Goethe once said, 'A liberal progressive at twenty, a cautious conservative at forty.' This is the way of the world."

"Ah," Takahito interjected, "Johann Wolfgang von Goethe, author of *Faust* and hundreds of superb poems of the German language."

"The same," La Rochelle conceded, feeling like a high school teacher not in tune with his students. "But when violence and carnage are on the agenda even the most discriminating among us have a change of heart."

"Indeed," Takahito commented primly. "I wonder about all this fuss regarding the death of millions. Is it some sort of delayed sense of guilt? Stalin killed off millions of kulaks to create a viable socialist society not controlled by personal wealth, and the sacrifice was well worth it. During the reign of terror in France those who, by their speech or mannerisms, were identified as supporters of the ancient regime were summarily executed because the French Republic leaders set their hearts on creating a new society, one governed by liberty, equality, fraternity, where rank and privilege counted for nothing. The aristocrats and their minions simply stood in the way. They had to be removed. Even in merry old England during their civil war the Cavaliers slit the throats of the Roundheads after the initial molestation and torture, and vice versa. But in the end after Charles I had been beheaded and the Royalists routed, England was a more equitable, better country. Progress is never bloodless, Dr. La Rochelle. Death for some ushers in a new life for many. This is the logic of history."

Takahito went on and on, adducing fresh examples and glorifying victories for mankind as a whole in the wake of purges, bloodbaths, and genocide.

La Rochelle listened spellbound. It was clear the young man had read widely and it was equally clear he had accepted a militant socialist ideology, no questions asked. Takahito fluently conversed in Japanese and English, and he also possessed a ready command of French and Spanish. Currently, in addition to his other studies he was learning Russian. His accents were decidedly Bostonian, no other drawl or brogue lying within the realm of possibility. In years past all his American nannies had come from Boston, and later all his American tutors hailed from the same town. For the most part Takahito's speech was the patrician English of the devotees of Brahmanic culture, but now and then his diction broke into words or tones whose provenance was unmistakably proletarian Boston—the Boston of Irish and other immigrants, of brannigans, barroom brawls, insults held in reserve and when the time was ripe volubly conveyed. He was well aware of his heterogeneous linguistic heritage and chuckled, looking the National Security Advisor straight in the eye when his polished high-class delivery was suddenly thrown off track by the intrusion of a colorful patois telling so much in so few words. As La Rochelle kept listening he became convinced that the young prince was endowed with a considerable histrionic talent, his imperial birthright signaling a grievous loss to the stage. "Still," he thought, "I came here under different colors."

"You've intimated, Prince Mikasa, that at times violence is a necessary component in the improvement of society."

"I sure have."

"Well then, tell me what beheadings, hangings, or other humane forms of terminating the other fellow's life are necessary for the betterment of Eastern Amernipp?"

"Your condescending irony is ill placed, sir." Takahito lifted his head and was staring at Siegfried with merciless ill will.

"Is it really? Well, tell me how the abolishment of monarchy and the execution of the imperial family will serve in the noble cause of improving the lives of Eastern Amernippians. Surely when blood is shed, it's for a good reason. Tell me the reason, Prince. I'm dying to know."

Takahito shook his head in obvious disgust.

"Let me teach you a lesson in the unofficial, unsanctioned history of my country. Since the beginnings of time millions of our people have been slaughtered like animals by their masters, lords, princes, emperors—men maimed and sadistically slain, women raped, tortured, disfigured, and left to die. Their blood would fill not one but a hundred Tokyo Bays. We must never allow ourselves the privilege of forgetting. I can see millions of those suffering faces right before me; I can see blood dripping from their mutilated limbs—millions and millions who perished for what? The lord's whim? An emperor's false ambition? The feudal code? The samurai code?"

"This happened a long time ago, Takahito. Let's lay the past to rest."

"You're wrong. The great religions of the East teach us to embrace the mighty forces that shore up the moral order of the universe, and they teach us to strike a balance. Everything has to be paid for; everything has to be accounted for. Otherwise there's disharmony and chaos in the universe."

"Frying the emperor and the empress in oil won't bring the millions you spoke of back to life."

"Maybe not. But a balance has to be struck, and there are millions of my compatriots living today poverty-stricken, helpless in the clutches of global corporations."

"Listen to me, Takahito. We are only concerned that you do not lend aid and comfort to those who want to achieve their goals by violent means, assassinations, acts of terror. We can't allow you to become involved for the good of Eastern Amernipp."

"I am already involved."

"That man, Tarako Lepra—"

"He's been much maligned in the Japanese and world press. He wants to build a new society. He is for us what Lenin was for the Russians."

"But he is a revolutionary."

Takahito waved the comment away, and a primly sardonic smile curled up round his lips. "You're banging Sayko."

"I beg your pardon."

"Stop being a stuffed shirt, Doctor. We are two men of the world having a frank conversation."

La Rochelle gulped down the contents of the whisky glass and was at once overtaken by hiccups, while Takahito set about procuring a jug of water and another glass and began to pound his guest on the back.

"That's enough, enough," the American blurted out. "I didn't know this was known even to the happy few."

"It isn't, with the exception of the empress, who makes it her business to know everything that doesn't concern her, and one or two confidants. As for me, Sayko is Sis and we talk. She cries on my shoulder. Lately she's been crying a lot, and I am well advised to have a spare shirt with me when I see her."

"Princess Sayko has favored me with her friendship, and I believe her to be entirely happy."

Takahito gave out a chuckle and made a deprecating gesture. "Sis loves you very much. Frankly I don't understand what she sees in you: flabby and overweight, gross, self-centered, arrogant, thinking he's the cat's pajamas and all the rest. Still, it's her business."

"Now look here, young man—" La Rochelle raised his voice, looking daggers.

"Why don't you make an honest woman of her?" Takahito asked nonchalantly. "Nothing would please her more than a walk to the altar."

"Impossible, I am already married." La Rochelle gave every indication of wishing to quash this particular topic.

"I know, to a Millicent Kirby." The young prince was gloating over the visitor. "Say, is one to believe the story of her threatening to chop off your nuts if she found you with another woman, and this at a presidential reception inside the White House?"

"Where did you hear it?" La Rochelle's discomfort was mounting.

"It's all over Tokyo and an opening gambit at many a dinner party. You know this town lives on gossip."

"As I said before, I am already married. The matter is closed."

"Not by a long shot. You can divorce Millie, and your attorneys will handle the case without your ever putting a foot inside the courtroom. If you love my sister, that is. If you don't that's a whole new ballgame."

"I love Sayko," La Rochelle spoke quietly and earnestly. "But our stations in life are so disparate, she being the granddaughter of the emperor of Japan and sister to the future emperor . . . "

"When my turn comes," Takahito interrupted noisily, "we Japs will have the good sense to have converted our anachronistic monarchy into a republic and a socialist welfare state."

"And me being an American politician, an immigrant lacking even a noble pedigree, let alone a royal one."

"Sis doesn't give two hoots about your pedigree, or rather the lack of it. She's not like that. She loves you more than life itself, and she wants to be your true wedded wife." He paused. "As I said earlier I don't understand what the hell she sees in you, but that's her business. They say love is blind."

"And they are right," Siegfried ranted.

Takahito refilled his guest's glass with the precious, specially prepared spirit and fetched for himself a tumbler of ice water from the refreshments table.

"To be perfectly honest with you, Dr. La Rochelle, I really don't give a damn about the imperial family, any of them with the exception of Sis. The whole damned lot can die of natural causes, preferably before their time, though it would be to the country's advantage if they were executed. At least the emperor, the empress, the crown prince, and the crown princess. This would help restore the moral balance in the universe, and would allow millions of victims to find peaceful eternal rest. But things are different when it comes to Sis. I don't want her hurt; I don't want her to suffer. I know what is ailing her, and I am entering the lists. Maybe this'll turn out to be a weakness on my part."

"It's more like an almost invisible trace of common decency in your grotesque makeup."

"Have your fun, Doctor, but I am offering you a deal."

"Oh!"

"The emperor and the empress would like Prince Mikasa, Takahito to his friends, to become once again a tame little boy wielding no weapons, no accessory to political murders, no perpetrator of merciless violence, though he may continue to cherish his outlandish liberal and socialist beliefs and try to put them into practice by peaceful parliamentary means. But woe unto him if he crosses the line. And to this purpose the emperor and the empress have secured the services of a super-diplomat, one Siegfried La Rochelle, architect of the indissoluble union between the United States and Japan before whom incense is burnt and golden trumpets flourish not seven but eight days a week. How am I doing, Doctor?"

"Uncommonly well, Prince."

"Well then, I have no qualms about renouncing violence of which I was known to disapprove so long as my thoughts are free."

"Thoughts are free!" La Rochelle exclaimed with gusto. "*Die Gedanken sind frei.* This was the slogan of the succeeding generations in the country I came from, Germany. For centuries only thoughts were free in Germany, while we lived under the boot of the church and the absolutist rulers. Poor Germany, we deserved better." And he shot out these words again, "*Die Gedanken sind frei*. It's different in the States, of course."

"No, it isn't, and you know it better than me. You live under a tyranny. Not even your thoughts are free. How could you allow it to happen?"

La Rochelle was staring into space in utter silence.

"I shall simply inform Tarako Lepra that from now on, while still remaining a dedicated supporter of the movement, I shall not participate in the planning and execution of terrorist acts. Lepra will understand. He is bright, he understands history, and he understands people. Yes, he is an ex-jailbird. But in the filthy yards by the docks, as my grandmother calls our meeting places, this is a badge of honor. He's been persecuted by a government that has tried to shut him up. But he will carry his message to the people. He and the movement will overcome."

La Rochelle nodded in agreement and was watching Takahito expectantly.

"This is my part of the bargain, and now it's your turn." Takahito was on his best behavior and spoke with studied courtesy. "If you wish to keep up with Princess Sayko you should consider yourself engaged to her and nuptials should take place before too long. I am not being narrowly middle-class, but I know what will make Sis happy, and I am on her side. This doesn't mean that I am set against you, far from it. I am in hopes of addressing you before too long as my brother-in-law.

But if marriage is definitely out of the question you should break off the liaison reasonably soon and be frank and honest with the Princess. This mustn't be a shotgun marriage. I rather fancy it will be a marriage of love, since she swears she loves you and you swear you love her. Sayko is not very good at playing second fiddle. Nor am I for that matter. This is the way we are."

"You made your position crystal clear, Prince Mikasa. I just want to ask you a very trivial question." La Rochelle was in full control of his temper.

"Yes?"

"What is the Japanese word for blackmail?"

Not a muscle twitched on Takahito's handsome countenance as he rolled off the word in question.

"Dr. La Rochelle, you may want to mull over what I said. You may need time to ponder."

"Certainly not. Captain Siegfried La Rochelle of the 82nd Tank Brigade, United States Army, is ready to give his answer to Prince Mikasa now, without a moment's delay." And he stood to attention.

Takahito also stood up. "You have the floor, sir."

"I would like to marry Princess Sayko if she will have me. The location and character of the wedding are details to be addressed at a later date. I will propose to my fiancée tonight and will appear before the appropriate member or members of the imperial family to offer a formal proposal of marriage. It is my hope that, the consent of the princess forthcoming, we can be married within the year. My present marriage will have been dissolved during this period of time."

"Sis will advise you who to speak to. Probably just to the empress because the emperor's mind is going and in addition he is totally deaf."

"Very good," La Rochelle snapped in a military fashion, shifting his body weight from one foot to the other.

"D'you know that bit coming from Millie's lips that she'd chop off your you-know-what is like a breath of fresh air in a room full of asthmatics? The next time I am in D.C. could you introduce me to her?"

"Absolutely not. There's that glint in your eye marking you as a blackguard and a lothario. I wouldn't trust you around Millie. I wouldn't trust you around any woman."

"I'm sorry to hear it. Still, we are even now, Professor."

"Yes," La Rochelle gravely agreed. "We are even now."

/   /   /

Snow comes early to Wyoming and not as a delicate wrapper, as it does where other folks make ends meet, licking the oval landscape, bordering highways and rooftops in a hasty embrace, but like a mighty canopy of thick, impenetrable whiteness pulled down with a single stroke from the heavens themselves to the sagebrush flats, the craggy hills, and what lies in between. It was now the end of August and many a country road was impassable, mounds of collected snow rose haughtily outside towns and villages, Wyomingites telling one another without a twitch of emotion that winter had set in.

These were happy days for the Chadwick family, now again reunited, Nathan no longer suffering from bouts of depression and outbursts of rage, Linda contentedly ruling the roost and Agnes, who had just turned thirteen, in seventh heaven. Progressively, Nathan's work involved him more and more with public figures, members of the Wyoming legislature, members of the House of Representatives and of the U.S. Senate, with officials of all sorts. The men and women he met with and spent long hours talking and listening to were for the most part loyal supporters of Chief Justice, but they pinpointed numerous areas where changes needed to be made without advocating sweeping reforms or a return to the U.S. Constitution of 1787. Among these were greater authority assigned to law courts and to trials by jury; modest revisions in the Higher Education Acts opening the door more widely to lowgovies who sought admission to colleges and universities; new executive orders allowing more freedom to trade unions; and reorganization of the Sex Police and the Faith Police with concomitant emphasis on the rights of the accused. These loomed large. In the discussions that followed congressmen and congresswomen, senators, and other public figures were at pains to stress that the modifications in the governmental structure they favored were calculated to improve it in limited concrete ways. No thought at all was given to superseding it by another governmental structure.

As Nathan listened to some of his new bedfellows he had a distinct impression that a major shift in strategy was being mounted, a shift aimed at chipping off one by one the most unjust and anti-democratic hallmarks of the political system under which Western Amernipp lived without firing off broadsides. In some instances the Fabians of the

twenty-first century resorted to highly ingenious yet plausible justifica-
tions for their amendments: they claimed trial by jury of one's peers
afforded a wider field for expression of faith and of religious feelings in
general than an ordeal because in the former the sight of the accused,
now in God's hands, evoked in the jurors the whole gamut of religious
sentiments from hatred of sin, fear of hell, to hope of redemption, belief
in divine grace, and the ultimate possibility of salvation, the ordeal
heavily constricting faith on all counts. New blood in universities
would increase the ratio of converts and martyrs-to-be, new fields
would be harvested, new lakes and rivers to be plumbed for riches yet
unknown. Similarly more slack would help the unions climb higher and
higher on the religious ladder; respect for the rights of the accused
resulting in the SP and FP investigations rising to a higher level of efficiency. All other amendments proposed and discussed well into the
night with Nathan were accompanied by impassioned speeches prov-
ing beyond the shadow of a doubt that the speakers were inspired by
the arduous loyalty and devotion to the principles of New Jerusalem
and to Chief Justice personally.

Nathan strongly approved of the amelioratory measures, as one of
the group named the wide variety of motions, projects, and amendments now freely under discussion, but he was at a loss as to how they
would be received by the government and whether they were really a
spark leading to greater things. But as he crisscrossed the country in the
fall meeting with friends of the Center for Democratic West and with
many others who did not share his political beliefs, he sensed again and
again that the mood of Western Amernipp was changing. Newly
formed political organizations, some newspapers, guests on talk shows,
and many a private citizen advocated modest reforms in tune with the
exalted ideals of the theocratic state preached often and so eloquently
by Chief Justice. There was very little demand for a fundamental change
and those spoiling to storm the Bastille were a tiny minority, but there
was a widespread desire to take numerous matters under advisement,
examine the validity of recent executive orders, probe thorny problems
to the bitter end till only the husk remained, and lay a steady hand on
the government's shoulder when the government was up to its antics or
worse, all this without crossing the line.

What struck Nathan with great force was the political maturity of
the electorate of Western Amernipp, its almost uncanny understanding

of what could be said or done without incurring the wrath of the theocratic D.C. and the vengeance of Chief Justice. In the last four years the previously naïve, myopic, blundering population of the United States, adopting a new statehood, that of Amernipp in 2082, had graduated to a highly sophisticated electorate, well informed and perceptive, no prey to illusions or fantasies, and equipped with a radar-like security system warning it of what could be said and done and what could not on penalty of governmental repercussion. The American nation had advanced to a level of political consciousness unknown in its entire history—discrimination and wisdom garnered by eager minds in the years filled with tragic events and circumstances.

The changing mood of the country was one thing, but alongside a new form of protest made itself felt in dozens of clubs and associations springing up all over the West, devoted compadres watching the government's every move like angered hawks. In Boise, Idaho, was founded The Brotherhood of Tinkers of the West, which went to great lengths to root out corruption among public officials and publicize irregularities in the business conducted in law courts. Montanans were tickled pink when at last the opening ceremony was held in the newly painted offices of The Sword of the Big Sky in Helena, dedicated to the exposure of egregious cases of injustice no matter where they occurred and the punishment of guilty parties. The Dakota Shooter, operating from Bismarck, set its sights on acts of physical abuse or worse perpetrated by the government and usually went to court seeking damages. In New Mexico what had started as jolly meetings over coffee and doughnuts after church blossomed into a fraternal organization and was given the apt name of Keeping Faith. Its members had pledged to help one another, and non-members as well, in solving whatever difficulties they experienced in dealing with the government. Branch offices of Keeping Faith were being established all over New Mexico, and almost immediately the noble enterprise crossed over to Wyoming and Nebraska, to Nevada and Idaho, then to the other western states. Similar organizations bonding perfect strangers in a common cause sprang up between the Canadian border and the state line severing Texas from New Mexico and in the vast territory stretching from eastern Nebraska through Washington and Oregon to the brine of the Pacific. As on so many previous occasions so now too the West was standing tall and leading the nation.

In addition a keen realization of the dangers threatening the country, burdens and labors commonly shared, and the daily interdependence of practically all the regions of that immense land spawned a new spirit of camaraderie outshining good fellowship of old. A new spirit was born in the American West, a new spirit of togetherness, of cooperation, of one-for-all and all-for-one, of mutual understanding, of mutual effort. The West was part of a great nation, but in the momentous year 2083 it also stood as a nation apart and a very special one. The closeness between its inhabitants, the pervasive recognition which the great majority of them showed for the similarities and differences fashioning them, and above all common resolve in times of crisis, to which they all spontaneously subscribed, set them apart from much of the highly advanced industrialized segment of the planet, a throwback to an earlier simpler era, to a real or imaginary tribe living in happiness long before the invention of machines, computers, and above all of bureaucrats.

Nathan traveled to other parts of the country, to the South and to the Northeast, and he kept his ear to the ground. He was learning more and more about the changing mood of Western Amernipp and about where the shoe pinched. In Georgia he spent a day in the company of Huston's old pals, clerics like him or men and women retired from the legal and other professions. They were far from being enthusiastic about the unashamedly theocratic state of affairs, but they were too old, they insisted, to do anything about it. In the Carolinas similar voices were heard, senior citizens of limited means complaining about the rising prices of foodstuffs and prescriptions. Here and elsewhere the mood was one of resignation, but it was often laced with a bitterness that did not seem to go away. What greatly surprised Nathan in parts of the South and in the Northeast was the absence of meetings and parades extolling religion and Church and State Party. Citizens were putting up with the iron fist of the government and learning to live with it, but they could not be induced to wave a festive banner or raise a cheer. This state of apathy, Nathan thought, could in time become a breeding ground for resolute opposition culminating in open revolt.

As he traveled, he encountered every shade of conformity and nonconformity with governmental edicts, and in isolated pockets he witnessed feelings seething and ready to explode. In Cleveland he spent the evening at the home of Joe Pitkin, a young rabbi and his family, and he was taught a lesson in dissident thinking and plotting. Esther, Joe's wife, a dancer and choreographer by profession, was so vociferous in her condemnation of Everett Huston and what he stood for that Nathan feared for her and her family's safety. Joe was equally outspoken, and their two daughters, Natasha and Kimberley, aged eleven and nine respectively, speaking in low voices, pronounced Chief Justice to be a bad gray wolf and his minions a wolfpack to be shot on sight. As Nathan listened to the girls' highly articulate invective he reflected that in a different century they could have played key roles in a great national upheaval, being in addition to much else spokespersons for Danton and Robespierre, though he could not decide which girl would best represent which statesman.

In two towns in Maine he was a witness to spirited demonstrations taking the government to task for offenses grave and small and ending in a minute of silence honoring the fallen victims of the regime and a public prayer for the restoration of the true United States of America. Nathan returned to Cheyenne inspired and invigorated, his head full of stratagems, schemes, new notions. Then an impulse stirred in him that was half expectation and half resolve: perhaps things were coming to a head, perhaps it would soon be time to strike as never before, risk everything on a single card and God willing . . . God willing.

As he was hugging Linda she told him an urgent telephone message from Omaha had been left earlier in the day asking that he call back as soon as he received it. He recognized the voice at the other end as belonging to one of his confederates in Nebraska, employing on this occasion an innocuous sounding code. "Tarako Lepra is with us in Omaha," the confederate was saying. "You know he's forbidden to cross city limits of Tokyo, but he slipped out without being noticed, he hopes. He flew over to Canada as a stowaway on a cargo plane and our friends in Vancouver arranged his transportation to Western Manitoba whence he crossed illegally to North Dakota, was met by the Bismarck cell, and brought here. He would like to meet with you. I understand the two of you have been corresponding."

"Anytime."

"We could deliver him to your home bound and gagged tomorrow around dinnertime. I don't know how long he is planning to spend in your company."

"He can stay with us as long as he wishes."

"Fine. And one more thing: can you make yourself responsible for his being driven back to the Canadian border?"

"It goes without saying."

"The place in question on this side is north as the crow flies from Hannah, North Dakota. Our friends to the north will take it from there."

"I know the location. We are staying in touch and travel information will be passed on to you."

"Check and thank you."

"Check and my thanks to you." Nathan hung up and headed for the kitchen to tell Linda about the imminent arrival of a houseguest.

Lepra and Chadwick had indeed been exchanging letters for more than two years, but neither had the slightest notion what to expect from a personal encounter. When shortly after 7 P.M. on the following day a car with Nebraska plates pulled up outside his house and a tall, broad-shouldered Asian jumped out, Nathan had the satisfaction of being very nearly certain that his guest's illegal stay in Western Amernipp was progressing without a hitch.

Tarako was tall indeed, six foot three or four, Nathan reckoned, his flesh being mostly muscle, Nathan was willing to lay a wager, even though little of it was visible from under a heavy winter coat. Once inside the house and after introducing the visitor to Linda, Nathan's guess was fully confirmed. The Japanese man was trim, held himself erect, and his body did not seem to display even a single ounce of fat beyond what was absolutely necessary for an organism in its prime. When he took off his jacket Nathan could not help but notice how athletic-looking his guest was, his biceps forming hardened mounds all the way from the elbow to the shoulder, and what was seen of his hairy chest looked also hard and wiry, an inflexible steel-like armor against vicious attacks. In the aggregate Tarako's body projected the uncanny and extraordinary strength of a member of a race wholly separate from the acknowledged ones inhabiting the discovered continents, but also stringent discipline that controlled and guided it, thus making the body an even deadlier instrument, each of its twists and punches tested and calculated in advance. His head was well proportioned, the face spare and skinny and the dark green eyes unusually prominent, unusually animated and luminous.

Linda and Agnes took an immediate liking to the visitor, and at dinner Linda surpassed herself, pouring forth quantities of small talk and posing innumerable questions. Tarako's answers were brief and direct, and it was clear he had no stomach for making polite noises. But his candor made the mother and daughter admire him even more. He was an orphan, he said, an illegitimate child by all accounts who never knew his parents, brought up exclusively in orphanages in Tokyo, some supervised by the state and others by Christian missionaries. He had received the most rudimentary education only, but from the age of twelve or thereabout he had been educating himself, reading by night and whenever he could seize the time, reading hungrily and voluminously the great works of Western civilization: Plato, Hobbes, Locke, Rousseau, and then with redoubled zeal Marx and Engels, Lenin, Trotsky, Mao Tse-tung, and their disciples.

When he was fourteen he was approached by a stranger who offered to provide him with books and took him out of the orphanage now and then to meet children of the members of splinter groups of the communist party. When at the age of sixteen he was sent to work in a shoe factory he promptly joined the Trotskyist Alliance and soon rose to a position of a trusted functionary and leader. He planned and organized terrorist attacks both in Japan and abroad, and when Amernipp was created in 2082 he was ordered to make contact with Trotskyist and other revolutionary groups in North America. He had visited the Western Province on several occasions, always illegally, had come to know some communist and anarchist activists, but so far he had not been able to find a common ground with his opposite numbers on Western Amernippian soil.

"Your people," he began, piercing Nathan with a scathing glance, "are not interested in a social revolution. They don't give a tinker's damn for Lenin's and Trotsky's ideals."

"That's true," Nathan replied. "Our first priority is to take this country back to the principles of the Constitution of the United States, and the year is 1787."

"I know. But your constitution was only the beginning. It didn't create social justice. It was another capitalist obscenity."

As they were tasting their dessert Agnes asked, "Mr. Lepra, could you tell me some Japanese fairy tales? They are thrilling, aren't they?"

"Maybe so," he replied, "but I don't know any. I wasn't brought up on fairy tales. I can tell you tales of proletarian struggles in my country. They'll keep you on edge."

Agnes shook her head. "No, thank you. I'm in no mood for sob stories."

Just before they rose from the table Agnes asked, "How old are you?"

Linda glanced reprovingly at her daughter. "Honey, we don't ask personal questions of people we hardly know. You should know better."

Tarako burst out laughing. "That's all right. In a new society we'll be able to ask any question we like. I am thirty-four—just turned thirty-four several weeks ago."

"And what is your occupation?" Agnes persisted, doing her best not to notice the look on her mother's face.

"I am secretary general of the Eastern Amernipp chapter of the Trotskyist Alliance. In the last twenty years or so I tried my hand at all kinds of jobs, most of them menial, but now I spend most of my time fighting for social justice."

"That sounds real important," Agnes commented. "I have only one thing to ask of you. Please brush up on your Japanese fairy tales. I'll ask you again, and I won't take no for an answer." All smiles, she sailed out of the dining room.

Later in the evening, sipping bourbon in Nathan's study, the two men returned to an earlier topic.

"In most countries today, the rulers and the ruled can't see five feet ahead of them. The same rotten capitalistic system is in power. Its days are numbered. Let me ask you again: will you join us?"

Nathan took one sip from his glass, then another and let his eyes wander over the walls and ceiling. "No," he let the word fall with finality. "And you know the reason."

"American society right after the revolution was rotten to the core. Why reach out for something that is criminally wrong? Your political system today is a farce—the same double standards, the same forms of discrimination, the age-old master-slave division. Do you want me to go on?"

"No, I've heard this line before, more than once."

"You see, Nathan," Tarako was refilling the glasses, "Trotsky was right and Stalin was wrong as he could be. Only worldwide revolution can realize our hopes. It's not a matter of building just one socialist state, which happens to be your native land. It's revolution in every country we are aiming at, without exception. The focus must always be on the world as a whole. This is the only pragmatic way. Otherwise we get what happened in Russia at the end of the last century, socialism corrupted by nationalism, by its own hierarchical posturing, by its own managerial methods and ingrown ambitions. The socialist state crumbled into dust because it became its own *raison de' être*, its own alpha and omega, and ceased to be yet another stage and testing ground for world revolution. Shortsightedness is always a failing we pay dearly for, but in this case we paid with the blood of millions. Like the great religions of the world, socialism or Trotskyism, to give the movement its true name, addresses itself to all the inhabitants of planet earth, to all countries great or small where human hearts beat in anticipation of social justice and better life. No community is excluded because our goal is universal and rests on the moral order of the world. Won't you join us, Nathan, in the pursuit of our noble goal, nobler than any other in this poisoned and diseased world of ours still waiting for its liberators, its ragamuffins and sansculottes to strike a blow for justice?"

Nathan gave the appearance of extreme seriousness when he replied. "I want you to know I admire your sentiments and the improvements you've engineered in Eastern Amernipp by parliamentary means, especially in the lives of the indigent and the dispossessed who lived without hope. But you still talk about a bloody revolution, about sending the imperial family to the gallows, about tons of blood flowing?"

"The Japanese monarchy has to go," Tarako said in a level voice. "For centuries it stood for tyranny, oppression, unheard of cruelty."

"But today . . . " Nathan ventured.

"Today the emperor is a figurehead. It doesn't matter that with every passing day the one presently sitting on the throne gets to be more and more imbecilic. He's also deaf as a post. This too doesn't matter. He symbolizes centuries of vicious criminal rule; he carries within himself the crimes of all his predecessors, the injustices and transgressions of his court from year one. Blood calls for blood, and punishment should fit the crime. Once the imperial family is put down and the old regime ousted, a new sun will shine on all our people, and a new age will be ushered in, severed for eternity from the bad old days. We have to do things right, Nathan. We have to do things right."

"You wanted to cover with me a host of other subjects," the host reminded his guest.

"That's right, but I don't want to rob you of your sleep."

Nathan's face tightened in a derogatory grimace. "I can sleep another day. Fire away, Tarako."

They were soon engrossed in a serious discussion, a new subject called to life on the heels of one just flogged to death, and they did not stop until, with the faint light of a winter morning breaking in through the openings in the curtains, they heard Linda's voice as she was getting Agnes ready for school.

Chapter 5

Groves of Academe

In New Jerusalem, on whose behalf Everett Huston and his allies labored day and night, canons of literary criticism changed beyond recognition, and appreciation of texts old and new drew strength from the articles of faith that the government wore on its sleeve. Religious themes and motifs were eagerly sought out in literary works of all genres and were magnified or deflated at the discretion of official readers and censors. Some authors became favorites of the regime, others were cold-shouldered, and others still, relegated beyond the pale. Although the trio composed of Phineas Léger, Homily Grister, and Ganymede Pillows, which headed the Department of Wholesome Literature, swore by objective criteria in evaluating what had been written in the past and what was being written at present, in actuality conflicting views, personal judgments, wild biases, and prejudices ruled the evaluating process and made literary reputations the sport of kings.

Works that had stood the test of time and had delighted millions of discriminating readers were all of a sudden demoted to the level of dubious pulp fiction or shoddy *théatre de bulevard,* considered wholly lacking in religious values and stylistic excellence, while barely noticed compositions whose readers could be counted on the fingers of one hand were unexpectedly elevated to the highest regions, nay shown to a seat on Mount Olympus. The classics fared no better. There was a concerted assault on Geoffrey Chaucer one year on account of his godlessly tolerant perspective of sinners of all ages, on Edmund Spenser the next charging him with gross immorality, and Homer was banned in Western Amernipp, the litany of his alleged offenses being so long that few could call it to mind. One sweltering summer Rabelais was pilloried and during the torrential wind-swept fall that succeeded it, Jonathan Swift.

Detractors of the Department of Wholesome Literature pointed out that the bedlam reigning there was caused by a total lack of qualified personnel, citing one story out of a host of similar ones of a newly hired reader, a young man of high moral character personally recommended by Chief Justice, who upon being given the assignment of determining Tolstoy's place in the literary canon grew so bored reading *War and Peace* that in less than an hour he angrily tossed the book out of the window and immediately put in for a transfer, the only vacancy occurring in Drains and Sewage, to which the young reader betook himself with alacrity. Seasoned and well-informed critics as they were, Léger, Grister, and Pillows nevertheless had too much on their plate in the way of truly substantive matters to find time for reading books and rendering critical judgments. They referred such tasks to their assistants and others, and the results were mixed at best.

Things had been moving at the usual snail-like arrhythmic pace in the Province of Letters until an event in the first week of September 2083 stood everything on its head and demanded new oaths of loyalty from Huston's supporters. Much against his better judgment but seeing no way of bowing out gracefully, Chief Justice finally agreed to accompany a motley party of his grandchildren, grandnephews, and grandnieces, all of them high school sophomores, juniors, or seniors, to a theatre in Philadelphia. The play they saw was Shakespeare's *Love's Labour's Lost*, and Chief Justice could barely contain his indignation at its frivolity, bad taste, and rank immorality. It was for him a devastating experience. Yet loath to be a wet blanket and determined to preserve his standing as a benevolent *paterfamilias*, he held his tongue while the young people were practically jumping out of their skin with infinitely more noise than necessary, extolling the production and the play itself—wonderful acting, those divine costumes, and gee verbal fireworks that sent shivers up and down your entire body. Even little Eric, the youngest of the lot and in his grandfather's estimation more levelheaded than his brothers and cousins, was spellbound and hollered one tribute of praise after another. Huston kept smiling and making small talk, realizing that the young people's enthusiasm for Shakespeare vic- ariously generated more good will for him as the adult in the group and paymaster. To end the evening in style he took the whole gang for fancy ice cream and soda, their tongues ceaselessly wagging, the magic of the theatre holding them fast.

Several days later he summoned his three lieutenants and recount- ed the infuriating and humiliating experience. "Something's got to be done about Shakespeare. He corrupts men's minds, he corrupts chil- dren," he fumed.

"We can close down public theatres and ban private performances. It's widely known the stage has been a hotbed of immorality since day one," Grister suggested.

"I'd tread carefully there," Léger interposed. "If we do that we'll seal the fate of genuinely religious drama, mystery and morality plays, church histories, and so on."

"I agree," Pillows joined in. "If Shakespeare promotes vice, we should go after Shakespeare and not after the stage."

Huston smiled wanly. "My gut feeling tells me this case is different from the rest." He paused and for several moments his pale blue inquis- itive eyes were focused on each of them in turn. "Homer was a low- down Greek, a nobody. Were he among the living today, he'd be refused a visa, and as for the green card, well, he'd be waiting for one forever and a day. But Shakespeare, I am given to understand, is called by throngs upon throngs The Bard, whatever that means. Anyway, he's one of us, a sterling American. Banning his writings in Western Amernipp would not do. It would decidedly not do. It might backfire."

"Banning Homer has backfired already," Léger interjected. "Have you read the recent editorials and listened to the EDTV?"

Huston made a pooh-poohing gesture. "What the hell do I care about the howlings of bums and longhaired jackasses?"

"You should, Ev. The mood of the country is changing."

Huston strode to where Léger was sitting and patted him on the back. "You've been known to cry wolf, Phineas, when your dyspepsia is acting up. Is it bad today?"

"Not particularly."

"Well then, let's keep an eye on target. The way I see it, guys, don't make no waves playing down Shakespeare's verbal skills. The fella has a way with words, none can deny it. But his content is a whole new ballgame: no respect for the Almighty, godless triviality all round, lechery that comes out of every pore of his characters' bodies and can't be stopped no matter what, shameless razzle-dazzle that keeps religion in a dungeon and gives full rein to every degenerate pastime and game you can think of. That's Will Shakespeare for you."

"This being the case . . ." Grister began hopefully.

"This being the case," Huston echoed magisterially, "we gotta think of something special, for the culprit ain't no ordinary culprit and extenuating circumstances will drive any state attorney worth his salt to distraction."

"Meaning precisely what?" Pillows, ill at ease, thrust the question forth blusteringly. "Meaning precisely what?" He thrust it forth again.

"We gotta understand place and time," Huston went on unperturbed. "W.S. lived in a barbarous time, the sixteenth and early years of the seventeenth century. He was born in England, a barbarous country at that time where men and women alike doubted the existence of the Lord and denied His presence in hearth and home. Self-indulgence, vanity, and all the other vices led the English by the nose and to perdition of course. This was a long time before the Great Awakening that shook the American colonies in the early and middle decades of the eighteenth century and even longer before the great religious revival that showed us the true way some thirty years ago. Shakespeare lived and died before the great dispensation, before the word of the Lord became flesh and lived amongst us. He is not to be held culpable for his daunting and shoddy secularism. He didn't know any better; he was a prisoner of a godless society, a child damned by vicious and perverse parents."

The others nodded noncommittally, unwilling to trust their thoughts to words.

"But a man of his skill deserves our attention," Huston proceeded, his tones rising in gravity, "and the corpus of his writings could be of inestimable value to us and to generations to come."

"So?" Pillows blurted out.

"So," Huston stood straight and erect, towering over their sitting selves, his arms thrust forward, the palms of the hands pointed at their faces in a solemn gesture of dominance and comradeship. "So," he repeated, "Shakespeare's plays and poems will have to be edited, revised, corrected when the need occurs, so that they may become what they should have been from the very beginning—a monument to faith and a panegyric of the Almighty."

"So you want all thirty-six of his plays rewritten, right?"

"Sure, and the sonnets and other poems too. Any objections, Phineas?"

"No, but it's a Herculean labor. It'll take man power helluva time and effort."

"Sure! In the service of the Lord much is demanded. The Lord checks on us every minute of the day, and the Lord don't take kindly to dawdlers and slugs. Therefore I want ye to get off your goddamn butts and put together a committee of readers and editors, and it better be a blue-ribbon one and nothing less, or else your goddamn asses will be in the sling." He paused, his concentrated gaze shifting from Phineas to Homily, from Homily to Ganymede, and back and forward again. "Cast your net far and wide. I wanna have good men and women of all kinds and from all walks of life. I wanna see somethin' like a national crusade and nothin' less."

"We ought to review the fundamental principles of this editorial job. I'm sure the committee will be most obliged," Phineas shot out, leaning forward.

"Why?" Huston queried, the grimace planting itself on his countenance being aggressively scornful. "Why, the task before the committee is clear as the day is light." Then he shook his enormous shoulders and hollered in their faces with all the latent strength of his lungs, "This meeting is closed!!!"

/   /   /

The committee was formed without delay, and it did indeed include partisans of Chief Justice in different walks of life. There were several seasoned civil servants betraying very little interest in literature in general and in Shakespeare in particular who were beholden to Huston in a variety of ways; there were several professors of English, classics, religious studies, and art who had earned his complete trust and who, he knew, would steer the committee in the right direction. A number of well-known theologians, both Protestant and Roman Catholic, graced the exalted ranks and so did script writers whose méter was rooted in paeans of Christian devotion and in religious extravaganzas. At the last minute several new members completed the quorum, men and women of diverse occupations whose presence, Huston proclaimed, would inculcate into the committee that breadth of perspective that a national crusade rightly called for. Among them were two janitors: John Scaggs, who had spent many a year at MIT and upon its transformation into an asylum for the unbalanced, not legally insane as such yet posing a danger to society, stayed on as chief janitor, and Wyn Purdue, of long duration at Hofstra University, though her employer had changed colors to those of a closely guarded hospital for homicidal alcoholics. By unanimous vote and with Huston's blessings the committee appointed Léger, Grister, and Pillows as ex-officio members with all the rights and privileges attendant upon regular members. Now at last the carefully selected body could get down to business.

After choosing a chairperson and vice-chairperson in quick succession, then secretary and treasurer, and setting down the schedule of meetings and dates, the committee went off-record for the remainder of the first session. They listened to general comments, pet ideas, cautionary tales, and whatever else individual members felt inclined to dredge up from the depth of their psyches and share with their colleagues. The first wrinkle appeared on the agenda when the two janitors, John and Wyn, expressed doubts about the viability of the project.

"Will Shakespeare was no incense-burning bugger. He wrote to entertain us. And 'cause he had helluva between the ears he taught us a thing or two. Why change him into something he ain't?" John asked.

"My motto is, 'If somethin' ain't broke, don't fix it.' And Will ain't broke; he's standing tall beaming at us," Wyn exclaimed, gazing round the table. "Let's leave the guy in peace. He's done one helluva lot for us, so let's leave his comin's and goin's as they are. He don't need no bunches of flowers and no canopy."

At once a chorus of angry voices rose in protest.

"You don't understand the first thing about the barbarous conditions in sixteenth century England. The country was a cesspool and a gutter," shouted a professor of English.

"By rewriting Shakespeare in accordance with the laws of God we raise him to a higher status and we improve also our own civilization," an irate theologian scowled. "Be on your guard, Wyn and John. The Prince of Darkness never sleeps."

The two janitors remained largely silent as the professors and the scriptwriters, the civil servants and the theologians out-grimaced and out-shouted them and one another. When the meeting was nearly over several committee members addressed John and Wyn politely and sympathetically.

"We all understand how you feel," one of them let fall.

"Live and let live. It was a dandy rule before we came to our senses."

Another courteous critic confronted the nonconformist pair.

"Please sleep on it but remember we are doing God's work, and the two of you wouldn't want to set yourselves up against the Lord."

"We sure wouldn't," John and Wyn replied in unison.

The man smiled and shook hands with each of them. "We want you on board because you have much to contribute. Till the next meeting then."

"Till the next meeting," they said, and then thanked the man for his kind words.

Early in their proceedings the committee decided by a substantial majority they would first prune, edit, and improve the corpus of Shakespeare's plays in a chronological order, and then pass on to "Venus and Adonis," "The Rape of Lucrece" and other poems, and finally to the sonnets. The Bard's dramatic output posed a most exacting challenge, and once past it they would feel less pressured. But before casting their eyes on *The Comedy of Errors* they placed that slightly later and dissolute comedy *Love's Labour's Lost* before them. It had offered the stimulus and justification for the entire project, and its rakish performance in Philadelphia earlier in the year shook the Republic of Letters to its very foundations. It was altogether fitting that this unholy play should be at the top of the list, and Chief Justice heartily concurred.

In the course of the second meeting the committee divided itself into no fewer than eight subcommittees, each charged with specific and well-demarcated duties. The first five were entrusted with whatever pruning, editing, and improving was necessary in each of the five acts of the play, with a subcommittee for each act. The sixth examined the feelings, emotions, and sentiments in the work as a whole. The seventh looked at its thought content and, broadly speaking, its philosophy. And the last one put under the microscope its overall mood, its ambience, as well as particular dramatic devices employed in the play as a whole, which would be retained or expurgated as faith and the laws of God ordained.

The chairperson and vice-chairperson were delighted to see the work of the different subcommittees overlap. They saw it as a golden opportunity for both rigorous scrutiny of segments of the play and for spirited discussion of their relationship to the entire text. Some committee members patted themselves on the back for being so inventively concrete and specific and at the same time so far-reaching and general, and words of praise and encouragement traveled fast and at fixed intervals from Chief Justice himself. Slowly, a new shape emerged from the clamor of heated discussions. *Love's Labour's Lost*—it had been decided that original titles would be preserved in all instances—was no longer recognizable, but it waved the most sublime flag ever granted to mankind, that of absolute obedience to the commands of the Almighty and of New Jerusalem, at long last one sure reality on this planet.

In the expurgated version, King of Navarre's speech announcing his intention of living with his attendant lords for three years as celibate scholars, his court becoming "the wonder of the world," and "a little Academe" was considerably lengthened and strong religious convictions were added. The King together with Biron, Longaville, and Dumain would spend these three years in prayer and religious contemplation, doing his very best to understand better the greatness of God. The Princess of France and her ladies-in-waiting, Rosaline, Maria, and Katharine, appeared as angels singing hymns in praise of God and aggressively supporting the men's choice of celibate life. The subcommittee in charge of Act II went to great lengths to lend a dramatic quality to the men's expostulations about chastity, divine grace, and the evils of sensuality, and it surpassed itself in portraying the women's part. At first the four male characters and the four female ones engaged in spirited duets. The King of Navarre and the Princess of France exchanged their very similar beliefs about faith and martyrdom. Biron and Rosaline canvassed the power of prayer and the ways of reaching God directly; Dumain and Katharine spoke on charity and compassion; while Longaville and Maria debated from the same side of the fence, though employing dissimilar arguments, total rejection of the senses. In the middle of Act II two choruses were formed, male and female, and they extolled the power of faith and the intellect, decrying the sensory part of human nature.

Make our faith a sturdy kingly oak
That never sways with winds or tempest wild,
And our intellect a massive rock
That stays the waves piling on high,
sing the men.
And the women respond:
Tear from our sinful limbs nerve and sense
That drag us down to wild beasts' lair,
For feeling never shows a visage fair,
And we are begging for faith's recompense!

In like vein this exchange continues until shortly before the end of the act the two choruses merge and sing with a single voice.

Raise us, oh Lord,
To heights of godliness
Where what is base is promptly overthrown,
Where our incorporeal beings thrive
In God's own peace and shining holiness.

As soon as Act III opens there is a fly in the ointment. It comes to light that Don Adriano de Armado, whom Shakespeare calls a "fantastical Spaniard," is in reality the Devil in disguise, and a gross sensualist to boot, engaging off-stage in perverse sexual practices with the country wench Jaquenetta, the She-Devil and Armado's confederate. The pair's mission is to lead the four men and the four women from the path of holiness to every kind of profligacy and thence to ultimate damnation. At the outset the He-Devil and the She-Devil ridicule the King, the Princess, and their retinues as cowards ruled by tyrannical conformity, too frightened to live life to the fullest and being no more than impotent slaves under the yoke of the inhumanely austere and anachronistic religious establishment. Their oratory is powerful, their arguments well aimed, leaving the two royals and their lords and ladies-in-waiting on the defense and downcast. Next the devils attack their would-be victims individually, bringing to light embarrassing incidents in their private lives, hardly the acts of probity that are their acknowledged badge of honor. The pair is assisted by the schoolmaster Holofernes, the comedian Costard, and the constable Dull, all three in the pay of the

Prince of Darkness. The assaulted characters mount a feeble defense invoking the mercy of the Lord and the glimmer of redemption that would never be snuffed out. But their situation is precarious. In what he considers to be the *coup de grâce* Armado challenges his opponents anew: "Abjure your church, deny God, and your lives will be spared, your reputations untarnished, and not a word spoken here known in the outside world. Persist in your errors and the heavens will come down and crush you."

King Navarre is gazing in the faces of his courtiers watching for a signal or a tip, but they are frozen into impassivity. Then he barely hears the swish of a dress and turns round. The Princess of France has taken two steps forward and is now standing alongside. She takes his hand and they advance two more steps, the infernal band glaring at them.

"You can take our lives, and you can ruin our reputations, do as you please; but King Navarre and I will never abjure the church and deny the Almighty God. You evoke in us disgust and contempt, nothing more."

The Princess speaks in a clear, firm voice, and the King presses her hand and kisses it. And so the act ends in a standoff, the heavy curtain rolling down, the two parties looking to another day.

For months after the work of *Love's Labour's Lost* had been completed, the committee overseeing Act IV had been congratulating itself and others joined in. It had hit on a splendid idea. Threats and blackmail had availed little, and Armado had to surpass himself if victory was to be his. Accordingly, Act IV is a tour de force of temptation: snapping his fingers and reciting spells, he conjures up before the four men magnificent feasts where the rarest delicacies are served, visions of political power far above their present station, and finally gorgeous gardens of joy where beautiful maidens dance in homage to Eros, impatiently awaiting the King and his courtiers to make them experience sensuality at its most intense and refined. Before the Princess and her attendants Jaquenetta invokes visions of social prominence that outshines their present status, of coffers filled with gold and jewels that would make them the richest ladies in the world, and of scores of handsome youths ready to satisfy, as no one else can, their physical desires. The men and the women can have all of it for the asking, the bargain calling only for a single abjuration and a denial. The magnificent visions conjured up before the four male and the four female characters dazzle their senses and make a powerful appeal. Armado and Jaquenetta press their suit and summon one brilliant vision after another to subdue the excited spectators. The invoked figures tempt them again and again, and the objects and places grow out of proportion before their eyes—mammoth calls to raptures beyond compare. Sparkling, seducing dialogue flows from the mouths of the tempters while the King, the Princess, and their attendants waver, their defenses getting weaker with every passing minute. The suspenseful juxtaposition of the two camps takes much time and space, and in the months to come members of the subcommittee made no secret of their immense pride at having made full and inventive use of various surrealistic and expressionistic techniques that gave Act IV an extraordinary dramatic quality. Their modest affirmations were long remembered. As the act draws to a close it is touch and go. But the Almighty intervenes.

Armado and Jaquenetta take a respite and Moth, the former's page, revealed as God's messenger, pours a sleeping potion into their drinks. The pair does not awaken before the end of the play, if they awaken at all.

The powers of darkness having been chased away to the antipodes by a divine legerdemain, the royal personages praise again virtue and faith. At the outset of Act V the four male and the four female characters join forces and laud the institution of religion, the presence of different churches, and above all the omnipotence and omniscience of God. Holofernes, Costard, and Dull are nowhere to be found, and Moth appears for a few seconds flying high in the air, the messenger returning to heaven, his mission accomplished. Unlike the other acts, Act V has the character of an oratorio—recitatives, arias, and choruses playing a major role in it. All scenery has been removed, and we are now in no identifiable location. But as the subcommittee tried to stress the point, we are now in any place we choose, and the bareness of the stage, together with carefully chosen singing and music, emphasize the universality of the human condition independent of geography and history. The Holy Spirit permeates all things as the four women are about to enter a convent and the four men to take holy orders.

Subcommittees six through eight had not been idle either; Boyet's speeches in Act II, Scene 1, were amended so as to present the Princess of France as a saint whose mission it is to transform the world. All traces of mirth and humor had been expunged from the text, and any sign of

frivolity promptly transmuted into lavish earnestness. The mood of the
entire play is now grave and devotional, and scholastic ideas both real-
ist and nominalist are liberally scattered in the text to strengthen its
intellectual framework. No one, try hard as he may, could say this was
William Shakespeare's early comedy, written in all likelihood in 1593
and bearing the title *Love's Labour's Lost*. An entirely different creation
is in the hands of the committee, and it will soon be given to the world.

Just before the curtain comes down all the characters join in a brief
but pithy recitation:

At all times everywhere
The Lord over the world presides
His commands to obey instructs,
For they are infinitely wise.
But to us in Western Amernipp
His favorite country far and wide,
He sent his coadjutor benign
Everett Huston to save mankind.
Thrice blessed we
With such felicity,
To have in our midst God's coadjutor benign
Saving mankind.

The addition of these verses was approved by a unanimous vote, and
when the fruit of their labor finally lay before them they all felt they
had done a yeoman's job.

Love's Labour's Lost was rewritten in thirty-three days, a record time,
and the remainder of Shakespeare's output awaited their devoted attention. But first related matters had to be settled. Huston consulted with
the committee as to the disposition of the old texts going back to the
First Folio of 1623. Should they be allowed to remain in libraries and
in private hands even though they were undoubtedly an offense to public morals or should they be withdrawn from circulation altogether?
The committee was divided, the majority opting for a speedy with-
drawal, while a sizeable and very vocal minority led by John Scaggs and
Wyn Purdue urged in the strongest possible terms leaving the old, the
truly Shakespearian texts, alone, letting them rest where they had always

rested, an uncorrupted monument of The Bard's genius and a national treasure.

Huston was irked by this divisiveness and again summoned his three lieutenants. Phineas Léger and Ganymede Pillows counseled caution, allowing things to remain as they were and leaving the final decision to the discretion of the public and the institutions that served them, libraries of all sorts, colleges and universities, archives, and so on. Only Homily Grister remained adamant in his conviction that all the previous editions of Shakespeare ought to be confiscated forthwith and destroyed, the expurgated version being the only text allowed for educational purposes and for other purposes, whatever those other purposes might be. Huston bit his lip. "I guess it's too much to ask for a united front. You guys are running haywire," he scowled.

Still he had to make a decision, and it was clear it would be his decision alone. Later in the day he dictated an executive order calling under the law for the return of all editions of Shakespeare in public and private possession to a designated government office in each community by January 1, 2084, the order including also videos, films, and audiocassettes. A separate information sheet widely distributed promised speedy shipments of the revised version of Love's Labour's Lost displaying Shakespeare's genius at its most striking and spectacular to bookstores, libraries, schools, etc. as soon as the version came off the government printing press. Other writings of Shakespeare would be shipped in large quantities as soon as their revisions had been completed and the printing effected. Unburdening himself to those closest to him, Huston confessed he was elated at the prospect of God-fearing Amernippians being no longer corrupted by that fella W.S. and having within their reach a string of new editions brimming with wholesome ideas.

For some time Chief Justice had been beset by requests and entreaties to found a new literary journal. At first he turned them all down without a single comment, but as they multiplied he began to feel he owed his well-wishers an explanation, however curt. He had always considered literary journals to be an ignominious waste of paper and energy that should have been channeled to more estimable ends. As for the editors of such ventures, more often than not they turned out to be troublemakers. Still there was something on his mind that militated against a stark refusal, and it concerned Phineas Léger. In the previous six months, he could not but help notice that Phin's attitude had changed. When they met the usually voluble writer and journalist, "Never at a loss for words," as many had said, was strangely tightlipped. Yet he always managed to weave in the line, "The mood of the country is changing. Take note, Ev," in an unmistakably foreboding manner.

Huston was puzzled but also saddened by the change in his friend's outlook. He dismissed the thought that it was due to Phin's ill health, his dyspepsia to be precise, this particular condition being regarded among their friends as an ever-timely jest since Phineas Léger was strong as a horse and prey to no ailments of any description whatsoever. There was also a corollary situation. *National Forum,* of which Léger had remained uninterruptedly editor-in-chief and which had always staunchly supported Huston through thick and thin, had of late developed a more independent attitude. It took exception to some of his pronouncements; it printed articles by avowed critics of the government who should have been jailed but had somehow eluded dragnet; and worst of all it set itself up as treasurer and distributor of funds collected in every part of the country to help victims of the regime. Sitting stiffly in his office and mulling over these matters, Huston regretfully concluded that as of the middle of October 2083, he could no longer count on *National Forum* as an ally and friend.

Another publication, another journal, not seeking a warmer place in the sun and cleared of the interminable ifs and buts, might be just what was needed. Huston consulted numerous associates and was told that what had been tentatively projected was a literary monthly entitled *The Yale Encyclical* to be edited and published in New Haven, Connecticut. When he inquired as to its content he was informed that the first two issues would be devoted exclusively to panegyrics of himself, the third to panegyrics of religion and the government, the fourth issue introducing a more diversified subject matter yet unfailingly encomiastic of theocracy and the laws of God. Huston's earlier reservations were laid to rest, and he enthusiastically endorsed the new publication, whose full title was *The Yale Encyclical: Review of Literature and the Arts.* Shortly thereafter he received a letter from the editors saying that in the present desperate mood into which the country had been plunged by the enemies of the state a serious, prudently edited journal standing proudly on the side of the angels only could bring stability to the life of Amernippians and assuage their worst fears. Huston's thoughts turned at once to Léger's often repeated remark about there being a new mood in the country. He wondered if there was a connection between the two. Enclosed with the letter was the editors' statement of purpose, and Huston was taken aback while reading that stylistic excellence was just as important in evaluating manuscripts as nobility of thought. Pressing his lips together, Chief Justice gave out a shrill deprecating noise. Was he being taken for a ride after all?

Then he focused on the names of the editors, some twenty of them, and wondered at there being so many. He recognized a handful of names, faculty members at newly installed institutions of higher learning who had never faltered and through the years had supported him to the hilt. He recalled a lengthy meeting he had had with one of them, Alvin Doppelschwartz, back in the sixties and his subsequent bold stance as marshal of the national faculty association, best epitomized by his leading marches in at least a dozen cities, the marchers carrying signs trumpeting the soul-saving message, "American professors stand with Chief Justice and with God Almighty." Now, after an interval of years, the memories of that meeting came alive again in his mind, and he could see Alvin's well-proportioned figure standing before him, then dashing round and about, finally sitting down only to rise a second later and start dashing this way and that. Apparently the man was incapable of sitting still. Like larva passing through several molts then reaching the chrysalis stage and finally giving birth to flying adults, so the recollections of that meeting rose in Huston's mind from dormancy to expansive maturity and nurtured his brain.

Alvin was of German-Swiss origin, he reminisced vividly, and his grandfather, whose name was on the tip of his tongue, had been a house painter in Zürich. The son, Alvin's father, a bit of a rover at the best of times, had tried his hand at many a trade but always returned to the relative stability of earning his keep as a one-man cleaning detail in one of Zürich's less prestigious moviehouses. But the day came when, cheesed off to the very eyelashes at the reality and myth of Helvetia, he pulled stakes and accompanied by his girlfriend, also a native of Zürich, sought fortune in the New World. Settling down in New Jersey and going through the simplest of marriage ceremonies, he was soon hired by an expanding cleaning concern, popularly referred to as Mr. Clean of New Jersey. Fortune smiled. His methodical efforts were appreciated by his employers, and before long he was placed in charge of training young recruits in the intricacies of home, office, and super-area cleaning. The excruciatingly boring years in Zürich polishing everything under the sun till it sparkled or walked of its own volition were now paying off. He impressed customers and competitors alike by his grave manner, which categorically belied glibness and dishonesty, and was promoted ahead of schedule to supervisor and then to junior executive. His wife, not to be outdone, excelled in her own chosen province, explaining to at least half of the female population of the state the arcana of preparing genuine Swiss pastry.

But their greatest satisfaction lay elsewhere. Alvin's father was proudly bouncing on his knee his two-year old son, and his wife, with unmistakable Swiss precision, was planning his future. Another memory swept into Huston's consciousness and then another: the parents were fervent Roman Catholics but devoid of any hostility toward other Christian denominations. Not so Alvin. He had an *idée fixe* on the subject of Protestantism; he detested Protestant churches, and he detested Protestants as a people. He did nothing to hide his bigotry. Still, Huston reflected with a smile, this did not lessen his unabated loyalty to the principles of theocratic government in Western Amernipp nor his unabated loyalty to him personally as a Protestant.

The other memory Huston found even more amusing. According to his own account Alvin had decided on an academic career early in life when he was still in short pants. His father was horrified and his mother wept. They wanted their son to be a watchmaker, an occupation worthy of a Swiss, which had never lain within the father's grasp, and not an antisocial bookworm. Words passed between father and son, mother and son, and husband and wife, but the responsibility for the dismal state of affairs could not be pinned on a single family member. And Alvin persisted, holding nothing back, immune to reason.

Then Huston remembered something else, also from Alvin's own account. His father was a man of few words, judging others according to the principle of silence being man's honorable posture, with any deviations from it, unless propelled by necessity, blackening his character and reputation. But Alvin was an irredeemable chatterbox, finding it impossible to hold his tongue anymore than to sit still. This time Huston chuckled not once but several times, his secretaries at the other end of the office looking hopefully up in anticipation of a memory to be shared. But Huston went on communing only with himself. Alvin's well-worded justification of opening one's mouth whenever one felt the itch, delivered years earlier, now rang in his ears like an injunction from on high. The mercurial young professor had argued against wasting time on familiarizing oneself with the subject matter one was about to embark on.

"Just talk, talk about it, talk around it, and don't stop," he had advised. "As we talk we gain knowledge of what it is we talk about. Bring an open and empty mind to the floor, and it will soon be filled with vital data so long as you keep on talking. Data comes to us from thin air, through a particular kind of osmosis, though the hand of God is always present. Keep on talking about a thing you know nothing about, and you'll soon be an expert on it. Great Catholic mystics understood that, and they understood too that God acts in mysterious ways. The secret is to keep talking and never shut up. The rest will follow."

Huston reviewed Alvin's words with eager nostalgia. "What a character!" he exclaimed. "What a character!" Then his gaze focused on the other signatories of the letter. Tom Rosencrantz, a classicist, he remembered well, asking intelligent questions, occasionally voicing reservations but in the end toeing the line. Huston had always been convinced that Tom was much less concerned about the final outcome of any given case than about the propriety and breadth of the discussion leading up to it. The final decision may have been a foregone conclusion and Tom knew it, but he would not be deprived of the satisfaction of advancing arguments and counterarguments, of adducing examples and presenting new information, all of which carried no weight whatsoever, and could carry no weight circumstances being what they were. Tom knew it too, but he was in love with empty forms and some of those who knew him well insisted that empty forms were more to his liking than real forms encasing the substance and the goal because in this way he was absolved of the necessity of making moral judgments. In the end, he always went along.

At the very bottom of the page Huston spotted two names, those of Robbie Burger and Hershey Bar, which evoked in him very different memories. Both men were professors of English and for many an academic no better than hired hands. On two occasions they had ratted on students who had risen in clattering protest against the required religion classes, pretending at first to be body and soul on the side of the protesters; their role in the arrest of several faculty members who had openly challenged the government was dubious at best; and they regularly leaped into print filling academic broadsheets with wake-up calls to rally round Chief Justice and the government. Burger and Bar's pre-eminent achievement was that of snitches, and Huston devoted a fleeting thought to their precise qualifications for the editorship of a high-aiming literary journal. Nevertheless, the team, as he reviewed their names again, inspired confidence and, if blessed with a no-nonsense quarterback, could go far. Huston scanned again the letter and tried to determine best he could the approximate age of each editor.

A gnawing realization made itself felt in the very center of his consciousness—a realization that many others in government and in higher education experienced and which always brought with it mists of incensed embarrassment. Beginning in the mid-seventies the practice of purchasing academic degrees set in and soon elbowed out the stodgy orthodox one. Highgovies by the hundreds either bought doctoral dissertations readymade, properly typed and formatted to the last comma or dot, or had them ghostwritten. At many new universities brought into existence after the old ones had been shut down the traditional procedures of appointing dissertation committees, of comps and dissertation defenses had all but disappeared. A candidate presented himself or herself before a university cashier, paid the required fee, and was awarded the degree. Some universities still held commencements where M.A. and Ph.D. degrees were ceremoniously conferred upon the ranks of fledgling academics about to join their senior colleagues in lifelong intellectual pursuits, but others had dispensed with them altogether.

Two mammoth concerns located in New Jersey supplied the needy for a price with every stripe of school or academic writing from a junior high school report to a doctoral dissertation on the most abstruse of subjects. Papers to be handed in for a wide variety of courses were available in large quantities and custom-made ones could be easily ordered. Business was booming and the proprietors had wisely instituted rolling discounts favoring customers in accordance with the frequency of orders placed on a yearly basis. Grade school, junior high school, and high school itself were not exempt from these purely monetary encroachments taking the place of individual intellectual effort, but the new trend was at its most widespread and flourishing at colleges and universities. It was generally recognized that some of these institutions were no more than money exchanges or retail stores handling information, knowledge, and intellectual content in general with the briskness normally reserved for pig iron or toilet articles. As the self-respecting insiders of the scientific community in and out of Academe constantly averred, this state of affairs tainted the humanities and the social sciences only, the physical sciences remaining pure as the driven snow and marching to the old trusty drummer.

Scrutiny did not entirely confirm these rosy beliefs, but even within the departments dedicated to the study of national literatures, sociology, political science, and other disciplines within numerous universities at which the accusing finger was most often pointed there were honorable men and women following the academic tradition of study and research at its shining best, not heeding the mammoth corporations of New Jersey. Interviewing committees facing candidates at conventions had to have their wits about them and something approaching a sixth sense since documentary records including testimonials and recommendations were more often than not inconclusive. Some committee members resorted to coded notes such as 4/16/16 standing for d/p/p, dissertation probably purchased, or 4/16/78 d/p/gh, dissertation probably ghostwritten, and various others. The train bearing American higher education and everything it stood for, which earlier in the twenty-first century had run so smoothly, began to puff and falter, making unscheduled stops, losing speed, its driver complaining of poor visibility. The wheels were still on the rails, but schedules could not be kept, itineraries were constantly changing, and the driver could not make head or tail of the orders he was logging in. His principal concern was to keep the train moving, just moving, nothing more.

Work to put *The Yale Encyclical: Review of Literature and the Arts* in the saddle went on at a swift pace, and on November 10, 2083, the new journal was officially inaugurated, the first issue being planned for release a week before Christmas. A festive crowd assembled in New Haven, and a lavish parade wound its way from one end of the town to the other. The editors, the staff and their guests, the invited dignitaries, and well-wishers marched proudly on carrying huge portraits and photographs of Chief Justice in a manner reminiscent of the Chinese people's adoration of Mao Tse-tung over a hundred years before. They also bore equally huge signs reading, "Oh Lord, bless our review and Chief Justice too." That particular fall in New England delighted most inhabitants on account of being the mildest in more than a hundred years, and the day of inauguration was unseasonably warm and sunny with not a single cloud marring the majestic azure of the sky. Some of the paraders wore academic gowns, some exhibited exotic or colorful garments, some were topless or bottomless irrespective of gender, and many of those who had opted for displaying themselves both in a topless and a bottomless fashion wore narrow blue ribbons across their torsos scrupulously covering their navels. Some bore wind or string instruments on which they played, but melody was never coordinated and a cacophonous effect followed. Segments of the parade sang at the top of their lungs, here and there three or four consecutive rows resorted to acrobatics and boldly restructured modern dance, jugglers were plying their trade in front and fortune tellers in the rear, while a sizeable part of marchers in the middle gave a vivid rendition of Saint Vitus' dance.

Pedestrians on both sides of the street catching a glimpse of the parade were for the most part reserved and displays of exhilaration were rare. As the marchers passed by what had been the campus and the buildings once occupied by Yale University, later converted on Huston's order into a lunatic asylum, they and the pedestrians alike saw through the iron fence patients sitting quietly on benches and deck chairs, perusing newspapers and books or conversing amicably with one another—the very acme of rationality and decorum. Some passersby were overheard expressing surprise at the circus-like atmosphere of the parade, hardly corresponding with Chief Justice's puritanical views of conduct. By staging bacchanalia the revelers were inviting a terrible retribution—they warned—unless, of course, they had gone stark raving mad, or was it Chief Justice himself who had finally abandoned all pretense of sanity? However in the days to come more understanding comments were exchanged: whether approved by the Savior of the Country or conducted without his knowledge, the New Haven parade was—it was stressed again and again—a clear sign of the changing mood of the country and a signal to many to enter the lists. The adversaries of this hopeful prognosis painted a doomsday scenario and gained some adherents, but for the time being at least, they formed a distinct minority. Still, on all sides tempers flared and tongues wagged as seldom in the past, and it was universally agreed that the inauguration of *The Yale Encyclical* was an event to be remembered as long as the human race was alive and kicking.

/   /   /

On the very same day on which the motley crowd irked and aston-ished the burghers of New Haven, Wyn Purdue and John Scaggs were sitting in the living room of his house in Cambridge. John had just fin-ished pouring out two double bourbons on the rocks and handed Wyn her drink.

"Thank you, my love," she said, getting a firm grip on the glass and blinking profusely.

"Down the hatch," John said.

"Righto," Wyn concurred.

The Shakespeare Revision Committee was presently preoccupied with *Richard III*, and a drastic change had come over the two janitors, not entirely unexpected, since they had already stood their conformist beliefs on their head and then demolished what was left.

"I don't want to work with them crazies no more," John let out.

"Nor do I," Wyn joined in.

"Will Shakespeare's got a ripping tale to tell in each of his plays. Why turn it all upside down? Ain't he entitled to a little respect? In a free country man is free to say what he pleases."

"That's right, John, except we don't live in a free country no more."

"Maybe one day," John ventured.

"Maybe so, maybe so." Wyn placed her dainty hand on top of John's massive one. "I think we ought to resign from that crazy committee," she almost whispered. "I don't want to have it on my conscience remaining a party to a lowdown fraud turning William Shakespeare's nuggets into hard, dry shit. We'll claim reasons of health."

"Hell, no!" John shouted. "I wanna come clean. I wanna tell them what's on my mind. Are you game, girl?"

"Aye, now and forever, John."

He got hold of writing paper and they jointly penned a letter of resignation, he reciting beforehand what he wanted to put down, she making changes in it and dictating her part. It was a one-page letter, but it was complete and to the point. They made it plain that rewriting Shakespeare's plays, or anyone else's literary output for that matter, was the lowest trick in the book, and forcing parsons and nuns into places where they had no business being, building altars to Chief Justice and God Almighty by every smelly cowpie was not only plain crazy but also plain crooked and demeaning to man's dignity and common sense. They wrote: *And for these above-mentioned reasons we, John Scaggs and Wyn Purdue, resign from the Shakespeare Revision Committee and urge other members to do the same.* They both signed the letter with a flourish, and John clipped it to the mailbox to be collected by the mailman on his morning round.

"Flora Gibson came to see me the other day," Wyn began out of the blue, sipping bourbon.

"That neighbor of yours who never stops yapping? What did she want?"

"Just a neighborly call. Her son is in the military and writes his mom that they now have more lectures on religion than on self-defense and the art of combat."

"I am not surprised. Huston will soon be issuing crosses, Bibles, and crucifixes in place of automatic weapons."

"Jimmie—that's her son—tells her half of the officers are laughing their heads off, and the other half call it high treason. She's in touch with that fella in Wyoming . . ."

"Nathan . . .?"

"That's right, Nathan Chadwick. He's raising a lot of dust."

"I know. When the pot overflows . . ." John left the sentence unfinished.

"I am so happy we sallied forth out of that balmy committee."

"Me too. And now what is your pleasure, Wyn?"

She let her eyes rest unhurriedly on his craggy face and the powerful neck.

"Let's make love, John. Let's make love while we still can."

In a flash he knew there was nothing else in the whole wide world he would rather do. He stepped forward and put his arms round her.

/   /   /

Editors of *The Yale Encyclical* kept their promise, and on December 17 stacks of the first issue were ready to be mailed to subscribers and delivered to bookstores. With exemplary speed all the panegyrical entries—directions had specified a panegyric of Chief Justice in verse or prose, not exceeding two pages—had been read and the winner chosen. The winning entry graced the first page of the journal, along with the name and a short biography of the lucky litterateur printed in golden letters. In this instance the winner was a young lady of twenty-two putting her tender age to ingenious stylistic uses and rubbing the Muse with both hands. Her laudatory piece consisted of one line, "Me love Chief Justice," repeated twenty-one times, the aggregate triumphantly asserting her tender age. The judges were duly impressed by the young lady's power of feeling, her stylistic conciseness, and the force of her arguments. Their verdict was unanimous. She took tea with Chief Justice on New Year's Day and he pronounced her a very accomplished young person. In the months to come the winning entry was circulated to English departments at carefully selected universities and to literary clubs and associations, with the admonishment that it marked a revolution in stylistics, a breakthrough in rhetoric, and the discovery of literary paradigms the human race had been avidly looking for.

Chapter 6

Chief Justice Goes Upon a Journey

At the outset of each calendar year Chief Justice undertook a journey lasting two to three weeks, starting off from Raleigh, North Carolina, then heading directly to its southern cousin and from there to Georgia, Alabama, and the Heart of Dixie. From Jackson he would proceed in a stately fashion northward through Tennessee and Kentucky, thereupon either swerving left toward Indiana, Illinois, and Iowa or swerving right, aiming at Ohio and Pennsylvania, crossing the Mason-Dixon Line at the previously determined and punctiliously observed moment. On the way he visited old friends, listened to reports of what young folks were up to, picked up local news and gossip, was told who was up to no good and who merited a reward, and shook as many hands as was humanly possible. In some towns he stayed longer than in others, and a sealed itinerary was known to undergo changes not once but several times during any given trip, bending to the events of the day.

To cover longer distances Air Force One or Super-chopper One stood in readiness with their highly trained crews at Huston's beck and call. Otherwise, much of his traveling was done in a specially constructed limousine dubbed Lim One, there being twelve such limousines kept for his exclusive use in Washington D.C. A new one awaited him on each landing strip he had just flown onto, intending to continue the journey by land.

Customarily Huston took with him no papers and no homework of any kind, and he was accompanied by two trusty male secretaries only, a political and a theological one, identified as "polsec" and "theosec" respectively, each of whom had vast data at his fingertips. Occasionally Huston chatted and joked with the two young men and with the driver, but more often than not he was immersed in thought—reflecting, ruminating, planning. These tours relaxed and invigorated him as nothing else did, infrequently giving him a new perspective on a particular thorny issue or on things in general. Recently he had taken a fancy to traveling by land because of its leisurely pace and the ease of making unscheduled stops, taking to the air only when it was absolutely necessary.

Leaning against the softest of feathers and the finest of silk while the limousine was wending its way through central Kentucky in the second week of January 2084, Huston reviewed the achievements of his administration since its inception. He had inherited a dissolute and godless nation lost in the labyrinth of its self-destructive liberal policies, constantly hearkening to the licentious principles of the Constitution of 1787, where religion was an old wives' tale and God Almighty a malodorous cadaver everyone wanted out of his backyard. Six years up the road the American and later the Western Amernippian nation made a hundred-and-eighty degree turn. Faith in the almighty God had been rediscovered: the crucial importance of churches in national life reasserted with vigor that knew no equal; Satan, his tail singed, put to flight, and New Jerusalem stood on the verge of celebrating its glorious birth. Next Huston delved into individual areas of the national rebirth, artfully blending the general and the particular: at long last God's commands came to be obeyed and vice almost entirely stamped out. The Sex Police and the Faith Police had accomplished much, much more than what had been expected of them, and as time went on they were winning new laurels while the clinics, the centers, and the condos, those unsung chambers where the battle was at its fiercest, were sanctifying the hearts and minds of the people.

Faith, religion, and virtue triumphed everywhere in Amernipp, and Huston came to the realization again—his back pleasantly tickled—as he had done several weeks earlier, that the country of which he was rightly proclaimed savior was standing at attention eager to fulfill another of God's commands—to shed its earthly shell and enter the Godhead. But how precisely this was to be effected Huston was far from certain. He remembered with fervid emotion how the Almighty had appeared to him several times in a dream, how He praised His faithful servant Everett, and how He promised that the entire nation of Amernipp would be lifted up on high to be one with God. "But how, how, oh Lord?" he cried despondently, perspiring as never before after the vision had vanished, and falling down on his knees he begged to be enlightened. "Enlighten me, oh Lord. Shed light where there is darkness, for we believe in you and our paltry minds droop and wither without your guidance." But when the Almighty appeared again in a dream His words were identical and no modus operandi revealed. Once or twice, as Huston recalled, He appended the phrase "time draws near," or words to that effect, and Huston was forever in a quandary. Picking the brains of his wisest advisors and straining his own intelligence to the limit, Huston concluded that Amernippians' unification with the Godhead could happen in one of several different fashions.

First in line was the distinct possibility of the entire territory of Western Amernipp being lifted up, placed on a divinely magical carpet and transported to Paradise. When he had rather foolishly, as he later regretted, broached this possibility to La Rochelle, the National Security Advisor compared it in his own offensively irreverent manner to lifting a pizza out of the box by its extremities. Huston remembered vividly La Rochelle's uncouth laughter as he was uttering the word "extremities," that constant laughter that pained and horrified Huston to the very depths of his soul.

Another possible solution involved the ascension of the entire population of Western Amernipp to heaven after the manner of Christ's ascension. This would make sense since of late the country had moved infinitely closer to Jesus Christ than it had ever been, and the Almighty might wish to let His grace shine on the inhabitants of the country as a whole and make them coequal with His own son, the Redeemer. If so, God's love for the human race would be made manifest as never before in the long centuries of human error and His forgiveness be a boon one could scarcely hope for. Huston wondered whether ascension entailed dematerialization, whether only the souls of Western Amernippians would find their way to heaven, or their bodies as well. The orthodox Protestant view taught that Christ ascended to heaven as Himself, which meant in spirit and in body, since he had previously and after the crucifixion appeared to his disciples in the flesh. Ergo his ascension would incorporate both spirit and body. But, Huston reminded himself, Christ was God the Son and He was free of sin, ergo He entered, or rather reentered, heaven without the need of purification or disembodiment. However, even the best Amernippians were stained by sin, which was the ineluctable condition of man, and could never be placed on the same level as the Son of God. If they were to be redeemed by God's grace their bodies would be cleansed and their spirits made pure, and Huston was asking himself whether a period of punishment of the guilty, of redemption and forgiveness here on earth, would not antedate God's admission of the Western Amernippian population to the glory on high.

The longer Huston mulled the matter over the more convinced he became that surely dividing the population of Western Amernipp into segments, some of which were ready or nearly ready to enter the Godhead while others had perforce to march through the valleys of punishment and penitence, was not merely equitable but no less than a direct command of the Almighty. Surely there was a world of difference between someone like himself, a stalwart defender of the faith, the Lord's fervent worshipper and His obedient servant, and someone like Siegfried La Rochelle, an atheistical genius whom he, Huston, tolerated and often supported for the simple and sole reason that he, La Rochelle, had conducted American foreign policy with matchless skill and success and had made Amernipp the mightiest of all empires known to man.

Legions of breadeaters who followed in his, Huston's, footsteps however awkwardly and disappointingly yet never ceasing to cherish his high ideals, stood surely closer to God than the self-indulging pleasure-seekers who looked up to La Rochelle and the likes of him and were not man enough to break loose from the morass of the senses. And when it came to his, Huston's, true peers, men and women who lived by faith and carried out God's commands to the letter, the contrast could not be starker. To insist that saints and sinners would be treated in the same fashion by the Lord amounted to the travesty of His wishes— Huston's conviction in this regard had finally attained the muscularity and certitude that were God-given—and he joyfully felt the presence of the Almighty in every pore of his body and in every heartbeat.

But how would these dispensations be implemented? Who would assess penance, and by what yardstick? Who would determine whether the individual was fit to enter the Kingdom of God? Who would determine whether the damned were truly damned for eternity? God, of course, Huston responded at once to his own doubts without thinking. God and no one else. But, if so, would it be too much to ask of the Creator of Heaven and Earth that He take man by the hand and guide him through the canyons of uncertainty and the gullies of doubt? So far in the matter of entering the Godhead, the Supreme Beneficent Ruler had confined Himself to general statements that admirably pinpointed His eternal goals but left man uninstructed about their implementation, about the ways and means, about the nitty-gritty. Huston was still in hopes that one day soon the Almighty would dig in His heels before him and unfold the entire plan of becoming one with the Godhead down to the last detail. He was still in hopes—how could he be otherwise?—but the hopes, like plum trees unshaded from the broiling sun on a vast parching plain, were getting more and more desiccated, their internal juices drying up, no rain coming to the rescue.

Huston pinched himself in the arm to keep alert and went on reflecting. Of course it was entirely possible that God would forgive everybody his and her offenses and by an act of divine mercy gather the entire nation by His side and take it to His heavenly abode. Perhaps the Father of mankind would dispense with hell and convey his chosen nation, Western Amernipp, straight to heaven. Such a course was possible, Huston nodded to himself, but unlikely. There had to be Last Judgment and division of the souls into two main categories, the saved and the damned. Hence there was a strong likelihood hell really existed. As for the righteous souls, they might be ordered to wait in Paradise until the Second Coming of Christ, Resurrection of the Body, and the Last Judgment. This would be the orthodox view Protestantism had received from the Almighty, had evolved under His tutelage, and had preached to the world under His command ever since the days of Jesus Christ. That much was clear. Heaven, hell, God's infinite mercy, body and soul, ascension to heaven after the manner of Jesus Christ, material world and dematerialization, sainthood and the wages of sin, penance and absolution—these were concepts highly relevant to the promise made by the Lord to his faithful servant Everett Zacharias Huston, who now smacked his lips in self-congratulation, perhaps much more than simply being highly relevant. In truth they constituted both the essence of God's promise and the very bricks the faithful servant would use in building yet another monument to the glory of the Lord. Huston smacked his lips again, much louder this time, and the two secretaries exchanged knowing glances. "Yet when everything is said and done, there is much murkiness in my mind relating to the divine pledge," he muttered to himself.

"The Lord spoke in powerful tones when He informed me," Huston delved into recent memories, "that because of the extraordinary services rendered by the government and the people of Western Amernipp in the cause of religion it was decided on high that this nation, this New Jerusalem led by me, was to be rewarded in a singular and unique way. This country deserves salvation as no other, and it will be transported to the heavenly regions taking its place on the right side of the Lord." Huston remembered these words well since they were spoken by the Almighty on no less than four occasions, always in a dream which came abruptly to an end once they had been spoken. It was impossible to ask questions or beg for a clarification. The Lord spoke *ex cathedra* and apparently would not demean Himself by entertaining questions. "If I could only face You not in a dream, oh Lord, but in the light of day," Huston whispered, "and hear from Your own lips instructions for me and my people, then my mind and whatever energy I possess would be ruled by You and Your will would be done." But neither now, nor in the past when a similar orison was offered, was there any response from the deity who for all practical purposes could have been deaf as a post.

Another thought struck Huston: "Suppose the Lord was indeed grooming Western Amernipp for the rewards of heaven, and if so bliss eternal in the life to come could only commence once this miserable existence in the valley of sorrow had been snuffed out. Ergo, wasn't it plausible to assume that the Almighty would first envelop the bodies of Amernippians in eternal sleep and then let their souls ascend to heaven?" Yes, this was plausible enough, and it would neatly take care of the problem of the body, of dematerialization and so forth. In consonance with the orthodox Protestant view souls of Amernippians would await in Paradise Second Coming of Christ, Resurrection of the Body, and Last Judgment. True enough! Yet Huston was only partly satisfied. Gnawing at the back of his mind was a disconcerting half-belief that perhaps inherent in the Lord's message was an implicit expectation that Everett Zacharias and his like-minded friends would take it upon themselves to help in the fulfillment of the divine dispensation by doing some preliminary spade work that would smooth the edges, provide headcounts, or do whatever else was needed. "After all we are no more than servants of the Lord," he uttered in a stage whisper, "servants of the Lord and nothing more."

Then an impulse stirred in him that put all the other impulses to flight—the impulse to press forward, to dominate, to command. He saw himself on a hundred playfields marshalling thousands of young men and women, reminding them of the gravity of the occasion, prepping them on what to say when the CO put his foot on the grass—*the CO*, not one of those clowns with bars and stars on their uniforms, but the man upstairs, creator of heaven and earth and of the puny human race, which got things wrong and had to be whipped into faith and obedience, the old horsewhip being as ever the gentlest of tools. Their uniforms and blouses fluttered in the wind and he, God's vicar on earth, the Savior of the Country, inspected his battalions, young men and women of high character who had pledged themselves to obey God's commands without question and fulfill each of His wishes.

"Surely," he argued with himself, "here is sanctified flesh that will bear no false witness and can be put to excellent use in implementing your orders that man and the Godhead join forces and become one." And he added softly so as not to be overheard by his secretaries, "Show me the way, oh Lord, and reveal Your designs to me for I merit Your confidence more than any man alive." Again Huston saw himself marshalling the troops and being second-in-command to the leader who needed no introduction. He discharged his duties conscientiously, and with every whiff of air sensed the zeal and devotion of the troops. "The Lord is proud of you," he roared in all directions. Then the power impulse left him as suddenly as it had taken hold of him, and he was reclining on the comfortable seat, a little puzzled and musing.

The country's imminent admission into the holy bosom of the deity had been on everybody's lips for some time now, and it was widely believed that Chief Justice had reached an agreement with the Almighty on terms highly advantageous to Western Amernippians and had in his pocket a step-by-step chart of the operation. How could it be otherwise? In parts of the country Huston was considered coequal with the Lord, and not infrequently beliefs were articulated that it was he, Chief Justice, who ran the show in the universe, the Almighty being no more than a sleeping partner. While the great majority of citizens held to the conviction that on the planning table every *i* was dotted and every *t* crossed, they nevertheless bombarded the Savior of the Country with questions, suggestions, requests. His clerical staff had to be doubled to respond individually to every letter, fax, e-mail, or telephone and radio message, and devoted civil servants had to be practically ordered to go home to bed since they were falling asleep over their desks or lying listless on the floor.

In the midst of all this Huston was both elated and worried sick. On several recent occasions he had again begged the Lord in lengthy prayers for an inkling as to how the country's admission into this dominion would be effected, vividly painting the wretchedness of his own situation due to his total ignorance of the specific designs of the Lord. In return he heard in a dream vision the familiar sonorous voice giving him the same general message of joy as before and nothing more.

In the meantime, correspondence mounted. The governors of Alabama and Alaska let it be known, apparently after conducting numerous polls in their respective states, that the alphabetical way of proceeding was the most judicious. Alabama would be the first to be lifted up in glory and absorbed by the Godhead hook, line, and sinker, then Alaska, and so on in alphabetical order. This would allow the population in each state to make farewell arrangements, decide what to take with them and what to leave behind, see friends in the other parts of the country, attend to various legal matters, and put their affairs in order. The governors were cogent and insistent, and although Huston reviewed their request sympathetically he could not commit himself.

From some of his cronies in Texas who had stood and were still standing very close to the throne, Huston received a lengthy epistle via snail mail claiming that the momentous steps should be taken in accordance with the rank of each state, the size of its economy and its area serving as the two criteria. Texas was the largest state in Western Amernipp if you rightly excluded acres of ice that surrounded the Alaskan shores, which no man in his right mind would call terra firma. As for the Texas economy, it towers over that of the other states like a Texas Ranger of old towered over the bad guys and his holstered competitors alike who knew nothin' from nothin'. Again Huston bestowed much sympathy upon the epistle, and again he deferred his decision.

From New England a series of e-mails reached him unedited and jumbled up but making the point clear: the imminent event was of such monumental importance that it was only fitting it should be planned in a historical context, in the context of American history. History was not a dirty, lifeless mat on which people wipe their feet, it was a cascading waterfall where each cascade derived from the preceding one and gave movement to the one that followed. The past, the present, and the future were one continuum. Past events shaped the present and the future, and future events, anticipated or unanticipated by us, imprinted the present and the past. Understanding of the present human condition involved understanding of the past, which in every fleeting moment became the present and the future. Time was one, unbroken, undivided, and history was the past, the present, and the future, all rolled into one, unseverable, standing up heroically to the sleazy demigods and kingpins of partition. If entry into the bosom of the deity was to be effected by region, e-mails went on, then New England, the cradle of American freedom and independence, should be at the top of the list, to be outvoted only by the thirteen colonies that had first risen in revolt and now were standing shoulder to shoulder claiming the first berth on the ferry. Huston shrugged his wide shoulders and let out a whistle. "Freedom, independence. Some people never learn," he muttered. "Hankering after those godless times will do you no good, New England." He tossed the e-mails onto the inactive pile.

Next he scanned a letter from an old friend in New Orleans, for some years now a high-up in the state office of tourism, who claimed no precedence but counseled that Louisiana's entry into the never-never, as he called it, be coordinated with Mardi Gras. "The state sure needs monies and we can charge all them tourists that thirst for a little culture double for a holy jaunt from which no one returns and for a ride in our fair city they won't forget if they live to be a hundred," he wrote. Huston chuckled. "Luther was always a bit of a doubting Thomas and a prankster. The never-never, the holy jaunt! My, my! Luther hasn't changed over the years, and he looks after his state like always. Good ol' Luther." Huston placed the letter with the others destined for further consideration.

Profusion of written and transmitted communications made it impossible for him to examine each of them separately, and he picked and chose searching for new awe-inspiring ideas and spectacular tributes to the Almighty. He was often disappointed. From the Garden State he received smug accounts of the symbolism of dairy products with particular emphasis on the role of milk in the religions of the world guaranteeing a place of honor for its inhabitants on the holy voyage to end all voyages. Many other states lauded their industrial and technological successes and some inquired whether sample gadgets and instruments, daunting examples of their skill and ingenuity, could be taken along to promote earthly know-how in heaven. Missouri's chamber of commerce, for reasons which Huston was unable to fathom sent him, a bulky catalogue of their newly produced wines, which earned high marks at tasters' meetings and were beginning to compete internationally against better known brands from countries priding themselves on their centuries-old tradition of wine-making. The president of the chamber of commerce added a postscript in longhand to the effect that these new wines were often used for sacerdotal purposes and that in any event he was dispatching two cases of Missouri's finest to the Savior of the Country as a small token of the veneration in which he was held by the people of the state.

Huston's office workers told him bluntly that many letters and messages received were off the wall, and they were astonished that men and women in high positions could have written them. A sizeable part of the correspondence, office workers continued, sinned in another fashion: either through absentmindedness or by design, the writers confused the momentous event of being united with the Godhead, an event that was unique in the history of the world, with a county or industrial fair, or on a larger scale with an exhibition of the marvels of the fourth quarter of the twenty-first century. One of the temporary office workers engaged to sort out mountains of incoming mail asked, "May I be frank?"

"Please do," Huston replied. "By all means be frank."

"Well, sir," the young man began, "some of your correspondents haven't got a clue what you're after. Hasn't your office publicized the matter? After all, blending in with the Godhead doesn't happen every day."

"Of course the event received maximum exposure. I thought it was common knowledge."

"As things stand now it's common ignorance, Chief Justice, no more, no less."

"How do you explain this horrendous mix-up, Hal?" Huston inquired sadly, still hoping there was a simple explanation for it, invalidating nothing.

"Actually it's Hamlin, sir, not Hal, Mom's maiden name, the Hamlins of Beloit, Wisconsin, squires of the county, a family of some standing, as Mom never tired of telling us youngsters, and greatly superior to the plain Kraut-like Grossmenschers, Dad's family name."

"Poor boy," Huston let fall without thinking.

Hamlin spoke resolutely, "I've been out of that stinking family fold for years now, and I never looked back. Amy and me will be married in June, and both my old man and his missus can go to hell."

"You know, Hamlin, the name Grossmenscher strikes a chord," Huston spoke softly, reminiscently.

"Dad and Mom were both in the military."

"Regular Army?"

"Wisconsin National Guard." Hamlin gave out a scornful laugh, "She was an officer, a captain, and he was just a plain foulmouthed sergeant."

"I bet this didn't make for harmonious family relations."

"You're right, Chief Justice. They went after each other like two starved hounds fighting for the non-existent bone. Now and then in the middle of a row she'd order him to salute her 'cause she was an officer and all that, and he'd start throwing things at her—pots, pans, plates, anything he could lay his hands on. There were times both drew blood, made up, and started anew."

"My God," Huston sighed again and again. "Didn't social services, the police . . . ?"

Hamlin hooted with laughter. "At first social workers and the family council paid frequent visits. But, after a time, as things didn't get better, they gave up on us."

"Eventually . . . " Huston started off in a very understanding manner.

"Yes, eventually they split, ten years too late. I was leaving home when the divorce hearing was held, and my two elder sisters and a brother were already living on their own."

Huston sighed again. "I remember now why the name Grossmenscher stuck in my mind. There was some sort of military publication and—"

"That's right, Chief Justice," Hamlin joined in. "*Wisconsin National Guard Newsletter,* edited for years by one Lieutenant and later Captain Marjorie Grossmenscher, my own biological mom."

"Thank you for the information, Hamlin. It's a small world. I take it you've gotten over the family situation . . ."

"Yes, and as I told you, sir, I've never looked back. Amy and me will be in marketing, but we are still at school so we sign on for temporary jobs like this to buy basics and pander to Amy's irrepressible lust for haute cuisine."

Huston laughed. "I know what you mean. Years ago during my first marriage my wife got it into her head that our entire family should sub- sist on French food exclusively, not only everything being prepared in the Frenchy way but the ingredients, every one of them, being Frenchy as well. That meant we stopped buying groceries at the usual stores and visited instead special establishments where all kinds of fancy foreign foods were on display. It cost a bundle, and I was at the time an under- paid preacher. I felt the pinch, but this madness raged for three full months before I finally put my foot down. Well, we reverted to eating cheeseburgers, Boston beans, and sweet potatoes, but don't you believe for one moment, young man, that my wife took it sitting down. She raved like a maniac and accused me of barbarism. Just imagine that. As I said, things went back to normal, but a scar was left on our marriage that took helluva long time to heal."

"Thank you for taking me into your confidence, Chief Justice." Hamlin smiled broadly. "I am honored. It puts the wind in my sails."

"I am happy you are working for us even though this is a tempo- rary assignment." Huston's swift hand patted Hamlin on the back and shoulders. "And now for your analysis of those goofy responses."

"Right, sir." Hamlin straightened himself up, glancing at loose sheets of paper clasped in his hand. "A great many letters and messages you've received do the correspondents very little credit. That's why I asked you whether there was prior knowledge of the earth-shaking event."

"There was," Huston replied with verve, yet feeling that the ground was sliding from under him.

"For many of them," Hamlin continued in an unemotional, clinical manner that gave no clue as to his judgmental position, "the only thing that matters is to make a little extra money. This applies both to large corporations and small businesses, and to private associations of one kind or another that sponsor a particular humanitarian, educational, religious, or medical cause. Dollars and cents come first, but many recognize to that end gimmicks must be used. Those out there take Amernipp's unification with God Almighty, which may be a turning point in the relation between Him and us, as a super-gimmick, something that will bring pots of gold. For you this is an event like the birth of Christ or the Resurrection; for them it is a nerve-tingling ride on a gigantic roller coaster that will draw millions cash in hand. I don't want to be rude, sir."

"Go on."

"Few believe the Lord Almighty will clutch the Western Amernippian nation to His bosom and find a place for it in this three-person body. Few do because it defies the imagination."

"Anything else?"

"Only to advise you, sir, to teach the masses honesty and forthrightness, veneration of the Almighty, and respect for religion. But don't count on them because they are after the fast buck, and will sell you and your grand visions for two bits. Instruct them to set modest goals for themselves in ethics and religion and keep their feet firmly on the ground. Thank you very much, sir."

Wrinkles began to ooze out and intersect on Huston's forehead and cheeks, and his tone was harsh.

"It appears, Grossmenscher, that your religious education has been criminally neglected. I am greatly disappointed in you. Report back to your supervisor and don't forget to remind him that you are here strictly on a temporary assignment. Entertain no hopes of permanent employment on my watch. Good-bye to you." He threw his arm forward in an unceremonious gesture of dismissal.

Huston's journey had proceeded to Iowa, and Huston was reliving the magnificent reception he had been accorded in Burlington and Mt. Pleasant. He had stayed for three days in Burlington rubbing noses and shoulders with hundreds of backers, and he vividly remembered the religious pageant the local high schools had put on in his honor. It had been a moving occasion, and he had gone backstage to meet and congratulate the actors. Iowa City was studiously avoided, and after a brief stop in Cedar Rapids they were heading for Waterloo where another round of festivities awaited him. Huston recrossed his legs, exchanged a few words with the secretaries, and focused again on the review of his achievements, comparing, assessing, prognosticating.

In the last several months he had gotten numerous messages from Raoul Borgia, the pontiff of the Roman Catholic Church, always heartening and saying the right word at the right time. Huston wondered if Borgia was telepathically-minded since he was abreast of what was going on in his, Huston's, mind on any particular day and also whether he had spies planted in the inner offices reporting to him on the flow of confidential business. He recalled the faces of his closest assistants, among them the face of a young man, a fervent Roman Catholic, who did indeed travel often to Rome on pilgrimages of all sorts. Could he be the secret agent? As for the mysteries of telepathy, perhaps the answer was much simpler and hinged on the affinity between the two minds, Borgia's and his own.

Huston smiled cryptically. In any event, what was happening or not happening did not constitute clear and present danger. The pontiff had offered Chief Justice excellent advice on a variety of subjects and much classified information which would have been hard to come by. Chief Justice was grateful for both and planned meetings, on neutral ground preferably, so they could talk freely as they had done in Geneva. More than that he planned new areas of cooperation, new joint undertakings, a new you-scratch-my-back-I'll-scratch-your-back set up, a new freemasonic lodge. But one phrase of Borgia's had been pounding in his brain as soon as he had caught sight of it in e-mail, and he soon began to quote it to others and then pass it on as his own, "In the service of the Lord much is permitted and nothing is forbidden." A mere motto, a maxim, but it quelled all doubts and sent them to pastures new!

Like a dog hard on its luck making a beeline for the kennel, so Huston's thoughts hurried to and refocused on the ways and means of entering God's kingdom while body juices were still streaming up and down, loath to give up the struggle. When Huston had brought up the subject with Homily Grister before embarking on the interstate trip he had been assured that everything was in order and that most likely the Almighty held the answers in readiness and would impart them to His faithful servant in His own good time. There was nothing to worry about, Hom had insisted, and the Almighty was merely testing His servant. When, disappointed and frustrated, Everett called Hom from Iowa, reassurances were repeated and a euphoric picture painted.

Still Huston felt uneasy. He enviously recalled that his good friend, the president of the Church of Latter Day Saints, received on the average sixteen revelations from the Almighty everyday, including Sundays and other holidays. Admittedly some of them were trivial and had to do with proper pricing of toilet articles, poor quality of various brands of shoe polish, and new and healthier methods of diluting fruit juice. Even so the Almighty was on post, no bureaucratic delays on His side of the fence, and when everything was said and done He treated his Mormon servant fair and square, meeting him on an even ground. Why couldn't the Almighty extend the same courtesy to another faithful servant of His, one Everett Zacharias Huston? Why, why? Resentment surged in him, but he met it head-on, beseeching the Almighty to give him strength to rout the infernal gang, beseeching Him for forgiveness, beseeching Him for grace.

Soon he was absorbed in prayer oblivious of his secretaries' chatter, oblivious of the questions the driver was asking. When some time later he glanced out of the window dusk was falling, and he realized they were approaching Waterloo. He must have packed some shut-eye along the way because he felt refreshed, and in addition he was in a more optimistic frame of mind. The Almighty would not let him down, of this he was certain now, and the notion of some citizens of Western Amernipp being damned or sternly punished before their time struck him as absurd. The Almighty had given His pledge that the Western Amernippian nation would sing His praises in the company of angels after entering His domain, and Huston could feel in his bones that the Almighty had meant the entire nation, no exceptions allowed. This was the Western Amernippians' reward for stamping out vice and making the country New Jerusalem in every respect. No other nation on the face of this planet had ever risen so high in the Almighty's estimation, and no other nation had been so rewarded. This would be another Ascension Day in imitation of Christ's ascension into heaven forty days after Easter, and it would be equally momentous, for the collective body of Western Amernipp was holy just as Christ's body was holy. And the time drew nigh.

His reception in Waterloo was warmhearted, and on the second evening of his stopover he put in a personal and urgent call to Borgia. The line was clear as the day was bright, and he almost suspected that his friend was not in the faraway Vatican but in the adjoining room.

"Holy Father," he began apprehensively, "I would like to ask your advice. I need your advice. I need the benefit of your wisdom."

"But of course, Chief Justice, this is the reason I am here, at the service of the entire world, but especially at the service of my friends."

"Let me come straight to the point."

"A straight line is dearer to the Lord than a tortuous one."

"Thank you, Holy Father. You know very well that the Almighty has promised to reward Western Amernipp by raising it up on high and setting it in His Kingdom of the Blessed. I have received promises, assurances."

"Of course. But tell me again how were they conveyed."

"In dream visions, but with extraordinary clarity. Upon awakening I'd commit each of them to paper."

"I don't quite see where the problem lies, my friend."

"The ultimate goal is manifest, but how precisely will it come about, Raoul? Shall we ascend limbs and all? Or will only our souls be received by the Almighty? And the entire nation at one go or by stages, by installments as it were?"

"I see."

"I besought the Almighty time and again to give me a signal, a hint. I implored Him most respectfully to disclose to me the actual manner, the *modus operandi* of our nation's entry into His Kingdom, but to no avail." He paused and drew a deep breath. "My people are getting restive, soon they'll hang me in effigy or worse. I thought the Almighty understood."

"He does, He does, Everett. His ways are mysterious, but if He made a promise He'll keep it."

"But when? When and how?" Huston scowled.

"In His own good time, that's all I can say. Implore Him most humbly to enlighten you. He will . . . in His own good time."

"In the meantime what else can I do?"

"Pray to the Lord and venerate the Lord. One other thing."

"What?"

"Reassure your people that the day of entering the Godhead is drawing near irrespective of the actual modus operandi. Let them be ready . . . and tell them to keep their noses clean."

"Will they listen to me?"

"They will if you tell them to . . . or else."

"I see. Anything else?"

"Yes," there was a brief silence at the other end, and then Huston heard again Borgia's voice. "You should be more conscious of the extraordinary honor the Lord saw fit to bestow upon you. You and your entire country will become one with the Godhead. You have been singled out, wisely no doubt, because the Lord is always wise. But I can't hide from you my astonishment at this particular dispensation of the Lord. I would've thought had the Lord wished to confer this unique distinction on a people he would've chosen us Spaniards, because we stand closer to Him than any other people in Europe. Why has He passed us over in favor of a wild bunch of tobacco-chewing cowboys? His decision is divine law, but it defies our infantile human reason."

"It's a petty point," Huston remarked softly, "but in my country tobacco-chewing went out of fashion many years ago."

"Maybe so, maybe so," Borgia replied with verve. "But on the allegorical level my point still holds true."

"I admire the way you so easily shift from the factual to the allegorical and back. Surely it must've taken years of training." Huston's tones were as soft as before.

"It has taken no training at all," the answer burst out frighteningly. "I simply follow the commands of the Lord."

"I get it," Huston commented in a noncommittal tone.

"Remember this, my friend," Borgia went on. "Among the Catholic nations of Europe we are preeminent in religious spirit and devotion to the Lord. No other Catholic country comes up to our ankles even. Other Catholic countries in Europe and outside of it are either degenerate, or barbarian, or have taken such a potent dose of secularism that they are at present hopelessly losing their way in the maze of self-indulgence, corruption, and liberal teaching. But Spain is a rock and will never be swept away. Remember this, my son."

"Thank you for your encouraging words, Raoul. They really mean a great deal to me."

"You're welcome. I am ready to swear on the graves of all my ancestors that the day will come when you will be privy to every detail of the Lord's logistical operations. Be patient. In the meantime I'll pray for you."

"Thank you, and I hope the Almighty, in his infinite wisdom, omniscience, and all the rest, will be more receptive to your prayers than He has been to mine."

"Now, now," Borgia spoke like a kindly teacher to a straying pupil who nevertheless shows much promise, "there's no need of that, no need at all. Go in peace and follow the Lord."

/ / /

Two days later as they were leaving Waterloo after an early breakfast the secretaries briefed Huston on urgent business that had come up the day before and during the night.

"Am I not entitled to a vacation, a brief vacation free of paperwork?" he complained, making the most of it. "Everyone in Western Amernipp gets three or four weeks free away from all the hustle and bustle, and with pay too. But not Chief Justice; oh no, that wouldn't do, would it now? Wear down the old curmudgeon till he drops, then hurry to his funeral to see he's really dead. I know your game. Can't put one over on me."

"Scathing criticism by the Wyoming legislature of the way civil rights have been trampled underfoot, the Speaker of the House and the president of the senate holding a joint press conference in Cheyenne, and the disarray this caused in Washington merited your being informed," the political secretary announced stiffly.

"And broadsides from the Society of Friends against your administration, a barely veiled attack by the provincial of the Dominical Order on your character, and demonstrations in several Jewish communities were for me reason enough you should be told," the theological secretary reported unctuously.

"Yes, yes," Huston exclaimed, nodding repeatedly. "My thanks to both of you. Not to inform me would be dereliction of duty. These are grave matters. Thanks again, fellows!"

While the two young men were offering collateral information Huston could not help concluding that Fred, the polsec, would make an imposing state attorney, laying down the law, forgetting and forgiving nothing, while Larry, the theosec and the more jovial and voluble of the two, was surely bishop material. In fact Huston had heard through the grapevine that young Larry already looked upon himself as a bishop, a bishop without a see to be sure, but a bishop nevertheless, in his own eyes if in no one else's.

Matters at hand consumed time and necessitated messages and telegrams to numerous parties, among them Dr. Hertzfeld Chief Rabbi, Siegfried La Rochelle, head of the Ecumenical Council, the F.B.I., Secretary of Internal Security, and the current head of the C.I.A., the change in leadership in this organization being so frequent and regular that Huston could not keep track and was usually two or three names behind. La Rochelle with his usual frivolity had compared the steady ingress and egress at the C.I.A. to a cute eighteenth-century ballet-chantant in which young swans enter the lavish abode of a woman reputed to be beautiful and mysterious and leave in a hurry, each crediting her with a different but deadly blemish. La Rochelle had entitled his piece: "*Que cherches-tu chéri daus le chateau des pouries?*"

"Damn you, Siegfried, and your clever profligate jokes," Huston cried out to the consternation of his secretaries. "Damn you."

The latest business kept them busy till nearly noon, and when everything had been duly pigeonholed Huston leaned eagerly toward the driver and asked, "How much longer to the state line, Carl?"

"Twenty minutes or so."

"Good, I'd like to make St. Cloud by nightfall."

"No sweat, Chief Justice."

They lunched lavishly in Mankato where at the others' invitation Carl Hessler, the driver, told them about his army days, first in Italy with a small detachment of Rangers and then in the Balkans, in Spain, and finally under the guideon of a spearheading U.S. Army division landing in the Middle East.

"Yeah, the Arabs were different from our boys," he responded dutifully to a question. "When on the offensive and when things were going well for them, they had more zeal than anyone else. But on the defensive and things getting kinda dicey they withered on the vine."

"Tell us more about the engagements you were in, Master Sergeant," Huston begged him. Carl obliged and, hard-pressed, owned up that he ended the campaign against the Muslim armies with three purple hearts and the military cross. "That's just being at the right place at the right time," he added smiling. A few minutes later Carl volunteered a recollection of his own. "It was the very end of August of that year, and we were pinned down at Samarra. The third division was to come right behind us but, I guess, it had a change of heart. The generals decided to wait for forty-eight hours. Well, it was touch and go, and the Muslims outnumbered us ten to one. We sent frantic messages to whatever units we were guessing might be in the vicinity but nothing doing, and the Arabs thought they were on the offensive again. Nothing could stop them. And then out of the clear blue sky lo and behold Captain La Rochelle tears in with his tanks right behind the second and third Muslim line. He saved our hide. He'd gotten word the third division wasn't moving forward and put two and two together. Smart guy."

"Quite a war hero, that fella La Rochelle," Huston conceded with a forced smile.

"I don't know about that," Carl said quietly. "But I can tell ye he knew what he was doing, and that's more, much more than can be said about lots of 'em higher-ups."

An uneasy moment intervened. "Would any of you gentlemen care for more dessert?" Huston inquired with all the bonhomie he could muster. "No? In that case let's meet by the car in ten minutes."

Spread out on the soft seat of the limousine and flanked on all sides by softness and comfort unimaginable, Chief Justice was relaxing to the point of drowsiness. Then he got hold of himself, and his mind returned to the leisurely review of past events and their consequences, to reflection and planning uncircumscribed by a temporal frame, to ambitions burning his psyche like white heat, unfulfilled and perhaps never to be fulfilled. One of the most poignant disappointments of his tenure of office was Eastern Amernipp's unflinching refusal to join in the noblest of undertakings—merging with the deity, being raised to the status of angels and enjoying eternal bliss. Huston's henchmen had contacted Japanese deputies, members of the cabinet, high officials, but without even a ghost of a positive result. Eastern Amernippians had turned up their noses. They considered the entire venture to be a joke in the worst possible taste, a farce, a skit for the burlesque.

Undaunted, Huston stood his ground, suspecting most politicians to be either simpletons or crooks or a mixture of both. Shortly thereafter he dispatched a delegation to Tokyo made up of eminent theologians and church leaders representing different denominations and attaching Léger, Grister, and Pillows to it in the capacity of rainmakers and troubleshooters. Their Eastern Amernippian counterparts were highly placed keepers of the Shinto flame, Buddhist masters, world famous scholars of Japanese history, religion, and culture, and several distinguished Harvard and Oxford-trained Japanese Occidentalists, two of whom were converts to Christianity. The commission had gotten off to a good start. The Japanese listened attentively as the Americans expounded on the sanctification Western Amernipp received from God as a reward for stamping out vice—sanctification that would lead them to the heavens and that would lead the Japanese there too if only they joined forces with their Western brethren. Certain measures would have to be taken, of course, certain new laws promulgated to bring Eastern Amernipp closer to God, but this could be easily accomplished, the Americans felt, and the rewards surpassed the wildest dreams of any Japanese.

With infinite patience and courtesy the hosts reminded their opposite numbers of the essence of Japan's three major religions, Shinto, the different branches of Buddhism, Confucianism and Neo-Confucianism; of the three compilations of beliefs and customs, the *Kojiki*, the *Nihongi*, and the *Yengishiki*; of the final goal of the religious man under Buddhist dispensation, which was escape from existence into blissful non-existence, nirvana; of the system of ethical teaching, which was the cornerstone of Confucianism with its stress on *jen*, translated roughly as sympathy, and on avoidance of extremes. The Japanese religious traditions, they went on, emphasized internal development of the individual in this lifetime, a steady attempt at moral self-improvement benefiting not only any given individual but the human race as a whole and a steady search for further knowledge and a better social order. "This being so," chairperson of the Japanese delegation resumed, "there is no provision in our faiths and cults for ascensions into heaven, because every man or woman carries the embryo of heaven within himself or herself, and it is his or her responsibility to make it bloom. The idea of the entire Eastern Amernippian nation being raised on high by the Christian God and deposited in a Christian Paradise strikes us as most bizarre, grotesque in fact."

"It is the command of the Almighty God!" Grister, leaning forward, shouted defiantly at the Japanese. "Command of the Almighty God received by Chief Justice Huston, head of Western Amernipp."

"Did anyone else in Western Amernipp receive a similar intimation?" the Japanese chairperson inquired.

"No, and there was no need to." Grister was brushing this line of questioning aside. "Chief Justice is God's anointed, and God communicates with us through his servant, the head and ruler of Western Amernipp."

"All right," another member of the Japanese delegation spoke up. "How is this entry into heaven to be effected? Will the population be put to death and then miraculously revived and transported to higher regions to enjoy eternal bliss on the right side of the Lord?"

"The actual manner according to which God's pledge will be redeemed is a closely guarded secret shared only by the Almighty and Chief Justice," Grister replied with difficulty, holding his temper in check.

"This is plain wrong," another Japanese joined in. "The people of Western Amernipp have the right to know."

"If we in Eastern Amernipp agree to your proposal, we'd want to know every detail of this intriguing journey, which calls to mind science fiction fantasies so much in fashion at the beginning of the twenty-first century."

Léger preempted Grister and, bowing low to the Japanese, spoke in a silky tone. "Let me assure my compatriots of Eastern Amernipp that everything is under control. The Almighty has outlined several options and these are being carefully studied. Very soon the Almighty will make the final decision and Chief Justice, better known as Savior of the Country, will communicate this decision to the citizenry. Everyone will be fully informed. I am sure you are fully aware that in Western Amernipp the government has no secrets from the people."

The Japanese on the other side of the table formed a long row of impassive faces, well-bred reserve and Oriental inscrutability acting in unison as two mentors of their deportment.

"That merging with the Godhead," one of the Christian Occidentalists shot at the visitors, "will it take place before Second Coming, Resurrection of the Body, and Last Judgment, or after?"

The Americans were divided and different answers were awkwardly advanced. Then Grister broke in. "What does it matter when our union with the Godhead will happen? The Almighty decides, He alone, and what He does is for the good of His children. I can only tell you we will be united with the Godhead very soon, and if you guys ever see the light, you too will be on the receiving line."

"I am merely asking because Christian theology contains definite stages in the life of the soul from the moment it is released from the body until Last Judgment." The same Occidentalist pressed the point.

"You're splitting hairs. Questions of this kind are totally irrelevant!" Grister shouted, looking daggers.

"On the contrary, they are highly relevant." The words were uttered by an elderly gentleman immaculately and formally dressed playing with a statuette of Ferdinand and Isabella being addressed by Christopher Columbus. "I find it disquieting that you know next to nothing about the logistics of this glorious event and that you are so poorly informed about the tenets of Christian theology."

"You watch it!" Grister snarled. "You watch it!"

"This is the last thing I intend to do," the same gentleman continued. "It is very unlikely that we on this side of the table will join with you in this, this . . . " He left the sentence unfinished. "But as your compatriots we wish to warn you. Unless this venture is a hoax to milk Hollywood and tabloid press—which may very well be the case—what proof do you actually have of God's promise to elevate the entire Western Amernippian nation to some divine or angelic level? Babblings of a choleric old man suffering from delusions?"

"How dare you! *How dare you!*" Grister had lost all self-control and was hollering wildly at the Japanese, his knees already on top of the table, sending a signal he would leap fighting onto the other side where the enemy was entrenched. Léger and Pillows pulled him down and made him sit up. Another member of the Japanese delegation spoke to the same topic but from a slightly different angle.

"I would like to know whether your Chief Justice has a history of mental illness. In addition to being a professor of comparative literature I am also an MD. The question is important. We Eastern Amernippians should know where we stand."

Barely were these words out of the speaker's mouth before Grister, on his feet again, was shaking his fist at the Japanese shouting, "You bastard! You are all bastards, good for nothing! You should be fried in oil. Ignorant bastards, nothing more!"

With difficulty Léger and Pillows pulled him down and held him pinioned. Phineas covered his mouth with his hand and growled in his ear, "Not another word, Hom, not another word, or else."

Casting a searching look at his colleagues sitting to the right and to the left of him, the Japanese chairperson stood to his feet and brushed a bit of fluff off his lapels. "Because of the unusual nature of today's meeting," his voice was firm and neutral, "I am ordering a twenty-four-hour recess in our proceedings. Please adjust your watches. We shall meet right here in exactly twenty-four hours. Hopefully this recess will allow our American compatriots to regain their composure and learn better manners. I thank you all."

Huston remembered every word, every syllable of what had been said, very distinctly. He digested and redigested it. He practically knew the entire proceeding by heart having heard it from Hom and Phin and Gan, and from the others. In addition he had read and reread the transcript more times he could count. And now as he was sitting amidst softness itself those recollections came rushing into his mind, overwhelming it and making it clear that his reliving them once more was his bounden duty, no excuses accepted. Huston gloried in his friends' bold undertaking and was not in the least angry with Hom for having lost his temper. Hom was acting as a friend, and after all what were friends for? "The Nips were asking for it, and they got their comeuppance," he muttered to himself. Immediately an irrepressible conviction wrapped itself around his brain that Eastern Amernipp was at bottom a barbarous country, something like England under Elizabeth I, and that the best way to deal with it was to kick it hard in the ass. The meetings that took place after the punitive recess were inconclusive and often counter-productive, including Hom's last stand. Huston shed a quiet tear when in his mind's eye he saw his friend erect and dignified calling to the Japanese delegation:

Jesus Christ is come to save ye
Jesus Christ is here to meet ye
He will raise ye up on high
To the meadow where angels lie
Waiting for the trumpet call
He will save you one and all
Da capo.

Sadly the Japanese were not in the least moved and questions asked of the Americans were the same old questions, poisoned by disrespect toward the Savior of the Country and criminal belittlement of Western

Amernipp as New Jerusalem. Following the last meeting of the commission the two sides had bidden each other farewell with icy politeness.

As they were passing through one small town after another in southern Minnesota, Huston called to mind the last act of this grotesque drama. He had had one last card to play—again his recollections were vivid and precise to an unusual degree—an eyeball-to-eyeball meeting with the emperor who could override the cabinet and parliament by dint of his prestige and not because of a constitutional provision. Huston had consulted with La Rochelle whom he found, to his great surprise, to be very courteous and helpful. "These days," the National Security Advisor was saying, "the emperor is no more than a figurehead, and he does what the prime minister tells him to do. Also you have to bear in mind that he is very old and senile and one hundred percent deaf. It would be more politic to sway the PM to your side. He could then persuade the old boy."

"Impossible. We have approached the PM, and he showed us the door."

"I see. Then best of luck with the old boy and keep things simple. He is very religious, you know, in the old Shinto way, and he might be receptive to a spiritual message. Also, remember, Ev, that unlike some members of the royal family this emperor has never leaned toward Christianity."

"This is my call then," Huston exclaimed. "But he's still brainy enough to beat the Russian ambassador at chess, nine to one I hear."

La Rochelle smiled indulgently. "Everyone in the diplomatic community knows what's going on. The canny Wyacheslav wants to ingratiate himself with the old boy, so he persistently allows himself to be beaten. He was the world champion a few years back, you know, so no one is fooled except the old boy himself. One has to give old Vinogradov credit; he never misses a trick."

"Are the Russkies on the rise again?" Huston asked with alarm in his voice.

"Not in the least. It's all about trade agreements. Import, export, and fishing rights. Nothing to worry about, Ev."

"I am relieved. Thank you for all your help, Siegfried."

"You're welcome and good luck with the old boy."

Huston remembered very clearly that the day before flying to

Tokyo he had spent mostly in prayer. And he remembered with clarity, soon turning into disgust, what had happened subsequently. He and the emperor spent four long hours in the latter's private quarters, each man accompanied by his interpreter only. As Huston was calling back to mind the painful scene, his repugnance of everything Oriental under the sun mounted and in a matter of seconds grew into a terrible hatred—hatred of the emperor and his family, hatred of the Japanese nation, hatred of the entire yellow race, hatred of anybody who was not white, an Anglo-Saxon, and a Protestant, hatred of spicks, wogs, wops, micks, gooks, kikes, and the rest of the scum.

His opening gambit had been a statement of moderate length emphasizing the value of spirituality in private and public life, and when it had been translated and duly inscribed on tablets the emperor nodded and replied with a statement of his own calling on all religions to work together for the benefit of the human race. Charitable institutions, schools, and universities were foremost in his mind, he said, and then, grasping Huston's hand, he said it again. The next half hour was filled with banalities of every conceivable ilk on the subject of charity and faith, and Huston was ready to swear on a stack of Bibles that the hereditary ruler of Eastern Amernipp was quoting from an assortment of state documents drafted for him by politicos intent on enhancing his international prestige without giving him an iota of real power. Huston waited and listened patiently and then in a flash got down to brass tacks.

"Western Amernipp has been singled out by the Almighty and will enter the Godhead," he began. "This is our reward for stamping out vice and creating New Jerusalem on the North American continent."

"Excellent, excellent," the son of the gods commented.

"Western Amernipp and Eastern Amernipp are one," Everett Zacharias continued without pausing even for a second and eliciting no response from his host. "We are brothers."

"To be sure, to be sure we are brothers," the most exalted personage piped up.

"What I am proposing is inspired by brotherly love of the kind never recorded on the parchment of time."

"Yes, yes, brotherly love," the son of heaven joined in delightedly.

"Your Majesty, we want Eastern Amernipp to unite with us on this heavenly journey so that our entire country, Eastern Amernipp and Western Amernipp acting as one, will enter God's dominion and enjoy eternal bliss." Then he began to explain in general terms the nature of the sacred voyage ordained by God Almighty and the extraordinary benefits accruing to the Eastern Amernippians who, like their brethren the Western Amernippians, had been singled out by the Lord. When he turned his head and glanced at the wrinkled and furrowed countenance of the Son of Heaven, it displayed puzzlement and doubt while his interpreter was frantically filling out the tablets. "Jesus Christ is calling to all of us, for He is the Savior and Redeemer of the entire human race," Huston was shouting, "and the Almighty will be raising our country on high!" As he went on he watched his host closely, and he noticed a beatific smile taking shape and lightening his face from ear to ear.

"Brotherly love!" the emperor cried out, elated, "brotherly love! We must sign a pact you and I to help those in distress in your province and in mine. We don't pay our debt to charity. We don't do enough." His eyes were sparkling, and his features glistened with joy. All of a sudden he looked younger by many years, the burden of office no longer weighing him down, his worries dispelled, disappointments all but forgotten. He jumped up from his seat, threw his arms high in the air, and cried out in that high-pitched voice of his, "Brotherly love, brotherly love now and forever."

It was at this point, Huston now recalled with uncanny precision, that his heart had begun to sink.

Presently they were dashing past Hutchinson, and Huston made up his mind not to give the imperial visit another thought. Much better that way, he gave a stern piece of advice to himself. Upon returning from Tokyo he gave an account of what had happened to Phineas Léger, and his learned friend was at his most philosophical.

"You win a few and you lose a few," he counseled. "This happens to all of us. Forget about Eastern Amernipp. It doesn't deserve your good will anyway. Forget it and move on."

"Easier said than done," he told Phineas, but he tried to follow his advice.

Carl Hessler, the driver, and the two secretaries were in touch by phone with Huston's hosts at St. Cloud, exchanging information. Huston was looking forward to staying there for two nights and touching base with old friends and associates. In fact, this town, which had witnessed the early realizations of his theocratic vision was filled for him with memories that were precious and intimate. They involved both comrades-in-arms in whose vocabulary the word "impossible" simply did not exist and several women who played a role in the various stages of his life. It was all ancient history, of course, very ancient history, but this did not diminish the importance of St. Cloud, which was for him a haven and a memory bank. Huston began to relax again to the point of drowsiness, and again he pinched himself, regaining his earlier alertness.

There was one area of national life that, for reasons that were multiple and complicated, had received less attention from him than it deserved, as head of state, and also from his lieutenants, the scientific community. When the theocratic government was first being established six years earlier, scientists and technocrats were among the brightest lights of the militant avant-garde that tore down the old liberal and democratic fabric and imposed religion and the rule of clerics as a *sine qua non* of national life. It was largely due to the efforts of scientists and technocrats that the U.S. Constitution of 1787 had been at first excoriated, then nullified, and finally burnt to ashes in public squares all over the country, the citizenry being urged to bring with them all the copies of the old rag they could find to the public burning, the government printing office obligingly churning out additional copies to add fanfare to the solemn patriotic event. In this manner things continued for close to three years, and Huston became thoroughly used to looking at scientists and technocrats as his trusty troops. They had proved themselves.

When the Scientific and Technocratic Association was formed, its members could be counted among the best brains in the country and the most loyal of subjects. And then two years ago chinks began to break out in the armor of that much revered institution. First came demands for higher salaries and new fringe benefits exceeding the expectations of even the most favored highgovies. Ganymede Pillows took it upon himself to speak to the association about fiscal responsibility and was booed. Other high government officials followed suit and met with the same contemptuous reception.

Finally Huston betook himself to the grand offices of the association to get things straightened once and for all and extract a pledge of reasonable behavior on the part of its members. He was interrupted as soon as he opened his mouth, jeered at, and repeatedly shouted down.

The spokesmen for this monolithic body roared their assessment of the shamefully unjust situation at him and did not stop. Soon only their roar could be heard, and Huston gave up any attempt to speak. After an hour the spokesmen changed course and to the vigorous applause of the crowd read the list of their demands, which was not subject to discussion but to approval only. It included much higher salaries, free highgov education for their children, housing allowances, discounts on numerous luxury goods they wanted to purchase, immunity from investigation by the Sex and the Faith Police, and creation of luxurious rest-and-recreation centers within the confines of Amernipp and abroad for the exclusive use of scientists and technocrats.

Numerous members of these two professions worked for the government and many others for private firms contracting out to it, the economic life of Western Amernipp being a maze of private and governmental initiatives, interconnecting, overlapping, working in unison, and shoring up one another—a maze that few could understand but which those in the know, like Ganymede Pillows, pronounced the most enlightened and efficacious form of capitalism known to man under which maximum of private enterprise was benefiting from governmental oversight, which in turn was guided and stimulated by this very enterprise. The thriving economy of Western Amernipp depended on the labors of scientists and technocrats now driving a hard bargain, and they knew that their concerted counteraction would drive the country into a recession, into dramatically rising unemployment, into a depression even. The government would not brook it, and the masters of the slide-rule and of the most sophisticated instruments in existence knew it and played their card to the hilt.

As all these circumstances and events were slowly parading inside his brain, Huston became acutely conscious of a gnawing pain in his left side. "Yes," he whispered to himself, "these are stabbing memories." One was better off without them, but he could not banish the flow of piercing images. He asked for a glass of water and readjusted his body on the seat. What happened in the end—he was again reliving the past—was hardly creditable to the government: a compromise was reached shamelessly favoring the scientists and the technocrats in exchange for their solemn promise to keep the wheels of the Western Amernippian economy running full tilt.

Since that consequential encounter two years ago—Huston was back on track recalling every detail—the community of monetarily aggressive experts and specialists had been fast becoming a state within the state, not even bothering to pay lip service to the principles of Chief Justice's theocracy under which the country now lived and prospered. The community's newspaper, *The Scientific and Technocratic Times,* read by a substantial portion of the nation's intelligentsia, printed skits of religious leaders and of churches and devoted several issues to controversies between science and religion, going back to Galileo and giving full coverage to Charles Darwin, Thomas Huxley, and other courageous spirits fighting bigoted and ignorant clerics invariably painted as villains of the piece.

Confidential agents reported to Huston on the lamentably low church attendance in communities heavily inhabited by scientists and technocrats and on their almost unanimous non-participation in religious activities. Members of these two fraternities and sororities could no longer be touched by the Sex and the Faith Police and they were running amok. Huston had been profoundly shocked—he again vividly remembered—by the rank picture of godless and criminal secularism, but at the same time he was hard put to do anything about it. Phin and Gan advised that the matter should be handled with kid gloves, and even the usually combative Hom tended to agree.

All three were apprehensive about upsetting the applecart, and so was Huston, although he kept his cards close to his chest. "And yet, something's got to be done about it. Lord knows it's been dragging on for nearly three years," he spoke to himself in an undertone. "The Union is in jeopardy, and both the science boys and the techno boys must be whipped into shape. The present situation is intolerable." He finished addressing himself, and henceforth his plans and resolutions cut across the inside of his head mutely leaving a thick trail of collateral joys and regrets, like an ornate float in a grand parade that leaves some folks ecstatic and others drooping as it passes. "Right, something must be done," he thought with emphasis. Then he recalled a conversation he had had with La Rochelle some three years before, when the science-technocracy business was just surfacing. He had expressed some apprehension to Siegfried of the scientific ideology posing a danger to the state, and the National Security Advisor laughed in his face.

"Set your heart at rest, Everett. The great majority of those well-heeled boys and girls have no ideology of any kind. They probably don't even know what the word 'ideology' signifies. In addition, they have no sense of ethics, no morality, no honesty. They are after lucre, pure and simple, and after building up their profession because with it comes money and power." Huston thought at the time La Rochelle's words were unduly harsh and said so. Siegfried laughed again. "Your run-of-the-mill scientist will do anything, including murder, for a new lab or a new superatomizer. If those guys had lived in the last century, why, they would've been happy working for Hitler, Stalin, Mao Tse-tung, anyone fitting them out with well-equipped berths and giving them all the toys they need."

Reviewing the situation in the privacy of his limousine Huston concluded that Siegfried had been right. At no time had scientists-cum-technocrats posed the slightest threat to the state, at no time had they joined the scattered liberals in protest, at no time had they championed a democratic cause. They had been conformists par excellence, apolitical, a powerful silent minority living in their own world, now and then coming to the aid of the state in tracing those lost souls that hankered after the Constitution of 1787, after civil rights, after free elections and the democratically constituted government. So far so good, Huston concluded, but their secularism run wild was a public disgrace. They would have to be chastened—chastened and rehabilitated. And then a thought struck him that perhaps the Almighty's silence about the actual manner in which Western Amernipp would be lifted up and merged with the Godhead was due to his, Everett Zacharias Huston's, remissness in stamping out all the vice in his country. "It isn't You, oh Lord, who has let me down," he cried inwardly. "It is I who let You down."

He put the scientific community at the top of his agenda and reviewed the matter of presidential, senatorial, and congressional elections that he now considered a senseless anachronism. He decided on the spot that from now on members of the U.S. Senate and of the U.S. House of Representatives would be appointed by him personally, and presidential elections would simply be scrapped. Jack Woods could return to his native Georgia and keep bees. He, Everett Zacharias Huston, was head of state and needed no figurehead looking over his shoulder or cooling his heels in the wings. 2084, he decided, would be the year of streamlining, of tightening the reins.

A ray of certainty shot up his body scourging all speculation and doubt, and with tears in his eyes he thanked the Almighty for His latest epiphany. He knew now that the Lord would convey to him the detailed scenario of Western Amernipp's entry into heaven as soon as he had put the house in order. Certainty buoyed him up and swelled his breast, and he felt younger by many a year. One other thing had to be attended to: Siegfried La Rochelle was a thorn in his side and would have to step down. His monumental diplomatic labors had been accomplished and now any eager State Department Jack or Jill would be able to conduct the country's foreign policy. On July 4, 2084, he would make a number of very important announcements to the nation, and tucked in among them would be the resignation or dismissal of Siegfried La Rochelle.

Sliding sheets of snow on both sides of the road reflected the moon in the darkness of the evening, and the large luminous orbs hanging high over the median—bits of old-fashioned theatrical scenery—held his attention, when Huston heard Carl's cheerful voice resonating the length and width of the car.

"Chief Justice, we are now crossing the city limits of St. Cloud."

"Thank you, Carl. It was a good run," Huston said, and his face brightened again.

book
three

Chapter 1

Unus Contra Omnes

Strictly speaking, there is no spring in Wyoming. Snowfalls that started in the preceding August or September did not relent in January or February anymore than in the succeeding months, and the March equinox is a mark as valid as the date forged on an ancient Egyptian tomb by an archeologist hard on his luck and in need of buckets of dough to heal a very personal matter involving a ravishing member of the opposite sex. Snow keeps falling in April and May, causing no eyebrows to be raised in June and July, and terms like very early winter, early mid-winter, late mid-winter, very late mid-winter, very late and early winter, and their variants are cavalierly employed by those who as children had been instructed in the art of dividing, subdividing, and categorizing the outside world without the slightest clue as to what made it tick and what temporal frames it embodied. A couple of old-timers had been in the habit of opining that Wyoming winters breed a better relation between man and nature than winter in those places where seasons rise and fall with the regularity of square dancers changing places, because man is exposed for eight or nine months to the same rhythm of nature, is surrounded by the same natural forces, interacts with them, builds his resistance to them, but also comes to know them in a manner that engages both his conscious and subconscious mind, making him nature's debtor and half-brother.

In Wyoming, the same old-timers were overheard opining that here granddaddy Jean-Jacques' war cry came to fruition more sweepingly than in any other spot on the face of the planet. In the Equality State man is closer to nature than in any other part of Western Amernipp, and there is a bond between the two that knows no equal. A Wyomingite treasures his independence like his last silver dollar, but the snow and the mountains, an abundance of the freshest air in the universe, the craggy slopes, and the vast open spaces shape him subtly and indelibly without in the least encroaching on his freedom.

It was the beginning of March, and Nathan Chadwick had just finished two long radio consultations with fellow democratic activists in Montana and the Dakotas, the frequencies being changed constantly so as to escape governmental surveillance. Leaning back in the chair in his study in Cheyenne he reflected that most of his coworkers, as well as sympathizers in western and non-western states, urged him to organize industrial strikes, marches, sit-ins, and other forms of organized protest. In the last several months the Wyoming legislature had boldly taken the government to task citing numerous cases of civil rights violations, and "Freedom or Tyranny," a week-long conference hosted by the Center for Democratic West in the middle of February, had attracted twice as many participants as had been anticipated, many of them coming to Cheyenne from faraway states—Connecticut and Vermont, Maine and Michigan, Alabama and Mississippi.

By an overwhelming majority the candidates had passed a resolution calling on the Center to mobilize supporters nationwide to exert maximum pressure on the government to shame it into reforming its ways and redeeming itself morally. An angry chorus had roared in Nathan's ear that the mood of the country was drastically changing, that desertions from Huston's ranks were on the rise, and that lowgovies ideologically united and disciplined as never before were waiting for a signal from him, Nathan, before bursting into an armed offensive, no-holds-barred, against Chief Justice and his minions.

"We are sitting on a powder keg," friends were telling Nathan. "Let's see to it that when it explodes it takes with it the other side, not us. How long can we wait?" Nathan was listening with both ears to the advice he was getting and to the news from Washington. When Huston had been handed the third protest from the Wyoming legislature he agreed to meet with a delegation, and if on schedule the meeting would take place within twenty-four hours. Nathan was not exactly pinning his hopes on this meeting, but he thought it could be a start. In the past

Huston had always defended his position by asserting that carrying out divine orders and bringing the country closer to God easily outranked all this "civil rights and secular justice nonsense," as he put it. If only he, Huston, could be convinced that the authority of religion would remain undiminished in Western Amernipp while modest steps would be taken toward equality before the law, free elections, and the restoration of the Bill of Rights, a peaceful evolutionary path could be found out of the present deadlock.

"If only Huston shows a modicum of good faith and a glimmer of understanding," Nathan kept repeating to himself, "the revolution may be avoided." In a day or two at the latest he would know what precisely transpired in Washington at Huston's meeting with the Wyoming parliamentary delegation, and this might very well decide the future course of events. Nathan understood to the fullest that the day of armed intervention might be fast approaching, but he was determined to exhaust all the possibilities of a peaceful settlement, however incomplete or slow moving.

Earlier in the day his spirits were dampened by the news of a showdown between Huston and his two well-known opponents, the general secretary of the Society of Friends and the provincial of the Dominical Order, which had taken place the day before and in the course of which Chief Justice threatened the two men with imprisonment unless they renounced what he called their insurgent speeches and deeds. Both men said they would not, and for the time being the matter was in limbo, but not likely to remain there for much longer. Nathan clenched his fists, and his thoughts dashed to the valiant men and women of the Wyoming parliamentary delegation who very soon would be facing the wild beast in his lair. "This may very well be a last-ditch attempt," he mused. Then he straightened himself up and hollered clear across his study, "Our hopes and prayers go with you, guys!"

/   /   /

"Come on in, come on in," Huston rapped out with a sneering laugh as a handful of visitors stood quietly in the doorway waiting for a welcoming gesture. "Delegation from the legislature of the great state of Wyoming?" he inquired, nodding vigorously before anyone had the time to answer. "How was your trip?"

"Fine, Chief Justice, just fine," the tall middle-aged woman in front whom Huston took to be the leader, or at least one of the leaders, of the group replied in a no-nonsense voice.

"Why, this must be Helen Markham," Huston piped on delightedly. "We met many years ago, but I never forget an intelligent face. A pharmacist in Rock Springs, if I am not mistaken?"

"That's right, the same," Helen Markham answered curtly, making it transparently clear she considered small talk an utter waste of time.

Huston shook hands with every member of the delegation and heartily bid all of them to sit down. "We have things to go over that are more serious than life itself, but before we begin I wanna be certain each of ye is comfortable."

"Snug as a bug," somebody said, and the others assured the host they were indeed very comfortable.

"My first task," Huston began on an earnest note, "is to make sure you understand I am a teacher first and chief executive and head of state miles later. My job is to see to it that you grasp what is essential and let what is inessential fall by the wayside."

The only other woman in the delegation, who identified herself as Fodora Calico, G.P. practicing in Douglas, spoke up. "I rather surmise your definition of what is essential and inessential and ours are worlds apart. But go on, Chief Justice."

"They needn't be . . . they needn't be," Huston rasped. "If only ye folks could see the light."

"We are listening," the doctor spoke firmly, her smile adding just a touch of warmth to the dialogue. "Proceed."

"Ya gotta understand Western Amernipp climbed as high on God's own totem pole as is allowed, and before too long the Almighty will reward us. We'll be transported to heaven; we shall be angels savoring eternal bliss."

"Why have eighteen citizens of Wyoming been thrown in jail for taking part in a peaceful demonstration?" Helen asked.

"And why is your band of rogues conducting illegal searches and seizures in private homes?" Fodora followed suit.

"To keep ye out of trouble, friends. Ye know full well the old liberal, democratic straw man was burnt to ashes years ago, and there ain't a trace left. Come to your senses, join our side, which is the Lord's side 'cause the Lord don't hold with liberal politics and democracy."

"We live in a tyrannical police state, Chief Justice, and it's your doing. One day you'll have to answer to a real court of law." The words came from a thin man with graying hair sporting a neckcloth.

"Oh." Huston fashioned both his hands into a sign of amused contempt. Then his face lit up. "Why it's Tom . . .Tom Hicks the rancher. You have a nice spread north of Casper, Tom. Long time no see."

"That's right."

"Well what are your plans, friends?" Huston was again addressing the entire delegation.

"We want to return this country to what it once was. We want to return it to the Constitution of 1787. We shall fight for free elections, for the Bill of Rights, for equality before the law." Helen's voice was level and controlled.

"Is this your last word? Maybe you'll change your minds?"

"Not a chance in a million," Fodora said showing little emotion.

"You leave me no option," Huston made every attempt to sound courteous and understanding. "You made your bed, and now you have to sleep in it. I follow the Lord, and what the Lord commands is done. This script could've had a different ending. But you, folks, have no respect for the Lord."

/ / /

The red telephone grotesquely shaped like a small boat on a stormy sea began to emit its well-known grinding bawl on La Rochelle's desk, one second an electric drill inching through a cement floor and the next two sterns furiously rubbing against each other at the mooring sight battling for a cable or a line. Red telephones used exclusively for Chief Justice's direct communication with members of the cabinet had been constructed to his exact specifications, with Chief Justice examining and approving each detail. La Rochelle answered the phone on the third bawl, unwilling to appear too eager.

"Siegfried, what the hell's going on with the Canucks?" He heard Huston's furious voice.

"What d'you mean, Everett?"

"He's asking me what I mean! How d'you like 'em apples?" Huston roared again. "Every two-bit politician in that benighted country is talking against us, and the prime minister's leading the charge.

Canadians are parading up and down main streets shouting anti-American slogans, and Beau Merveille, good ol' Beau, our man in Ottawa's been pelted with rotten eggs and rat excrement."

"I know, and the reports I get are more comprehensive than yours."

"Well what is the reason? What has unleashed those SOBs?"

"I have to backtrack to make it clear to you. First I'll explain, and then you can ask questions."

Huston grunted a reluctant consent.

"Do you remember those conversations about international trade we had three, four months ago?" La Rochelle began.

"Sure do."

"Well, Canadians had their eye on several southeastern Asian markets—high tech, software, but also agricultural machines. This goes back at least six or eight months. It was a cinch, and they were counting on it. Big, big orders. But we stepped in and underbid them. Those markets became our markets, and the Canadians were left holding absolutely nothing. You recall at the time I strongly opposed us competing with the Canadians on that turf, but you overruled me. That idiot friend of yours in commerce told you a bunch of crap and you believed him."

"He's a highly respected expert on international trade," Huston grunted again.

"In theological circles maybe, but not on Wall Street."

"There you go again," Huston grunted with even greater vigor.

"That underbidding operation was a fiasco from the word go. The private sector demanded compensation from the government because they had to lower their prices, so we made very few bucks. In some cases we couldn't deliver on time, and this riled the Asians to no end. In fact some governments and private concerns in Southeast Asia went back to the Canadians, over our strenuous opposition of course, and they told us to stick our opposition up our own smelly rear ends. At one go we gave our own big business a black eye, we lost face in Southeast Asia, and we antagonized the neighbors to the north, all this because one Everett Zacharias Huston wanted to play the part of Napoleon of international trade, about which he knows as much as a retarded skunk does about post-Wagnerian opera."

"Are you through?" Huston shouted. "Are you through?"

"Far from it. There have been other recent occasions when we underbid the Canadians for no reason at all except to make you feel important. Remember, our policy should never be to conquer or dominate the entire world. Other countries have the right to success and great national wealth just as we do. At different times because of your untamed vanity we insulted and turned old friends into enemies: Australians, New Zealanders, Brits, Russians and others. Your intrusions into foreign policy and international trade and finance have always been a disaster. If you have any love for your country keep your cotton-pickin' fingers out of international politics. Pray to whatever deity, Christian, pre-Christian, crypto-Christian or other will listen to you, though I very much doubt whether any self-respecting one would sink so low as to listen to you, let alone answer your prayers."

"You lowdown Kraut. There'll be no room for you on the shining ferry."

"The ferry, oh yes. Are we going fishing?"

"You bastard!" Huston shouted.

"One more thing: our relations with Canada need to be normalized. Tell Ambassador Merveille to call me within the hour. I am going to handle it personally, and you will not, I repeat, *will not* interfere. We'll make modest concessions to the Canadians in the domain of foreign trade. They are entitled to it after the dance we led them. Also I'll be talking to the Russians, the Brits, the Australians, and the New Zealanders. Again holes have to be plugged, and I'll handle it personally. Not a peep out of you. Understood!?"

He heard Huston's tense voice. "Beau will call you within the hour." Then one expletive after another punctuating the recurrent phrase, "You bastard, you bastard!"

Siegfried replaced the receiver and dialed the high security number. He gave instructions hastily in a firm official voice. "This is Dr. La Rochelle, National Security Advisor. Please connect me with this number in the imperial palace in Tokyo." He gave the number very distinctly and then repeated it. "Highest priority, no recording to be made, secret official business, and I need a scrambler." Several seconds later he heard Sayko's voice.

"How are you, darling?" he asked.

"Very lonely without you, but your letters came. Small consolation." She was mincing her words.

"Sayko, things are progressing very satisfactorily at this end. My attorneys tell me we'll makc the date for the final decree we were hoping for, obstacles are being removed one by one, and we can be married as per schedule."

"That's wonderful, Siegie, truly wonderful," she chirped in. "Grandmother, the empress, I mean, is being very helpful."

"Bless her diamond-studded imperial corset."

"What did you say, Siegie? I didn't quite grasp the meaning."

"Nothing of importance. Anyway, things are moving on and the end's in sight."

"Are you still sleeping with the Kentucky bitch?" Sayko asked, her voice now sounding very serious, very concerned.

"No, of course not. How could I?"

"I would be absolutely furious if you did. But she is still living in your house?"

"Actually, Sayko, it's our house, hers and mine. But we occupy separate bedrooms and have very little to do with each other otherwise."

"But she is still around, cooking your meals, pouring you a drink after your official duties have ended," Sayko went on with fuming insistence.

"No, she is not much around."

"Liar! I can always tell when you lie because your eyelids move sideways."

"And do they move that way now?"

"Of course."

"Dearest love, listen to me. In a few weeks Millicent will be moving out for good. She'll be rejoining her family in Kentucky. I'll probably never see her again, and—"

"Oh yes, I remember now," Sayko interrupted, less serious now, "the family's in the liquor business . . ."

"Something of the sort."

"And you're not chasing other women around Washington?"

"Of course not. How could I? There's only one woman in my life—the divine Princess Sayko—and I have the good fortune to be speaking to her now."

"I wish I could believe all that malarkey."

"You must believe it. It's the truth."

"Listen to me, Siegie, because I am absolutely dead serious. I expect you to be faithful to me now and in the future. If you're not, I don't know yet what I shall do, but it will be the terror of the whole world, the living terror that passes all reason and imagination."

"I am faithful to you because I love you, Sayko. How about a little trust?"

"Do you think you deserve it?"

"Of course I do."

"Hmm, hmm, hmm . . ." Sayko refused to commit her thoughts to words. Instead she began to hum a tune from a recent and well received musical. "When are you going to pay a visit?"

"Not this coming weekend, but the one after. I'll come on Friday evening and stay through Sunday."

"Very good," she replied with all the command of a first-rate CEO. "The news about the divorce is good too. I think it's time you were introduced to the empress."

"It will be a great honor, I'm sure," Siegfried mumbled, taken aback.

"I'll make all the arrangements and you will, of course, be on your best behavior. Till the weekend after then."

"Till then, dearest." Siegfried was anxiously waiting for another word from Sayko. But the line went dead.

/   /   /

Leaning over his desk, Nathan Chadwick caught sight of the two transparent buttons on his receiving-transmitting radio set in the corner light up and block letters MIC formed themselves on the small screen next to the power and tuning knobs. He walked over to the set, pressed the reception handle, and a familiar voice came through.

"Nathan, this is Kevin. We have an eighty second corridor. The delegation from the Wyoming legislature which met with Huston this morning was arrested on his orders an hour ago. All seven are now in D.C. Detention Center 11, designated for housing those guilty of serious crimes against the state. Our contacts in the criminal division tell us the charge will probably be sedition. We are rounding up legal defense, and next of kin are being notified."

"Did Huston offer an explanation?"

"None," Kevin snarled. "Visitation rights have been suspended. For all practical purposes the seven are held incommunicado. We'll keep you posted, and you take care of the rest."

"Right, Kevin. Does Beta Gamma code remain in force this week?"

"It does. We have to end now. Good luck, Nathan."

"Look after yourself, Kevin."

"Over and out."

Nathan walked back to his desk, sat down behind it, and remained absolutely still for a good ten minutes without so much as moving a muscle. He had been surprised by Huston's move not because he had credited him with higher ethical standards but because he had expected more criminal subtlety from Chief Justice at this particular juncture—more duplicity, more resourceful Machiavellianism. He had expected him to try to divide and rule, or to set one faction against another, to try bribery or even intimidation, but not to clap unceremoniously in jail those who had called on him with grievances and complaints.

However, this was what happened, and the road of negotiations was no longer open. Nathan had feared that the moment would come when only armed insurgence could restore a democratic government to Western Amernipp and everything that went with it hearkening back to the U.S. Constitution of 1787. And now that moment had come. Further maneuvering was bound to be a waste of time, and selection of the most effective strategy and of the most effective tactics was what really mattered. There would be bloodshed, of course, but the time for passive resistance and reasoned arguments had long passed.

In the next forty-eight hours Nathan met with the executive council of the Center for Democratic West, with the leaders of the Wyoming legislature, with the governor of Wyoming, and with a number of key supporters who lived in Cheyenne or traveled to it from towns in Wyoming and surrounding states. Furthermore he traveled to Nebraska, Idaho, and Montana to plan strategy and tactics and held lengthy radio and telephone conferences with liberal activists in North and South Dakota, Colorado, and New Mexico.

Slowly a strategy was emerging. In Wyoming, Nebraska, and South Dakota, National Guard was mobilized, was issued weapons and live ammo, and took an oath on the constitution of each state that proudly replicated the Bill of Rights. Three days later Montana, North Dakota, and New Mexico followed suit. The six aforementioned states combined now had some 370,000 men and women under arms, well-trained, well-equipped, and imbued with patriotic spirit. By an overwhelming majority the Wyoming legislature passed a referendum on five major issues in which every voter in the state had the right to participate. The ballot would read:

Do you want a return to free elections? Yes or no?

Do you want a return to political parties freely competing in the political arena? Yes or no?

Do you want a return to equality before the law and to due process? Yes or no?

Do you want the abolishment of the Sex Police and the Faith Police? Yes or no?

Do you want the division of our society into highgovies and lowgovies abolished so that each individual, irrespective of his or her religious and social status, might enjoy the same legal rights and the same educational opportunities? Yes or no?

The referendum was scheduled to be held on March 25, and on March 15, the same day on which it was passed by the legislature, that very legislature put the five issues to the vote first in the house and then in the senate, the result being an overwhelming victory for the yeas. It was a day of jubilation in the Wyoming legislature and soon a day of jubilation in the entire state.

The first priority was the release of eighteen Wyomingites arrested during a peaceful demonstration and with them the release of all political prisoners, numbering more than five thousand, detained on a variety of charges without legal representation and due process in thirty-eight states. Nathan went on national TV, began to describe the situation, and called on the administration to free all political prisoners. He was immediately cut off, the network curtly informing him that his broadcast was cancelled for reasons of national security. He knew no other national network would allow him to complete the broadcast, but a Texas TV station picked it up and as he was speaking relayed it to satellite stations all over the country, rebroadcasting the complete text immediately following the live address. This particular Texas station and the affiliates were easily accessible to viewers in large urban centers, only rural areas remaining at a disadvantage, their population being a fraction of that inhabiting cities and towns. Moreover within days, and to Nathan's intense satisfaction, his broadcast appeared in print, in pamphlet form, and was both sold for a few pennies and distributed free of charge to curious multitudes, the expense being absorbed by the Association of Independent TV Stations.

Very soon waves of congratulatory telegrams, letters, faxes, e-mails, and radio and telephone messages burst upon Nathan in his home and in the Center for Democratic West, deluging all else. The majority came from western states, but there was a sizeable influx from the North and Southeast, from the Midwest, from the Deep South, and from Texas and California. Many writers and speakers urged firm action, military if necessary, to bring Huston's regime to a speedy end. They understood civil war was all but inevitable, and the sooner the country was made aware of it the better. Many offered their services; they would be proud to join the ranks of liberating armies.

Once again Nathan spent some time alone, examining the options, and then met for all-night sessions with key advisors. Two days later he was closeted with the governor of Wyoming and the commanders of the Wyoming, Nebraska, and Idaho National Guards. Their discussions were mostly about tactics and logistics, about transporting seventy to eighty thousand men to Washington D.C., arresting Chief Justice and other members of the government, occupying government buildings, imposing martial law if necessary, and formally announcing the dawn of a new democratic state superseding the tyrannical theocratic one and governed by an interim democratic government. If fired upon the National Guard had orders to fire back, and once it was in D.C. all available media would be employed to call upon the government forces to come over to the side of the liberators and serve the legitimate government of Western Amernipp. Freeing political prisoners would be one of the first priorities.

Encompassing all these matters and others, the planning for flying the National Guard to Washington went on at a brisk pace, and it was decided that the first landing would involve three states only—Wyoming, Nebraska, and Idaho—some seventy thousand men, while troops from North and South Dakota, Montana, and New Mexico, eighty thousand men give or take, would be on high alert, guns ready to be flown into the capital at an hour's notice if needed. At the last minute Colorado welshed on its promise, advocated sending petitions to Chief Justice, and had to be dropped out of the calculations. Nathan made a bid for one more broadcast calling on the government to adopt nationwide the results of the Wyoming referendum, and the others gave him their unanimous support. It was now March 31, the broadcast was scheduled for April 2, and with no satisfactory answer arriving from the government by midnight of April 4, the first wave of National Guardsmen would take off from airports in Wyoming, Nebraska, and Idaho at 0500 hours on Friday, April 5. Everything was in place and morale was high.

/   /   /

Huston spent Sunday, March 31 and Monday, April 1, in consultation with Léger, Grister, Pillows, and other key advisers. Nathan's erupting activity had taken him by surprise, and he had a strange gut feeling it would not wane soon.

"Ignore him," Phineas counseled. "That's the wisest course because—"

"A new mood is coming over the country," Huston finished for him.

Phineas laughed sardonically. "Something of the sort."

"I am with Léger on this," Ganymede ventured, eyeing the two of them caustically, "but for a different reason."

"Oh?" Huston queried.

"Chadwick is springing a trap for you, Ev. He's good at springing traps, and he's taken into account both possibilities: your under and overreacting."

"Surely my ignoring him would clearly be under-reacting, so what's the trap?"

"He'd go for you from behind, mobilizing public opinion, insisting on impartial audits of government books, investigating your laxness in dealing with the scientific community. He could cause embarrassment."

"And if I overreacted?"

"He'd address the nation again and again. He'd become a real pain in the ass."

"You're not really offering a solution, Gan."

"Hear me out to the end. Yes, I said ignore him, meaning don't exacerbate the situation and . . . give in a little. Arrange a temporary truce. We want him off our backs for a while till we regroup."

"Give in how little or how much?" Huston asked impatiently.

"A little," Pillows resumed. "A reprieve in the case of the seven Wyoming legislators and some other political prisoners would do very nicely. Reprieve with all kinds of conditions attached but ground-clearing nevertheless so that our boy can go see his buddies and be patted on the back. Right now, Everett, forget about being a lion or even a bear. That's for children's books. The age demands that you be a serpent. No more, no less."

"Oh thank ye, thank ye from the bottom of my heart," Huston articulated, still a little mystified but seeing an object or two he could take the measure of.

"Serpent's the thing," Ganymede wound up in a drawling singsong, and Huston gave him one of those glances that eminent psychiatrists give to uneminent patients.

For some time now Homily Grister had looked pained, shifting the full power of his merciless gaze from one man to the next and keeping all three of them under observation. "I've had enough of this hogwash to last me a lifetime. Do I make myself clear?" He spoke brusquely, apparently dead-set against listening to any of them and gasping in anger. "Ignore him, ignore the danger, ignore the gun that is pointed at your brow! My, my, my! This is no time for making apple pie beds for your bunkies and for other cute preppie games. This is serious. The tiger's at the gate; all you want is to play the fiddle while Rome is burning."

He stood up and appeared to be taller than he really was. He towered over them and bore the unmistakable stamp of the leader whom the nation had chosen to take command in the hour of dire need. He was a man of destiny, and they were his minions. Still standing he let the words fall harshly and gratingly as if he feared that polish and gloss would detract from his elemental strength and from whatever strength they possessed, hoping against all the instincts in his body that between the three of them they might after all be able to fire a shot or wield a heavy iron bar. "Chadwick has the power and capability to bury us, and you just sit there, waiting for what, for whom? For the Holy Ghost to load your bazooka, and maybe you'll hold a powwow on whether to fire it from the right or the left shoulder. Drastic measures are called for, and all that nonsense about not hitting below the belt don't apply. It's him or us, and I say it'd better be us."

"Agreed!" the three men called out. "Agreed!"

"Then this meeting that takes us nowhere is adjourned, and let's start another this very minute to get down to brass tacks on how to kick Chadwick and his friends hard in the ass, very hard."

"Agreed again!" Three voices rose in a tumultuous unison. "Agreed again!"

When, two hours later, Huston finally found himself alone he experienced an overpowering sense of satisfaction. Hom had laid it all out. The plan was complete, and it was a good one. It was war, war where no quarter was to be given and the rebels, those guilty of high treason, caught and sentenced to hard labor or exterminated. Federal troops in large numbers would move to troubled areas, the population in Wyoming and other western states might have to be evicted from their homes and placed in detention centers, martial law might have to be promulgated. Hom had laid it all out. There would be no half measures, and the traitors would be crushed. Huston needed time to digest everything Hom had said, to familiarize himself with the tactical details of all the operations, but he wholeheartedly approved of them. This campaign that Hom had so meticulously planned had all the hallmarks of success. Perhaps once and for all the enemies of the state would be routed, law and order permanently restored. Here was a silver lining over the sea of trouble, and he was immensely looking forward to communing with Hom's thoughts later in the day.

There was another reason for Huston's sanguine disposition on this particular Monday, April 1. At the crack of dawn he received word that a new inter-arts journal had been founded devoted to him personally and to the ideas and beliefs he held sacred, *The Massachusetts Chipmunk: Literature, Painting, Music, Film*. Editorial policy was announced in a pithy sentence: "*The Massachusetts Chipmunk*'s sharp teeth cut through falsehood, deception, ineffective thinking, and get to the truth."

The journal was a godsend. From its inception *The Yale Encyclical* had praised Huston's private and public persona to the skies, and its tenor has been encomiastic. *The Chipmunk* would have an opposite yet complementary goal: it would attack Huston's enemies, it would excoriate them, destroying their character and holding their achievements and beliefs up to ridicule or worse. It would never be accused of pulling its punches. Huston sank into his comfortable armchair and stretched his feet out onto the footstool. *The Massachusetts Chipmunk* would show those bastards who had the temerity to censure him what's what. It would show 'em.

Then another happy thought struck him. In the last two nights the Almighty had appeared to him, as He had appeared to him on previous occasions, a tall silver-bearded man wearing a long ornate robe, but now much more talkative than before. He emphasized at great length the extraordinary honor soon to be conferred on the Western Amernippian nation, the mystery and uniqueness of the Ascension. He did not delve into divine logistics proper but inched toward it and, Huston was convinced, would have done so if only He stayed a little longer. A wave of fervent hope and redoubled faith engulfed him, and he could feel in his bones that the Lord was watching over him and would soon, very soon, confide in His humble servant. Energy by the bushel streamed into his body, and his mental faculties were made sharper, stronger, ready to tackle riddles no man had ever solved. He joined the palms of his hands and thanked the Lord.

/   /   /

Tim Hysart was bending over La Rochelle's desk showing him a variety of official papers and then arranging them into neat piles on the National Security Advisor's spacious desk. "This came by courier from the Canadian Embassy only a few minutes ago." He held before La Rochelle's eyes a sheet of thin blue paper with several lines of longhand toward the top and an illegible signature at the very bottom.

"Oh that," La Rochelle sighed, "the PM's confirmation. I am glad we have it."

"Was restoring Amernippian-Canadian relations to their pristine state a hard nut to crack?"

"Hardly. The Canadians wanted a way out of the impasse just as we did. They said they wouldn't hold a grudge, and I said we wouldn't hold a grudge. They said what happened was water under the bridge, and I repeated it word for word. After that everything went smoothly. They were very pleased those new African markets were theirs, exclusively theirs, and no one could say boo to them. In fact the markets sealed the deal."

"I see," Tim commented with a nod. "Am I right in assuming that your talks with the Brits, the Aussies, and the New Zealies are also going well?"

"Quite satisfactorily, thank you, Tim."

Hysart began to laugh gustily, mock-heroically pounding his chest with a clenched fist. "So, in less than a week you undid all the harm brought on by the madman."

"You're very complimentary, Mr. Senior Assistant. I wonder whether this being April Fools' Day has anything to do with it?"

"You never can tell, sir, can you?"

"I am too old to play word games," La Rochelle put in with a twinkle in his eye. "Still you may have a point. If you look inside this one basket, only the Russian Federation remains. But this'll take some doing. I may even have to fly to Moscow. Huston did a first-class job in bungling Russian-American relations every inch of the way. I had no idea he could be so thorough."

Hysart laughed again. "Conventional wisdom has it the madman is at his most destructive when he tries to be helpful."

"That's close to the mark," La Rochelle agreed. "But he is still head of state."

"Only because of his Secret Police, the bootlickers who have invaded every sphere of national life and the populace, which is sleepwalking and won't wake up. For crying out loud, Siegfried, this was once the United States of America, and where are we now?"

"I know, I know," La Rochelle said very softly.

"I am hosting a meeting tonight, in my apartment, 8 P.M., and I'd like you to come." There was fire in Tim's voice.

"What sort of meeting?"

"Myself and my like-minded friends will examine ways and means of restoring what was once the Great Republic."

"You're not serious, Tim. You work in this office, under my very nose, and behind my back you're what? A rebel, an insurgent, a traitor?"

"In our cell we prefer the term freedom fighter."

"Indeed! I dare say you do. Don't forget the government we serve is the legitimate government of Western Amernipp, and it enjoys support of the overwhelming part of the citizenry. I carry out orders like everyone else."

Tim stepped back to his own desk and stood there transfixing La Rochelle with an accusatory gaze, his arms akimbo. "Stop talking like the Nazi high ups at the Nuremberg Trials. They all said they were just carrying out orders, poor lambs, they knew nothing about massacres, genocide, the final solution. They were just obedient servants of the state, carrying out orders. My heart bleeds for them."

"For your information, young man, civil rights and the judicial process are on the ascending slope. Well-informed sources predict the very structure of our society may soon be drastically changed, changed for the better, and something approaching freer elections may see the light of day. We must have patience, Tim, we must have patience."

"I'd say you're losing your marbles. Elections are either free or they aren't. There's nothing in between. And we haven't had free ones for years."

"We must allow all those excesses," La Rochelle went on in a warm, dignified manner. "The blind zeal, the unswerving allegiance to our leaders burn themselves out. Yes, burn themselves out like refuse lying in a field to which a match is applied. Once this refuse has burnt itself to ashes and there is nothing left of it, a new lease on life will come. It will come, I know it. There's an old saying that evil destroys itself, and this is a case in point. We must have patience, Tim."

Hysart still standing by the desk was shaking his head vigorously. "You're dreaming . . . you're dreaming. Everything with regard to civil rights, the judicial process, free representation and elections is on the downward slope. The madman will never forgive Chadwick for what he is doing. Nathan will be lucky to get off with life imprisonment, and there will be wholesale arrests, new forms of repression, speedier and more effective strangulation. The madman is counting his victims before he pounces again. Mark my word."

"This is hogwash. You don't know what you're saying."

"Damn you! It's folks like you that keep the madman in power." Tim was beginning to raise his voice.

"I must remind you, you are involved in high treason. You, a trust-ed government employee," La Rochelle censured him with dignity.

"Balls! Go and fry your egg, a couple of eggs if you wish." Tim moved very close to La Rochelle, the coat of his dark business suit touching his boss's shoulder and arm. "Something has occurred to me," he snapped.

"I am sure there isn't enough gold in the world to assess its net worth."

"Stop being a court jester for a brief minute and listen to me with both ears."

La Rochelle sent Tim a highly disapproving look.

"We Americans and the Germans are not so far apart, especially when it comes to citizens' relation to the state, to the government, to authority. The Germans fell for Hitler, and they couldn't have enough of the Führer. Men were wetting their pants and women were creaming their panties at the very sound of his name until the very end, until the moment he swallowed a cyanide capsule. We Americans fell for the madman, and we can't have enough of him. But the chances of his swallowing a cyanide capsule are remote, particularly since things are going so well for him, and he is surrounded by bedfellows whose devotion is absolute. To be sure there is some dissension, some opposition to the tyranny the madman has locked us under, but numerically and power-wise it is tiny. It can only wax and maybe tilt the scale when all of us do exactly the opposite of what Dr. La Rochelle counsels, Dr. La Rochelle being a weathercock that must be read in reverse every hour of the day."

"You are displaying abominable taste," Siegfried enunciated very deliberately, placing heavy emphasis on each word.

Tim ignored the remark and with the help of body language sent a signal that he did not give a hoot for what Siegfried was saying. "Be on time tonight," he began on a serious note. "Back in New England where I come from we take a dim view of those who flaunt the politeness of kings, and we don't give a damn how many emblems of honor the individual is wearing on his or her sleeve or how many are tucked in the underwear."

"How many will be there?" La Rochelle asked.

"It's difficult to say. Many will be your juniors in age and rank, but there will be a cross section—teachers, professors, government workers, business people, scientists, labor leaders, the clergy, ordinary citizens with no attachable labels, both highgovies and lowgovies."

"How long has this been going on?"

"For over a year, and our numbers are growing."

"I'll be there to have a look. But don't put me down right away for membership. I want to see for myself, reconnoiter."

"Of course," Tim replied, smiling broadly. "You'll want to calculate the odds, after all you are a very prudent, farsighted man who usually lands on his paws."

"There are times, Hysart," La Rochelle rapped out looking daggers, "when I can do very nicely without your sarcasm. Very nicely, thank you."

/   /   /

On the morning of Tuesday, April 2, Nathan Chadwick broadcast to the nation courtesy of Texas Independent Television and was pleasantly surprised that he was not interrupted, the broadcast being allowed to run its course and then relayed to affiliates. He repeated the demands made in the earlier broadcast and requested that the government respond to these demands no later than midnight, Thursday, April 4, saying nothing about the planned troop movements. He doubted there would be any response from the government, and the circle of key advisors and supporters concurred with him that the die would be cast at 0500 hours on Friday, April 5.

The remainder of Tuesday was spent in further military planning and coordination, National Guard commanders putting finishing touches on their daring operation. Wednesday promised to be another day of futile waiting, and Nathan, with his eye on the momentous event scheduled two days hence, busied himself with routine matters.

Then the unexpected happened. Shortly before one P.M. Wyoming time a national address by the attorney general was announced on all TV channels to be immediately followed by a national address by no lesser a person than Chief Justice himself. The attorney general spoke for twenty minutes exactly, informing the country that the seven Wyoming legislators held in custody in Washington D.C. were being released, and so were the eighteen Wyomingites mistakenly arrested in connection with a political protest. Both parties were being flown to Cheyenne at government expense. Furthermore, making a show of being elated by what he was reporting, the attorney general promised imminent release of some two hundred political prisoners held in federal prisons and a review of the charges leveled against all other political prisoners currently in federal custody without giving their number or any other information.

When it was his turn to speak, Chief Justice greeted his fellow citizens with ebullience, singling out several states and a dozen or so individuals for praise on account of their achievements in various walks of life, and he had warm words for the governor, the legislature, and the people of Wyoming who carried on the great Amernippian tradition of hard work and self-reliance that might fittingly—he returned to it twice—serve as an undying example to other parts of the country and to the world at large. He drew a graphic sketch of Nathan, commending him as a valuable member of the community, never shirking a civic duty and the first to come to the aid of others.

At the end of his address, which was considerably shorter than that of attorney general, he announced the appointment of an extraordinary commission whose members would be drawn from many different professional, religious, and ideological quarters and which would be charged with the task of reexamining the relationship between the individual and the state fairly and impartially, with particular reference to the legal process, the matter of elections, the divisions within Western Amernippian society, and the role of law enforcement in the world. He assured the public that, like Caesar's wife, the extraordinary commission would be above suspicion, asked for patience and understanding, bade a hearty farewell, and disappeared from view.

The two addresses were like shells exploding far too early and in the wrong place. Among Nathan's supporters opinion was divided. Linda, who had listened to the speeches with her husband, made no bones about where she stood. "It's a trick!" she cried. "The old buffoon has something up his sleeve. Don't fall for it, Nat, keep your cool."

Elsewhere suspicion of Huston's motives was also voiced, but release of political prisoners and the promise of a commission swayed many minds. When on the morning of Thursday, April 4, the seven Wyoming legislators and the eighteen detainees were flown to Cheyenne in an Air Force III usually reserved for generals and their staff, their reception was jubilant, and public opinion began to favor waiting for what might happen next. Only a minority still backed a military intervention, but even they agreed postponement was highly desirable. Accordingly plans that were to come into fruition at 0500 hours on April 5 were cancelled, and in the next several days weariness and aimlessness took hold of the activists. These were palling days.

Eventually they rallied, new decisions were made, new courses of action advanced and laid on the drawing board. Nathan appointed the Center for Democratic West to be the watchdog of the extraordinary commission, scrutinizing its every move and logging the progress it was making. On the same day he called into being a special committee charged with the responsibility of watching closely the government's treatment of political prisoners and collecting all relevant information.

Two weeks later the news conveyed by these two bodies was hardly encouraging. The extraordinary commission had not been formed, and there was no indication of the list of possible members being drawn up. Treatment of political prisoners remained as shabby and inhuman as it had been in the past, and there was no word of two hundred of them, or of any number for that matter, being released. On the contrary, hundreds of new political prisoners were being rounded up, and the review of charges leveled against the old prisoners was not taking place.

The outlook was dismal indeed, except for what the Wyoming legislature had put down on their agenda, thus buoying up the would-be liberators and astounding the nation. On April 25, at the extraordinary joint session of both houses of the legislature of the Equality State the five articles of the referendum, previously approved by the state and by the statehouse, were enacted into law effective May 25, 2084. Now Wyoming would be what the United States and Amernipp had once been, a democratic land where political parties competed with one another in free elections; where equality before the law was the order of the day and every Wyomingite was protected by due process and civil rights; where unconstitutional and pernicious police forces like the Sex Police and the Faith Police no longer existed; and where there were no first-class and no second-class citizens, the division between highgovies and lowgovies having been abolished, every inhabitant of the state enjoying the same legal rights and the same educational opportunities.

May 25 was several weeks away, but groundwork to implement the five articles of the referendum started immediately. Future politicians sharpened their teeth to perform meritoriously in debates, young lawyers boned up on that part of American jurisprudence with which they had had no more than a passing acquaintance, and school principals frantically created new classes to accommodate highgovies and lowgovies under the same roof. As for the Sex Police and the Faith Police, a contingent of the newly formed state militia paid them a call

at their offices asking that they leave forthwith, taking all the impedimenta with them, and not return, which they did.

A new spirit was abroad. The people of Wyoming set about con-
summating the transition from lawlessness to the rule of law and gave
it their best shot. A new self-confidence, a new pride, new soaring
ambition pounded in their breasts and a myriad of chores, big and small,
waited at the door. "Right, it'll have to be done," was invariably heard
when yet another undertaking was pinpointed. Chief Justice and his
administration showed no sign of wishing to interfere in the internal
affairs of the Equality State, and normal channels of communication
between Washington and Cheyenne were left intact. There was one
wrinkle, though, in the fast-changing political landscape: all federal
funds were held back, no explanations given, and the newly reorganized
democratic land was left to its own devices and resources. In 2084 federal standoffishness mattered little because of a large surplus lying in the
state's coffers. But the pinch would be felt in the following year. The
hazard was understood by all, and the leaders of the gem of the West
labored tirelessly to bring more business to it from the four corners of
the earth, make it more attractive as a tourist's haven, and they drilled
night and day for more oil.

As heaven and earth were moved to render Wyoming economically self-dependent, congratulatory telegrams and messages by the hundreds were delivered daily at the state legislature, the governor's
mansion, at Nathan's home, and at the Center for Democratic West. In
the world beyond the boundaries of Western Amernipp, particularly in
Scandinavia, in Russia, Australia, New Zealand, India, Pakistan and, of
course, in Eastern Amernipp, the chief executive of Wyoming and its
gallant legislators were seen as men and women of steel, semi-gods and
semi-goddesses almost. They were hailed as a brave new race who
emerged from the rugged Rockies at the behest of the primeval lords
of the universe to bring peace and justice to that part of North America
that for hundreds of millions of years had been their favorite spot on
that difficult and temperamental planet called earth. Nathan was for
them a prehistoric mountain man, pure and simple, one day shot out
unto the heavens clinging to the arrow of an Indian chief's bow, and
once in the celestial abode a favorite of the primeval lords, their
Ganymede, until the day when the moral order of the universe had to

be enforced and Nathan was dispatched to earth, liberator of Western Amernipp, but vicariously redeemer of the entire human race.

In secular circles, at colleges and universities of the Western world, the political adventures and misadventures of the American Equality State became a burning topic, passionately debated in classrooms and generating mountains of unreadable prose. At long last Wyoming found a permanent and highly honored place on the world map. Political scientists, historians, economists, constitutional scholars, demographers, and agriculturalists crossed swords and vied with one another in extracting meaning from the rich experience of this sparsely populated western state, in advancing theories, postulating paradigms, and predicting the future.

In the world's eye the western neighbor of Nebraska and South Dakota became a cause *celebre* and an inexhaustible source of raw material to be put to scientific, pseudo-scientific, scholarly, and pseudo-scholarly use. Vast numbers of noisy visitors, tape recorders, and film cameras at the ready to study local conditions firsthand, descending on Cheyenne and other towns, further bolstering the state economy, and they were urged to come again. Many did.

This bubbling lull in the boisterous saga of his state was a good time, Nathan thought, to give himself and his family a short vacation combined with a lecture tour. Linda and Agnes were highly receptive to the idea, and the Chadwick family piled their belongings in the much used and much loved station wagon and set out for the unknown, returning twice from the outskirts of the town to pick up Nathan's lecture notes sadly forgotten in the bustle of the holiday spirit.

"I'd like to go further afield," Nathan said as they were approaching Fort Collins, "further afield."

"That's all right with Mom and me, Daddy," Agnes said. "Go as far afield as you wish. Go to the ends of the earth."

Chapter 2

O Powerful Western Fallen Star!

Between Ft. Collins and Denver their plans for going further afield were crystallized and a consensus reached. They hurried southward on I-25 making short stops in Colorado Springs and Pueblo only, arriving in Raton well into the evening to put up for the night. Nathan had no lectures to deliver nor meetings to attend in Colorado, and they were glad to have crossed the state line into New Mexico. Three busy days followed. Nathan lectured twice in Albuquerque, once in Santa Fe, and conducted two workshops on civil disobedience, one in the latter and the second in Taos. In addition there were receptions, discussions, official dinners and luncheons, open meetings to shake hands with new recruits and closed ones to revamp old strategies.

Reunions with those who had put the Keeping Faith initiatives on a statewide footing, throwing the gauntlet of solidarity before the thugs of Washington, were charged with emotion. Several lowly Roman Catholic priests with no easy access to the seats of power thence haughty prelates lay down the law circulated in the crowd, old hands at protecting their flock from religion gone stark raving mad. In New Mexico Nathan and Linda were among friends, and past experience easily joined hands with the most inventive gambles now set in flight and caring not a jot for the verdict of history. And Agnes, thrown into the company of adults and making the best of it, was tickled pink on the third day of their stay in the Land of Enchantment at being able to spend several hours with Swen, a boy in her class the previous term in Cheyenne whose family moved to Taos.

On the fourth day the vacationing family set out for Texas, with Linda commenting that this was the strangest vacation of all the strange vacations she had lived through and had heard about. In Dallas, Houston, and San Antonio Nathan was kept very busy, but luckily his interlocutors had children his daughter's age, and Agnes was soon lost in a swirl of activities and games much to her liking.

Texas was a new territory for Nathan, and he knew by name no more than a handful of supporters. The interested parties he was meeting now for the first time lacked the thought-out commitment of his western neighbors but were willing and ready to go an extra mile. Significantly Nathan discovered almost at once that in reality there was not one Lone Star State, but two as dissimilar as one could imagine. He dubbed them Texas I and Texas II.

The former was decidedly Huston's country, and in it the governmental machinery was in full gear, encompassing with a single sweep of a powerful arm the individual's entire life, his or her ambitions and dreams, political cravings, daily routines, carefully mapped out agendas of conduct and religious engagement. Texas I was a monolith—Nathan could not remember anything like it anywhere else in the country—and it had the air of permanence, of having always existed in this exact form and of being destined to last through eternity and beyond. The officials, politicians, religious leaders, and other pillars of society whom the crusading Wyomingite closely observed and occasionally exchanged a few words with all radiated the absolute self-confidence that comes from knowing one is on the right track and has received the blessing from the highest.

The denizens of Texas I went about their business reminding themselves every minute of every hour that they were doing God's work, work to which each of them was called by his or her name, work which alone was honorable and worthy of a child of the Almighty. In this world doubt was anathema, philosophical speculation a grievous offense, thought itself an unpardonable weakness corroding and finally destroying the individual's religious fiber. Faith and obedience were the only dispensation. Faith and obedience pointed the way, the only way, for there was no other.

When in Texas I teenagers were inducted into religious clubs to serve Chief Justice Huston, the Savior of the Country, and Jesus Christ, they embarked on their new duties with a sense of assurance that, Nathan thought, could not be paralleled in any other part of the country. In the states Nathan knew, allegiance to Huston's theocracy grew out of many different reasons, some selfish, some altruistic and idealistic. In Texas I, however, this allegiance was fired by religious faith only, unalloyed by baser motives, and the sense of adherence to the truth its population experienced was unique and unshakable. Nowhere else, Nathan concluded, did religion triumph in such a pure form. To adulterate it would be to any self-respecting citizen of Texas I worse than committing the most heinous of crimes.

Here and there overlapping the extremities of Texas I, encroaching on it from three sides, lay Texas II, puddles of rainwater forcing themselves onto the coffin-shaped mass of hardened sand standing on even ground but bruised by potholes and crevices alternately hastening and retarding the flow of water. Texas II was bristling with animation. There was laughter galore, jeers, and a hundred and one intimations and pieces of everybody's mind freely given, doubts and reservations excitably expressed, assertions and beliefs held sacred vented in the face of those who made a captive audience and in the face of those who made no audience at all, jests and flashes of wit flying this way and that like bloodthirsty mosquitoes.

The division between Texas I and Texas II was not principally along socio-economic lines, though these played a part. Manifestly, the real reasons, and there were presumably many, defied analysis so far and awaited lengthy examination of thousands if not millions of Texans of both genders and of all ages, to be followed by complicated tabulations and the use of the latest instruments measuring human responses to a variety of stimuli, as well as mind readers. Fortunately such a project lay in the future.

In Texas II Huston and his regime were for the most part considered a necessary evil, though of late the pendulum began to swing backward and voices claiming Everett Zacharias was an evil and should be removed were heard more and more often. Still, all this good will and common sense gave rise to no strategies bent on shaking off the theocratic yoke and returning the country to the principles of 1787. Texas II was aglow with good intentions, but an organization was badly needed to whip those intentions into a concerted effort and a plan to make a dent in the existing structure.

Accordingly, Nathan spent his weeklong stay in Texas organizing cells of resistance and organs of information. In working with the former he was handicapped by a widespread reluctance to hatching conspiracies, cloak-and-dagger operations, and everything else that accompanied clandestine ventures against the established authority. Many of those who sympathized with the cause would rather march on Washington carrying sidearms only and face the enemy along the Potomac man-to-man than spend a couple of hours in a smoke-filled room. Nathan valued their candor and their predilection for laying everything up front, but he went to great lengths explaining that the government was not playing by the rules and that secrecy and other tricks of the conspirator's trade were an absolute necessity.

When the Chadwick family shook the dust of El Paso off their shoes and headed for Arizona and California, the Lone Star State could boast of a nucleus of organized resistance to governmental tyranny growing by the day and looking confidently to the future. Nathan did not tarry in the Grand Canyon State because his associates in New Mexico had already worked closely with their friends in Tucson, Phoenix, and Flagstaff with excellent results, and he was saving his fire for the Golden State.

In San Diego, Nathan sensed that opposition to Huston was more articulate, more sophisticated, and much better organized in California than it was in Texas, and his impression was confirmed upon arriving in Oceanside, River Side, and finally in Los Angeles. The more than two centuries-old tradition of direct democracy, insistence on popular vote, and resort to referenda had created in California a set of beliefs and attitudes conducive to the censure of unpopular authority, be it on the county or state level or aiming at the federal government and all the trimmings. Furthermore, because of the abundance of newspapers and media networks rising to gigantic proportions, the process of communication in the Golden State was more immediate and easier to conduct than anywhere else in the country.

There was no monolith in California championing Huston; there were instead dozens of gradations of opposition against and of support for him, displaying an assortment of related options among which the hope of accommodation was burning bright, a give-and-take arrangement from which both parties would emerge winners. The Californians were willing to negotiate, to claim and to concede, but paramount in numerous local public opinions across the state was also an eagerness to restore the basic rights to the people of Western Amernipp no matter what the cost. Nathan was quizzed again and again about the value of further dialogue between the government and the opposition, about exploring every avenue, about leaving no stone unturned. Yet breaking through all the parliamentary hubbub was a conviction that once all the peaceful means had been exhausted, only one honorable course of action remained: armed intervention.

In northern California, and in San Francisco in particular, there was much less patience with seeking an accommodation with the Savior of the Country. The leaders and rank and file alike did not mince words.

"You have patience to burn, Nathan," cried some backbenchers in the course of the last meeting held in San Francisco on the eve of the Chadwicks' departure. "You have patience to burn 'cause without it you're lost," they cried on. "You gotta have patience for the snow to melt. But it don't."

"Right! It don't!" Nathan shouted back.

"And you gotta have patience for the sun to come out. But it don't come out."

"That's right," Nathan shouted back. "The sun don't come out."

"Well now," the persistent backbenchers were at it again, "here in California we got other concerns, Nathan, so you'd better trim your sails. 'Cause we are out of patience."

"I'll sure press to my heart every grain of wisdom you guys have honored me with. And may a skunk piss in your beer."

All in all it was a most satisfactory meeting, and it ended in a prolonged libation. Before leaving the state Nathan made a mental note placing Californian detachments in the first line of battle in any future conflict. Now more than ever he would not march without them. The next morning they bid farewell to the Bay Area and, making very few stops on the way, slid at a leisurely pace on I-80 through Nevada and Utah to Wyoming and its proud capital.

They returned home on May 26, one day after a positive vote on the Wyoming referendum made it the law of the land. They had been on the road for twenty-four days, having left on May 2, and at dinner Linda told her husband, who was strangely silent and sheepish-looking, with a forced smile, "Now that this vacation is over some of us need a good rest."

Soon Nathan marveled at the changes that had taken place in the state during their absence. For the most part these changes provoked no violence, no recriminations. The transition had been orderly. To Nathan's great surprise the leveling of the population, the abolishment of the highgov and the lowgov status and the resulting equality before the law of all inhabitants of Wyoming provoked few diatribes and complaints from the former highly privileged citizens. A handful of Huston diehards who saw the handwriting on the wall had pulled stakes as early as March and April and had taken themselves to parts unknown where their old loyalties would be respected.

But the majority of those first demoted and then invested with universal rights accepted their new status without a murmur. In parts of the state, especially in the ranching country, former highgovies expressed individually and in deputations their extreme joy at the turn of events and swore up and down that for years now they had opposed in one way or another glaring social injustice but, alas, had been helpless to do anything about it. Few were believed and hypocrisy, magnified by greed and eagerness to lay the blame on others, went a long way in restructuring Wyoming society, placing hundreds of families beyond the pale. This ostracism, which in certain instances amounted to a boycott, had no bearing on the legal status of the individuals involved, but it effectively debarred them from public service, from occupying high positions in the private sector, and from membership in the more exclusive clubs. A new term was coined, highgovie bleeding heart, HGBH for short, and it was liberally applied.

In post-May 25 Wyoming, social forces were distributed in a starkly novel manner. Now the social crest was occupied by those who had fought against Huston's tyranny and who had put their lives on the line—associates, coworkers, and friends of Nathan Chadwick. Thousands of those who had minded their own business and had not been active collaborators were forgiven, their sins of conformity and inactivity, if any, forgotten.

But those who had profited financially or otherwise by following Huston and his minions and who had been government agents were hunted down. Even though the governor together with the majority and minority leaders of both houses of the Wyoming legislature called on May 25 for a new spirit of unity and for letting bygones be bygones, bitter memories could not be easily laid to rest. Without consulting Nathan, the Center for Democratic West prepared a lengthy white book listing thousands of Wyomingites who—the evidence was over-powering—had engaged in acts injurious to the state, had been paid servants of the tyrannical dictator or at best were guilty of dereliction of duty, looking the other way when their self-respect as human beings and citizens dictated the opposite course of action. Relentlessly the accused were indicted and tried in specially constituted tribunals. To avoid mass hysteria and witch hunts the Wyoming Supreme Court appointed a commission to investigate the entire gamut of offenses vio-lating civil rights in Wyoming and superimposing the might of the fed-eral government thus perverting the constitution of the state of Wyoming, causing pain and suffering, and infringing upon the inalien-able rights of citizens to life, liberty, and pursuit of happiness from the day the Huston regime came to power until midnight of May 24, 2084.

The high court was hoping to diffuse the cartridges of hate and revenge that the former victims were now firing at their former oppres-sors, but without much success. The *White Book* led to more and more litigation, and the state of Wyoming became a legal beehive and a par-adise for lawyers. As a well-informed foreign journalist put it, "One part of Wyoming is bound and determined to keep another part of it in jail, and there is no reprieve in sight."

Actually, reprieve came. The Wyoming Supreme Court stepped in, nullified the *White Book*, and declared that the commission that it had appointed should be the sole arbiter in the matter of alleged govern-mental abuses. Tempers cooled and cases brought before the commis-sion were investigated fairly and expeditiously. Wyoming welcomed a new lease on life.

Still, the national situation did not change a jot. Thousands of polit-ical prisoners, including many Wyomingites, continued to rot in deten-tion centers; there was no sign of imminent reforms; nothing suggesting that Washington was contemplating a more liberal or compassionate policy. In fact Huston's grip on the country was perceived to have tight-ened. The administration went by the slogan "Business as usual," and avoided at all costs any references to the Equality State. For all practical purposes Wyoming had ceased to exist. "Maybe its entire population has been drowned in the melting snow, or maybe it has been devoured by wolves," quipped some Washingtonians.

Sitting in his study in the last week of May, Nathan decided that something had to be done. The government had reneged on its promises, and its word could no longer be trusted. That same evening he addressed his closest associates in the offices of the Center for Democratic West, and a town meeting was set for the following Saturday, four days hence.

/   /   /

Timothy Hysart leaned back in his chair, lit another cigarette, and neatly piled up the current folders on the far side of the desk. He rose to his feet and crossed the office to where the National Security Advisor, his brow clouded by puzzlement and disbelief, was examining handwritten papers through a magnifying glass. "If I am disturbing you, say so," he began, but La Rochelle at once waved a jolly hand and motioned his senior assistant to a chair. "I've been looking again at the minutes of the latest Moscow meeting," Hysart began again. "You were brilliant, there's no denyin'."

"I wouldn't want to deny I was brilliant," La Rochelle put in modestly. "Why should I? I was brilliant, my usual self, nothing more." He laughed raucously.

"But I gather the other side was not exactly made up of ninnies?"

"Far from it," La Rochelle went on a little more seriously. "The ministers of trade and energy had done their homework, and old Govaritchov didn't miss a wink."

"I understand the president of the Russian Federation is quite a character."

"You can say it again, Tim, you can say it again. What the Russian stage has lost the Russian political arena has gained. But of course there's more to it than that."

"So you faced a real challenge, if I understand you correctly." Hysart spoke slowly, his eyes focused on La Rochelle with extraordinary persistence, with extraordinary curiosity.

"Yes, you might say that," La Rochelle agreed. "What I found interesting about that latest Moscow meeting was that the last few days were an exercise in personal diplomacy, the kind of thing that went on in the eighteenth century when heads of state or their foreign secretaries would negotiate tête-à-tête and try to outwit each other without the benefit of previously drawn up reports, analyses, and so on. Just two men verbally fencing, using the resources of their personalities and wit—a duel of wit."

"And you won," Hysart cut in, delighted.

"The Russians didn't leave empty-handed. They got much from us, but we also got much from them. Perhaps more they were initially willing to give. Perhaps more we deserved."

"Ha," Tim let out appreciatively. "Again, my heartiest congratulations, and keep up the good work."

"Thank you." Siegfried immediately held up a sheet of paper covered with scrawls running in all directions. "I've been reading the latest reports from Luigi Baldieri, our man at the Vatican."

"I suppose those reports are so hot they can't be entrusted to a member of the embassy staff who can write legibly or knows how to use a word processor." Tim gave out a prolonged laugh while bending forward to decipher the scrawls.

Siegfried smiled weakly. "Something like that." He again fixed his gaze on Baldieri's report and muttered, "I am beginning to wonder whether the Pope hasn't taken leave of his senses." Tim, smoothing his hair in a machine-like fashion, was looking at him coldly, inquisitively. "A week ago the Pope issued a call to Roman Catholics everywhere to join his International Catholic Brigade. He wants to use the troops to march on Rome and bring the government to its knees."

"This is because of the dispute between the national government in Rome and the Vatican about those measly subsidies to Roman Catholic schools." Tim was searching his memory.

"That's right. The Vatican thought the subsidies were ludicrously low. They wanted more."

"As I recall," Tim put in jeeringly, "the two sides nearly cut a deal a couple of weeks ago."

"Correct. But at the last minute the negotiations broke down."

"So now Borgia is at the point of invading Italy? And that International Catholic Brigade of his, will it be made up of armed troopers or of monks and priests blessing the crops and singing hosannas?"

Siegfried glanced again at the handwritten letter. "Luigi tells me the brigade will be armed with the latest automatic weapons, will carry cannons, and the volunteers most in demand are those with prior military service. Borgia already has thirty thousand men under the papal flag, and new recruits are pouring in by the thousands."

"Will either side back down?"

Siegfried shrugged his shoulders. "President Villafranca knows where his duty lies, and he has at his disposal the Italian armed forces. The tricky part is that the enemy are not the Germans or the Muslims but the church, the holy Catholic Church. He will be under pressure to make concessions."

"Church militant!" Tim exclaimed. "Is it conceivable, sir, that members of the Catholic Brigade will really fire on the Italian army, defending the republic, and on fellow countrymen?"

"Not only conceivable but certain," Siegfried rapped out. "Remember that in the papal brigade foreigners will greatly outnumber the Italians. And those foreigners will have no attachment to Italy whatsoever. It's an international force. Luigi says that theoretically induction into the brigade is restricted to Roman Catholics only, but this rule has already been waved aside and no doubt will be waved aside again."

Tim nodded. "So the brigade will be manned by mercenaries of all sorts, by the lunatic fringe, by bigots and criminals."

"That's the size of it."

"Will the United Nations pour oil on troubled waters?"

Siegfried was silent for what seemed to Tim a very long while. "I doubt it," he said at last. "The UN's record in such matters has been one of uninterrupted failure. I'd put my money on an elder European statesman or on several elder European statesmen working together, or on some other body that has guts and diplomatic know-how."

Tim was viewing Siegfried questioningly. "Such a body may be difficult to locate." He let the words fall matter-of-factly.

"Very difficult, and time is running short. Luigi offers but one silver lining: two days ago Spanish cardinals met in conclave in Saragossa, and there was a heated discussion. They had been apprised of all the facts."

"This is not the last chance?"

"No, not by a long shot. But options may diminish in number as we go on if Borgia is allowed to remain his old self."

"I understand," Tim said softly and made ready to return to his own desk.

/ / /

"It's all Chadwick's fault," Huston sputtered the words out furiously, squeezing the remaining drops of juice from a quarter part of a desiccated lemon into a teacup. "Without Chadwick there would've been no secession and no revolt and our detention centers would be empty. He's the bastard responsible. He stirred up honest folks, told them fairy tales, and then led them down the road to perdition. He poisoned men's minds."

"I am not so certain Chadwick alone is to blame," Phineas Léger commented, sipping tea and then handing his cup to Huston's confidential secretary to have it refilled. "I'd say it's a number of people in various states but primarily in the West, and most of all in Wyoming."

"I'd tend to agree with Phin," Ganymede Pillows raised his voice, then rose from his chair and walked several times up and down the length of Huston's spacious office in the Supreme Court Building.

"Are you suffering from cramps?" Huston inquired.

"No, far from it. I just wanted to flex my muscles."

"Oh." Huston turned toward Homily Grister, sitting on a sofa some distance away. "What do you say?"

"Chadwick may have been the first and he may have blazed the trail, but now he's just a face in the crowd." Homily sounded self-important and wholly convinced of the veracity of what he was expounding. "In Greek mythology Hydra had many heads, but not thousands. Wyoming's secession and revolt is led by thousands of heads, and cutting one or a couple will accomplish nothing."

"So what are you telling us, Hom?" Huston sounded impatient and disgusted.

"Sooner or later federal troops will have to be sent to Wyoming and other western states. Martial law may have to be imposed, if need be the population kept in penal camps for the time being. These are the measures that face us, not half-measures."

"That's risking everything on one card," Phin broke in. "What if the country rises against us, millions marching on Washington shoulder to shoulder? What then?"

"This won't happen," Homily scowled. "This will never happen."

"And why not? We've had revolutions in this country before. Why not another one?" Homily gave the impression of being dead set against yielding an inch.

"Because this time God is on our side, that's why. And if you don't believe it, fella, I can't think of anything better than sending you to one of our detention facilities."

"Gentlemen, gentlemen," Huston began soothingly, "calm down. Please calm down."

"Not if I have to listen to that damned turncoat!" Homily roared and shook his fist at Phineas.

"Gentlemen, gentlemen," Huston begged again. "Do I really have to remind you that all four of us are of the same party?"

"Are we?" Homily fired away and then fell silent.

"I'd be against occupying large parts of the country, half a dozen states or so with federal troops. There must be subtler methods. Maybe arresting the ringleaders, all of them, if you like . . ." Ganymede left the rest unfinished.

"Now you're talking," Huston snapped approvingly.

"Sanctions against the rebellious states could be an effective option," Phineas added, nodding in the direction of Ganymede. "Withdrawing federal support, embargo on what they sell to other states and abroad, encouraging big industries to move elsewhere, undercutting consumer buying power, that sort of thing. This would hurt them."

"Good, very good," Huston's appreciative words came quickly.

"These are half-measures!" Homily bellowed from the sofa. "Half-measures, and you guys should be ashamed of yourselves."

"Overpowering force brutally employed does not create a positive impression." Phineas looked from one face to the next expecting a measure of approval.

"Yes, yes," Huston joined in briskly, "but I'd like to go back to what I said earlier, Chadwick being the prime evildoer. Methinks without him the opposition would suffer an immense setback."

"If you shackle that damned cowboy, people will take to the streets. Do you really want that, Ev?" Ganymede clearly invited further dialogue.

"I stand with Ev when it comes to the offensive anatomy of one

Nathan Chadwick," Homily bellowed again. "Maybe he ought to be cut up root and branch like Ev says—root and branch."

Huston smiled amiably. "Thank you for your advice. You gave me much food for thought. And now it's time for me to consult with meself and do some thinkin' and calculatin'. More tea anybody? I'll see you all at the reception tonight, and this has been a very helpful session. Till tonight then."

/ / /

The hands on the two enormous wall clocks in the National Security Advisor's inner office were creeping relentlessly toward figures six and twelve respectively, and as they were at last touching these figures Timothy Hysart rose from behind his desk and walked noiselessly to where his boss was sitting, stacks of official papers barricading him on all sides.

"Siegfried, I didn't want to disturb you earlier, because the Russians and the Vatican engrossed your mind for hours."

"Yes, Tim."

"But actually I have something to tell you that may mean more than meets the eye."

"Go on."

"Father has turned over a new leaf. He's sided with the opposition. Last Sunday he preached a sermon on Matthew 7:15, 'Beware of false prophets—'"

"'Who come to you in sheep's clothing but inwardly are ravenous wolves,'" La Rochelle finished the verse for him.

"That same evening Father had a long telephone conversation with Emily and told her he'd been blind and deaf far too long, and he now joins the ranks of those who want Huston out. He also spoke very candidly with several members of the congregation."

"So," La Rochelle shot back, vastly amused, "Reverend James Hysart changes course, and you think it to be significant in a wider sense."

"I most certainly do. Father never does anything without some concrete reason which can benefit him in a material sense."

"So you think—"

"Yes, that Father held his finger to the wind to see how it blew and decided it was time to switch sides. It was a calculated move caused by self-interest."

"I think the question is does your father have any proof that Huston is on the way out, or does he sincerely believe Huston can't be of any further use to him?"

Tim rubbed his chin nervously before replying. "I suspect a little of both. He's a crafty old fox. He can read what's in the wind."

"You're probably right. From what I know the opposition to Huston that is directed by Nathan Chadwick and his closest associates is made up of a number of spheres encompassing the center. The one closest to the center boasts of activists, militants, doers of one kind or another, although a doer can also be a thinker. The next sphere is tamer and not so trigger-happy but wholly devoted to the cause. As we move away from the center each new sphere carries with it more territory and a higher membership of freedom fighters. And when we reach the last sphere, the sixth or the seventh, we are talking of millions of Western Amernippians inspired by the same ideals as those who are close to the center, though admittedly some of them may be sleepers or reservists. It is entirely possible your father made his way to one of these spheres, and let's hope he'll be a godsend to his fellow conspirators."

Tim shook his head vigorously. "I doubt it. When I spoke to Emily after last Sunday she said she couldn't believe her ears when Father called her. My sister is hard to fool, and she had a distinct impression Father was putting on an act."

"What would he gain from it?" Siegfried asked cautiously.

"It's difficult to say. He could infiltrate various cells of resistance and then rat on them. This would catch Huston's eye, and he'd be royally rewarded. Surely Chief Justice could do with another snitch, particularly a man of the cloth."

Siegfried smiled non-commitally.

"You know that Father burned incense in Huston's face for years, but in the end he felt he'd been passed over."

"Well, perhaps your father is out to get Huston, pay him back for the meager wages of neglect," Siegfried ventured on a merry note.

"Very unlikely. This would take courage, and my father is a coward."

"Well, we'll have to wait and see, won't we?"

"I suppose so," Tim blurted out and reeled on his heels. "I have a gut feeling things will be happening soon, very soon. We are living on borrowed time. It's all very, very eerie. For all practical purposes the state of Wyoming has seceded from the Union and adopted a constitution that is anathema to Huston and his gang. Yet no one is cracking the whip; no one is evoking the sanctity of the Union; no one is making the slightest effort to bring the rebs to their knees. Huston has officially made all kinds of promises to Nathan that Nathan knows will not be made good. Yet Nathan parades his saintly patience to the world like a ceremonial robe the returning monarch is dead set on being seen in and touched by the more of his subjects the merrier. Why doesn't Nathan call Huston to account? Why?

"New arrests are being made every hour, and our political detention centers are filled to capacity. Yet the administration insists the electorate is ninety-nine percent loyal to the state and that only criminal elements create disorder. Talking about disorder—how about a dozen or so jailbreaks planned and organized from the outside to show the jailers not everything is hunky-dory? And finally, what about that uplifting jaunt to a better world? Is anyone taking reservations? Are we going by land or sea, or flying supersonically body and soul, or maybe just soul, body having been left in cold storage as insurance against excessive spirituality? I don't mean to paint a doomsday scenario, Siegfried, but we are in limbo, and we couldn't ask for a worse place. Still, our days are numbered, and when shit hits the fan it'll be a sight to see. And that's just around the corner."

La Rochelle was leaning against a bookshelf lost in meditation. "The odd thing is," he spoke at last, "I too have a presentiment, a presentiment of things finally breaking as never before, soon, very soon."

For once Tim was lost for words and just stood there attentive, courteous. "Are you going to Huston's reception tonight?" he finally asked. It was a relief to get away from the doomsday scenario.

"Both you and I are going," La Rochelle announced with a twinkle in his eye.

"Thank you for taking me along. But in view of what he knows, is it wise?"

"It would be unwise not to go. And we can't have that, can we now?" La Rochelle's tone was smoothness itself.

"No, sir."

/   /   /

Friday, May 29, was a radiant day in Cheyenne and indeed in the entire southeastern corner of the state. Because of the unseasonable operation of the sun the heavy snow that had fallen earlier in the week was now melting by the ton, and trucks were braving the slushy creeks and crumbling snow piles, white underneath but touched by a gauze of dust above, while passenger cars maneuvered this way and that to stay on firm ground. Troops of Cub Scouts marched merrily to assembly points and next to Washington Park the slanting meadows were all black, the blaze of the sun having dissolved the overlaying blankets of ice crystals to the last speck. It was almost eleven o'clock in the morning, and a quantity of pedestrians could be seen about, many of them on their way to a shopping mall.

But this was also the day before the town meeting at which momentous matters would be aired, and many a citizen of Cheyenne had a bump in his or her throat—such excitement, anticipation, and hope not throbbing in their innards every day. Planes took off and landed on schedule at Cheyenne airport, and a mini-super-helicopter with no markings swirled over the city, then made an abrupt left turn and began a sharp descent, landing on level ground just outside the main gate to Washington Park. Two men jumped out dressed in closely fitting black clothes, leotards to a casual observer, each carrying a long thin leather bag, perfect receptacles for golf clubs or fishing tackle.

The elder man pointed to the street behind them. "It's number 1264, right in the middle. He is alone. His wife Linda will be out of the house until 1:30. His daughter Agnes may be in, but we have no orders for Linda or Agnes. It's a piece of cake. We'll follow the line of trees."

/   /   /

At the precise moment when the two men were starting to run along the cover of trees, Timothy Hysart burst into La Rochelle's inner office, out of breath and spasmodically waving his arms.

"They are going to shoot Chadwick this morning at his home in Cheyenne!" he gasped. "Team's already in place."

"Who's in charge?"

"Section 6, anti-terrorist."

"Did you manage to get the time of the operation?"

"Not exactly, but it's this morning, Cheyenne time. Eleven A.M. was given to me as the likely docket."

La Rochelle glanced at his wristwatch. "It's now," he rapped out. "Tim, call Nathan's home, the FBI office in Cheyenne, and the local police. I'll try Section 6 and Huston himself. And that friend of Chadwick's—Kevin . . . Kevin something," he added briskly.

"Kevin Schultz, Nathan's deputy," Hysart confirmed at once.

Tim was already putting the three telephones on his desk to good use as La Rochelle was dialing a number.

"Section 6? I must speak to Colonel Stephens." After a brief pause a gruff voice came on the line identifying himself.

"Colonel, this is Dr. La Rochelle, National Security Advisor."

"How do you do, sir? A few days ago we were talking at a reception about our army days."

"Yes, yes, Colonel. But this can wait. I am calling you regarding a matter of extreme urgency."

"Yes, Dr. La Rochelle."

"Your section has been entrusted with a closing order on one Nathan Chadwick in Cheyenne, Wyoming. I can give you the address if you wish."

"No need to. I remember the order."

"Listen carefully. I am countermanding this closing order. Radio your operatives immediately."

"I am sorry, sir, but I can't do it. This particular order was issued by Chief Justice himself, and he alone has the authority to countermand it."

"Listen to me, man. This order was issued in error; it must be revoked. An innocent man's life is at stake!" By now La Rochelle was shouting into the receiver.

"I am sorry, Mr. National Security Advisor, but my hands are tied."

"Damn you!" Siegfried shouted again and slammed the receiver down. Presently he was dialing another number. "Gertie, this is Dr. La Rochelle. I must speak to Chief Justice at once. This minute! It's very urgent."

The silky voice came back. "I am very sorry, Doctor. But Chief Justice is in conference with the top brass. He is not to be disturbed no matter what. I am to log in all incoming calls and messages. He'll attend to them tomorrow and Monday. I am very sorry."

"Thank you, Gertie." Siegfried replaced the receiver.

Tim was already standing by his side. "Bad news," he whispered and was pierced by a furious, venomous stare. "In Nathan's house and at Kevin Schultz's the phone is dead. So it is at two other close associates of Nathan's. The law in Cheyenne—city cops, highway patrol, detectives, and so on, as well as the FBI—will not be accepting calls for another hour. Same in the statehouse. Prerecorded messages that came from the government exchange make it plain it was a carefully planned operation."

"I don't rightly know which round it is, but we lost again," La Rochelle said in a flat voice.

"Yeah," Tim followed him with bitterness. "It makes one wonder if we are doing anything right."

/ / /

The two men in leotards halted, and the older was whispering last-minute instructions to the younger. Then they remained perfectly still for a few more seconds as the tall figure of Nathan Chadwick came out onto the porch and stood there looking vaguely around. They watched him with intense curiosity, with *schadenfreude* that kept them glued in place. When Nathan went back into the house, the older man said, "We'll go in through the backdoor. It's better that way," and they resumed their trot. They moved nimbly, rhythmically, like dancers, and the distance between them and the house, diminishing with every second, was less than fifty yards. They redoubled their efforts.

/ / /

Agnes entered the living room and at first did not see her father lying on his back on the floor, his head almost touching the door leading onto the porch. Thick blood was trickling down from two holes in his chest onto his sportshirt, pullover, and trousers. Two bullet wounds, one in the left temple and the other in the back of the head, were hazy and dry. Only Nathan's ears and nostrils, as if in compensation, released a profusion of thin warm blood. Agnes knelt by the body, lifted her father's hand, and kissed it. With the fingers of the other hand she dialed 911.

/   /   /

Nathan Chadwick's funeral, held in the first week of June in Cheyenne, was a grand affair, the grandest the city had ever seen. It seemed the population of Cheyenne had tripled overnight, not through additional births but in some unfathomable mystical way, and when one added to it mourners from every corner of Wyoming, from some thirty other states, and from countries as distant from one another as Canada, Mexico, Britain, Australia, New Zealand, Spain, Portugal, Italy, Iceland, Turkey, Greece, the Scandinavian nations, Belgium and Holland, the Russian Federation, and numerous lands in Africa and Asia, one was talking about more than a quarter million souls paying tribute to an individual born and bred in a sparsely populated western state. He had never been to Europe, Asia, or Africa but was remembered and saluted in every land where freedom and common decency were deemed worth fighting for. Some mourners came from afar individually or in groups as private citizens, others were part of state or national delegations with all the attendant fanfare. Crowned heads flew from their European palaces following their own instincts, but also because their subjects clamored for it, and there were more heads of state, prime ministers, dignitaries, and notables of every imaginable ilk rubbing shoulders on less than half a square mile of the city of Cheyenne than on a like area at any other time in American history.

The large British contingent was headed by a member of the Royal Family, President Sergej Govaritchov of the Russian Federation commanded his own crew and, formerly a quartermaster officer, he infuriated his subordinates by allegedly being in different places at the same time. He behaved like a typical American politician on the stump, shaking hands, hugging passersby, bussing babies, praising to the skies whatever was shown to him, and exuding kiloliters of geniality. He hit it big with men and women alike, and his aides were taken aback when old codgers with the smell of liquor on their breath patted him on the back saying, "You settle down here among us, Sergej. You belong to Wyoming, and we'll find you a job, something simple, to keep the wolf from the door." At the sound of these words Sergej felt it was his bounden duty to shake more hands, hug more passersby, buss more babies, and exude twice as many kiloliters of geniality as before.

After many hours of heated persuasion by the empress, the prime minister, Princess Sayko, and his closest advisors, the emperor finally gave his reluctant consent to his grandson, Prince Mikasa, to be included in the Eastern Amernippian delegation to Nathan Chadwick's funeral. "I do it against my better judgment," he exclaimed thrice, immediately placing the prince under the prime minister's tutelage and exhorting him not to spare the rod. The prime minister found this exhortation difficult to adhere to as Takahito was nearing his seventeenth birthday. One very special mourner from Eastern Amernipp whom Nathan—no matter where he might be—would want to be present at his burial was unable to attend. Tarako Lepra was again in jail, and the government did not wish to take the risk.

Two European countries were deliberate absentees from the international tribute and remembrance, France and Germany. It was bruited that the French and the Germans, under the leadership of President Jacques Merdeacac and the German chancellor, who was the Frenchman's acknowledged toady, were reviving the Empire of Charlemagne and could not spare a single dignitary or diplomat for this melancholy transatlantic voyage. The camembert-sauerkraut empire, as the future superpower was dubbed in newspapers on both sides of the Rhine, not only gave a preview of an extremely ambitious foreign policy but made no secret of planning to annex portions of neighboring countries, Belgium, Holland, and Denmark, a slice of northern Italy, and a canton or two to be ripped out of the Swiss Confederation, if the Swiss could be easily hoodwinked. In speech after speech Merdeacac outlined what the new European colossus would bring to the international arena. France had wisdom and experience in foreign affairs and in managing and conciliating the community of nations, which had once and for centuries been the French prerogative. Germany's powerful economy would spearhead a new alignment of European industrial output and trade watched over by the Paris-Berlin Axis. Above all, the New Franco-German state would be a counterbalance to the amateurish policies of the Americans and to the outdated ideas of the British. It would reestablish the rule of intelligence in world affairs and put on the world map a new political, economic, and cultural superpower ready to take on the cowboys and the shopkeepers. At long last Europe would come into its own.

At home the administration's decision to ignore Nathan's funeral and pretend there was no such thing surprised no one, least of all Linda, who knew the facts. Official Washington had no time for what was happening on the outskirts of civilization in buffalo country. More sadly, because of one of those scheduling conflicts that plague men in high places, Siegfried La Rochelle had a prior and very important commitment in Tokyo on the day of Nathan's interment, and he was obliged to keep it. Bravely and tactfully, Timothy Hysart deputized for him.

After the church service the cortege made its way very slowly through the city's main streets and then, by the V.A. Hospital, turned into a wide country road leading to the cemetery. The open coffin rested on a catafalque that had been placed in the middle of a long and wide cart, drawn by four horses. Round the coffin lay precious mementoes—Nathan's riding boots, his hunting rifle, his camping hat, the tape recorder he had first used while working for the local radio and TV stations, his handgun. Linda, Agnes, Nathan's brother, and two sisters walked immediately behind the cart, and following them thousands upon thousands of mourners advanced in silence. Here and there the walking throngs made room for enormous limousines proceeding at an extremely slow pace carrying the royal and presidential guests.

Further down, the governor, surrounded by his department secretaries and numerous members of the state legislature, walked resolutely on as if to tell the world that Nathan's death, a terrible tragedy though it was, was also a call to action. Right behind him came, in strict formation, police, firefighters, city workers, and garbage collectors. The entire current student body, staff, and teachers of Abraham Lincoln High School, which Nathan had once attended, were next in line. Other official contingents followed, and at the very end of the procession, more than two miles away from the coffin, rode a company of Casper Troopers, young men and women in dark blue uniforms, white sashes thrown over their shoulders, with precision and flair that would have done credit to Vienna Riding School.

At the cemetery eulogies followed one another at a stately pace, and at one point the head of the Swedish delegation made the announcement that Nathan Chadwick was being put forward as a candidate for the Nobel Peace Prize. An appreciative murmur rose in the crowd, and other speakers duly took note. Prince Mikasa translated sentence by sentence the prime minister's eulogy, which he later pronounced to be the shallowest piece of empty rhetoric he had ever been forced to listen to. Still many other speakers surpassed themselves in giving a credible assessment of Nathan's achievements, of the dangers he faced, of his strengths and weaknesses. The honoree was honored in a highly perceptive and unconventional way.

On the day of the funeral Linda remained dry-eyed, as she had been ever since her husband's assassination. But when flanked by her daughter and the pastor of their church and his wife, she saw Nathan's coffin being lowered into the grave, something inside her exploded. "Why, why?" she cried mutely. "Why did his life have to end this way? Why and why again?" Tears welled up in her eyes, and even before the end of the service she was escorted to a waiting car.

Some visitors from abroad stayed in Cheyenne for another day exploring the town and its environs or meeting with members of Nathan's staff, or talking to their opposite numbers from other countries, or simply resting. President Govaritchov stayed on for two more days, a fountain of geniality as ever, highly delighted when the city of Cheyenne presented him with an old Colt .45, two retired sheriffs recounting its history and use in the old days. Later in the day the mercurial Takahito could be seen surrounded by a bevy of giggling girls trying a variety of Western hats on him, each wider than the last, tying a cartridge belt round his waist with a holster on each side, and fussing over him. Other visitors blended in with the crowd, sought out friends or relatives, carried out what they had planned to do or acted on instinct. The weather was glorious, and when the time came at last for the visitors to leave many were sorry. It had been a sad occasion, but the funeral was so stately and featured such an outpouring of national and international feeling that it would not be easily forgotten. In fact, in later years three separate associations of mourners of Nathan Chadwick were formed, and they met regularly. They kept the flame burning.

Everybody in Wyoming believed Nathan had been killed on Huston's orders, and this was also the widespread belief in many other states. But to prove it and make a case that would stand up in court was another matter. The killers left no clues behind, and the murder weapon, an automatic T36 equipped with a silencer, could be found in great numbers in army and National Guard depots and at some police stations. Cheyenne detectives examined very thoroughly the Chadwick house and retraced the movements of the two agents—they determined that two men had been involved—from the time they jumped off the mini-super-helicopter to the time they boarded it after the commission of the crime. They wanted to follow the helicopter trail to ascertain its base and registration, but the federal government refused to cooperate, and the detectives' repeated requests for information germane to a murder inquiry were ignored. The feds hazarded a guess, though. The Chicago FBI office contacted the Cheyenne detectives and advanced the hypothesis that the killer or killers were most likely local derelicts, possibly with a long record of petty crime, who for one reason or another bore Nathan Chadwick a grudge. The FBI's advice to Cheyenne CID was loud and clear: "Turn Cheyenne skid row inside out. You won't believe what'll turn up."

Kevin Schultz, on whom Nathan's mantle had now fallen, called several meetings of all Wyoming activists and asked them how long, in what manner, and with what resources the search for Nathan's killers should go on. At each meeting there was a consensus that unfortunately the perpetrators were beyond the reach of the law because they were protected by the Grand Seal of Western Amernipp and by Everett Zacharias Huston, Savior of the Country. Painful as it would be to all concerned and especially to Nathan's immediate family, energies should be expended, the majority argued, on solidifying the extraordinary gains of May 25 and on making the land more solvent. There were few dissenting voices, and in the early days of June 2084 this became the official policy of the sovereign state of Wyoming.

Political moves, novel initiatives to increase state revenue, educational reforms, and revamped health insurance plans were all carried out by analyzing data, applying statistical methods, and making educated guesses and predictions. Scientific bases and dimensions underlay every step in the socio-political-economic progression on which Wyoming had embarked, and the results, positive or negative, or a mixture of both, were tied to the thorough studies that preceded each decision, each new step taken. This was the complex world of quantitative and qualitative data, of judgments made with the help of evidence collected, of scientific thinking, coldly examining facts, and drawing proper conclusions. Here labs and prides of experts, supercomputers, and other highly sophisticated machines reigned supreme.

But beginning with the day of Nathan's assassination another phenomenon surged to the skies and then descended on the inhabitable world, tearing up old protocols and igniting men's hearts. In life Nathan Chadwick had been a daring defender of American values, successful at times and wretchedly unsuccessful at others. In death he became the first citizen of the world, an idol, and a role model. Norwegian schoolgirls sang songs about him; in Iceland three town halls were named after him. In the war-torn countries of Africa the oppressed multitudes invoked his name as a messiah and urged their leaders to model themselves after him. On the Indian subcontinent his name was uttered in the same breath as that of Mahatma Gandhi, and the fascination which the deeds and memory of John Brown had exercised on European nineteenth-century revolutionaries was now transferred to Nathan who in many parts of the globe came to be admired as a super-revolutionary, a commander of the just. Less than a month after the funeral, in an act unprecedented in his country's history, the British monarch raised that son of the West to an honorary peerage, and he henceforth was known in the British Isles as Lord Nathan Chadwick, Earl of the Wild.

It appeared that Nathan had something to say to almost every single living soul, and each soul drew his or her particular lesson from his own personality in which reality and myth, fact and fiction, freely commingled. To some people he was Spartacus come to life, to others a reincarnation of Albert Schweitzer, even though he had never practiced medicine. In many quarters he was viewed as a consummate parliamentarian outwitting the opposition every step of the way; in others as tribune of the people crushed by cynical bosses and finally murdered by them; and in Eastern Amernipp he was counted by reverential crowds among Shinto deities. Pacifist, social reformer, Rousseauist, astute party leader, humanitarian, strict constitutionalist, conscience of the world, war hero who had earned his spurs with distinction, moral teacher, friend of humanity, saint, fighter to the last drop of his Wyoming blood—he was all these to different folks in the four corners of the earth, and they acclaimed him each according to his or her lights.

Nevertheless there was one particular category, many agreed, into which Nathan could perforce be squeezed, though some laughed it off with a word while others rambled on and on about it as if there was no tomorrow. Here at last was something approaching a consensus regarding one major aspect of his psyche: Nathan was an eminent and very distinctive American drawing strength from the ancient and limitless mental resources of the New World, from its sense of democracy, not an abstract concept but the preferred way folks on the American shores wanted to live and be governed by; from its neighborliness, not a cate-chistic doctrine but a conviction born of experience and common decency that neighbors deserve the same consideration from us as we from them; and what must never be forgotten—from a deeply-rooted belief that all men are created equal, that pedigree and high connections don't amount to an ass's pissdrop when it comes to fundamental rights.

Seen in this light, Nathan Chadwick was heir to those outstanding Americans who had taught foreigners, particularly Europeans, a thing or two, and had left an impact on European affairs, men like Ben Franklin or Teddy Roosevelt. That the legitimate government had turned against one of the most gifted citizens of Western Amernipp, had persecuted him, and in all likelihood was responsible for his death, preyed on the minds of Europeans, Asians, and Africans and spawned many different judgments, some harsher than others, their common denominator being the differentiation made between outstanding indi-viduals and the government in Western Amernipp, the former making notable contributions to civilization and the latter putting the former beyond the pale. More broadly, the censuring voices proclaimed from abroad that in America individual effort was strangled by regressive authority.

/   /   /

In Washington in the first week and half of June the relations between Huston and La Rochelle grew worse by the hour. Chief Justice had not told the National Security Advisor that on July 4 of the current year he was dropping him from the government, but he sus-pected that the canny foreign relations ace had found out about it any-way. He was right. La Rochelle was kept informed hourly of Huston's moves and plans, and this particular decision had not caught him nap-ping. He had suspected it for more than a year, and he was prepared. Presently he was ruminating as to whether the ongoing conspiracy to oust Huston from power had national backing or whether it was anoth-er flash in the pan. He could not decide. As he hoisted his head he became aware of Tim Hysart practically touching the side of the desk, breathing heavily.

"If I am not disturbing you," Tim said very quietly.

"Of course not. What's up, Tim?"

"I'd like to return to the family saga, because it's sending a signal."

La Rochelle nodded.

"Something very strange is happening to Father. Several weeks ago he came across for the first time—this shows you how abreast he is of the world of letters—some books of Studs Terkel. You know, those American oral histories that date back to the second half of the last century, books like—"

"Yes, I know, Tim, I read them all," La Rochelle interrupted gently. "Go on."

"Well Father became engrossed in them, and in a matter of weeks he became a liberal progressive convert. I've been told he's working very closely with the friends of the late Nathan Chadwick here in D.C., and he attended the last meeting of the group. More than anything else in the world he wants Huston out, deposed, exiled, executed, whichever."

"Saul on the way to Damascus, eh," La Rochelle quipped.

"Possibly," Tim reluctantly agreed. "There's something else. First Baptist Church of the Holy Tabernacle—that's Father's church—has thrown its weight behind our disloyal opposition. At Father's behest it is helping victims of political oppression, providing food, lodging, safe houses. Emily and I spent hours trying to make sense out of this absurdity."

"Why absurdity? Your father had a change of heart and therefore—"

But Tim, stepping back from the desk and shaking his head vigorously, cut him short. "That's very naïve and it won't do."

"Oh?"

"I don't believe people change overnight, least of all my father. All those stories of extraordinary and pious conversions, of seeing the light and the rest are hogwash."

La Rochelle remained silent, but he was watching his senior assistant like a hawk.

"In the end Emily and I came to the same conclusion," Tim continued. "The old humbug finally saw the writing on the wall. He's calculated Huston will lose, and he wants to be on the winning side."

"And the signal your family saga is sending?" La Rochelle inquired.

"Precisely this: democratic forces, I prefer to call them the American Party, are gaining strength and momentum. The old balance is no longer in force. I am sure Father has counted noses and calculated the odds. The old buffoon has done his homework; he always does. His decision is indeed sending a signal, and it is a signal you can stake your reputation on."

"If what you say is true how do you see the end of Huston's rule, Tim?"

"I don't think there'll be one dramatic and deciding event, something like a march on Washington and the American Party troops taking over and throwing Huston and his gang in the clink. No! That's movie stuff. Much more likely it will happen over a period of time, a relatively short period of time. Recent desertions from the government ranks have been noted. There will be more desertions. Concurrently there will be constant jabs at the establishment, defying orders, local insurrections, strikes, political prisoners in detention centers taking hostages, and lots of demonstrations."

"And then what?"

"The government will have to make concessions, small ones at first, bigger ones later. Otherwise they'll be wiped right off the map."

"I see."

"And don't forget the menacing example of Wyoming, which sends cold shivers down Huston's spine. For all practical purposes those guys told Huston to kiss their ass. Other states may take the cue."

La Rochelle walked a short distance to the nearest bookshelf and leaned against it, his countenance frozen into extreme seriousness. "What you say is credible, though I'd rather hear another explanation of your father's motives. I don't want to condemn a man whom I hardly know."

"That's very gentlemanly of you, Siegfried." Tim gave out a quick jeering laugh. "But believe me, Father doesn't deserve such gentlemanly treatment."

La Rochelle adjusted his glasses. "Today is Monday, June 8th, the beginning of a new week. My intuitive powers are embryonic at best, Tim, but I can't shake off that feeling of foreboding that gripped me as soon as I woke up. I fear something terrible will happen soon, very soon. I hope I'm wrong."

"Does your feeling tell you something a little more specific?"

"No, it doesn't. It's just an overwhelming sense of foreboding."

"I understand, but I have to tell you I am feeling rather sanguine today. Things have taken a turn for the better, of this I am convinced. Maybe we are entering the last phase of our shameful bondage."

La Rochelle made an accommodating movement of hand.

"By the way, the group meets again tonight. Can you come?"

"I'll be there," La Rochelle replied, his habitual buoyancy all but gone, and he returned to his desk.

/   /   /

In the early hours of the morning of the day on which Siegfried La Rochelle experienced a keen sense of foreboding Princess Sayko and Prince Mikasa left their respective quarters in the imperial palace in Tokyo and very nearly collided in the vestibule, neither of them looking in front but instead dispatching affectionate glances at the highly ornamented walls and ceiling.

"Look where you're going, Takahito!" Sayko cried, making a gesture of dismissal with both her hands.

"Look who's talking," Takahito shot back, sending a signal with the little finger of his right hand for Sayko to step aside.

"More respect for your elders and betters, boy," Sayko rebuked the young man, "or I'll see to it your behind resembles a tartar stake."

Takahito made a prolonged guttural sound. "You wish, you wish," he raised his voice in contempt.

"Anyway, what are you up to?" Sayko asked. "I was given to understand you sleep till noon after your frequent nights of debauchery."

"Since you have no understanding it is impossible for you to understand anything under the sun. Still, because we men have to humor women and animals, I'll tell you. I am on the way to see my tutor. A very important session."

"I am on the way to see a computer expert. Those latest supercomputers drive me mad."

"I see, and otherwise all is well with you?"

"Perfectly well, thank you."

"I am told the date has been set."

"Oh yes."

"I am sorry it will be a private affair."

"This is the way Siegie and I want it."

"By the way, Sayko, what is the date?"

"You will be told when the time comes, brother dear."

"Aha. We are already entering the world of half-truths and deception."

Sayko made a pooh-poohing sound. "All in good time. And how was your trip to Wyoming for the funeral of what's-his-name?"

"If only I could've poisoned or strangled the PM before we got there, it would've been all the more enjoyable. It's a beautiful part of the country, you know."

"Yes, yes, so I've heard." They were on the point of going their separate ways when a familiar figure attracted both their attention. The empress, attired entirely in black, accompanied by her favorite lady-in-waiting only, similarly attired in black, was getting into her Rolls, while the chauffeur held deferentially the door.

"Where's Grandma off to so early in the morning?" Takahito was genuinely surprised.

Sayko gave her brother a long, patronizing stare. "She will be communing with the spirit of her dear friend."

Takahito scratched his head. "Oh yes, I remember. A Canadian sailor, sis. Did I get it right? But the name eludes me."

"Commander Quentin McPherson, of the Royal Canadian Navy," Sayko put in softly.

"Was the body ever recovered?"

She shook her head. "He lies buried somewhere on the bottom of the Pacific Ocean."

Takahito straightened himself up. "Poor Grandma."

They watched the Rolls slide slowly away, and Sayko placed a hand on her brother's shoulder. "Grandma had a shrine built for the commander, and she visits it often. He was a June child, and today is his birthday. Each birthday Grandma places a bunch of his favorite Japanese flowers inside the shrine. She hasn't missed a single year."

"I take it she had a soft spot for Quentin," Takahito uttered the words with understanding.

Sayko looked down at the floor and smiled faintly. "He was the love of her life."

Chapter 3

Interludes

Linda managed as well as she could after Nathan's death, receiving moral support from all quarters, but turning to Agnes more than to anybody else for understanding and assistance. Ever since that terrible Friday mother and daughter drew closer to each other and faced the challenges of widowhood and of the parent permanently severed from his daughter together. It was a new bond that neither the mother nor the daughter had experienced before, and it was a blessing for both.

Agnes would soon be celebrating her sixteenth birthday, and boys were very much on her mind together with a not wholly crystallized ambition of becoming a pharmacist. She was a slim, dark-haired girl, a little taller than ordinary, not particularly attractive, but possessed of a vivacious personality. Her face, as many of those who knew her well asserted again and again, changed so drastically in aspect and expression in short periods of time as to become unrecognizable to mere acquaintances.

Agnes drew those she was fond of into her magic circle, but she had no staunch friends of her own gender and though she dated with all the energy and passion of youth she had no steady boyfriend, only male friends for diverse occasions. Linda was telling her daughter she ought to settle down with a single boyfriend, but Agnes rejected this advice as it limited her movements and would, she feared, land her in a suffocating morass of cheap sentimentality. She was popular with boys and girls her own age but not to a very high degree, and at times she was looked upon as an oddity of a special and pleasant kind, but an oddity never-theless. More often than not she found instances of vows exchanged among her schoolmates laughable and demeaning, but she held her tongue and no one had ever accused her of being a gossip. To the dis-criminating few among the high school population she was a tad dif-ferent from the rest, but she harmed no one and those boys and girls who knew her better than the others said they had enjoyed her com-pany and would be happy to repeat the experience, which some of them did.

Agnes was not even moderately intellectual and was not drawn to art. As she matured, her goal of becoming a pharmacist became more crystallized, and already while a sophomore and junior in high school she worked part-time in one of the largest pharmacies in Cheyenne. Politics disgusted her, and her favorite recreational reading was science fiction fantasy. She was good at math, chemistry, physics, and the sci-ences generally, and volleyball was very close to her heart. She carried on serious conversations with her friends, but her only true confidante was her mother. From her Agnes had no secrets.

She knew her father's murder was a blow so hard that it would take her many months and possibly years to come to terms with it, howev-er lamely. She felt a blind rage, and she was in a quandary whether this blind rage would ever go away. Perhaps not, perhaps never!

Her life was struck by the worst possibly tragedy, but in addition, earlier in 2084 another pall of gloom hung over her health and well-being: her epilepsy returned with a vengeance. Several attacks occurred in March as well as in April and at the end of May. Agnes's condition worsened, causing the doctors grave concern. Convulsive attacks accompanied by loss of consciousness grew longer and more frequent. At times Agnes had a premonition that an attack was on the way, but at others she seemed to be in the best of health just before it happened. Doctors in Denver had no ready answer and no new cure, but they were of the opinion that the traumatic experiences the patient had recently undergone were at least partly responsible for her condition. They prescribed the same treatment that their colleagues had pre-scribed several years before, and Linda made an appointment for her daughter to see a highly recommended specialist in Chicago, in the lat-ter part of June, who had recently achieved a remarkable success both in research and in handling numerous cases of epilepsy.

Agnes endured the effects of her illness bravely, standing guard against disruption of her academic schedule and her private life, but she was far from being optimistic about the medical prognosis. She had read deeply on the subject of epilepsy in medical journals, and she knew there was no miracle cure, the whole field being subdivided into jealously protected bailiwicks, none of which could boast of a better record than any other.

Just before venturing out of Wyoming on their "vacation" Agnes met a young man whose home was also in Cheyenne but who was now a pre-med student in Denver. Walden was eighteen, thus being her senior by slightly more than two years, and he took a very serious interest in her. Agnes liked him but searched for hidden reasons for his attention. She concluded that, coming as he did from a zealously evangelical fold, he was inspired by pity and compassion for her, and she had no use for either. Or, since he was grooming himself for the medical profession, he'd want to pick up a guinea pig or two on the way to observe from close quarters and then sermonize about it. Agnes belched impolitely—she could not remember when she had belched last—at the thought of being a guinea pig. Her mother spent much time and energy advising her that more likely than not Walden's intentions were simply romantic—pity, compassion, and guinea-pigging playing no part in the equation.

Agnes demurred, dismissed her mother's advice as do-gooding twaddle, and very soon sat down to a heart-to-heart with Walden, telling him it would be best for all concerned if they stopped seeing each other immediately after the present meeting was over. At first Walden sat very quietly listening to Agnes. Then he professed his love for her again and again swearing he was carrying out no mission of mercy and no research into epilepsy. After that he made a terrible scene shouting insults in her face, the least offensive of them being that she was a pigheaded, lowdown bitch and ought to be locked up. It was Agnes' first exposure to unrehearsed and unexpurgated male fury, and even though she had no intention of changing her mind, at least for the time being, she was impressed by her friend's candor and hell-for-leather attitude. "He's a real man," she thought, "just like Daddy, but he hides it under those impeccable manners of his and all that Ivy League trash."

"You'd better go now," she said when his fury had spent itself. But her tone was warm and she was eyeing him with curiosity.

He swung the door open, and then he roared at her sitting ginger-ly across the room and looking so very alluring, "Go to hell! *Go to hell!*"

Looking after Agnes was now a fulltime occupation, but in addition Linda had another fulltime job as a resource person for Kevin Schultz and his staff, as their memory bank, as their trusty advisor and testing ground. Having been a confidential helper and coworker of her hus-band's in his struggles for the old democratic U.S.A. for more than twenty years, she was uniquely qualified to assist Nathan's successors in their renewed struggles toward the same goal. Linda had no political ambitions of her own, but her grasp of the political situation, her knowledge of names, places, of obstacles encountered and steps taken to overcome them was pure gold to the conspirators. It was only when she became entrenched in her new role that she realized how all-encom-passing her marriage to Nathan had been, where for the most part work undertaken was joint, Nathan's and her own forming one indivisible whole, private concerns merging with political concerns and vice versa.

From the perspective of time lapsed Linda reflected on her good fortune of having found a mate who had satisfied her needs and desires and who had always taken her into his confidence as she had taken him into hers. A widow now still under forty—she had celebrated her thir-ty-ninth birthday in the wake of her husband's death—she had no incli-nation to marry again or to embark on a serious relationship. She was surrounded by male friends, friends of many years on whose assistance, should the need arise, she could always count.

Presently she began to spend more and more time in the company of Kevin Schultz for purely professional reasons, and at the same time she tried to be sympathetic, knowing that Kevin was in the midst of a messy and painful divorce. The hours of intimacy the two of them shared did not blossom into a lasting relationship because she pulled back and retreated to her cocoon of a mother and advisor-at-large, but also because she soon realized that at that juncture of his life Kevin needed a mother and not a wife or a girlfriend, and she was loath to be one. One day the two had a very serious talk and decided that their romantic contact was at an end permanently while the professional one would, of course, continue. The decision was really Linda's, and Kevin reluctantly agreed seeing that he could not persuade her to change her mind.

In the weeks and months to come Nathan's widow came to appreciate how frustrating it was for Kevin to hold his end of the bargain. He was head over heels in love with her, and she wished he would rush into an affair, any affair, to erase her picture from his mind. But he did nothing of the kind.

Agnes, in her epileptic condition that did not seem to improve an iota, claimed much of her mother's attention, but in addition Linda was happy to be working with Nathan's former associates because it gave her something to do. She was not unduly nostalgic about the years of her marriage. That part of her life had ended, and she very much doubted whether it could be duplicated even in part in a union with another man. Dwelling on it, attempting to relive the highlights of the marriage and make them tangible and inspiring, would in the long run only bring pain, pain and suffering. She was telling herself she had to adjust as best she could to her new circumstances, her new environment. She did not face a void, and she was not broken in spirit.

Yet she understood that her future life would be lived in a lower gear, that much of what had made her life so abundant in the past was irretrievably gone, and that adjustments, yes, adjustments had to be made and new goals pinpointed. Without delay an initiative of self-preservation, of regaining her strength to stand up to new challenges took hold of her and served her well, like a pilot bringing a ship safely to port from a tempestuous sea. Linda made a vow to live in the present, to take the measure of her situation, to approach whatever was surging in front of her on her own terms, and above all to be her own self always, every hour of every day, to crush the thorns in her path underfoot and partake of the mellow fruit.

When she had been married to Nathan neither of them spent much time alone. In contrast they often used a phrase that in due course became their profession of faith, "Being alone together," which they fulfilled to the letter. But now Linda spent more time being alone, by herself, reflecting, weighing pros and cons, planning. She was far from becoming a recluse but treasured those hours of tranquility when she could be alone with her thoughts. Mother and daughter continued to have no secrets from each other, but in addition Linda struck up a friendship with Helen, Nathan's sister, and the two of them were often seen in restaurants and ice cream parlors talking their heads off.

Wyoming's newly won independence and its new political structure, a bone in Huston's throat, acted as a magnet to the surrounding states and elsewhere. At the very beginning of May, Nathan had received news of a considerable pressure being exerted on state governments in Nebraska, the Dakotas, Idaho, and Montana to follow Wyoming's example. In each instance state leaders were calculating the odds. Later in the month more exciting news came from New Mexico, California, Oregon, and Washington. Here too large crowds were clamoring for the return to the principles of 1787 and for the adoption of a referendum modeled on that of Wyoming, which with the stroke of the pen would restore cherished rights and liberties. At the beginning of June Kevin hosted in Cheyenne a conference of representatives from ten western states at which projected changes in their constitutions, jurisprudence, and social structure were discussed and debated at length. It was also proposed that any given state should not act by itself but that as many different parts of the country as possible should act in concert, reinstating what had been trampled underfoot when Huston had come to power. Representatives at the conference envisaged a coalition of fifteen to twenty states motivated by the same political philosophy and demanding identical reforms. In this way, should the sun of liberty shine on the newly unshackled territories, a sizable segment of the country would be throwing down the gauntlet before the tyrants, standing guard and protecting American honor. From this nucleus rays of freedom would travel east and south, the conferees were in hopes, and before long the entire country would coalesce round it, a score of heroic states sparking off the second American Revolution, equal to if not surpassing in glory the thirteen colonies that had sparked the first.

Reports from other states were also encouraging. In Wisconsin and Michigan, in Iowa, Minnesota, and Illinois, in Virginia, and other parts of the South, there were men and women of goodwill who did not shrink from danger and self-sacrifice. But they had to be trained, taught how to present the message of American democracy to smug close-minded majorities fearful that any political change would undermine their economic status. This applied to highgovies and lowgovies alike and the latter, beneficiaries of recent financial and job-oriented adjustments, often made common cause with highgovies and damned all change.

Neo-conservative trends emerged in a variety of professions and occupations, among MDs and scientists, in the engineering circles, in the ranks of auto mechanics, factory workers, and manual labor. Higher salaries or wages with concomitant longer vacations and better medical coverage were the perennial goals worth demonstrating for, but civil rights, impartial justice, freedom of speech, free elections, and majority rule were to millions of city dwellers and of heavily populated areas incomprehensible gimmicks helping no one and getting honest folks into trouble.

Comments most often heard in those overflowing centers of teeming humanity when so-and-so and so-and-so were arrested or endlessly interrogated by the Sex or the Faith Police blamed the victims and not the authorities. "They only have themselves to thank for it, they brought it on themselves. Careless! Careless considering how things are," were the typical inferences drawn absolving powers-that-be and urging Tom, Dick, and Harry, Susan and Jane to mind as they made their way through jungles of liberal temptations and across spy-ridden minefields.

From Maine to Virginia, across Indiana and Michigan and westward over the lake to Wisconsin and Minnesota palls of conformity and obedience covered human life so tightly that only the bravest of the brave broke loose and many perished in the attempt. Virginia was currently celebrating its hero-worshipping week, and entranced crowds lingered before forty-foot high portraits of Chief Justice, praying, quoting biblical verses, pledging allegiance, and boasting what they would do to his enemies. Elsewhere in Dixie the situation varied from region to region, from state to state, but throughout the God-ordained authority of the Savior of the Country hung thickly in the air like a gigantic axe held by invisible strings, proud of its well-earned reputation of not having missed even once the traitor's and the liberal's tainted neck. Voices of protest were heard in the South, but in the main they were muffled and uncoordinated, sporadic outbursts of wounded consciences that had had enough, for the time being at any rate.

Kevin remembered well a meeting held several months earlier at which Nathan had outlined a nationwide program of education in democracy, its intrinsic nature, its organizational framework, participation of as many members of the community in its day-to-day and year-to-year activities being its necessary basis. Other urgent matters had intervened, and the program had never been launched even on a limited scale. Now Nathan's words began to haunt Kevin. Yes, in many parts of the country education, preparation for democracy, was badly needed. With the exception of allied states, strengthened by the addition of California, Oregon, and Washington, the rest of Amernipp was thoroughly indoctrinated in the philosophy of tyrannical theocracy and did not aspire to anything better.

Kevin vividly remembered words spoken by Nathan and also by some of his academic advisors attempting to explain the country's apathy when it came to pressing for needed reforms and seeking a fairer political system. Kevin recalled that explanations varied but that the bulk of what he had thought to be particularly enlightening could be arranged under three headings, which in part overlapped. Under the first two headings the speakers played the part of the devil's advocate, but the arguments marshaled under the third one were unbiased and the speakers were straight shooters.

I. The social and business structure of Amernipp is so complex and so interrelated, it is such a jigsaw puzzle of choreography, that traditional means of ensuring the highest productivity and efficiency, many of which stem from democratic principles and assumptions, are no longer viable. The Western Amernippian economy, responsive as it is to national and international pressures and to the ups and downs that are the inevitable hallmark of the business cycle, has evolved its own checks and balances and its own oversight, which are rooted in the laws of supply and demand. This being the case the judicial process in the field of the national economy and in the business world has become a dead letter, an embarrassing anachronism. The economy of Amernipp is regulated by new methods, respectful of individual rights but calculated to reach the optimum of productivity and profits.

II. After three centuries of what can only be called a democratic bushfire, its flames abated and were finally extinguished. In the eighteenth, nineteenth, and twentieth centuries democratic practices stimulated business initiatives, protected the individual from governmental abuse, and were the mortar holding the edifice of state together. But in the extremely complex world of the twenty-first century, democratic practices impede industrial expansion and progress on all fronts. Judicial process scrupulously observed, the so-called free elections, equal representation, freedom of speech, the right to a speedy trial, and other rights of the accused impinge on the authority of the state, interfere with legitimate business pursuits, and turn established order into confusion and chaos. National business can best be conducted when legislators are appointed by the head of the state, when the head and his officials enjoy broad discretionary powers and when lawbreakers, no matter what their ideology may be, are swiftly brought to justice. Offenses against the authority of the state are particularly heinous, and those who commit them deserve no mercy. Expeditiousness and efficiency are the war cries of Western Amernipp, and democratic practices can only weaken our resolve as a nation and destroy our fiber as a God-fearing people. It is worth remembering that the last ten years saw unparalleled industrial growth in our country, accompanied by the virtual disappearance of unemployment, a tripling of the GNP, and an unprecedented enrichment of the entire population of Western Amernipp. Our material achievements have been truly breathtaking.

But don't let us forget spiritual achievements, which lie at the core of our national character: the last ten years witnessed a religious revival in our country, a religious regeneration, a rebirth of faith like no other. Today we can truly call ourselves children of God. We live by God's word and He watches over us. Democracy with its godless secular sting is truly the work of Satan, and it behooves us to combat it with all our strength. The Almighty will reward us, and news reaches us daily from the heavens that our nation will soon be elevated to an angelic status. The nation that was under God will be with God, dwelling in God.

III. When one places what has happened to Western Amernipp in the last forty years in a broader historical context, it is impossible not to notice parallels with other powers, other empires, other mighty states flexing their muscles. After all, political organisms do not remain the same centuries upon centuries. They change, some drastically, some less so, and often abruptly in the wake of earthshaking events. The evolutionary process on the British model takes place seldom in the Western world, much more often things just explode, and no one is any wiser as to its real causes. The Great Awakening of the 1730s and '40s was the direct ancestor of the powerful religious revival of the 2060s. There are all kinds of similarities, all kinds of common traits, but there is also a fundamental difference: our revival two generations ago came after the horrors of two world wars, after the Holocaust, and after prolonged periods of ruthless totalitarian rule in Germany, Italy, Russia, Japan, China, and a little later in North Korea, in South America, and in the emerging countries of Africa and Southeast Asia.

History is like a malfunctioning vacuum cleaner; it absorbs everything on its way and stores it after a fashion. But it cannot be emptied at one go, and the best it can do is to leave a trail of what it has collected on the clean new path which points to the future but is at once soiled by the refuse of the past. This malfunctioning vacuum loses nothing, just as history forgets nothing. Any authoritarian regime in the saddle in our own century must perforce have taken note of the horrors of the last century, and that is why Huston's regime is so bloody; it bears imprints of Auschwitz and Buchewald, of Soviet gulags, of Japanese POW camps, of Pinochet's torture chambers, and of much else.

Every new dictator learns from previous dictators consciously and unconsciously, what happened in the past fashions the future, and the curious thing about it is that we simply can't put the past to the side, forget it, pretend it never existed. Some of us wish we could, but we can't, things just don't happen that way. In different ways all of us are legatees, and each man's legacy is nailed to his back. As soon as Huston started playing games with secret police, wholesale arrests, absolute power, dissolution of duly elected legislative bodies, he lay himself wide open to the implants of his fellow dictators who were beckoning to him from the grave. He was a quick learner. He made them proud.

However, there is another way of looking at the last two

generations in the life of Western Amernipp in a broader historical context, which is apersonal and cares not a whit for individual culpability or lack of it. In the history of some mighty nations the initial parliamentary or elective system gave rise in time to imperial rule because the republican framework was inadequate in dealing with the expansion of the state and an impediment to the new imperial ruler. The Roman Republic ended with Julius Caesar, and even if Caesar had wanted to preserve it, as obviously he had not, it would have been impossible for him to do so if he were bent on pursuing his policies. The whole republican apparatus stood in his way. Caesar's ambition drove him on, but new historical forces were also afoot and an empire was the next shape of the Roman state. Western Amernipp's tragedy was that its first emperor was not Augustus, but a man combining the worst features of Nero and Caligula and of the mediocre emperors of the next three centuries. But a change from democracy to theocracy, or to some other totalitarian system, was in the cards. In retrospect, little could have been done to avert it.

Kevin pondered the academicians' speculations and wondered whether anything in them could be of value in helping ameliorate the present situation. After a while he went back to Nathan's oft-repeated words urging a nationwide program of education for democracy. They struck him as eminently practical. He walked over to the large map of the country hanging on the wall where different shades of dark and red signified the degree of loyalty to Huston or to the old democratic principles. Somehow, in one way or another, the reddish areas must be enlarged and intensified. "In one way or another," he muttered to himself. His eye fell on the Commonwealth of Massachusetts, and he winced at the sight of so many gradations of dark from one end to the other. Several weeks before, new minutemen had been organized in Massachusetts, carrying no weapons but armed with zeal that their admirers pronounced to be equal to moving mountains. Judging by sheer numbers the commonwealth was solid Huston country yet it spawned two of the Chief Justice's fiercest critics, widely respected and eminent figures who denounced him publicly and from the pulpit, the provincial of the Dominical Order and the secretary general of the Society of Friends.

There were other protests too. Toward the end of 2083 a dozen Protestant ministers from New Bedford, Yarmouth, Plymouth, Worcester, and Springfield banded together forming the Commonwealth of Massachusetts' Center for Democracy. They distributed a newsletter, arranged for lectures, meetings, and discussions, advocated an all-out fight against the theocratic regime employing peaceful and whenever possible legal means, and shunned violence at all cost. They won a measure of support, mostly at universities and colleges, and a grudging respect from their opponents on account of their courage and high ethical standards.

Immersed in daily routine behind his desk, Kevin recalled to a tee the ghastly aftermath of their work. Just before Christmas two of the twelve met with fatal accidents on the expressway; two were killed while their homes were allegedly being burglarized. Another was found in an unsavory part of town with his head bashed in and an inordinately high level of alcohol in his blood, which astonished everybody including the police chief and presiding judge, since it was widely known that Reverend Clement Burr's lips touched nothing stronger than ginger ale. Of the remaining seven, three were dragged to a vacant lot in the middle of the night and repeatedly clubbed; their limbs and backs permanently injured, they would be confined from that point on to wheelchairs. Two drowned in shallow waters, which again caused astonishment because they were young, physically fit, and excellent swimmers. The last minister had been abducted from his church, knocked unconscious, and left tied up and naked on the edge of a forest in a snowstorm. He was not discovered until two days later, still breathing, but only just. The next day he died in an OR of pneumonia and of multiple injuries to the pulmonary artery and the thorax. The perpetrators of these crimes were never brought to justice.

As Kevin mulled over the acts of vengeance directed against the twelve ministers he knew they were not in any way isolated cases. Similar acts had been perpetrated in western states and elsewhere, always with the same purpose: to punish and to discourage.

Pushing folders and individual sheets of paper to the side, Kevin began to review the situation. Five western states bordering on one another were moving closer and closer to the adoption of the Constitution of 1787 and to a confrontation with the federal government, arms in hand if need be. Five other states—New Mexico, Arizona, California, Oregon, and Washington—were close behind. From the heap of folders, official documents, loose sheets, and letters awaiting his signature Kevin lifted a writing pad containing the size of the National Guard in each of the ten states, their ready equipment and weapons, the number of transport planes and super-choppers at their disposal. His eyebrows were contracted to the limit, and he was breathing heavily. He was reaching the same conclusion for the fifth or sixth time, namely that only military action could bring Huston's regime to an end. Military action and nothing else, for the man was slippery as an eel. Again he fixed his gaze on the figures and data pertaining to the National Guard, and he concluded as he had done several times in the past that the West, eleven states as of now, had a fighting chance. Kevin continued to attend to his numerous duties throughout the day, but now and then debilitating doubt gnawed at his resolve, a two-pronged doubt: would this tyrannical government ever crumble even if its opponents went an extra mile, and was he, Kevin Schultz, equal to the task?

Like everybody else in the movement Kevin had been under the spell of Nathan's dynamic and charismatic personality, and what added to its lasting effect on close friends and coworkers alike was Nathan's unwillingness at any stage of the game to take himself unduly seriously. The chief of freedom fighters had been endowed with a natural modesty, and this only strengthened the influence he exerted over the others by dint of his brains, his organizational capacity, and his unswerving commitment to democratic principles.

As for Kevin, he had always realized that he was the very opposite of Nathan, as a personality that is. He was a plodder, going about his work thoroughly and scrupulously, inspiring no audience large or small, winning few converts, and generating no brilliant ideas. He was the organizer, the watchdog, the ideal second-in-command whom a fickle destiny catapulted onto the throne. When shortly after Nathan's death he was informed he had been recommended by the departed idol as his successor and confirmed by a majority vote his first instinct was to run. He was literally shouted down and told that in trying times one does not shirk responsibility. He claimed he was not quite the timber for that high office, and he was shouted down again and told to report for duty.

He recalled with affection that in the short period of his occupancy of the office of leader of the democratic opposition and director general of the Center for Democratic West he received wholehearted support from practically everybody, backbiting being non-existent. He was grateful for this show of loyalty, nevertheless remaining of two minds about his qualifications for the job. When very recently he broached the subject to Linda she replied that Nathan had indeed talked to her about it, and she paraphrased his comments. "The trail has been blazed," Linda said, "and the railroad track laid in the right direction. What is needed now is not an explosives expert or a pioneer, but a reliable locomotive driver." This gave Kevin pause, and Linda made a point of telling him again how highly her husband had always spoken of him. Kevin shrugged and blew his nose. "Maybe I am not the best man for the job," he told himself, "but I am the only one. I'll give it my best shot and let others judge me."

His mess of a divorce would soon be over with, and he would be free to marry again. He swore loudly and touched his temples. The only problem was that the woman he wanted to marry, passionately and right now if it could be arranged, did not want to marry him, and he was absolutely uninterested in anybody else. Linda made her position clear, and he respected it. One day while their intimacy was still alive he told her he had fallen in love with her years earlier, but for obvious reasons could not make it known to her. She had evinced no surprise but had wanted to know whether his feelings for her had anything to do with the crisis that he and Marilyn later faced. "No," he had said with finality. "Marilyn and I had a heap of problems, but nothing tied it directly to you." He recalled that upon hearing these words Linda had given him a very odd, mistrustful look. He could have sworn then that she had plain refused to believe his statement.

A few days later she begged him that they ought to bring their short-lived affair to an amicable close. Kevin was fully convinced that Linda would never change her mind. All that talk about the ameliorative role of time, of time the healer, of time that brings a new lease on life was just empty talk, at least so far as he was concerned. His fate had been woven not by benevolent powers but by malicious and wanton deities. First, several years of an unendurably miserable marriage in the course of which he had fallen in love with the wife of one of his closest friends; then, after his friend had departed this world, a short-lived embrace from the widow for whom his love was boundless, followed by a rejection. "The only thing for me to do is to bury myself in my work," he mused. "But it hurts, it hurts like the dickens."

/ / /

In the most cheerful of moods, Siegfried La Rochelle bowed over his dessert plate and with the help of a minuscule fork explored the kernel of the multicolored dish where strawberries and round Swiss mini-chocolates glacés sprinkled with brandy lay embedded in marzipan.

"This is really awfully good, Tim. Thanks for bringing me here."

"My pleasure, sir, and even though I can't boast of your culinary discrimination, I'd say that desserts at the Montespan are unique. Those who know say so."

"But the soup and the entrée were also delicious," Siegfried mildly protested. "Surely all the chefs deserve praise."

"True, but Jules—Monsieur Jules to his underlings—is one of a kind. He was snatched from the Dindon where he was a generalist so to speak, supervising steak and filet dinners alongside his beloved desserts. The Montespan made him an offer he couldn't refuse. He is now entrenched in desserts, has two assistants working under him, and wouldn't lift a finger in the preparation of a main course even if it'd been ordered by the richest man on earth."

"I see."

"And he made his desserts truly *spécialité de la maison*," Tim went on with obvious enjoyment.

"So the Montespan is still in its salad days, if you forgive a mixed metaphor?" Siegfried asked still jabbing and prodding with his minuscule fork and spoon.

"They opened three months ago to the day and their reputation has soared high, very high. In the interim they managed to inflict such wounds on the cocky opposition that there isn't a restaurant in D.C. that has the guts to take them on. And dessert is, of course, the pièce-de-résistance and Jules a star."

"Thank you again for inviting me. It's been a rare feast," Siegfried spoke warmly and held out his hand.

"You're very welcome, I'm sure, and besides it was a pleasure."

Over coffee Tim leaned forward and the grave expression darkening his face bespoke a return to more serious subjects. "There is a scuttlebutt in the corridors of power that you'll be leaving your post, I mean retiring, soon—very soon. Any truth to it?"

"I've been toying with the idea, but my mind is far from being made up."

"If you resigned, this would wreak havoc on our foreign policy. It would be nothing short of national disaster."

"You exaggerate, surely."

"As a matter of fact I don't." Tim's hand rose in a richly emblematic approbation, drew oblongs in the air, and touched lightly Siegfried's shoulder. "Listen, Mr. National Security Advisor, your beef with Huston is common knowledge, but he'll never fire you. He might just as well cut off his right arm. Stay on, lead the country to safety across a new and then another minefield. You owe it to us."

In response the National Security Advisor smiled cryptically and beckoned to a passing waiter, asking for another pot of freshly brewed coffee.

"There's another reason why we want you to stay on, and that's no secret to you." But Siegfried's pudgy visage disclaimed prior knowledge and cast a questioning glance at Tim.

"Stop flirting, oh mighty Dr. La Rochelle. Stop flirting and come down to earth," Timothy Hysart called out heatedly. "We want you to be one of the leaders in our insurrection against Huston. We want him ousted, yes, ousted for good. I've been authorized to offer you a seat on the Revolutionary Council. You accept, of course, right?"

"Tim, thank you very much for the offer. I am being sincere when I say I am honored. Yes, I truly am, but I'd like to think about it. I need a little time." He spoke these words out without a trace of emotion, but his interlocutor, suspicious and inquisitorial now, gave out a quick sardonic laugh.

"Don't take too long. When the stuff hits the fan it may be already too late." The younger man showed signs of impatience and then of frustration. "You're one queer guy," he muttered.

"I take that as a compliment," the older man muttered back.

Presently the younger man spoke less angrily. "It goes without saying your commitments are very extensive, I realize it. Nevertheless I'd urge a speedy decision in the teeth of those very commitments."

"What are you trying to say?"

"Tongues are wagging in D.C. that you tend a pair of shapely imperial teats in the very heart of the eastern province of our great and divinely blessed country. Is it either love or war, Siegfried, one of necessity excluding the other?"

"I would've thought this sort of gross, mildly offensive talk would've been out of fashion for years in the exalted circles in which you move. As for the question you pose, I simply refuse to answer it." There was more than a touch of severity in Siegfried's voice.

Tim refilled his guest's coffee cup and folded his own napkin. "Answer or don't answer as you please. It really doesn't matter. But in regards to what is in fashion and what is out of fashion, hear this: good things never die, never. They are just put in storage for the duration—long-term storage or short-term storage. That's about it."

"I see," Siegfried La Rochelle put in, discreetly clearing his throat. "I see."

/   /   /

Within a stone's throw of the Montespan, where world-famous culinary creations tickled the palate of gourmets—it was now fashionable for the rich and discriminating to fly to Washington D.C. from places as distant as Texas, southern California, Florida, or Hawaii for the sole purpose of eating lunch or dinner at this mecca of all meccas and return home the same day—stood a tall and massive building constructed fifty-one years earlier and adorned by Doric columns on four sides. Commissioned by an American billionaire who late in life discovered the lure of Hellenic art, the Temple, as its owner called it, was to be his private museum of everything that merited the epithet Hellenic: sculpture, pottery, painting, furniture, musical instruments, rugs and fabrics, household items, kitchen utensils, articles of clothing, etc. However, when three years later the aesthetically-minded billionaire suddenly died of a stroke, his heirs promptly set about selling the *objets d'art* and the bric-a-brac for ready cash and the building as well. They showed very little interest in Hellenic art, or in any art for that matter, but rightly viewed their father's and grandfather's obsession as a cow that could be milked long and hard. They were absolutely right. Profits from sales were considerable, and a dozen or so items fetched very high prices, being sold to national museums and to private collectors of ample means.

The Temple itself did not stay on the market for long. Almost immediately large corporations and international banking concerns began to look it over, but against many an insider's expectation the buyer was no other than the Amernippian Rabbinate, which in the former museum of Greek beauty and versatile skill established its national headquarters, the offices of the Chief Rabbi of the country and numerous administrative and coordinating units. Because of the layout of each of the six floors, a combination of large and small chambers, of wide halls and passageways, the new proprietors were very pleased with their acquisition. They filled it with rather stodgy-looking furniture, hung all kinds of uplifting pictures on the walls, and saw to it that the parquet was polished and shining at all times.

There was only one point that evoked a spirited discussion and a variety of conflicting views. The wide wall of the foyer on each floor was ornamented by a relief displaying a scene from Greek mythology. The one on the ground floor portrayed King Priam begging Achilles for the return of Hector's body. The second floor played host to Odysseus spellbound by Circe; the third proudly presented King Leonides and his three hundred Spartans at Thermopylae; and crucial events and personalities of the ancient Greek world subsequent to the Persian Wars graced the fourth, fifth, and sixth floors.

Initially the reliefs had been greatly admired, but soon voices were heard advising and later urging their removal and substitution of Hebrew reliefs singing the glory of Israel. At this point factions were formed, some advocating recognition of eminent women in Jewish religion and thought—Esther, Rachel, and so on—a shamefully neglected topic, as some claimed. But others opted for a more traditional portrayal of the Hebrew religious tradition, while still others aired their pet views. Lengthy presentations and discussions ensued, but despite goodwill and a conciliatory spirit that were clearly in evidence no final agreement could be arrived at. The high priests dispersed and soon thereafter the chief financial advisor to the Rabbinate quietly announced that funds for the improvement of the existing buildings housing administrative and educational facilities had been depleted, and masonic additions of any kind whatever in the headquarters of the Rabbinate were out of the question for the foreseeable future.

Most of those who worked at the Temple accepted the verdict without rancor and a couple of enterprising newspapermen wrote pieces lauding the exemplary broadmindedness of the Jewish leaders in Amernipp, who had deliberately embellished their HQ with Hellenic motifs. "This is a signal to all mankind," wrote a third newspaperman, "that Western Amernippians of Jewish faith see the human race as one and indivisible, showing no lesser respect for Socrates than they do for Moses." These stirring words were often referred to, cited, and seldom contradicted. Quite naturally they eased themselves into the amorphous reservoir of contemporary wisdom and popular culture.

At the precise moment when Siegfried La Rochelle and Timothy Hysart were crossing the portals of the Montespan on their way out, Dr. Simon Hertzfeld was buzzing Betty Goetz, his confidential and treasured secretary.

"Betty, please call Kevin Schultz in Cheyenne and tell him we have to meet. It's urgent. I thought at first a week's delay wouldn't matter much but it does. If he can come to D.C., well and good, but if not I'll be glad to fly to Cheyenne or else we can meet somewhere in between. But it must be soon, very soon."

"I'll do it right away, sir," Betty intoned moving toward the door, "and I have to remind you that you have a car meeting with Rabbi Pitkin," she examined her wristwatch, "which is now."

"What! With young Joe?" Then Hertzfeld corrected himself. "Yes, of course, it comes back to me. I'm supposed to pick him up a few blocks from here, and we'll drive around having a highly confidential chinwag."

"I think Rabbi Joseph O. Pitkin is very clever in suggesting a car meeting."

"Who is that Joseph O. that you keep yapping about, Betty?"

"Why, this is Rabbi Pitkin's full name. Surely you know his middle name is Oscar."

Hertzfeld sent her a glance of absolute stupefaction. "By my troth, I know not. Still . . . 'old men forget', old men forget not only what is inconsequential but what is damned consequential. It's my fault. I forgot. But you didn't. Betty, the world owes you a great deal."

She smiled coquettishly and again consulted her wristwatch. "You should be leaving in the next few minutes. It's now two-thirty, and we shouldn't keep the rabbi waiting."

"Of course not. I had no inkling we had an Oscar in our midst. *Mortuus est* young Joe, *natus est* Joseph O. It makes all the difference. To get these mixed up would be a hanging offense."

"You know, Chief Rabbi, just about everybody who comes into contact with Joe lauds him to the skies."

"So you keep on telling me, you and the others. But joking apart do you know Joe simply loves all that cloak and dagger? He eats it up—secret meetings, secret chambers, messages in code or in invisible ink, wigs and false beards, the lot. Frankly, I'm surprised he didn't insist that both of us wear disguises."

Betty smiled again. "I'm sure he will next time."

Hertzfeld pulled one of the drawers in his desk open and took from it a pair of glasses in a case.

"Did you know that one of Joe's favorite novels is *The Scarlet Pimpernel?* I would've guessed even if he hadn't told me. A story of a wellborn Englishman who travels to Paris during the French Revolution wearing a hundred disguises and saves French aristocrats from the guillotine."

"Oh yes!" Betty exclaimed, clapping her hands. "Sir Percy and twenty Englishmen good and true, one to command and nineteen to obey, and the villainous Chauvelin, of course. What the Scarlet Pimpernel accomplishes is truly beyond belief. It's a ripping yarn. Bill loves it too."

"Another honest couple, Mr. and Mrs. William Goetz, seduced by this melodramatic nonsense. What a shame," Hertzfeld said as he reached for his hat.

"As if you didn't know, Chief Rabbi, Louise too has a soft spot for these energizing yarns." Betty was pressing the point.

"I know, though her principal weaknesses are English detective stories in which refined lords and ladies poison one another with ineluctable decorum in famous country houses."

"Your wife and I have had several serious discussions about *The Scarlet Pimpernel,* and it's always thumbs up," Betty went boldly on. "Bill and I are also very fond of the film versions, the one starring Leslie Howard being the best of the lot."

Hertzfeld pulled a face as gracefully as he could and made for the door. As he was swinging it open, Betty called, "Please hurry, we must-n't keep Joe waiting!"

He jumped into the elevator, was carried to the underground garage where, after fumbling in his pockets for keys, he climbed into a large and battered Chevrolet sedan badly in need of a wash, and was on his way. Several blocks away from the Temple he spotted a slender fig-ure in a doorway leading into a corridor he could vaguely distinguish, lit up by shingles and signboards. The figure wore a raincoat, collar upturned, and a hat cocked to one side, his hands buried deep in the raincoat pockets as if clutching a gun in each. "Straight out of Raymond Chandler or Dashiell Hammett," he muttered, pulling up at the curb and called out jovially, "Get in, Joe!"

"Let's move on with the traffic and stay on busy streets so as not to attract attention," Joe Pitkin advised pulling his hands out of the pock-ets.

"Are we being followed?" Hertzfeld inquired. "Got their number?"

"There is always a possibility, sir, there's always a possibility." Joe was all earnestness. "One can't be too careful these days."

They drove in silence for a good ten minutes and then, as a light was changing to green, they rushed forward shaking off the cars flank-ing them in the adjoining lanes. Joe turned his head, tensely watching the driver.

"Things are coming to a head, Chief Rabbi. And that means the council has to take a stand."

"Have you read the text of the address I delivered in New York two weeks ago?"

"I did one better. I was in the audience at Elijah Hall."

"And?"

"Your address was wishy-washy. It pleased no one. You counseled listening to one's conscience and bearing in mind the welfare of one's family and of the Jewish community. This was a call to inaction, to opportunism, and to cowardice."

"The council will not tell our people what to do. Nor will I, Joe. I shall not put our people in harm's way."

"Don't you know, Hertzfeld, that thousands of our fellow citizens are rotting in detention centers, that new arrests are being made daily, and that the only hope lies in a *coup d'état?*"

"I condemn injustice, Joe. I have always condemned it. My heart goes to all the victims of this undemocratic regime."

"You say you condemn it, but you won't do anything about it!" Pitkin shouted with fury. "Huston's henchmen murdered Nathan Chadwick and God knows how many others, it's in the thousands, and you turn a blind eye. You've been a fence-sitter and an ass-kisser for so long you don't give two hoots about day-to-day morality." He was not going to stop, but the Chief Rabbi interrupted.

"You may have forgotten that at my behest a special office was created at the headquarters. We try to help all the political prisoners, those still in jail and those recently released, and their families. We offer moral support, medical attention, financial and legal aid." His voice rose in anger. "Don't presume to teach me where my duty lies, young man. Go back and play with your toy soldiers."

Pitkin swallowed hard, held his tongue, and fixed a cold accusatory eye on Hertzfeld. When he spoke at last he had subdued his fury, and his words were dispassionate, deadly in their brutal directness, like bullets from the gun of a hitman who merely fulfills a contract and has no feelings about the victim one way or the other.

"This is what we want you to do, Chief Rabbi."

"We?"

"Yes, we. I am not acting alone. Several weeks ago I and my like-minded friends conducted a poll in numerous Jewish communities and organizations across the land gauging your effectiveness as Chief Rabbi. The results were largely negative. Few have confidence in you. The majority wants you out unless you reverse yourself completely. This is the text of the speech you are going to give tomorrow night on national TV. If you want to remain in office, that is." He handed Hertzfeld two typewritten pages. "If you refuse, you will be removed, excommunicated, most probably forced into exile. An election will be held within weeks, and you will be remembered as another Joe Schmuck who tried to be too clever for his own good."

Hertzfeld held the sheets before his eyes. "How long do I have?"

"Till midnight tonight. Call this number in Cleveland not later than midnight. I'll be at the other end." Pitkin forced a scrap of paper into Hertzfeld's hand. "Your not calling will be interpreted as a refusal. Remember that. We are playing for keeps. One more thing, old man—no tricks. Understand?"

"I understand," the Chief Rabbi replied with dignity. Then he turned sharply into a busy side street and parked the car in a vacant lot from which workers were removing tools and equipment.

"I'd like to go through that speech of yours now if you have no objections."

"Be my guest."

A few minutes later the reader of the speech he was requested to give, of whose existence a few minutes earlier he had been wholly unaware, began to cough and noisily clear his throat.

"I'm sorry. It's the lingering touch of bronchitis that doesn't want to go away."

"You should consult a physician," Pitkin said, a note of warmth breaking through the frost of orders and admonitions.

"Thank you." Hertzfeld paused briefly and placed a hand on Joe's knee. "A speech of this kind will only excite Huston to make new mass arrests. I shall be taken into custody and so will all the members of the council. As a consequence Jewish leadership will be crippled, and untold misery may be visited upon our people."

"And the alternative is doing nothing, I suppose. Let tyranny triumph." Joe's voice was being impregnated once again by fierce anger.

"No. Just the reverse."

"I don't understand. Explain."

"If you and your friends are convinced that diplomacy and horse trading will not succeed with Huston, then by all means start a revolution, which will probably lead to a civil war. But make sure you're in an advantageous position and that you're heading something approaching a national crusade. This will mean winning at least twenty or so states over to your cause. Make certain the odds are good. What you must never do is tell the enemy what your plans are. This would amount to madness. Don't send a messenger under a white flag to your opposite number on the other side informing him you're going to land troops on the beach at such and such a place at such and such a time. You tried to make me such a messenger, and I hope you've seen the light." Hertzfeld paused but it was clear he had more to say.

"The purpose of your TV address was to galvanize Jewish public opinion and present you as the conscience of Americans of Jewish faith. It would also have prepared them for action." Pitkin spoke calmly, but

Hertzfeld felt the young rabbi was beset by doubts. "I suppose the intention also was to give Huston one last chance."

"Wrong again," Hertzfeld broke in harshly. "He's had one last chance too many. Do you remember what happened to Nathan Chadwick? He tried to play by the rules and was swept aside because his opponent did not believe in rules, pure and simple. Don't make the same mistake."

"So what is to be done, Chief Rabbi?"

"Let me walk you back to Elijah Hall. I told the congregation listening to the voice of one's own conscience was of capital importance. But I didn't say those who did so were forbidden to band together for a common purpose, form alliances, make joint plans."

"So?"

"You either do not tickle Huston's throat or you go at him with everything you've got. And again you don't go alone. The time for conscience-searching addresses by eminent citizens about the plight our country finds itself in is long past. You either wait patiently or you act."

"Which of the two do you recommend?"

"I'll leave it to the leaders of the opposition, to the freedom fighters, to Kevin Schultz and his friends in Wyoming, to the activists in the other western states, and to you, Joe, and your tightlipped brothers-in-arms in Ohio and, of course, to the rank and file everywhere. By the way, I've been kept abreast of your activities, Mr. Joseph O. Pitkin. You have the makings of a leader, good and true."

"Thank you, sir. Could you stop by a public phone? I have several urgent calls to make."

"Certainly, but you are welcome to use the phones in my office."

"I'd rather use a public phone."

"I understand."

"What are your plans now?" Hertzfeld asked when Pitkin had come to the end of his phone calls.

"I'll catch the 4:10 to Cleveland, and tonight I'll be on the phone with Kevin for a very long time. Please give my best to Mrs. Hertzfeld. She and I have a common hobby—classical English detective novels and of late the spy novel, with particular emphasis on that ripping yarn by Baroness Orczy set at the time of the French Revolution."

"I'll be sure to tell Louise. But remember if she founds some sort of reading group or club she'll ask for dues. She's very money-orient-ed."

"Can you drop me by the Metropolitan? They have a shuttle to the airport every ten minutes."

"Certainly." The Chief Rabbi made new and stern demands on his large Chevrolet sedan. When he had parked by the glittering hotel entrance he looked Joe straight in the eye and scowled, "If it is war you guys decide on, I want to be in it. I volunteer now, and I'll report for duty when the trumpet calls."

"In your state of health? We advise against it," Joe pleaded.

"Balderdash. I can fire a semiautomatic better than any sharpshoot-er, and I want to be right in front where the action is. Got it, sonny?"

"I promise the matter will be reviewed," Joe said in a most concil-iatory manner.

"Hell, I don't want a review, I want action. If you cross me, I'll have you court-martialed. I still carry a lot of clout in the Armies of David. Or else I'll lay you across my knee and give you a good spanking. Take your pick, young Joe, take your pick."

"I have to think this one through," Joe called making a beeline for the shuttle bus and waving.

/   /   /

Princess Sayko was running along the corridor as fast as she could, and she would have collided with the empress's favorite lady-in-wait-ing just emerging from her mistress's private chambers if the lady had not stepped aside in the nick of time.

"I beg your pardon, Lady Tamiro. I'm very sorry. Did I hurt you?"

"Not yet, Princess."

"It's simply that events are moving at such a breakneck speed—"

"Just like your athletic body . . ." Lady Tamiro made an expansive gesture of welcome. "Please go right in."

The empress, reclining on a brightly embroidered couch, was wear-ing a dressing gown and attending to the day's mail.

"Well now," she exclaimed, "do you nowadays do your jogging inside the palace, Sayko?"

Still out of breath the Princess bowed and threw her arms high in the air. "Oh, Grandmother, things are really happening. We are by the finish line. All kinds of things!"

"Calm yourself, child, and tell me what precisely is happening, one thing at a time. Here. Sit by me on the couch."

Sayko did as she was bidden. Still catching her breath, her eyes sparkled and sent joyful messages all over the room.

"Well?" the empress let fall gently.

At last Sayko was equal to the task. "Oh, Grandmother . . . we finally have a date, and the arrangements are nearly complete. Siegie and I will be married on July 15 in that shrine you recommended on Kyushu, and he's buying through his agent that splendid country house nearby. I forget the name."

"Mon Plaisir, the one that used to belong to Marquess Opitoko years ago, seat of some of the grandest parties ever given in the kingdom. It's a very good choice," the empress commented approvingly. "Your frie . . . your fiancé has shown good taste."

"I am so happy!" Sayko cried excitedly, embracing the empress and smothering her with kisses. "Hear this, and your advice was again duly followed. It will be a dual wedding, Shinto and Christian, a Shinto high priest and a Christian minister officiating jointly. Siegie is getting some bigwig from his church for the other part, who is also president of the American Huguenot Association."

"This would be Dr. Leonard Chevalier, a highly cultured man and a fine historian. I met him years ago." The empress fell silent, and then laughed self-contentedly. "I must say, Sayko, your Siegie is scoring points." She laughed again. "Forgive me when I tell you your pet name for your future husband induces much amusement in me. When I first heard you speak it, I thought you were referring to a Pekinese or a poodle. It was only much later that I realized Siegie was no other than the mighty National Security Advisor and the architect of the union between our two countries."

"I am the only one who calls him Siegie. No one else has the right."

"I am sure, I am sure. But I have to confess that even today when I hear this affectionate diminutive I am liable to be overcome by a fit of giggles which only supreme effort can avert." The empress spoke with kindness.

"You're making fun of me, Grandmother."

"No, Sayko, I am not, and if this is your impression I apologize. We've known each other for so many years I thought I could be candid."

"When I call my future husband Siegie, the name is resounding with love and affection that has no equal."

"Of course, my dear child, and I promise from now on to be as humorless as King Canute when I hear this love-filled name. You are not cross, Sayko, are you?"

"No, Grandmother, I am not, but bear with me when I use names apparently fit for lapdogs to identify humans."

"Agreed." The empress hugged her granddaughter and kissed her warmly on the cheek. "What else do you have to tell me, Princess?" she continued, kissing her again.

"Actually there is something I would like to ask you about, and I am still on the subject of the wedding."

"Please do."

"Custom dictates that the father give away his daughter in marriage and in the absence of the father another male member of the family who is close to the bride." Sayko stopped abruptly.

"That's right. In this instance your father, the Crown Prince, is the obvious choice, and if he is unable to do it then the happy duty devolves upon your grandfather, the emperor."

Sayko's eyes were no longer focused on the empress. They roamed the room with something approaching an aimless determination, and they hardly rested on any single object for more than a second. The grandmother took prompt note of her granddaughter's strained silence but was unwilling to break it. However, as heavy seconds followed one another and even heavier minutes followed suit she broached the subject that she had expected the granddaughter to broach.

"I know you don't want your father to give you away. But you really have no choice unless the emperor can be persuaded to take his place, which is very doubtful. And something else: the fact that you have a distant and loveless relation with your parents has nothing to do with the formalities of the wedding, any more than your parents' displeasure at your marrying a foreigner and a commoner. There are certain rules and conventions to which the imperial family, and especially the imperial family, must adhere. I hope I make myself understood, Sayko."

"Yes, Your Majesty."

The empress leaned toward her granddaughter and held her hands. "I shed tears for many a year on account of the lack of understanding between you and your parents. I tried, but it is clear I failed. Worse than that. Your mother, my daughter-in-law, repeatedly accused me of driving a wedge between you and her. She told me in no uncertain terms that starved as I was for affection I was jealous of the love that might bloom between mother and daughter, that I was poisoning your heart and brainwashing you against your own mother, my daughter-in-law. Stuff and nonsense. I did no such thing, and just to set the record straight I was never in my life, not even once, starved for affection. Your father made a bad choice in marrying that stuck-up halfwit, and our bad choices have a way of haunting us for years to come." As the empress went on talking Sayko slid onto the floor and, pressing her torso against her grandmother's legs, lay her head on the grandmother's knees.

Looking into space the empress stroked Sayko's hair and cheek. "I was rambling," she poured forth. "Let the past stay buried." Then taking notice of the look of disgust on her granddaughter's face she spoke quickly and resolutely in the manner of one taking charge and immediately dispelling in the crowd the continually mounting fears.

"No matter what your personal feelings are about your parents I can assure you that at your wedding both of them will comport themselves with dignity and good taste." Sayko did not move a muscle nor open her mouth, and the empress, her keen eyes scanning the young woman crouching at her feet, snapped her fingers delicately and lay both hands on her shoulders. She spoke now with redoubled vigor. "Forgive me for being so slow and for understanding so little, child. It comes with age. You have already made up your mind once and for all that you don't want your father or your grandfather to give you away. You want your brother to do the honors."

"Yes, Grandmother."

"But he's barely seventeen."

"Does it matter? There are precedents for it in Japanese history."

"I know well the ones you have in mind," the empress countered. "In most cases the father was no longer living and the brother, much older than the bride, was in effect a father figure and her protector. Your situation is entirely different."

"Not really."

"Does it really matter who gives you away?"

"Yes, Grandmother, it does. The day of the wedding is the first day of my new life. I want this life to start on the right foot. I want next to me a male member of my family whom I trust, love, respect. Takahito is the only one. My father and mother remind me of those pitiful French aristocrats at the time of the French Revolution without a thought in their heads, endlessly insisting on their criminal privileges and getting their overdue comeuppance during the Reign of Terror. The kindest thing one can say about my father is that he is a martinet and a stuffed shirt. Mother is a mechanical doll, capable of bowing, curtsying, shaking hands, and of uttering a banal line whenever the wires inside her cross. I despise both of them."

"My, my, my. This is a temporary posture, I take it."

"Far from it, and with all due respect you are not as observant as you claim to be, Grandmother."

Self-effacingly the empress spread out her hands.

"I have felt like this about my benighted parents ever since the age of seven or eight," Sayko declared very firmly.

"I see."

"Do you really, Grandmother?"

"Don't be impertinent. I see there are obstacles in your way."

"I will deal with them as I see fit, and your help is not needed. Furthermore, stop treating me as a child. I don't like it. I too am being candid."

The empress knitted her brow. "We have been friends for I don't know how many years. It would be a shame to fall out over a relatively simple matter."

"I agree."

"What are your intentions as the adult that you are and a wife to be?"

"If the idiotic protocol choking the imperial family will bar Prince Mikasa from giving me away, then quite simply I shall not be given away by anybody. I shall walk up to the altar by myself, accompanied by no living soul, and be married to Siegfried La Rochelle before God and man."

"This will be seen by the nation and the world as a lamentable faux pas and blame will fall on our family. Do you really want the family to be censured and humiliated?"

"You're very good, Grandmother, but it won't work. Just to satisfy your curiosity, I am utterly indifferent to what happens to the family, yourself included. Let's be candid, as you had suggested."

For a few moments the empress was deep in thought, her fingers mechanically rearranging objects on a small side table.

"Neither you, nor the emperor, nor the government can force me to be given away by a person of their choice. Nor have you the authority and power to cancel the wedding." The Princess was again very firm.

"Sayko, believe me no one will try to cancel the wedding. You have my word."

"I thought it was appropriate to bring it up."

The empress stood up and stretched her arms. "All this highly charged chatter made me very thirsty. Would you like some lemonade?"

Sayko shrugged her shoulders, and her grandmother pulled at a bell. When a servant appeared she ordered lemonade for two. When it was brought in and they were sipping it she smiled broadly and patted Sayko's hands.

"I understand your first real job . . . with that international multi-billion-dollar corporation is going well, and I hear you're very active on the Tokyo stock exchange."

"Yes, the job is going well. I am still a trainee. Long hours, which are only to be expected."

"And Siegfried will not mind your spending more than half of your life in your office or in your study surrounded by telephones and super-computers?"

"Not in the least. He knows he is marrying a career woman. We sorted it out ages ago."

The empress refilled Sayko's glass and rearranged herself on the couch, while the granddaughter moved to an armchair, and she was now facing her grandmother.

"Please listen carefully," she began. "I'll do my best to have Takahito named as the family member charged with giving you away, but I can't promise I'll succeed."

"Go on."

"There are factors for and against it. The prime minister gave the emperor a glowing account of Takahito and how he had helped him, the prime minister that is, in all sorts of ways in Wyoming. So far, so good. But a few days later your brother queered his pitch with the government by speaking on Tarako Lepra's behalf and calling for his release from prison. The government stood firm, and when Takahito appealed directly to the emperor he was treated to one of those little talks—actually they can last hours—through which our sovereign corrects, rebukes, and puts to shame the young rebels."

"So it's all a little dicey."

"I'd say there is less than a fifty-fifty chance. If your plan doesn't pan out, you'll have to go it alone. But you know it already, and you're not in the least daunted."

"No, I am not," Sayko cried with spirit, "and I am very glad we talked the way we did."

"So am I," the empress concurred, and then she added, the words coming out of her mouth slowly and awkwardly as if they had been held in check by the witch of silence and released irregularly in dribs and drabs, "I was . . . I was forgetting you are no longer . . . no longer a child . . . I've been . . . been . . . deluding . . . deluding myself."

Sayko pressed her grandmother's hand. "I have one more bombshell for you. I've been keeping it for the last act."

"Take pity on an old woman, Sayko. Take pity," the empress grumbled, showing no sign of waning energy or resolution.

"You are the only one to know in the whole of Eastern Amernipp. And back in our Western Province no one is any wiser except Timothy Hysart, and he can keep a secret."

"Young lady, you are torturing me. Out with it!" the empress cried in desperation.

"All right, Your Majesty, I'll come straight to the point."

"Don't announce what you're going to say. Just say it."

"Right you are."

"Well?"

"This is strictly confidential, and you are not to whisper a word about it to a single living soul."

"Yes, yes, yes. Satisfied?"

Sayko nodded gravely, and all of a sudden she was transformed. No longer a discontented daughter and a rebel against conventions she stood there facing her grandmother, the empress, a euphoric woman in control of her destiny, sanguine to her fingertips, armed against any contingency, equal to any challenge. "Siegie will be leaving public life. He's had a bellyful of it. He's shifting gears."

"What will he do then? He's still a young man," the empress asked in amazement.

"He wants to be a farmer, here in Eastern Amernipp, a gentleman farmer. His agent is looking over some land right here and on the other islands."

"I see. Does Siegfried actually know anything about farming?"

"Well, Grandmother, he had a book about Japanese agriculture checked out for him from a public library in D.C. He's read the first four chapters and tells me it's all very simple and as easy as falling out of bed."

"Indeed!"

"His ancestors back in France, in Clermout-Ferrand, were farmers before they became artisans. So you see, farming is truly in his blood."

"Not to belittle in any way the call of blood, but wouldn't it be a good idea to send someone from our Ministry of Agriculture to see your fiancé and fill in the gaps?" the empress suggested. "I imagine there are parallels between farming in seventeenth-century France and farming in twenty-first century Japan, the one coming readily to mind being that in both cases you are dealing with the soil. But even so."

"Oh no, this would never do," Sayko remonstrated.

"Why not?"

"Siegie feels he knows everything and has an authoritative answer to any question, any question under the sun. He needs no teachers."

"But surely no man or woman can be an expert on every field of knowledge. This is juvenile fantasy run amok."

"If this were to pass, Siegie would make a terrible scene," Sayko spoke up at once.

"A scene with you?"

"No, not with me. With that unfortunate official from the Ministry. He told me in strictest confidence that in going back to farming he is touching the very roots of his family tree and experiences a unique sense of fulfillment. He taps the sources of his family history. He walks with destiny."

"You deserve credit, my clever granddaughter, for explaining all of it so well," the empress said very quietly.

"Remember there are only four of us in the know. Let's keep faith." Sayko was at her wisest and most practical.

The first lady of the land stooped over the bride-to-be and assured her that faith would indeed be kept. "I take it," she said next, "you will be working fulltime in international finance while Siegfried farms."

"Of course. I want a career. I want to be a professional in my own right, and Siegie understands."

"I am happy to hear it." The first lady of the land smiled encouragingly. "In these uncertain times it is essential that at least one of you be gainfully employed."

/   /   /

In early May two professors of English, Robbie Burger and Hershey Bar, joined Huston's inner circle. Previously they had been employed as snitches and agents provocateurs, always with positive results. Now they again trod the beat they knew so well, but they also investigated parties of dubious loyalty to the government, wrote confidential reports about organizations suspected of being less than snow-white, and did a spot of intimidation and extortion. In the early days of their academic careers, Burger and Bar had been dedicated teachers, had published regularly, and had served their respective universities in committees, on panels, and in continually thankless evaluations of curricula and educational trends, which invariably added to the list of one's enemies.

Gradually these commitments began to lose their luster and *raison d'être* and daily confirmed the pettiness of their existence. Burger and Bar wanted more, infinitely more—money and recognition of their efforts beyond the thick walls of academe. They wanted glitter, fame, a life they had never known but had dreamt about. As 2084 came around, they were ready for anything. They reminded Huston's emissaries of their past services, were twice interrogated no-holds-barred, and finally admitted to the august presence. Chief Justice was satisfied, the green light was given, and the two academics were put on the payroll. They were hardliners, counseling mass arrests and no quarter given to the enemies of the state. They warned their boss that with Nathan Chadwick alive, cancer would spread and no *cordon sanifaire* could keep it in check. He saw merit in what they advocated and brought them into the palace. Once inside they quickly climbed the ladder of success.

The Massachusetts Chipmunk had also earned its keep and more. It had mercilessly attacked in print those lukewarm in their praise of the

Savior of the Country and had positively seethed with fury when incense was not continually burning in his honor. Reputations were destroyed, criminal shortcomings of character laid bare for all to see, charges of malfeasance and embezzlement leveled. Few escaped patriotic whipping and there was no recourse. But then the editors of the journal allowed themselves to be careless and overstepped their bounds.

The widely respected provincial of the Order of Saint Dominic was accused of the molestation of young children of both sexes, of sodomy, and of witchcraft. The first charge could not be upheld since in the course of the investigation it transpired that the children who had allegedly filed complaints with a representative of the publicly spirited Massachusetts journal could not be located, their names appearing on no register in any grade, middle, or high school, private or public, in Boston.

The second enjoyed a brief moment of triumph as a young man and a young woman employed by *The Massachusetts Chipmunk* in a clerical capacity piled one heart-rendering denunciation of the provincial on another—how he had forced each of them to commit acts of anal copulation with him, how he had laughed in their faces when they had begged him to desist, and to top it all how at the point of a gun he had coerced both of them to engage in the most unnatural and humiliating sexual practices.

In court feelings ran high against the nefarious and perverse friar, and had lynching not gone out of fashion he would have faced his Maker there and then. Nevertheless as proceedings continued the prosecutors and their partisans faced one cold shower after another. The would-be victims could not testify with certainty as to the location where those terrible sex acts had been perpetrated. First they had named the provincial's official residence and, when told it had been closed down for renovation three months earlier, they asserted the shameful locus was a small bedroom adjoining the provincial's office in the main administrative building. But they could not be precise about the time, and a string of witnesses testified that during the hours in question the head of the order in Western Amernipp was alone behind his desk dealing with a variety of administrative matters, tea being taken to him at regular intervals and later the evening meal.

"Poor, very poor prepping," a juryman barked. "Prosecution lost the case. It ain't right."

Worse was to come. The two clerical employees first confessed they had been paid a substantial sum of money by the editors, but not to perjure themselves, merely as a reward for bringing an abject criminal to justice. Later they recanted saying that no money had changed hands, and the editors of the journal refused to answer questions in court on the grounds of self-incrimination. In the third week of the trial, as new contradictions in the sworn testimony of the would-be victims came to light, the judge, with the consent of the prosecution, threw the case out of court, ordering the bailiff to take the two clerks into custody pending possible charges of perjury and obstruction of justice. He warmly apologized to the provincial who later was loudly cheered outside the courthouse.

The third accusation, that of witchcraft, was relegated to an ecclesiastical court, but it never reached the docket. During a preliminary hearing the judges questioned the three accusers, two middle-aged men and a slightly younger woman, all three fulltime readers and assistant editors at *The Massachusetts Chipmunk,* about the evidence they were going to present. The three assured the tribunal that the provincial had been worshipping animals, inciting them to violence against the government and the august person of Chief Justice. He was up to his neck in sorcery and in league with the devil, they stipulated. The judges inquired as to the identity of the animals, which it was alleged were devils in disguise. It appeared that the provincial had habitually repaired to the south end of the main administrative building where he fed bread and cake crumbs to the pigeons. He also carried lengthy conversations with them in an unknown language. The pigeons reacted loudly making all kinds of sounds that were taken to be pagan incantations, paeans, and calls to bloodshed and mayhem.

"What is the language in which you communicated with the pigeons?" the judges asked of the accused.

"I spoke to them in Latin," the provincial replied. "For the most part it is the classical Latin of Virgil and Cicero, but I add a few colloquial expressions here and there—the patois of the marketplace, you might say—to hold their attention."

The judges expressed a desire to hear the provincial's Latin colloquies with the pigeons, and the accusers immediately stepped forward offering their tapes to the court. They had been shadowing the accused for some time, faithfully recording every word he had uttered in that unheard of lingo to the devils in disguise. The judges ordered the accused to replicate in court under oath his typical address to the pigeons and their vocal response. His replicated address corresponded closely to what was on the tape and an ornithologist of repute testified that the sounds made by the pigeons were the typical and expected ones in situations when food was offered to them. Still, the content of the provincial's addresses to the pigeons remained an enigma, and the judges ordered an English translation to be made, which in due course was read in court.

"Greetings to you my angels of the skies, of the highway, and of the garbage cans. I warmly greet you, my lovelies, my beautiful ones, swift of wing and swift of foot, sharp of eye, gristly of beak . . . I bring you breadcrumbs, soft and nourishing, and bun crumbs, crumbs of New England buns, but I sprinkled them with milk and honey and put them in a microwave, so they are one step closer to being fit for consumption by pigeon and the human species; as you well know our native New England buns are as hard as rock and nothing can break them. If only Odysseus had had a couple of those buns in his armory on the way back from Troy, why, he wouldn't have had to go through all that rigmarole with the sheep and hollering nemo at the top of his lungs. A couple of our finest would've sent the Cyclops into a state of eternal indigestion and eternal sleep—in perpetuity, in perpetuity. But national resources are rarely put to good use. Well now, if one of you my lovelies cares for a bit of gambling on a rainy day, go to the marketplace and bet a fin against any jackass swearing up and down he can actually bite and swallow one of 'em New England buns without losing all his teeth and half his throat into the bargain. Jackasses are fair game. But let us end on a high note: having partaken of the aliment the good Lord sends you, fly again to the skies, take the high road, and commune with the good Lord's creation, which He sanctified with His name, and show kindness to the human race for the Almighty has shown it kindness and more—love, compassion, and forgiveness, having sent His own son to redeem it, knowing full well the human race stood in dire need of redemption. Amen."

The prosecution tried to make hay of what they called strangely deistic and pantheistic thrusts in the defendant's address to the pigeons that undermined Catholic doctrine. But the judges had heard from the plaintiffs all they wanted to hear, and the provincial was unanimously acquitted of the charge of witchcraft. This was the last straw for the editors of *The Massachusetts Chipmunk*. "Now the gloves come off!" cried the editor-in-chief. "Next time that cocky friar will do business not with a summons but with a whip and blackjack."

Even before the new method of administering justice could be put into practice, events necessitated a bold action against another prominent critic of the regime, the secretary general of the Society of Friends. This became highest priority. He had been lambasting Everett Huston and the government for years, sparing no effort, but of late his censure had reached a new vitriolic pitch, and Chief Justice sent word something had to be done about it. The editors of *The Massachusetts Chipmunk* met in an emergency session, and a strategy was formulated. Three toughies were hired to beat the secretary general to a pulp, but not kill. Accordingly they set upon him one evening as he was already holding the latchkey in the door of his Boston home and would have executed their commission to the letter if it were not for a band of cruising teenagers who in the sprit of adventure jumped out of their cars, helped the would-be victim into the house, and then proceeded to beat the three assailants to a pulp, leaving them on the pavement bleeding and unconscious before jumping back into their cars. There were long faces in the editorial offices of *The Massachusetts Chipmunk*, and Chief Justice, who had no stomach for failure, was weighing the pros and cons of taking the blundering journal off the payroll.

"Yet these are temporary setbacks only," Huston was consoling himself, "not on a par with what has been gained." In the previous three weeks the Almighty had appeared to Chief Justice three times in his sleep, each time addressing him at greater length, calling him His favorite son and lauding him to the skies. It had been the third vision that stirred the Savior of the Country to the very marrow of his bones, and so momentous had been the words the Lord had deigned to speak on that occasion that he instantly committed them to memory and thereafter to paper.

The Lord had said to him: "The earth is corrupt and filled with violence, for all flesh had corrupted their way upon the earth. But you, Everett Zacharias Huston, are a righteous man, blameless in your generation. You walk with God. And through your example your country, Western Amernipp, has become righteous too—every man, woman, and child. Therefore I tell unto you, you and your country shall be sin-gularly rewarded for you are an oasis of good in the desert of evil and corruption. I have determined to make an end of all flesh, for the earth is filled with violence through them; behold, I will destroy them with the earth. But you will be spared and the country you rule will be spared. Therefore gather all your countrymen in the famous city by the sea and wait for a sign from heaven. It will not be long in coming. On the appointed day and hour the righteous will be lifted up on high and permitted to watch how the rest of the earth goes up in smoke, for the rest of the earth is evil and corrupt. And when the wicked have been punished I shall bring you and your people down to earth, and you will be a new race of angels, spreading the word of the Lord to all and sundry and converting them to the ways of the Lord. And ye, Everett Zacharias Huston, and your people will forever live in a world from which unrighteousness, vice, and imperfection have been banished, and ye shall dwell in the Lord."

Chief Justice was in seventh heaven.

Chapter 4

Under Orders

The new superbomber, Huston 84, just off the assembly line and named in honor of Savior of the Country, was cruising leisurely over Wyoming at thirty thousand feet, the pilot with satisfaction logging time gained as soon as they had crossed the Appalachians. Visibility was near perfect, the temperature was an unwavering sixty-five degrees, and the engines turned over flawlessly, living up to everything that had been printed in big fat letters in the prospectus. For this particular mission a crew of four officers had been chosen—pilot, copilot/navigator, photographer, and bombardier. The pilot, Captain Glen Merrick, glanced at the clock, pressed an intercom button, and spoke in a low-pitched, ringing voice: "Pilot to crew. For your information local time is 1104 hours so you know in case you experience an unshakable desire to send a picture-postcard to a sweetheart on the range. Over and out."

Instantly he heard a voice though the earphones: "Copilot and navigator to pilot; forty-five seconds to target one."

"Right, navigator. I am informing bombardier," the pilot replied. "Cliff, keep me posted every five seconds." He pressed another button. "Pilot to bombardier, forty-three seconds to target one. Stand by, Warren."

"Right, sir."

Captain Merrick smiled with satisfaction at the absolute precision with which the operation was progressing and clenched his teeth. "A few more minutes, and we'll be on the way back to D.C. and to a heyho weekend with the kids," he muttered.

Then an all-too familiar voice came through on the intercom. "Photographer to pilot."

"What's the matter, Kelly?" Merrick shouted back, making no attempt to control his impatience. "Broke one of your lenses or has the M.C. gone bust on you?"

"None of the above, Captain, but there's something very odd going on."

"What?"

"They told us at the briefings the entire population between Riverton and Worland would be evacuated before the strike. Well, I can see the ground like it was two feet away from me. I can tell you who didn't shave today. It's a bustling Friday morning, lots of cars on the roads, kids playing soccer by the river. We've just passed Lander, and we are over the small towns of Hudson and Arapahoe. Every swinging dick and all his friends and foes are in the streets, and there's a wedding procession winding away from the town hall. Why hadn't those folks been evacuated?"

"Listen, Lieutenant Kelly," Merrick no longer sounded irate, "just before we took off from Andrews the general pulled me aside and told me again this operation is to go on as scheduled. There will be no recall no matter what. This mission will not be aborted."

"Are we doing the right thing, sir?"

"We are under orders, Lieutenant. My team will not disobey orders."

"Thirty seconds to target one." The words bored themselves into Merrick's ears.

"Couldn't we at least contact Andrews and tell them what we see?" Kelly continued. "Maybe it was all an error and they'll reconsider."

"Fat chance of that! We are carrying out a direct order, Kelly. Make sure you get everything on film."

"Twenty seconds to target one." The words were pounding again in Merrick's ears.

"Pilot to bombardier." Merrick's tone was devoid of any emotion. "We are now seventeen seconds away from target one. Lieutenant Choytek, is everything under control in your berth?"

"Everything under control, sir."

"Good. Stand by. You'll be told when we are on target."

"Righto, skipper." The intercom fell silent.

Merrick reached Kelly by phone and made an attempt to assuage his doubts. "Ed, the mental health of the team is as important to me as its physical health. This kind of mission may arouse trauma in some, and no one is exempt. When we get back to Andrews, I'll be in my office for an hour or so, filling out forms, reporting by phone to the brass, and so on. Drop in and get off your chest whatever is bothering you. We'll have a drink and talk man to man. You'll find me a good listener. Okay, Ed?"

"Thanks, Glen. I'll drop by."

"Do it as soon as you put your gear away."

"Will do, sir."

"Good, I'll be expecting you."

Then Merrick felt a vigorous nudge in the ribs, and raising his head he saw the co-pilot, Captain Cliff Bousson, the earphones hanging idly from his suspenders, eyeing him pointedly. "Four seconds to target one, city of Riverton."

Merrick nodded and at once established contact with Lieutenant Choytek by phone. "Four seconds to target one, city of Riverton. We now begin the countdown. Do you read me, Warren?"

"Loud and clear, Glen."

Merrick enunciated slowly with dogged determination, "Four, three, two one, zero, go!" And as the bombardier, Lieutenant Warren S. Choytek, was releasing a twenty-megaton nuclear bomb on the city of Riverton in central Wyoming, the pilot turned the plane ninety degrees to the north and accelerated to the limit. They could all see an enormous mushroom cloud rising down below to the south of them growing larger and thicker with every second.

"Target two, city of Worland, is four minutes, seventeen seconds away," Captain Bousson announced in a flat voice, turning on the intercom. "As before we drop the package in the very center of town. Did you get everything on film, Ed?"

"Sure did, and I am still getting it."

"Good man," Merrick joined in. "I wouldn't advise anybody to go to sleep or bail out, but relax for the next three minutes, fifty seconds at which time we'll hit target number two. Take care."

When in due course they were poised high above the very nucleus of Worland the same procedure was followed to the letter as before, and an enormous mushroom cloud rose once again down below them while the pilot made a sharp turn eastward, accelerated, and put the plane on its way home.

"I made a rough calculation of casualties resulting from a twenty-megaton nuclear bomb being dropped on Riverton and from another twenty-megaton bomb being dropped on Worland, between 1100 and 1200 hours on Friday, June 19, 2084, today's date. I am not including victims of radiation because if radiation nullifiers are really up to scratch the number of radiation victims may be relatively low. I am merely counting the dead and the wounded. First target, Riverton, approximately eight thousand dead and six thousand wounded, and this includes the town itself and the immediate environs. Of the dead approximately 2,500 will be children, and the children bearing wounds of one kind or another will roughly number two thousand. Second target, Worland, approximately six thousand dead and 4,500 wounded; dead children numbering approximately 1,500 and wounded ones 2,500. This also includes the town and the immediate environs. Total: approximately fourteen thousand dead and 10,500 wounded, and this does not comprise possible radiation victims."

"Any questions or comments from anybody?" Bousson sounded grave but receptive. As it happened there were none and Huston 84, a marvel of up-to-date engineering, bore them in silence to their destination, interrupted by sporadic small talk.

The Red Cross and other organizations rushed at once to what had been the towns of Riverton and Worland. The National Guard was activated in Wyoming, the Dakotas, Nebraska, Idaho, Montana, and New Mexico and dispatched to the nuked areas to render all possible assistance. Volunteers in massive numbers poured in from other states, from Canada, and from countries as remote as Australia and New Zealand.

The estimates Captain Bousson had given to the crew during the return flight on June 19 had fallen short. In reality, partly because Riverton had played host that Friday to the local chapter of the Livestock Association and Worland to the Union of Retired Nurses, and for other reasons, casualties were higher than originally calculated. Two days after the nuclear attack the total number of dead in both towns was estimated at eighteen thousand dead and fourteen thousand wounded.

Captain Bousson had been on the right track, but he had used the population figures drawn from an outdated census, hence the inaccuracies.

The grim task of pulling bodies from under the debris went on night and day, but beginning on Sunday, June 21, mostly charred unrecognizable corpses were being pulled out and the painful labor of identifying them lasted for weeks on end. All the buildings in the two towns and many in the surrounding areas had been leveled to the ground, but the height of the debris varied from place to place—massive brick or stone structures having been pulverized only in part, an odd column or a fragment of a thick wall lying on top of the heap, sad relics of once proud urban architecture. Lighter structures had been reduced to rubble, and elsewhere pulverulent layers were ankle-deep, deceitfully looking like clean sand but hiding tiny particles of body parts and much else.

The smell of death was everywhere, a grotesquely oozing smell made up of matter burnt to ashes or merely charred yet laced in many places by whiffs of putrefaction, human or animal, which defied a facile explanation. Did a human or animal segment inexplicably survive the conflagration, decomposition setting in subsequently? Or did this segment somehow manage to crawl into the rubble? Or was it dropped there after the strike for a reason or for no reason at all?

In both Riverton and Worland the survivors set their hearts on returning to normalcy at the earliest possible date. Tributes were paid to the dead, numerous funerals attended by respectful relatives, friends, and strangers, tents provided by the National Guard became classrooms, while lawyers and bank managers met their clients under the summer sky. A large tent was designated as the courthouse and many of the wounded transported to hospitals in Lander and Sheridan. Religious services were held in all kinds of places, and most pastors made an effort to talk sense without being eloquent.

Within weeks and by a superhuman effort, all businesses serving the two towns and the adjoining communities were back in place, though in less grand surroundings. A clearing a quarter of a mile past the old city limit was named the new business district, and the old and new entrepreneurs displayed much inventiveness in fashioning their new offices and showrooms. Nor was entertainment forgotten. In vacant lots close to where the town hall, the Masonic Temple, and the chamber of commerce had once stood a movie theater operating inside a garishly decorated tent lured passersby: there were two in Riverton and one in

Worland. Dancing halls under canvas also popped up. Worland, though smaller than its fellow victim, boasted two such halls, one exclusively for square dancing and the other for ballroom pyrotechnics, while Riverton had to be content with just one. Makeshift liquor stores sprang up like mushrooms in both towns, and when amidst much fanfare Fred J. B. Pearson, that much lauded and much cursed Western impresario, owner and general manager of Rock Springs Escort Service Inc., drove to Riverton and then to Worland with a truck full of his girls and let them loose on the town, many a survivor hazarded an opinion that things were getting back to normal. They were.

When nuclear bombs were dropped on two small Wyoming towns, shock waves went round Western Amernipp and indeed round the world. Messages of condolence from numerous countries were ringing with indignation, and the Western Amernippian government was pilloried as never before, its head being relegated to the lowest circle of the political inferno, where tyrants and madmen dwelled. Huston did not seem to care. When assistants showed him the strictures he was subjected to, he curtly dismissed them while murmuring words that few could understand, something about a famous city by the sea, imminent departure, a signal to be given, the people raised up on high, soon, very soon.

At other times he just stared into space, flecks of perspiration glittering all of a sudden on his forehead and cheeks, saying nothing, lost to the world. At home there was also indignation, but the entire response was muted. Those who had previously opposed Chief Justice and who continued to oppose him had long ago given up any hope of injecting even a modicum of justice into the regime. They had come to the inescapable conclusion that Huston would remain in power forever—yes, for all practical purposes, forever—and that any stand against him, armed or other, was utterly futile. This defeatist perception of the home situation infected even the western states where desire for insurgence was ripe. The murder of Nathan Chadwick in Cheyenne on May 29th, and the wanton destruction of two Wyoming communities on June 19th taught a terrible lesson to all believers in democracy. It read: "If you want to stay alive, bow low to Huston and his gang. He can't be dislodged. Face the facts."

By the summer of 2084, years of political doubt and cynicism had reached their peak. The majority of the electorate had no confidence in the honesty of public officials, no confidence in the honesty of the press and the media, no confidence in the pronouncements of educators, or any other scholars for that matter, no confidence in the men and women of the cloth. There was a nearly universal consensus that no figure of authority, no matter what his or her province might be, rang true. In the eyes of the majority, authority—any authority measured on the national scale—presupposed falsehood and dishonesty.

Huston's supporters fared no better. They too came to distrust the administration, but they were bound to it by economic concerns and a commitment to perpetuate the status quo that favored them. The Western Amernippian state existed in a chilling ethical void; since the executive, legislative, and judicial branches of the government were seen as corrupt and utterly unscrupulous, the concept of what was right ceased to have any validity. Public life was a cesspool and would never be anything better. Gradually the word "right," used as a substantive or as an adjective, was disappearing from private discourse. It had disappeared from public discourse years earlier because the government had not even bothered to pretend it had been the watchdog of what was right. Language, which never stands still, was adapting itself to new circumstances, coining new expressions and phrases mirroring the actual state of affairs. Disorientation and a sense of void were widespread, and a palliative was offered from many a pulpit.

Since city hall had joined the devil's party—so the argument ran—many opted to turn their energies, their moral values and what was best in them to private concerns—to the family, to the sacred relationships between friends. Outside of private homes, so the argument rang, an irredeemable morass of iniquity and evil had spread over the country. But inside the nation's homes one could still build a life based on decency and apply the virtues of justice, compassion, forgiveness, and above all love, to make life all the more rewarding. The new philosophy struck a sympathetic chord in many hearts and was dubbed in certain quarters "hearth-and-home hullabaloo." Officially the government pronounced no judgment but secretly gave it a stamp of approval, since redoubled commitment to family and to private concerns in general militated against activism.

/   /   /

Linda was observing her daughter ensconced on the ottoman amidst scores of medical journals, reading several of them simultaneously.

"Walden is here," she said at last. "And if you refuse to see him, you'll be the silliest doe in the whole of creation."

"Mother, what's irking you? Of course I'll see Walden, he's a dear friend. I sometimes wonder about you."

"That will do, Agnes." Linda left the room.

"Well, hello there." Walden stepped into the living room bearing an oversize bouquet of red roses and two boxes.

"Hello, Walden, it's good to see you." As she was being proffered the gifts Agnes exclaimed, "All these for me! I simply adore red roses. And what's in the boxes?"

"Two kinds of chocolates. This one," he lifted the box over his head, "contains chocolates filled with brandy. Very smooth to the palate, I might add."

"So these are really for you, because I don't care for brandy or any other kind of booze," Agnes put in smiling alluringly.

"And this box," Walden held it flippantly between his thumb and index finger, "is filled with cloying sweetness, chocolates without vital juices, run-of-the-mill."

"These are truly for me," Agnes declared with vigor laying her hand on his chest. "This deserves a kiss." It was one of the longest kisses in the history of the human race.

After putting the roses in a vase and half-filling it with water Agnes turned again toward her visitor. "What are you up to these days?"

"Well, the whole Denver med school is in Riverton and Worland, and we pre-meds are in tow."

"In both towns at once?" Agnes asked amused.

"You might say that. We have shuttles between the two—cars, buses, superchoppers, planes, you name it. Yes, we are in what in happier times was Riverton and Worland at the same time, simultaneously, like magicians."

"When did you touch ground?"

"The advance party left Denver early Saturday, and the rest of us caught up by noon yesterday. Time flies at a time like this. It was only yesterday, but feels weeks away."

"The sight must have been horrifying."

"Nothing to buoy you up. There's one consolation if you can call it that."

"What?"

"Most of the dead died on impact, in a flash. The seriously wounded are another matter. Unfortunately. And the nullifiers proved reliable. Danger of lasting radiation has been eliminated. A load off everyone's heart."

"I think I'll have another chocolate." Agnes again lifted the lid.

"And I'll have another kiss."

"Just like that!"

"That's right." Instantly he held her in his arms pressing her body against his, kissing her passionately on the mouth and caressing her flesh.

"Walden, Mom's in the house," she whispered.

"I don't see the relevance."

"You should."

A little later, Agnes pressed Walden's hand. "Can you stay for dinner?"

He shook his head. "I'm due back in Riverton this afternoon. I got a lift on a Red Cross plane picking up supplies in Cheyenne, and the same plane is taking off in exactly two hours. I am supposed to be at the airport in an hour, to help with the loading."

"I'll drive you," Agnes said with pride in her voice. "But you must be starved, poor thing. Let's go to the kitchen and raid the refrigerator."

"Thank you, I could do with a bite," Walden murmured kissing her again.

Back in the living room he told her enthusiastically about his parents' change of heart. "You know, Dad's been a Huston supporter since I guess year one. Mom the same."

"What made them change?"

"Two events: May 29th, when your father was murdered and this mess, the nuclear attack on our own people. They said it turned their stomachs. After this they could no longer support Huston."

"Walden, what do you think will happen next?"

"Darling, things are coming to a head. There will be a civil war. It will be bloody, but eventually we shall win."

"And there is no other way?"

"None. Your dad tried to negotiate with Huston. Where is he now? The time for negotiations is long past. We either lie low and keep our powder dry or else we hit Huston with everything we've got."

They went on talking about politics and their families, about their future plans, and about so much else. But the dialogue was interrupted at frequent intervals and merry labors of vocal cords suspended. Instead lips touched and did all the talking. It was almost time for Walden to report to the airport when unexpectedly he tossed a question at Agnes. "You are the only child. When you were smaller, much smaller, did you desperately wish for a brother or a sister? Were you lonely?"

Her face was tense, and she was deep in thought. "No, I didn't. I tried to be friends with those kids my own age whom I didn't openly dislike so as to be in the crowd when I didn't want to be alone. But I had very few bosom friends. I guess my childhood and teen years were a little odd. What about you?"

"I was lonely a good deal as a toddler and later, one of the reasons being my parents' inflated sense of social standing. When they bought that large house in the high-priced residential part of town we were at first surrounded by families with whom Mom and Dad were eager to associate, and they had children I played with. But some of those families moved away, and the new neighbors evoked only contempt in Mom and Dad. They were not good enough for us, and their children weren't good enough for me. This was the spell in my life when I wished for a brother, or even a sister."

"Things must've been pretty ghastly if even a sister would've been welcome," Agnes observed acidly.

"Don't take it to heart." Walden laughed boisterously. "Anyway, this spell didn't last long. At the tender age of four I was enrolled in that fancy private academy where the best people of Cheyenne enrolled their legitimate and illegitimate offspring, and right away I made friends with the high and mighty and with the nobodies. Soon I found out the parents of both were very often snobs, just like my own parents, and there was a lot of jockeying for position and a picture on the front page of the local rag. But I was no longer a lonely kid, and once I had set foot in the academy my parents grew more and more tolerant of my new friends, maybe assigning a higher social status to their fathers than was really the case."

Walden stopped abruptly. "I'm sorry. I am boring you."

"No, you're not. We have to know more about each other. It's only natural."

"You loved your dad very much?"

"Very much."

"And you love your mother?"

"Certainly, they've been wonderful parents. But there were times I was a first class stinker."

Another silent interval took place. When it had ended Walden hoisted himself up on the ottoman and assumed a sitting position. "I'd say you've been uncommonly lucky to have had parents like that, Agnes."

"Were your parents not on a par?"

"I have no real complaints, except that so-called social standing and silly conventions mean so much to them."

"Still, they brought you up."

"Yeah." Walden again laughed jeeringly, boisterously. "I imagine your parents seldom quarreled."

Agnes made a gesture of non-commitment. "At least not when I was around."

"Mine quarreled violently and continue now. Usually it's about the most idiotic things in the world—whom to invite to a party and whom not to invite; whom to blackball from the country club and whom not to blackball. That kind of crap. And the rows are . . . are of long duration, objects flying now and then. I have to tell you about one row I was a secret witness to," Walden went on, warming to the subject. "This happened about seven or eight years ago. One evening I'd gone down to the kitchen to get something to eat, and the row was already in progress in the living room. Well, I didn't want to be seen so I hid under the kitchen table. Lo and behold, I saw Mom's feet and Dad's feet in the kitchen, maybe the acoustics by the fireplace were not all they were cracked up to be. They went at each other tooth and nail, and it lasted for hours. I never found out what the row was about, maybe they didn't know it themselves. Anyway, at long last the coast was clear, and I slipped out from my hiding place and crawled upstairs to my room, a bundle of nerves."

"Secret agent, what!"

"Something like that. I'll never forget Mom's parting volley at Dad. 'You are paid a great deal of money for examining people's sensibilities and brains, Philip, but I find you totally inept at understanding what makes people tick. You are a vegetable, well-dressed and watered regularly, nothing more.'

"He answered, 'I beg of you, Myra . . . I beg of you to try to control yourself. At least try to pretend you're a rational human being.' and she left off with, 'Go to hell, Philip, go to hell!' and so on and so forth."

"Both your parents were very nice to me when I was invited to tea."

"Sure . . . sure. They have their faint redeeming features. Besides, I think they like you, and it may be genuine. Also, both Dad and Mom admired your dad; they gave him highest marks."

"Thank you."

"Agnes, I'm studying to be an MD, and I try to understand as much of human nature in its diverse manifestations as I can."

"Sure."

"I think I may have put my finger on what ails Mom and Dad."

"Well, tell me, Walden. Don't just sit there."

"They are both frustrated to their fingertips. They'd rather be earning their living in a different way. At least he would. And she'd greatly love to be in her own chosen profession."

"I am still waiting. You're dragging your feet."

"All right, but you understand this mustn't go further."

"Walden, you insult me. It goes without saying what you tell me is confidential. What do they call it in a court of law?"

"Privileged communication."

"That's right. So what you tell me is privileged."

Walden leaned toward Agnes, stroking her hair and face, and another long, mute interval took place. "You see, love, my mother had wanted to be an actress. At Bryn Mawr she was president of the drama club, and she appeared in all sorts of plays. But when she left college her acting days came to a screeching halt. Perhaps she wasn't good enough for the professional stage. I don't know what happened, and I don't know the details. I am reasonably certain, though, that after Bryn Mawr she never acted again."

"How sad, how very sad." Agnes was gently stroking Walden's hand. "Is your mother still connected with the theatre in some other way?"

"Not that I know of. She's on the Wyoming Arts Council, and she reviews grant proposals that infrequently may have something to do with the theatre, but that's about it. I'm afraid for her Bryn Mawr was the beginning and the end."

"And your dad?" Agnes asked, keeping her curiosity in check.

Walden took both her hands in his and kissed them repeatedly. "It's another story of frustration. And equally sad. When he was at Harvard Medical School the standing joke was that Philip couldn't attend this or that lecture, this or that lab session because he was directing rehearsals. Dad wanted to be a director, a theatre director, and he set his heart on it. Actually he did direct numerous university productions of classics and contemporary plays, and by and large they were well received. He stuck to it when continuing in psychiatry."

"So your father is a regular MD?" Agnes inquired.

"Not quite. He has a medical degree but also an additional degree in psychiatry. He's a shrink caring for those who have already taken leave of their senses wholly or in part, for those who are presently taking leave of their senses wholly or in part, and in anticipation for those who already tied a knot on their hankies to remind themselves they are duty-bound to take leave of their senses any day now."

"And directing?"

"It fell by the wayside when he left Harvard. Again I don't know the whole story, and I don't know the details."

"Could it be," Agnes was proceeding very cautiously, "that those rows royal between your parents when so many insults are flung about and so many words diligently spoken serve as a sort of compensation for what Philip and Myra lost, lost irretrievably—the theatre, the stage?"

"Point well taken, Dr. Agnes, would you like to schedule both patients for a psychiatric examination? The world is full of frustrated folks."

There was another silent interval, and then Walden jotted down a number on a pad. "This is the mobile phone for pre-meds in Riverton and Worland. I'll try to come and see you next weekend, work permitting."

"I hope you'll be able to stay longer."

"Me too."

"And now it's time for you to rejoin your unit. Shape up." Agnes was at her most efficient and professional.

/   /   /

It was shortly after 8 A.M. on Monday, June 22, and Timothy Hysart was already at his desk catching up on the ambassadorial reports and digests of political situations in the four corners of the globe. Several days before Siegfried La Rochelle had simply disappeared without a trace after handing a letter of resignation as National Security Advisor to Chief Justice and taking French leave. The very next day he, Tim, was summoned by the Savior of the Country and subjected to the third degree.

"Do you take me for a moron, Tim!!!" Huston shouted, clenching his fists and advancing so close to the hapless senior advisor that their chins almost touched.

"D'you think I can't read between the lines, boy?!" he continued shouting. "You had Siegfried's confidence; you were privy to what went on in that damnable office of his; and you have the cheek to tell me you knew nothing of his plans to pull stakes and take off like a little birdie flying off to parts unknown? Tell me, tell me you knew nothing."

Tim had been on the point of saying something to Huston, what he could no longer remember, and at this point he had cared not what it was but Chief Justice stuck a hard, scrawny index finger against his throat. "In Western Amernipp those guilty of high treason face the hangman's noose!" he bellowed. "Or didn't Siegfried keep you informed?"

Sitting now in the relative safety of his own office with Huston and his gang several long blocks away, Tim's recollection of the suspenseful scene in the palatial state chambers only a few short days before grew razor-sharp. With extraordinary clarity he could see himself sitting awkwardly on the edge of a chair, a man already condemned and without a prayer in appellate court surrounded by hanging judges and executioners, and his thoughts and feelings on that occasion were being recreated now with the same extraordinary faithfulness. He had given up any hope of survival, and his instinct had told him to have his say because there might not be another chance.

"The National Security Advisor resigned his office because it is common knowledge that you, Chief Justice, were going to fire him on the Fourth of July." He had uttered these words in an unemotional manner and had looked round him without an iota of interest.

"How did La Rochelle come by this information?" Chief Justice snarled and the men behind him drew a step closer to the respondent.

"It's common knowledge. It was common knowledge at the time," Tim repeated. "If you don't believe me, go to any bar in the vicinity of the White House or the Congress. You'll hear it from the bartender as you order your first drink."

"There's little doubt La Rochelle got the information from someone in your office, boss," one of the men said. "That's bribing a federal official, a capital offense."

"That's right," Huston snarled again. "Would you care to tell us, Tim, who La Rochelle's source in my office was? If you don't open up instantly we have ways of making you talk. Trust me."

"It was and it is common knowledge, that's all I can tell you."

"I see," Huston pronounced the words with affected smoothness. "You've made your bed, and you'll have to sleep in it."

Tim shrugged his shoulders ostentatiously. "Believe what you want. I'm telling you the truth."

A moment of silence intervened and the ex-senior assistant to the French-leave-taking National Security Advisor expected to be dragged away from Huston's presence and thrown into a prison van. Instead he heard one of the men flanking Chief Justice say, "It's entirely plausible La Rochelle did his dirty work himself. In fact it's very doubtful he'd assign any of his assistants to so sensitive a task." The others murmured assent.

Hearing this, Huston turned toward his entourage and nodded. "You may have a point. This particular Kraut is a master of deception. So . . ." He pulled a chair from the wall and sat astride it facing Hysart. "You're a bright lad," he began with forced bonhomie, "so tell me . . ."

"Yes, sir."

"Is it acceptable behavior for a member of the cabinet to leave his post at a moment's notice without consulting with me, without leaving any recommendations for the future, without informing the cabinet of the state and direction of our foreign policy? Is it? I ask you."

"I am afraid I can't answer your question without having access to all the facts. I would have to know what precisely transpired between you and the National Security Advisor regarding the post he had occupied and your plans to install someone else in that post. I can tell you one thing right off—Dr. La Rochelle didn't break any laws."

"Oh! So now it's shyster Hysart I see. Are you representing the low-down Kraut?"

"No, I am not. But you're right about my being a lawyer. I graduated summa cum laude from law school, and I passed the bar exam."

"Congratulations. I want to ask you something else: d'you think the Kraut may have taken with him boxes upon boxes of classified documents, of papers that are top secret and whose falling into the wrong hands may compromise national security? La Rochelle could hold us to ransom, couldn't he? Pay up or else."

Tim let his eyes wander over the walls and ceiling before replying, just like a surveyor in a strange land turns his eyes to white cliffs and stately poplars for solace after watching a putrescent marsh where insects and lizards battle for dominion under the unbearably foul odors stirred up by the midday sun. "Chief Justice, don't take my bluntness amiss, but your suspicions are preposterous. How can you even fancy that Dr. La Rochelle would go to the highest bidder with confidential state documents? Siegfried is a true statesman. We've had very few of those lately, and he's earned his place in a small and select company of great Americans from George Washington down. He is absolutely honest. He is a devoted patriot. And what you say is a criminal smear not only on Siegfried La Rochelle's reputation but on the United States of America as such raised by said Siegfried La Rochelle to unheard of heights and given an appropriately dual name of Western Amernipp."

Huston was taken aback by what he heard and, rising to his feet, he drew very close from the right and left to the apologist of the recently vanished National Security Advisor, inspecting his face for any proof of guilt, contrition, or crime committed. But of proof there was not an inkling. On the contrary, the senior assistant to the no longer visible one appeared to have grown in self-confidence, stature, and combativeness. He finally said, "Under the circumstances I shall ignore your disrespectful remarks and veiled accusations since they spring from a mistaken but genuine loyalty to your chief—pardon me, your former chief. This time I shall not throw the book at you."

"Birds of a feather," a voice rang out from the back and stopped abruptly.

"Hear, hear!" A chorus gave it its blessing. Tim had a succulent repartee all prepared but bit his lip just in time.

"How much do you know about our foreign policy?" Huston posed the question not as an inquisitor but as a researcher eager to uncover and unravel all available data and secrets.

"A good deal. Siegfried and I have always worked very closely together. He had no secrets from me, in foreign affairs, that is."

"That's what I heard," Huston observed dryly. "How many more are there in your office who helped to formulate and execute our foreign policy?"

"I was the only one—Dr. La Rochelle had only one senior assistant—me. The rest of the personnel are junior assistants whose job it is to collate our diplomatic and intelligence reports, keep all the data properly arranged and classified if and when it is needed, and the clerical staff."

"I understand," Huston commented with conviction. "Tell me, where are today's trouble spots?"

"These days things are rather quiet. We have an ongoing dispute with the Russian Federation, subject fishing rights in the Bering Sea and to the north."

"Can it be settled?"

"Well, Dr. La Rochelle didn't want it settled because the dispute gave us an advantage."

"How?" Huston asked, stupefied.

"Sir, it would take too much time to explain."

"Would it? All right. I expect an explanation later this week. Anything else?"

"The Russians, the Brits, and the French have built factories in China putting out all sorts of consumer goods. We also built factories there, and competition is fierce. The National Security Advisor was working on it just before he . . . he resigned."

"I see."

"And I am in possession of all the memos and moves we are to make. Siegfried wanted to make common cause with the Russians, in this particular instance only, being not overtly anti-British and anti-French, but giving us more leverage. It's a complicated maneuver."

"You'll have to explain this one too."

"Yes, sir."

Huston stepped back several paces and motioned to his entourage to leave him alone with Hysart. "Tim, you look as if you are on the point of falling off a skyscraper sitting precariously on the edge of that underfed chair. Plump down in that armchair. . . . Better now?"

"Much better, thank you."

"Give me your undivided attention."

"Certainly, Chief Justice."

"We want you to fill in for a while, carry on Siegfried's work. You will be Acting National Security Advisor with all the authority your boss possessed. That is, if the prospect is agreeable to you."

"Yes, it is agreeable." Tim could hardly believe his ears.

"We expect from you a top performance so that Western Amernipp will again dominate the world, as it did in the past. There will be, of course, salary adjustments, etc. Keep your staff if you're satisfied with them, or hire new people. You have a free hand, Mr. Hysart. There's one catch, though. I want you to appear once a week before the cabinet to report on international events and keep us informed. We begged your predecessor to share with us his thoughts and his triumphs, but he was the closest approximation to a deaf-mute I can think of. And we in government are cut to the quick—yes, cut to the quick—when our only source of information regarding what our foreign policy is up to are the newspapers. There's a new regimen in place—yes, by golly, a new regimen—and we'll do things by the book. Any questions?"

"No, sir, and may I say I am honored."

Huston smiled—it was an unusually warm smile befitting the occasion.

"When do I start?" Tim asked, still half-convinced he had unconsciously strayed into the land of chimeras.

"This very minute," Huston replied and held out his hand. "Mr. Acting National Security Advisor, may I trouble you to sign this consent form? The official swearing-in ceremony will take place later in the week."

Tim spent the next hour reliving this strangest of all the strange experiences he had been subjected to, weighing pros and cons and brooding on what it might lead to. At uneven intervals he had pinched himself to gain assurance he had not been dreaming and finally accepted against his better judgment that he was indeed in a real world. Instinctively his thoughts converged on Siegfried La Rochelle who two days before his hasty departure had taken him on the *tour d'horizon* of Western Amernippian foreign policy and had followed it by a thorough examination of the dangerous and sensitive areas. Had Siegfried done it in anticipation? Had he known in advance that his senior assistant would be named acting advisor? And if so what had been his motives? Tim had no answers to these questions, and he quickly excluded from consideration any kind of collusion between his boss and Huston. One thing was certain: working for several years under and with La Rochelle rendered him eminently fit to carry out his new duties and maintain his country's dominant position in the world. Tim was looking to the future with optimism.

And now as he was sitting behind his desk, which had been Siegfried's desk, in his office, which had been Siegfried's office, on Monday, June 22, Tim's sanguine mood soared. Still, the ongoing battle for Old Glory and democracy had to be won. He remembered; he would always remember. Pressing a button activating the automatic long distance operator, he dialed a number.

"Hi, Linda, this is Tim Hysart."

"Hi, Tim, how are things with you?"

"So, so. I'm calling to find out whether Kevin is any better. I called him last week, but the doctors were with him and we couldn't really talk. Nevertheless, my impression was he wasn't well. Not at all well."

"You're right. He's made no progress to speak of in the last few weeks."

"I see."

"He's still very weak. At first the doctors thought a month's complete rest was all he needed. But it's more complicated, though there's nothing organically wrong. It all comes from months and months of overwork and acute depression had set in. He drove himself like there was no tomorrow. He tried to do too much."

"Is he still running the ship?"

"I am afraid not, Tim. He can't work and the future is uncertain. Specialists from out of state are also looking him over, and he's on medication, undergoes therapy, counseling, and so on. He's well looked after, but the outlook is grim. Helen and I went to see him yesterday."

"Helen?"

"Helen McKintosh, Nathan's sister."

"Of course, of course," he mumbled. "Poor Kevin. His divorce came through some time ago. Did that help?"

"Only for a day or two. Listen, Tim, I want to bring you up to date."

"Go on."

"Kevin's work has been parceled off among three new faces. Jose Carero is the chief deputy, and he's assisted by Curt and Ingrid Wolf. Before moving to Cheyenne, Curt and Ingrid were active in the Rock Springs area. I'll send you their addresses and phones in the usual way."

"Thanks. Anything I can do?"

"Keep us posted on what their and our D.C. is up to. In Cheyenne we find an occasional whiff of pollution and putrefaction of the big city to our liking."

"Will do. Take care, Linda."

Tim was on the point of hanging up, but her voice called him back. "Yes?"

"Some weeks ago I met your sister Emily. It was a pleasure."

"Oh?"

"This year AGA met in Denver. Emily was there reading two fascinating papers. I represented Wyoming medical technicians. She's a very bright girl that sister of yours. We let our hair down at the reception."

"Oh yes, you can say that again. In our family, Linda, all the brains went to Emily. The rest of us are brainless."

There was a touch of anger at the other end. "I refuse to play this male chauvinist game. Having said what you did, my turn is to protest and tell the world you are in fact extremely bright. You deny it hypocritically, and I raise the ante. So it goes. No thank you. Cheating at cards is more honorable than your ego-building gimmick."

"Just to put you in the picture, this game and others like it are played constantly in D.C. We are a city of players."

"Well, back to the game, smart guy. Remember me to you sister."

"It's always a pleasure, Linda, always a pleasure." Tim infused quantities of warmth into what he said and blew kisses with it.

Over the next two days he familiarized himself with the constantly changing international situation and studied copious reports on the much-anticipated Franco-German union. Despite much clamor for it in both countries the new empire of Charlemagne was going nowhere. Hundreds of irritating obstacles, petty or dishearteningly bureaucratic, stood in the way and progress was not in sight. On several occasions vital decisions had been postponed until a radiant dawn augured a new spirit and a breakthrough.

In the meantime President Jacques Merdeacac assigned himself to the task, especially dear to him, of putting the glory of France on display once more, this time in a uniquely original way. New laws were passed, and the French government made it abundantly clear through an educational campaign that those who broke them would not escape punishment. The first Monday of every month was designated as the celebration of the Age of Louis XIV. Every resident in France over eighteen was ordered to wear on his or her clothes some memento of the glorious monarch or of the age he had so gallantly dominated. It could be a replica of a fragment of the wig Louis had habitually worn, or of some article of his ceremonial dress, or of anything else he had had on his person. Conversely the memento could be a register of the victories *le roi-soleil* had won in the early years of his reign against the Spaniards and the Dutch, or a picture of Versailles or of one of the king's influential mistresses, who were household names. Any original or copy would do so long as it unambiguously conveyed to an ordinary onlooker its affinity to Louis, his court, or broadly speaking his age with the stress on the grand and glorious.

The first Tuesday of every month was reserved for Napoleon Bonaparte, and the same principle applied. In great demand were tiny reproductions of the large drum the emperor played solitaire on and had by him on the day of his famous victories—Marengo, Austerlitz, Friedland, and others. Also popular were the neatly folded opening pages of the Napoleonic Code and dozens of other copies raised to the level of relics.

Obedient to the demands of Father Time the first Wednesday of the month glorified the heroic and bloody French victory in the First World War and its outgrowth, the Treaty of Versailles. Ribbons proudly proclaiming "*ils ne passeront pas*" were on sale everywhere, as were pictures and miniatures of General Galliéni mobilizing Paris cabs to transport troops. The more serious-minded preferred illustrations and sketches of the Armistice signed by the Germans in the railway car of Marshal Foch at 5 A.M. on November 11, 1918, while those favoring statesmanship over warfare paraded portraits of Clemenceau and "the big four" at the Versailles Conference wheeling and dealing.

The fifth day of the week honored General Charles de Gaulle, first as the bold commander before the fall of France, then as leader of the Free French, and lastly as president of the French Republic. The fiercest and most inventive manifestations of the French patriotic spirit sprang from the veneration of this soldier turned statesman, and the Cross of Lorraine was put to multiple uses.

Jacques Merdeacac was delighted, and even before the program of national self-glorification had been put into practice he had adjudged it "a marvelous success." In a national address he named it "*Experience de la gloire nationale à travers des siècles*," EGNTS for short, and the abbreviation stuck as if embedded in wax.

He was also true to his punitive promises. The first offense was punished by a small fine; the second by a much higher one; and the third carried an automatic prison sentence without the possibility of appeal. The first to be incarcerated was a retired couple in Lyons, a baker and a schoolteacher, hauled away in a police van as neighbors shook their fists at the gendarmerie and tossed garbage cans at them. Soon many, many others in all parts of France followed, Lyons remaining the hotbed of discontent. Fines rose to immense proportions, and French libertarians bandying themselves together defied the law and declared it unconstitutional. Merdeacac's popularity sagged, but he was reassured by several generals and the ministers of the army and of war, as well as by his confessor, a Jesuit priest, that he was doing the right thing.

Nothing like it was happening in the neighboring country to the east. The German chancellor, reasonably comfortable at delivering fireside chats and speaking to small groups, was at a veritable loss publicly addressing the nation or making official pronouncements. On such occasions he seemed to dwindle, and his self-confidence evaporated. In consequence he progressively appeared more and more seldom in public.

He had one hobbyhorse though, and he would not let go of it. The chancellor was convinced that sauerkraut seasoned with certain nutrients came to possess extraordinary curative powers, that it frightened away cancer, regulated blood pressure, strengthened the heart, and smoothed the digestive process. Furthermore, according to research conducted by a team of doctors handpicked by the chancellor and working under his personal supervision, sauerkraut-cum-alia preserved youthful vigor in men and women and lengthened their lifespan. The research in question was still in its infancy, but it was already predicted that before too long men's average lifespan would jump to one hundred and fifty years and women's to one hundred and seventy-five years, this being predicated, of course, on both men and women consuming mountains of sauerkraut-cum-alia and the research yielding the desired results.

In his capacity as master dietician of the German nation the chancellor left his mark on two distinct yet related areas of national life. At his suggestion sauerkraut eating competitions were organized in two German cities and others were to follow in their wake. Secondly, the chief executive leapt into the television set and created a program with himself as the star expounding the virtues of eating sauerkraut, the more of it the better, and the more often better still, giving advice to families, distributing free literature, and answering questions.

The sauerkraut eating competitions went down well in many quarters, particularly with blue-collar workers who thought of them as sporting events like boxing or wrestling, hurling in the world's face Teutonic vigor and might. But the chancellor's TV appearances drew a great deal of flak, and when the research on the medicinal value of this common fare, which he had supervised, was exposed as bogus by a group of eminent scientists the house came down on him. He was forced to explain his actions to the nation, but he broke down in front of the camera and plaintively complained how hurt he was by uncalled-for attacks. At that point the country resolutely turned against him, and he barely survived the vote of non-confidence in the Bundestag—survived it by one vote because the opposition entertained grave reservations about their own man. Even so, demands for his resignation fell on the government like an avalanche, and newspapers on the right and on the left proudly proclaimed that the country whose revered heroes had been Martin Luther, Frederick the Great, Bismarck, Stresemann, and Adenaner could ill afford to have a crybaby in the chancellor's office. Still, because of party politics he was allowed to complete his term, which expired in 2086, making a solemn promise not to put forth his name as a candidate in that year.

Once this matter had been settled, the electorate made it abundantly clear it wanted to see as little of him as possible. He was now a lame-duck chancellor, and energetic campaigning had already begun for the highest executive office two years hence. As before the

"Europeans" in France and in Germany stood behind their grandiose plan of a union of the two countries, but in the latter politicians began to wonder if it would not be in the national interest to wait until 2086 when a real leader would be at the helm. As things now stood, and were the union to be consummated, the Frenchie would wear the pants. It might be politic to wait until the last had been seen of the German jojo and the two countries could face each other as equal partners.

Tim pushed the French and the German material to the side and hiccuped at the thought of sauerkraut, which he detested. In Italy, as he was learning now, the armies of the republic were poised on the northern bank of the Tiber facing the Catholic Brigade across the river. Italian forces were some 150,000 men strong, and Borgia's barely numbered one hundred thousand. Both were ready for combat but were waiting while the government and Vatican officials negotiated to avoid bloodshed. The Pope had boasted that his force, though numerically inferior to that of the corrupt and despicable Italian state, was militarily stronger. "My men have been trained as no other army in the last hundred and forty years," he was wont to say. Others believed him. The model for the Catholic Brigade had been Adolf Hitler's S.S. Corps, but the Pope believed the brigade surpassed even the S.S. "Our discipline is stricter, training with all kinds of weapons more thorough, and above all our ideology captures both the head and the heart," he preached to all and sundry. "The S.S. believed they were carrying out the Führer's orders. We know with absolute certainty we are carrying out the orders of the Catholic God."

The president of the republic was agonizing over what was surely going to happen. "Italians killing other Italians," he kept repeating, "is a blow I may not survive. No, if this happens, I don't want to live!" When he was told that less than thirty percent of the brigade was made up of Italians, the rest being drawn from other Catholic countries, and principally from neo-Fascist and neo-Nazi centers in Spain, Portugal, and South America, he did not bat an eyelash. "But Italians are enrolled in that force," he insisted, "and many will be killed by their fellow citizens." In fact the composition of the brigade changed weekly, and the recent additions by the hundreds from the Middle East gave it a terrorist character. The new recruits knew as much about Christianity or Roman Catholicism as the Man in the Moon. They had been whipped to a state of frenzy by their hatred of democracy, of parliamentary government, of Western society as such. Muslim fanatics, they saw their chance to raze to the ground a modern Western state that their fathers and uncles had invaded but could not destroy thirty years earlier. On both sides of the Tiber the armies stood waiting for a signal, and they could feel it in their bones it would not be long in coming. Tim tossed the Italian folders onto a side table and curled his lip in a sneer.

"If those Continentals want to blow each other up, why, they should get it over with. No use keeping the Angel of Death waiting." He muttered a few more pejorative epithets about the Continentals and was picking up a stack of diplomatic cables from China and the Russian Federation when his private telephone rang, the number being known to very few.

"Yes," Tim said languidly, hoping the caller would go away.

"Well, son," the all-too familiar voice burst forth, "glad you're working and not goofing off."

"How are you, Father? And to what do I owe the honor?"

"Events are moving fast, very fast, Son, and I thought you and I could devise a common strategy. We are on the same side, aren't we?" Rev. James Hysart betrayed unmistakable signs of excitement, and the gruffness, Tim reflected, was his way of calming himself and telling the world he was not driven by emotions run wild.

"What exactly do you mean by a common strategy?" Tim asked, keeping his voice down and sounding as official and impersonal as he could.

"Well, the Church of the Holy Tabernacle is our headquarters for promoting democratic action and for battling tyranny. By the way, we sent volunteers to Wyoming to help in any way we could, and we shipped food and clothing."

"That was good of you."

"Those poor souls are our brothers and sisters," the gruffness in James Hysart's voice turned to stone, and the words came heavily like the sluggish pounding of a hammer on an uncharted surface, the workman being lost to the world.

"You carry out your work, Father, and I'll carry out mine."

"Son, maybe you don't believe in soul-searching experiences, in epiphanies?"

"No, I don't."

"I want you to know several weeks ago I became a new man. Not only did I turn against Huston, but I began to review my whole life and saw for the first time where I'd gone wrong." At the other end of the line silence grew heavier by the second. "Are you still there, son?"

"Yes, I am still here, Father, but I have nothing to say."

"I wish you'd come to the Church of the Holy Tabernacle. The Almighty in all His wisdom will give you grace."

"Stop yapping nonsense." Tim was barely controlling his wrath. "When I was a child you forced religion down my throat, and when I balked you beat me black and blue. Thank God those days are long over."

"I thought I was doing God's work."

"I dare say you did. You treated Mother and me abominably and Emily, well Emily was a different proposition. You were so astounded that a woman could go to a med school and become an MD that you suspected a sinister, devilish design. Do you remember those little speeches you used to honor us with at meals? 'Hearken unto me, the congregation will come to order.' And then you'd start off with the verse for the day! Satan never sleeps and maybe women enrolling in med schools is a Satanic plot to undermine the city of righteousness, the faithful city. And since Emily was your daughter and she'd enrolled in a med school, perhaps Satan was getting at you specifically, an eminent man of the cloth and defender of the Almighty to the bitter end. All you needed was God's help and grace, but they never made it to your doorstep. Has God betrayed you, Reverend, and has Satan won? I leave it to your biblical and therefore unchallengeable sense of justice. Emily graduated from med school and began an honorable career. Surely in your book someone has blundered. Put a label on the culprit and march with the prophets, Holy Man."

"You hate me, don't you, son?"

"No, I don't. I have no use for you, and I don't want to have anything to do with you. That's not hatred."

"I acknowledge now I behaved badly toward your mother and toward you. If my saying it is not enough, do you want me to abase myself before you and beg for forgiveness?"

"No, I don't. All of it happened a long time ago, and there's no need to stir up the ashes."

"Thank you."

"But I want you to know I don't believe a word of that glittering jazz of your being another Saul on the way to Damascus."

"Son, I make one last appeal. Please come to church with me. Please."

"Request denied. I'd like to quote Lenin to you as I did several years ago: 'Religion is opium to the people.' And a world famous mathematician and philosopher had this to say about man and God: 'When a person has nothing useful or worthwhile to do, he or she turns to God.'"

"No matter what you do with yourself, Timothy, you will always remain my beloved son, and Emily my beloved daughter."

"That's very touching."

Tim heard his father hemming and hawing, and then a powerful authoritative voice came on the line. "What d'you think is going to happen now, on the political arena I mean?"

"It's difficult to say. Huston still controls the government, the army, and much of the country. But the nuclear bombing of Wyoming revolted one hell of a lot of people."

"Even though Wyoming turned traitor and seceded from Western Amernipp?"

"This notwithstanding."

"I understand private armies are springing up on both sides of the fence."

"That's correct, a host of military organizations have come into being in the Northeast, and the South is spoiling to fight for Chief Justice."

"And facing them if things really get rough . . . will be . . . " James Hysart stopped, inquiring.

"National Guard from the western states, militias and so on plus one hell of a lot of volunteers from forty states," Tim replied confidently. "Remember most of the silos are in the West. If we get hold of them, we'll have the advantage."

"I hope to God," James Hysart raised his voice in desperate emotion, "that the folly of Riverton and Worland will not be repeated by either side. May God have mercy."

"So be it."

"Timothy."

"Yes, Father?"

"My house is always open to you."

"Thank you."

"We are not parting as enemies, I trust."

"Absolutely not. But we are not parting as friends either. We are meeting and parting from each other as we have done for more than twenty years, as strangers. Accept it."

Tim heard muttering at the other end of the line but could not distinguish the words. At last the firm, resonant voice returned. "By the way, is Emily still living in sin with that married buck?"

"You mean Scott, the highly regarded heart specialist? Yes, she is. His divorce came through only the other day. I thought you might like to know."

"It don't make it right. Emily ought to be married herself and bear children. The Almighty created the woman for procreation. That's why He put her on this earth of His. Besides, so far as I can tell that Scott fella is the wrong color."

Without the slightest warning a fit of giggles took utter possession of Tim, and he went on and on giggling.

"This is no laughing matter," Reverend Hysart warned sternly from the other end. "Control yourself."

But Tim was unable to exercise any control. Finally he managed to blurt out between giggles, "Father, call Emily and tell her what you've just told me. Then call and tell me what she said. Fair enough?"

"Methinks I won't take you up on it, just this time. All the best to you, son."

"And to you, Father." The two men hung up simultaneously, not even a split second separating their respective actions, as if they had planned it together to a tee.

/   /   /

Shortly after resigning from the committee expurgating and theologizing the works of William Shakespeare, John Scaggs and Wyn Purdue set their hearts on forming a group, a body of their own, to promote the principles of democracy and tenets of the Constitution of 1787 among their fellow workers—university janitors, plumbers, electricians, cooks, and others. Even before they decided how to name their undertaking, it proved an uphill battle. John and Wyn had known hosts of university workers at Hofstra, MIT, and at many other eastern universities and colleges for many years, and could always count on their support in matters relating to their jobs and vice versa. But when the couple first broached the idea of a political organization many of their friends shook their heads. "Leave it alone," they vociferously urged the couple. "It ain't your responsibility. Hand it to the educated mob, them carrying briefcases and looking like they could use an infusion or two of red blood." John and Wyn were undeterred and preached that, "All of us are in it together" till they were blue in the face.

They won no converts to their cause, and the first meeting of the Association of University Janitors, Plumbers, Electricians, Cooks, and All Other Essential University Workers—the name they had chosen after a brief tête-à-tête—held just off Hofstra University's campus on a glorious Saturday afternoon, remained totally unattended. Not a single person had shown up. John and Wyn sat there chain-smoking and racking their brains about what else they could have done to bring in at least one guy and one gal, a token attendance of two if nothing more.

Earlier in the week they had quipped at work about the common front against tyranny being a matter far too important to be left to professors, and they had cracked a litany of anti-longhaired jokes all of which had been received with jovial smiles. The two janitors-turned-political-organizers had felt they were connecting with the audience, their own goals merging with the newly evoked goals of the public and sealing a common bond. Such were the happy thoughts of the days immediately preceding the first meeting. But when it finally took place it was a different story.

Still, John and Wyn remained undeterred, preaching to the unconverted and underscoring the fact that in a national undertaking like this one all segments of society must be involved, any one segment being just as vital as any other, victory being guaranteed only when the whole nation came together and marched to the same drummer. Gradually a notion got about that John and Wyn had a thing or two on their clipboards that was everybody's business and that without putting on airs they actually tried to raise the social status of university janitors, plumbers, electricians, cooks, and all others by plunking them right into the political process, no excuses and apologies offered.

Political awareness and a sense of responsibility were slowly spreading to university workers in other eastern states, from New York and

Massachusetts to New Jersey, Maryland, Delaware, and Rhode Island, to Connecticut, Vermont, New Hampshire and Maine, and to the vast stretches of Pennsylvania. Membership in the association grew modestly, and regular meetings alternating between Hempstead and Cambridge, with additional ones held in other states, were better and better attended. Then two events threw everything out of gear and put the two janitors' darling project on a new footing: Nathan Chadwick's murder on May 29 and the nuclear bombing of Riverton and Worland on June 19. Some of those wearing overalls were not entirely in the clear as to where Wyoming really lay, whether it jutted out from an Alaskan or Canadian shore, or whether it was a half-submerged island off the coast of Hawaii. But geographers with magnifying glasses put everything right, and many a university janitor, electrician, plumber, cook, and other was asking himself or herself where the next blow would fall.

John and Wyn's political schedule now included trips to surrounding states, more and more paperwork, telephone calls stacked one on top of the other, weekly sessions of the executive board created right after May 29, and regular meetings of the association on a fortnightly basis. All their free time was merrily consumed by politics, and they thanked their lucky stars they had not been arrested so far. Yet they knew they were kept under surveillance. Far too many meter men arrived out of the blue at John's house in Cambridge, and at Wyn's house in Hempstead, unidentifiable callers, allegedly from the chamber of commerce and various civic organizations, were constantly on her doorstep asking all sorts of personal questions, pushing their way inside and demanding to know the names of her friends and visitors. An old friend who worked for a telephone company told them there was no doubt their telephone was tapped, and a black car was parked for days on end outside Wyn and John's homes, presumably recording the flow of visitors and much more.

John came to dislike the mounting paperwork—newsletter, leaflets, announcements of meetings—and preferred verbal contact unencumbered by writing. Wyn, methodical and more clerically-minded, took the scribal duties in her stride and kept papers in order. The association was an entirely novel experience but it grew on them, and it gradually became an integral part of their lives and second nature.

How long would they be allowed to remain at liberty? they asked themselves again and again knowing that by now the government must have a very thick dossier on each of them. They asked nervous and desperate questions of each other and put them to the vote, as it were. But they had their answers ready, and they would not budge. No, they would not give up running the Association of University Janitors, Plumbers, Electricians, Cooks, and All Other Essential University Workers; no, they would not curtail their activities for reasons of safety; and no, they would not hand over membership lists and lists of donors; and if the government came nosing around they'd tell it to go and fry an egg.

And so the exhilarating work to regain nationally what had been so shamefully lost went on full tilt. Ever since the nuclear attack Wyn had been staying with John in Cambridge, keeping in touch by phone with her Hempstead neighbors, and the modest Cambridge abode became another center of dissension, a headquarters of anti-governmental protests, another rebel stronghold.

After a tiring day John confronted Wyn on the evening of Wednesday, June 24th. "I am going off tonight, girl."

"Going off? Where to, handsome?"

"I'm going to sign on. They're putting together a freedom brigade in Buffalo."

"Isn't there a place in Mass where you can sign on?"

"Nope. This is Huston country. All you've got here are New Minutemen, New Sons of Liberty, and Huston's bodyguards."

"John, you're fifty-eight. You've done your share in the Middle East campaign thirty years ago. If you sign on, you'll be killed, and where will this leave me?"

"I gotta sign on, girl, it's me duty. I gotta, and you gotta understand it. This is special, this comes once in a lifetime."

She came up and stood very close to him, tears forming in her eyes. "No, no, and no again!" she cried with passion, pounding his chest with her fists. "No, I don't want you to go, can't you get this through your thick skull, John Scaggs? If you sign on, I'll never see you again. I can already see your corpse all mangled lying in a pool of blood. No!" She threw her arms around him, kissing his face and neck and holding his hands fast lest he push her away and just disappear.

Very gently he disentangled himself and kissed her on the lips.

"Wyn, I gotta go, but I'll be back, turning up like a bad penny, don't ye know? Somehow I always manage to come back."

"Who's running the Buffalo operation?" she asked a little more calmly.

"It's the people of New York, and they need volunteers, need them bad. Yesterday I spoke to Jose Carera in Cheyenne."

"Who's he?"

"He's running the show in Wyoming, and he told me Buffalo needs guys with military experience."

"I thought it was Kevin Schultz."

"Nope, girl. Kevin's in the hospital, nervous breakdown or something. Jose has taken over."

"I still say you did your duty years ago, and you deserve some consideration. It ain't fair. It ain't fair!" She again held his hands fast so he could not get away.

"I'll be back," he whispered in her ear, and then he straightened himself up and sounded off. "Did I ever tell you how I came back from the dead? I don't rightly remember how many years ago, but it was during our last offensive some twenty miles southeast of Baghdad."

"No, I didn't hear that one."

"Well, division had me marked as dead, killed by machinegun fire, and I guess they passed it on to my unit. I'd hitched a ride on a tanker, and when my C.O. saw me he nearly fainted.

"'Sergeant Scaggs,' he says, 'you're supposed to be dead. Division says so, and you're disobeying a direct order. Division is a higher command, and when it passes information down to us peons it is the right information. Division is always right. What the hell are you doing, Sergeant, kicking and shoving that ugly mug of yours my way?'

"'Well,' I says, 'with all due respect me thought you'd be pleased to see me. Another experienced NCO snatched from the jaws of death and adding to the glory of the unit. Me thought you'd be pleased to see me.'

"'Don't give me that bull, Scaggs. Did ye know that Jenkins, my company clerk—he's from the same town as meself, Orono, Maine, that is—did you know he was the high school valedictorian?'

"'No, Captain, for the life of me I didn't.'

"'Well then, Jenkins here spent a good part of the day putting together personal information about those recently fallen, to be sent to next-of-kin and such like. And now we are told part of his hard and scrupulously executed work was all for naught. For naught because of your stubbornness.'

"'Well, what can I say?' says I.

"'Listen to me, Scaggs,' says he. 'I've been in the army longer than you, and I know how the army ticks. The army don't take kindly to contradictions and uncertainties. If a guy is dead, he's supposed to stay dead, and if he is alive then he ought to stay alive. There's nothing in between. Do you read me?'

"'Loud and clear, sir.'

"'Well then, you'd better return to your duties. I'm sure your buddies will be glad to see you in one piece.'

"'Thank you, Captain,' I said. As I was saluting and reeling on my heel, he was at it again."

"'You're from New York, Sergeant, and I don't mind telling you I don't care for you fellas. By and large you're a bunch of arrogant bastards.'

"'The captain may have a point,' I joined in ever so gentle-like, and his face broke into a funny kind of smile.

"'I'm glad we finally agree about something,' he spoke through his nose and kept smiling.

"'Yes,' I added in my gentle-like tone, 'we may be a bunch of arrogant bastards, but then there's so much we can rightfully be arrogant about. Why, we alone built this country, and before we came along all that graced our new land was a handful of starvin' redskins and a poisoned well or two Redcoats left behind as a lovin' souvenir.' I saluted again and off I am quick as lightning. He didn't even give me a glance."

"That's a fine tale, handsome," Wyn said, petting John's cheek. "But I am not in the mood. I see dark clouds everywhere."

He nodded wisely and held her hands in his. "This is what I'd like you to do. This here house is not my home, and it isn't your house either. It's *our* house. As long as I am on military duty I'd like you to live here and keep home fires burning. Bring your cats, if they are still breathing, and whatever else you need from Hempstead."

"What a terrible thing to say, John. Of course my cats are still breathing, what an impertinence. My cats are eternal; they will live forever."

"I won't argue with you, love. You just settle in and keep things around here flying. I have to get ready."

"Driving at night?"

"That's right. It's peaceful-like, and after midnight traffic will be light. I gotta be in Buffalo first thing in the morning. No tears, girl. No tears 'cause I'm coming back."

"No tears," she repeated, "and you take care."

Chapter 5

Wyoming Compact

It was Thursday, June 25, six days after the nuclear strike, and the country at large had had time to digest its physical impact and some of its consequences. The initial shock and disorientation had given way to a widespread and lacerating indignation that such an act could be committed at all in Western Amernipp no matter what grave offenses the people of Wyoming had been guilty of. Now for the first time words like barbarism, barbarity, savagery, and the like were beginning to be bandied about, at first without any resolve to bring the murderers to justice. At the back of many people's minds lurked a hope that no other part of the country would be similarly attacked, that somehow decency would prevail, Riverton and Worland remaining forever an isolated case of the government losing its head.

Such exasperated and self-protective sentiments stirred in many a breast, while Washington's explanation was simplicity itself. At a hastily called press conference on the morning of Tuesday, June 23, Homily Grister, deputizing for Chief Justice, announced that despite frequent warnings the state of Wyoming had refused to reenter the Western Amernippian Union and its treacherous secession had to be punished. Having said this he declared the press conference to be over and refused to answer questions. Frustrated reporters followed him all the way to his office door booming questions, the most frequent ones being why the population of Riverton and of Worland had not been evacuated before the strike and why had they not been given notice of the government's actions. But Grister remained deaf to the reporters' entreaties and shut them out.

There were no announcements or explanations on TV, and some interpreted it as a sure sign of Huston's inclination to play the incident down and give it as little publicity as possible, the reason being that unfortunately things had gotten out of hand. Yet contrary to what Chief Justice was credited with, the publicity the bombings received in the press and the media, both in the two provinces of Amernipp and abroad, was enormous. It was front-page news for weeks on end.

As it had been said in the illustrious dramatic work, Shakespeare's *Julius Caesar*, many years ago, subsequently cited and explicated on innumerable occasions, "There is a tide in the affairs of men / which, taken at the flood, / leads on to fortune"; and so it was in Western Amernipp in the year 2084. Almost hourly the mood of the country was changing. By Friday, June 26th, men were calling for an impartial investigation of the bombings and for holding the government accountable. On Saturday, June 27th, many parts of the country were bristling with discontent. Men and women rose in protest at public meetings and in the privacy of their homes demanding a different government, one holding no warrant to murder innocent Amernippian citizens at will, and a different political system, one not grounded in inequality and injustice.

Irreversibly the deeply rooted bafflement and horror insulated in a self-protective instinct shot upward to a new calling and grew into a profession of faith exacting punishment of the guilty parties and above all drastic changes in the political arena consistent with the American oral tradition stretching back to George Washington and the Constitution of 1787. Individual psychologies no less than collective ones full of blocked gangways, of corridors half-walled-in, of windows recklessly swung open, of roofs that had lost more tiles than was good for them now offered a speedy escape or a path to ascension from the decaying edifice that was sum total of everything that was done, thought, and felt within its walls from the very beginning.

It is rightly postulated that every single moment in the psychology of an individual or of a community is the result of all that has been experienced by him, her, or it until this very moment, the past irreversibly becoming the present and then the future. True enough! But our ability and methodology to understand this causative process is still in its infancy. In this particular domain, as in so many others, our knowledge is heavily circumscribed. We can kid ourselves that we understand how things are. But we have less than a clue as to how they came to be. This means that many political predictions we made are pure guesswork, the term "political science" as an academic discipline and an intellectual activity being one of the most infamous but unacknowledged oxymorons in the English language.

The progression taking place individually in the minds of millions of Western Amernippians and collectively in the spirit of thousands of communities of the land from emotive and self-oriented attitudes to those sanctifying freedom, fairness, and justice eludes a thorough analysis. Though it might be said that this progression was nurtured by the rich mix of half-forgotten political loyalties, half-forgotten political beliefs, lingering layers of American idealism, half-suppressed memories of what the country that had declared its independence on July 4, 1776, had stood for for centuries, and countless cultural, ethical, and religious imperatives and rules of conduct. It was also plausible to assume that the electorate took the tide at the flood in the spirit of practicality and thus moved on to fortune.

Whatever the reasons, by the end of the week many parts of Western Amernipp were yearning for a change of regime and a return to the old America as it had existed before Everett Zacharias Huston became a household name. Tense drama plays out not only on the stage but in real life too, and it can be just as gripping. In the summer of 2084 it was enacted in the cities, towns, and countryside of Western Amernipp with unparalleled fervor and suspense.

When on Sunday, June 28th, President Jack Woods addressed, from the steps of Lincoln Memorial, over two million people crowded into Washington Mall he knew that parts of the country stood firmly by his side. But as for the other parts, well, it was anybody's guess. Here congregated was the greatest assemblage of citizenry since the days of Martin Luther King Jr., and President Woods, wearing a newly pressed uniform of captain of the United States Navy, stood on the same spot on which the Reverend King had stood one hundred and twenty years before. Exuding self-confidence and smiling broadly, he began, his Georgia twang gaining in resonance with every passing word.

"My friends, our days of bondage are coming to an end. I am happy to tell you that national elections on November 2nd of this year will be free elections and that our two major political parties, and other lesser known ones, will be putting up candidates for national and state offices." As loudspeakers carried his words far and wide he was interrupted by tumultuous applause and kept being interrupted every few seconds. "I myself am the candidate for president of the United States on the Democratic ticket, and the other day I found out, how I won't tell you, that the Republicans have their own candidate for the presidency who will be my main opponent." There was another burst of applause.

"In all executive, legislative, and judicial matters we are going right back to the U.S. Constitution of 1787 and to the Bill of Rights. Starting now this great country of ours is again a country under God with justice and liberty for all, and as in the days before the regime of Chief Justice Everett Z. Huston took over we hold now and we shall forever hold the legacy of the Founding Fathers near and dear.

"As commander in chief I have already assumed personal command of the Armed Forces of Western Amernipp, and if these forces have to be deployed to defend our civil rights against the tyranny and savagery of the usurpers headed by one Everett Z. Huston, I give you my pledge they will be so deployed.

"As of now there are no two kinds of citizens in our country previously designated as highgovies and lowgovies. This cruel and irrational division has gone up in smoke. There are no first-class and second-class citizens in Western Amernipp. All of us, irrespective of our religious affiliation, our social status, our national origin, race, education, manner of employment, and whatever else may be distinctive about each of us, all of us I say are first-class citizens enjoying the same rights and privileges; and all of us are equal before the law.

"My friends, tomorrow a new dawn will break on our great country. The chains that held us captive have been broken, and Western Amernipp will be again a beacon of light among nations, home of the brave, land of the free!" The applause was tumultuous.

"My friends, may God bless each and every one of you, and may God bless Western Amernipp."

There was much astonishment in the next few days that the ousting of Huston and his government from the capital had proceeded without resistance. Woods ordered the army to occupy all government buildings and arrest the cabinet and senior staff within the executive offices of Chief Justice and his principal advisors. Thereupon he issued a number of executive orders, subject to congressional approval, after free general elections to be held on November 2, 2084. The legislative business before the Congress was deferred till after the elections, the chasm between highgovies and lowgovies was declared unconstitutional, and the Constitution of 1787 was restored as the law of the land as was the Bill of Rights.

The keynote of everything that now emanated from the White House was a speedy return to status quo ante, to the not so distant past when the United States of America and later Western Amernipp was a democracy respecting the rule of law. To deal with the Herculean labor of carrying on the nation's business until the November elections the president appointed a twelve-member executive committee with himself as head, on which served Jose Carero of Wyoming and a young rabbi from Cleveland, Joseph Oscar Pitkin.

One of the committee's very early decisions was to free all political prisoners and incarcerate, at least for the time being, the chiefs of the infamous political police that had wrought so much havoc. Disappointingly some of the big fish eluded the net. Shortly after President Woods' address from the steps of Lincoln Memorial, Chief Justice disappeared from the scene. It was rumored that he was somewhere in Dixie protected by members of his family and multiple bodyguards. Other justices of the Supreme Court also fled, and their whereabouts were a mystery. On the same day Phineas Léger flew to Canada to negotiate the acceptance of his new book with publishers and hold far-reaching discussions with editors of literary and political journals, while Ganymede Pillows, leaving nothing to chance, had taken earlier in the week his entire family on an extended European vacation. Of the trio comprising Huston's closest associates only Homily Grister was left minding the store. Unrepentant and defiant to the end he claimed he had had no prior knowledge of Nathan Chadwick's assassination, of the nuclear attack, and of the thousands of political arrests. He was just a simple foot soldier carrying out orders given by Chief Justice. He considered himself exempt from any responsibility. He was taken into custody.

Until further notice the foreign policy of Western Amernipp was left in the hands of Timothy Hysart, and with much fanfare Wyoming was accepted into the Union. In the early days of July President Woods met with numerous state and community leaders, and with representatives of diverse professional, labor, and business groups. He listened patiently to their problems, offered help whenever he could but insisted that the return to justice and democracy should be speedy and wholehearted.

At a meeting with university and college presidents of both public and private institutions, he read an executive order he had issued earlier in the day restoring old familiar names to institutions of higher learning that had been renamed or converted to other uses. Universities closed down by Huston were to be opened again, and he urged the presidents to do all in their power to start fall semester 2084 in the spirit which had animated American higher education in the days before the theocratic takeover.

The bloodless political transition proceeded expeditiously, but it soon became clear to the President and the Executive Council that Huston loyalists were determined to make a stand elsewhere. In New England and as far north and west as Wisconsin and Minnesota, National Guard and state militia were being mobilized under Huston's banner, and word went out that these forces were defending the legitimate government of Western Amernipp, their opponents being cutthroats and traitors with a price on their heads.

The middle of July witnessed the first skirmishes and then pitched battles between the New York Freedom Brigade and loyalist units secretly ferried from Massachusetts, Vermont, New Hampshire, and Pennsylvania to the northwest section of New York State. There the Freedom Brigade, the New Jersey Freedom Fighters, and the Maine Volunteers faced on three consecutive days the numerically superior rebel forces at Medina, Stafford, and Batavia. Casualties were heavy on both sides, and neither army could claim victory. But the rebels were stopped. Their plan had been to march from Buffalo and Rochester southeast across the state, impose martial law in captured cities and towns and advance to the edge of New York City; once entrenched the rebel commander would demand its surrender. The stalemate in the three-day battle foiled this plan, and for the remainder of the summer rebel forces in the northeastern part of the state engaged in skirmishes without mounting another major offensive. They were waiting for reinforcements from the Midwest, which were late in coming.

A greater danger threatened from the South. The southern states, blindly loyal to Chief Justice, coordinated their efforts and put in the field a well-trained and well-equipped force of a million and half men whose high morale would be the envy of any commander-in-chief. Faithful to the maxim that offense is the best defense, the rebel generals decided to stake everything on a single card, transport their force with speed to the vicinity of Washington D.C., win a decisive battle, and either enter the nation's capital as victors or dictate peace terms to the cowed democrats and constitution-lovers. It was a strategy that in a slightly modified form had been contemplated by Southern leaders during the Civil War and now, the second time round, the generals were more sanguine than ever.

The president and his commanders knew what lay in store. Additional troops to defend the capital were hastily brought in from the surrounding states, from the Midwest, and from the West. Democratic strategy was to avoid a major engagement and rely instead on a series of clashes along the front, which would tire and confuse the enemy. But the Rebels soon wised up to it. Their maneuvers sent a chilly message to the democrats: "If you don't want to put your lives on the line, we'll just march into D.C. and you guys can catch the next train to hell." A decisive battle was in the cards.

It was fought on the sixteenth, seventeenth, and eighteenth of July on the plains between Catlett and Calverton, forty miles northeast of Culpeper, Virginia, hence the name, the Battle of Catlett and Calverton. On the first two days the Rebels were testing the waters. They tried to outflank the center of the democratic force, its right and left flank having been sent twenty miles east and west respectively. But the democrats lengthened their lines in both directions even more and were on the point of encircling the Rebel center. Smelling defeat the Rebels withdrew to the very edges of Calverton, and next day attempted another outflanking maneuver, which was again thwarted.

The third day witnessed a fundamental change in tactics. The Rebels moved all the outlying units to the center creating a massive force that they thought would overpower the enemy assembled on two hills south of and just outside Catlett. Rebel artillery mercilessly pounded the two hills to soften and if possible decimate the enemy before a frontal attack, and aerial bombardment was also employed to aid in reaching the goal. But the Rebels miscalculated. They found out after the battle that the democrats had constructed large dugouts on the other side of the two apexes and had dug a network of deep trenches roofed at evenly spread out assembly points offering protection. Artillery shells and bombs did little damage, and when in late morning of the third day of battle, rows of tanks crept up the slope with the infantry in tow they were met by a seemingly unending barrage of anti-tank mortar and grenade-launcher fire. Dozens of tanks exploded and the infantry suffered heavy losses. Yet the Rebels would not give up that easily. They swung to the sides, regrouped, threw more tanks into the fray, and began to advance uphill reinforced by heavy guns and bombers.

What happened in the next twenty minutes was a massacre the like of which neither the Rebels nor the democrats had anticipated. In flames, rows upon rows of tanks turned into scrap metal as their crews, bleeding or partly scorched, were hanging out of turrets, seeking escape from infernal heat and bullets. Wave after wave of infantry carrying heavy machine guns, grenade launchers, and flamethrowers was moved down, the armor no longer offering protection. Yet the still mobile tanks ground forward and the infantry, more and more spread out and repeatedly hitting the ground to return the fire aiming just below the apex on the far side, served as living proof that bravery against impossible odds was its true nature, and that it knew no other. Here and there a dispersed platoon or two had climbed almost to the foot of the hill only to be shoved down by bullet or bayonet, the butt of a submachine or an enraged fist. The last few Rebel tanks were demolished, and when the fighting ended shortly before 8 P.M. on July 18th, thousands of Huston loyalists lay dead on the incline leading up to the town of Catlett.

On this third and decisive day of contest, which determined the fate of Western Amernipp for several weeks to come the Rebel casualties stood in the sixty percent bracket. The democratic ones were much lower, at twenty to twenty-five percent, though they had been higher on the two preceding days, rising to thirty or forty percent. But the nation's capital had been saved, the road to D.C. closed, the insurgents chased away.

The very next day the remnants of Rebel forces began to withdraw in the southwesterly direction, fearing a counterattack, and they pitched camp in the vicinity of Charlottesville. Their march on Washington had been stopped by men fighting as bravely as they themselves had fought and who perhaps had had luck on their side. But their resolve had not been broken, and as soon as reinforcements arrived they would be on the march again; this time the prize would be theirs. President Woods and his advisors read the Rebels' minds—not a particularly difficult undertaking—and concluded that should the next blow fall soon, in a matter of days or weeks, democratic forces as presently constituted in and around Washington D.C. might not be able to withstand it.

Prudence dictated that the seat of government should be moved to a new location, preferably one far away from Virginia and the Potomac, and situated in a territory friendly to the democratic agenda and where great manpower stood guardian and protector. Cheyenne, Wyoming, was selected and on July 22nd the White House, the entire United States Congress, and the skeletal federal judiciary, still being reorganized and reconstituted, were flown to the Equality State.

The news of the unusual number of feds descending on the state capital to stay evoked only a feeble though varied response on the part of the citizenry, similar to a sad shake of the head when a much traveled highway is closed because of inclement weather or to a terse word or two uttered by a family who has just found out their house had been invaded by termites. In bars in Cheyenne and across the state the news provoked no more than a belch followed by a speedy order for another drink to drown the painful prospect of overpopulation. On the range a well-aimed spit livened up a few choice unprintable words.

In town wizards prophesied an acute housing shortage, which was the reverse of what happened. The president, the vice-president, the cabinet, and principal aides and advisors were lodged in the governor's mansion; the Senate and the House of Representatives in several large downtown motels; the judiciary branch of the government was conducted to a nondescript bed-and-breakfast establishment just across the city limits where, as one judge put it, one was never certain whether the place was equipped with indoor plumbing or not. Still, merchants, shopkeepers, restaurateurs, and liquor storeowners rubbed their hands in glee, and the chamber of commerce had thousands of leaflets printed advertising any and all holes where the estimable Washingtonians could divest themselves of excess cash.

The free spirit of the West and western hospitality ensured polite conduct on the part of the natives toward the visitors, but very soon something like a common belief was gaining ground and was intemperately vocalized that since all of a sudden the wholesome city of Cheyenne had been invaded by hordes of very peculiar-looking individuals everyone should be on his or her guard. Over major downtown intersections huge banners were hung sending a daring message printed in all the colors of the rainbow, "The City of Cheyenne Will Protect its Women," and the city was quick to act. The police department, in conjunction with the Association of Retired Sheriffs, the Association of Retired Detectives, and the Association of Retired Policemen, with the blessing of several churches and the active cooperation of the state football team, formed a protection service for female inhabitants of Cheyenne who might find themselves alone in a city street during the day but especially after sundown. Every lady facing such a predicament would have an escort of at least one or possibly two able-bodied males, free of charge for as long as she was abroad. This measure went a long way in alleviating the fears of the male population for the safety of their wives, mothers, daughters, sisters, etc., particularly after two professors from a nearby university made statements to the newspapers and the media that they detected in a number of U.S. Congressmen brought to Cheyenne by a fickle destiny distinctive physical traits marking them as atavistic types and possible criminals according to Cesare Lombroso, a nineteenth-century Italian criminologist. Lombroso's theories, first enunciated in 1876, were no longer held in such high regard as in late nineteenth century but there remained a lingering interest in them more in academic circles than anywhere else.

At any rate, Cheyenne, Wyoming, was the capital of Western Amernipp for the duration, and the bristling skepticism and discontent its new status evoked in the populace surprised nobody. Some city officials pointed to a sense of pride the city surely felt at having been raised to such an exalted position. Perhaps. But if so it was pride so discreet and muted as to remain very largely unexpressed however powerfully it may have been inwardly throbbing. In the months to come this question of civic pride was regularly canvassed yet the final verdict eluded the disputants. Prudently, it was left to future generations.

Several days after the government's installation in Cheyenne, Justin Brewster, the appointment secretary, ran into the unimpressive room serving as the temporary Oval Office. He was out of breath and clearly put out. "Mr. President, two Wyoming gentlemen insist on seeing you at once. They say it's an urgent military matter."

"Who are they, Justin?"

"They claim to be officers in the Wyoming National Guard. Well-dressed and all that, but odd. Not our kind of people, Mr. President."

Jack Woods smiled. "Can you route them to the Secretary of Defense?"

"I tried, sir, I tried," Justin Brewster protested. "They'll see no one but you."

"All right, Justin. Ask Colonel Stacy to join me here, and then show our two friends in."

A few moments later, two tall, broad-shouldered men in their fifties crossed the threshold. "Mr. President," one of them said, "I am William Roanoke Sherman, captain in the 306th Special Troops Battalion in the Middle East Conflict more than thirty years ago, now brigadier general in the Wyoming National Guard, and a realtor by trade from Evanston, Wyoming."

"How do you do, General?" The president held out his hand.

"And I am Antonio Fernandez Bolivar, sir," the other man said, "like Bill, I was a captain in the 306th during said conflict. Now brigadier general in the Wyoming National Guard. Hardware store owner hailing from Gillette, Wyoming." The President shook hands with Bolivar.

"I don't know whether you met my military advisor, Colonel Douglas Stacy."

"No, we haven't," the two men said. "But the name strikes a chord," Sherman added. "Doesn't it, Tony?"

"Sure does," Bolivar agreed, and the three men shook hands.

"Gentlemen, please state your business and be as succinct as possible," the president began, waving the two men to the chairs by his desk. "I am snowed under."

"Mr. President, what I am going to say comes from both of us." Bolivar's delivery was slow, precise. "We have business associates in Virginia and in other parts of the South. We are reasonably well informed."

"Go on," the President urged him to proceed, his voice filled with emotion.

"It's common knowledge the rebs will make another attempt to take D.C., and this time they may be successful. The South is mobilizing like never before, and once they take over the capital they'll install their own government with Huston or one of his lieutenants as head." Bolivar was going to continue, but the President raised his hand and cast a pointed look at his military advisor.

"Colonel Stacy, please give us an update on what is being done to defend the capital."

"Yes, Mr. President. We are going to comb the surrounding states for volunteers, bring all the remaining federal troops to Alexandria and establish a long front from Dale City to Germantown protecting Washington from the west. We don't think the Rebs will come from the east by way of Annapolis and Baltimore."

"No matter how they get to Washington, they'll have a two-to-one superiority," Sherman observed tersely.

"That's true. Unfortunately, as you well know, a sizeable part of our armed forces sided with the Rebs. But we are making progress little by little, and new contingents will be arriving from New York and Maine."

"With all due respect, Colonel, this may not be enough." Bolivar had risen and was now glaring at Stacy.

"Aren't you being just a tad melodramatic, Brigadier? Besides, our intelligence tells us the earliest the rebels will be able to attack again will be a month from now. Logistical problems and all that."

"Are you sure your intelligence is top-notch, Colonel?" Sherman asked also rising and observing Stacy critically.

"We have no reason to believe it is anything but top-notch, Mr. Sherman." Stacy took several steps forward, positioning himself next to the President, his back turned against the two Wyomingites.

"Mr. President, that's why we came to see you," Bolivar sounded off, doing his utmost to keep his voice level and his gestures under control. "We believe we ought to hit the Rebels with everything we've got now, before they rest up, regroup, and grow in strength and numbers. Preemptive strike is our best chance."

The President kept looking intently at the speaker and his partner without making a sound.

"Here out west," Sherman took over, "we have the greatest concentration of federal troops loyal to you and the legitimate government, and the largest force of state National Guards and state militias, and sure as hell today we can count on Texas and California. We've got what it takes to kick the shit out of Huston's loyalists once and for all, and even though this may be flying off on a tangent, save the great republic from a shameful death."

Abruptly Stacy turned on his heel and faced the realtor and the hardware store owner in utter silence, his face dark and furrowed, his manner insulting. "The bulk of Reb forces is two thousand miles southeast of Wyoming in western Virginia and the Carolinas. Moving a million or million and half men from here to where the enemy is dug in—equipment, transport weaponry—will take weeks at best, not counting establishing supply lines. You are both mad, yes, stark raving mad. Leave soldiering to professionals, d'you hear me? Go back to your cozy realtor office, Sherman, and you, Bolivar, to your lucrative hardware business. You won't be missed."

This time it was Bolivar who spoke, and to face the President he pushed Stacy lightly out of the way and against the wall. "Mr. President, there are ways of conveying two million men from here to Virginia in a space of twenty-four hours, together with weapons, equipment, and transport. It can be done, Mr. President. It can be done."

Sherman advanced and looked the President straight in the eye. "We keep hearing you've taken a shine to our humble state capital, to your hampered quarters at the gov's mansion, and we are informed you've even grown tolerant of the riff-raff that fills our streets. We thank you from the bottom of our hearts for the milk of human kindness that is pouring out of your own heart like an overflowing creek and demanding one whole milk-train as the only solution. We are honored, sir, we are honored. But when all is said and done, your finger being on the trigger and the deer clear in your sights, wouldn't you rather sleep in your own featherbed and have the use of the real Oval Office at 1600 Pennsylvania Avenue? Give it a thought, Mr. President, give it a thought."

Jack Woods nodded lightheartedly and pressed a button on his desk. "Justin, arrange a conference two hours from now—myself, our two friends, Colonel Stacy, the secretaries of defense, of the army, and of air force, and the secretary of the interior. And most important of all I want chiefs of staff to be on it telephonically, of course. Run them to ground in that Baltimore hideout of theirs, and see to it we have lots of strong coffee. Thank you, Justin."

"Yes, Mr. President."

/   /   /

Sherman and Bolivar took possession of all army and National Guard aircraft in the western states, including those in Texas and California and, worthy successors to the French general Joseph Simon Gallieni of World War I fame, they commandeered every commercial and private plane in as many states as they could lay their hands on. Trucks and cannon were rolled onto huge transport and cargo carriers, lighter weapons and equipment were distributed among jumbo jets, and troops were packed into Zeppelins, airships, flying boats, and the pride and joy of more than fifty airlines. Executive jets, the precious flying possessions of well-entrenched country club members, private planes of every size and description were also in high demand and performed a yeoman's job. Bolivar and Sherman were taken aback by the enthusiastic response to their demand for more aircraft and still more aircraft. From flying schools to CEOs' spacious offices came a steady supply of dirigibles, and in many quarters it was considered bad form not to participate in the national effort. High society outdid itself in putting more and more private planes at the army's disposal, and corporate America, together with every other America, did its duty. With regret Tony and Bill had to turn away the superkites, enormous spreads of cloth equipped with a small motor, which had become highly fashionable of late in junior high schools all over the country, each of which the young scholars claimed, could carry at least one trooper, wind and weather permitting. But just about everything else that had an engine and flew was put to good use.

On Monday, July 26, from the airbases, airports, and makeshift runways in Wyoming, Colorado and Nebraska, in the Dakotas, Montana, Idaho and New Mexico, in Oregon and Washington, Texas, and California, took to the air thousands of planes, large and small. Soon they darkened the sky and came to resemble vast swarms of locusts. Their destinations were the recently closed down airbases in Lynchburg, Bedford, and New London in Virginia with hundreds of runways and landing facilities, as well as the adjoining flat fields for smaller aircraft. Flight time and landing time had been calculated to a split second and air-flotillas were flying according to a strict plan. By 2200 hours on Monday, July 26, two million men and women in uniform had been transported to the quiet Virginia countryside together with hundreds of tons of weaponry and equipment, the advance parties directing the newly-arrived to requisitioned buildings and thousands of tents.

The operation had gone off without a hitch, and Huston loyalists were caught napping. They had expected a thrust south from D.C., but this defied logistics and the laws of what was possible. How the hell did the democratic bastards succeed in bringing two million troops, armor, and heavy artillery to the loyalists' backyard? How the hell did they do it? The Loyalist Supreme Headquarters in Charlottesville was torn by dissension, and at first no strategy could be formulated. The loyalists were waiting to see what the democrats would do and act accordingly. But on the other side of the fence the Army of Liberation of the Midwest, South, and other parts of Western Amernipp, as the flown-in force was officially christened, was quicker at decision-making.

Secretly the President sided with Sherman and Bolivar, but he could not afford to antagonize his own chiefs of staff. Hence he devised a compromise: he had appointed the chief of staff of the army as commanding general of the Army of Liberation, and Bolivar and Sherman, with temporary ranks of brigadiers in the Army of Western Amernipp, as his deputy commanders, with broad though not entirely defined discretionary powers. He was at once warned by numerous advisors that he was playing with fire and was creating what had never succeeded in the past, a divided command. Woods listened patiently to criticism, kept his fingers crossed, and dispatched trusted friends to the commanding general and to his deputies, counseling mutual understanding, harmony, and unity.

Contrary to the advisors' predictions, the trio—two cowboys and the vinegar Westy as it was promptly dubbed—worked well in tandem. All three agreed that because of the liberators' numerical superiority it was essential to go on the offensive at once and aim at defeating the loyalists in a series of decisive battles involving at each stage large loyalist contingents, weaning them away from the desire to fight skirmishes or worse still resort to guerilla warfare. A large concentration of loyalist forces could be brought about, the trio thought, when there was a widespread feeling that the tiger was at the gate and the old dominion on the brink of annihilation. This would rally the generals and the privates and, God willing, Virginians at large.

Accordingly, orders were issued for a march on Richmond, and the liberators' intelligence flooded the newspapers and the media with bloodcurdling stories of the imminent vengeance to be visited on the population of Richmond, no quarter to be given. The ruse worked. The loyalists combined their forces, and the first battle was joined at Scotts Ford on July 28th, the second at Chula on July 31st, and the third at Macon on August 4th. All three were resounding victories for the Army of Liberation. The loyalists' dead and wounded numbered tens of thousands, and the prisoners taken exceeded one hundred thousand; the enemy's armor, artillery, and their tiny but heroic air force were utterly destroyed. Calling every available man and woman to the colors, the Southerners put up one more fight at Rushmere, just outside Richmond, on August 4, and were again brought down with colossal losses.

At this point organized loyalist resistance came to an end. There were no more ranks, and most of the officers were dead, wounded, or in POW camps. The victorious Army of Liberation entered Richmond and surprised everybody by not erecting gallows and herding men, women, and children into public squares to be machine-gunned. It was now up to the Red Cross and other charitable organizations, and the victors willingly shared their rations with the populace.

The specter of full-scale civil war had been chased away, but even though the South had been placated, violence and insurgence erupted in many other states. In Illinois and Wisconsin armed gangs of loyalists attacked post offices and government buildings, and Iowa erupted in a farmer rebellion, federal subsidies for farmers voted on by Jack Woods' administration being much lower than what the Iowans had been used to under Huston. All these upsurges of violence were local and could be put down by local means, though in Indiana, Ohio, and Pennsylvania the opposing forces were of battalion strength. In these three states the liberators embarked on an ambitious campaign of persuasion and education for democracy that proved to be highly successful in places, and the pendulum was clearly swinging in the direction of democracy, albeit ever so slowly. In upstate New York skirmishing continued unabated, but here too there were signs that victory was in sight.

President Woods had been hoping that rebellions and uprisings without national backing could be suppressed by local authorities, even though he had never discarded the possibility of sending large detachments of federal troops to trouble spots. But now another burning issue was forcing itself upon his overburdened mind, and he knew he would have to make a decision one way or the other because the fate of the nation hung in the balance. Defeating loyalist armies and establishing a democratic government at the point of the bayonet was one thing, but in a democracy the electorate should be able to vote and decide upon the kind of political system it wanted. Taught and inspired by centuries of American democracy and peering into the future, Jack Woods became convinced that it was high time the people of Western Amernipp were given the chance to register their will as to whether continued theocracy of the kind Chief Justice Huston favored or democracy as it had existed from the very birth of the nation until the recent dictatorial takeover was their preferred choice.

"Justin," Woods asked, "did we bring with us from Washington any experts on elections, absentee voting, initiatives, referenda, that kind of thing?"

"To the best of my knowledge, we didn't, sir. After all this was to be a very temporary change of venue."

"Yes, yes," Woods blurted out. "What about constitutional lawyers? Are they gracing us with their presence?"

"No again, Mr. President. They're all back in Washington." Justin paused and then a thought germinated in his brain. "The U.S. Attorney General brought along two senior members of his staff. Perhaps," he left the remainder of what he was going to say hanging in the air. Then he added: "There's of course the Wyoming contingent. Their state attorney is in town and so are the five justices of the Wyoming Supreme Court."

"Gotcha," Woods snapped. "This is what I want you to do, Justin. Set up a conference for 1800 hours today. Ask our U.S. Attorney and the Wyoming Attorney General to bring with them one or two bodies specializing in the election process and constitutional law. I'll call the Chief Justice of the Wyoming Supreme Court myself with the same request. Tell the housekeeper we'll be ten or eleven for dinner."

"Anything else, Mr. President?"

"Oh, yes. What's the state of the liquor cabinet?"

"Almost bare."

"Almost bare," Woods repeated mechanically. "It was full a couple of days ago."

"So it was, sir. So it was."

"I'll tell you what's happening. All those guys coming to brief me

or seek my advice really come here to get a free drink, or rather a succession of free drinks, when my back is turned. Without naming any
names we know who they are, don't we?"

"Well, sir, there are only two culprits. The rest are rated snow
white."

"Indeed. Not to put too fine a point on it, but ordinary down-to-
earth guys boozing it up in a lowdown Atlanta dive have nine out of
ten better manners than many prominent Washingtonians. And that's
God's truth, Justin, God's own truth."

"Yes, Mr. President. I'd better get cracking on that 1800 hours conference."

"You do that, son."

The conference got off to a good start, and what emerged the next
day was a one-page statement with a ballot appended. It asked in simple and concise English whether the voter opted for the continuation
of the theocratic regime, which was briefly described in objective language, or whether he or she opted for the restoration of the democratic political system, which was again briefly described and which
followed the principles of the Wyoming Referendum, of the president's
address to the nation on June 28th, and of his subsequently announced
program of political reform. The voter was asked to cross one of the two
squares, each one under the appropriate description of the political system he or she favored, print his or her name and address, and sign the
ballot.

All citizens of Western Amernipp eighteen years old or older had
the right to vote, and arrangements were made to send ballots to
American citizens residing in foreign countries. The document was
named Wyoming Compact, and it bore the seal of the state of Wyoming
and Grand Seal of Western Amernipp. Polling stations were set up in
every state, in all cities and larger towns, and in rural communities. Tens
of millions of ballots were printed, and election officials drawn in equal
numbers from the Democratic Party and the Republican Party supervised the casting and counting of votes. Inhabitants of each state voted
for the most part in their home state, but in the West many voters were
eager to place their ballots in rows of boxes neatly arranged on long
sturdy tables inside the Wyoming Capitol. Thousands traveled to
Cheyenne from Nebraska and the Dakotas, from Colorado, Montana,

Idaho and New Mexico, from Oregon and Washington, and strings of buses brought thousands from Texas and California.

Voting time lasted four days, from August 15 through August 18, and turnout in practically all the states was unusually high. Jose Carero was in charge of the entire operation, and he worked closely with officials in each state. He was the man of the hour. On August 20 all of the ballots were transported to Cheyenne, Wyoming, still the temporary national capital, and again recounted. Votes from American citizens living abroad were in the mail, and on August 26, President Woods was able to announce the results of Wyoming Compact in a national broadcast.

Eighty-two percent of all ballots cast and accepted favored a return to the democratic rule, and eighteen percent a continuation of the theocratic one. Democratic victory was overwhelming, and in Cheyenne and elsewhere there was much rejoicing.

Concurrently good news came from the Midwestern states. In Iowa the farmer rebellion had been all but quelled, and in Ohio, Indiana, and Illinois the loyalists were on the run. The situation in Pennsylvania and Wisconsin was much improved, and in upstate New York heavy skirmishes were decimating the enemy. The armed opposition to the administration headed by Jack Woods was now confined to small numbers of anti-democratic zealots, men and women for whom the Messianic figure of Everett Zacharias Huston and the community he had called to life represented the triumph of religion over secular philosophy, of spirit over matter, of the infinite wisdom of God Almighty over the trivial and shoddy ways of man; and their numbers were dwindling. This was not the end, not even the beginning of the end. But as somebody or other had put it over a hundred years ago in a similar situation, it was the end of the beginning.

The presidential campaign and the campaign for other federal and state offices was now in full swing, and the lately resuscitated political parties competed for the prize like men possessed. President Woods was a popular candidate, but so was his Republican opponent, a former governor of a large and populous state, whose good looks, vigor, and charm made a powerful appeal to all segments of society including women, married, unmarried, young, old, and those in between.

Washington, D.C. was no longer in jeopardy, and the president felt it was time to exchange the salubrious air of the West for the marshes of the District of Columbia. Accordingly on September 2, the president, accompanied by members of the executive branch of government whom he had brought with him from the capital, flew back to the capital. Before departing he appeared on Wyoming television thanking the government and the people of the state for their hospitality and help. He singled out for particular praise Jose Carero and his coworkers, brave and wise men and women in making Wyoming Compact a reality. His broadcast was universally adjudged a very nice gesture.

The United States Congress and the thinned-out judiciary left by air on September 3, and presently Cheyenne was again what it had always been, the capital of a large but sparsely populated western state, and no more. It served as the seat of Western Amernippian government and the nation's capital for forty-one days during one of the most hectic and tragic periods in the country's history, and it played a major role in restoring the country's pride and honor.

Weighty facts are often absorbed slowly by the mind, not like the featherweight ones, and trying to speed up the process may have the contrary effect. It took several years before the impact of those forty-one days was put in perspective properly and even longer before its historical and political value was assessed. But one day the event entered the collective memory bank and the cultural lifeblood of the state and then memories, recollections, hindsight, analyses, speculations, hypotheses, and fully baked theories blossomed and multiplied. The event was canvassed on every imaginable level, from kindergarten through the graduate school and beyond, in groves of academe. As for the commonsensical reaction of Tom, Dick, and Harry, Jane, Susan, and Kim, which may be brainier than one at first imagines, there was little doubt it contained more than an iota of noble pride and satisfaction that the job was well done. And so pride groweth and self-esteem with it.

By the middle of September most of the fighting had come to an end, isolated pockets of resistance still holding out while the last of the intransigent guerrillas dashed this way and that in the dark, set on sabotage. On September 15 President Woods went on national television asking all combatants to lay down their arms on or before September 22 and promising if they did so they would receive honorable treatment as prisoners of war. The news spread quickly, and already by September 19 the remnants of the armed opposition surrendered to the authorities. Only isolated guerillas remained in the field, and those would be dealt with by sheriffs and state police.

On September 24 the president made the happy announcement that the country was at peace and that law and order again prevailed; and on September 26, against the advice of his closest friends, he granted a general amnesty to all those who had fought in the military for the loyalist cause, this amnesty not including war criminals who would come under the jurisdiction of the courts. The last words of his announcement were a call for national unity. "Go to your homes, those of you whom we met on the battlefield carrying a different flag. Go to your homes, resume your productive lives, and make friends with your former enemies. We are again one nation, and may God bless Western Amernipp."

"That's well and good, Jack," the President's friends said, "a noble gesture, but it may cost you the election."

"I won't brook one part of the population keeping another part in jail. This is not what we fought for," Woods replied. "The civil war's over."

"That's right, and you're being just and magnanimous. Just remember there's a price to pay. The governor'll make a lot of hay out of your amnesty."

"What I am doing is in the national interest. Whether it furthers my interests as a candidate for president is relatively unimportant."

"Sure, sure, Jack. But the public is fickle. Right now it's out for blood. It doesn't want those traitors pardoned; it wants them swinging from the tallest trees."

"We have to learn to respect and love one another. We are one family. God's children!" Woods was emphasizing each word, casting hard, inquisitive gazes at his friends, and they knew his resolve was pure steel.

"That's right, Jack, but remember you've been warned."

"What would I do without your warnings and advice, guys? Why, I'm deeply honored." He was heading for the door, and their vigorously appreciative laughter reverberated in his ears.

Two days after granting amnesty to loyalist combatants Jack Woods took to the hustings in the southern states. His first stop was Richmond, Virginia, where he mingled with the crowds, talked to passersby in the streets, to customers and checkers in supermarkets, to office and construction workers, to cops and firefighters. He asked about unemployment and inflation, about taxes, about health coverage, and where the shoe pinched.

In the afternoon he addressed a restive crowd in a football stadium, and in the remaining hours of daylight held a town hall meeting in the city park where even standing room was at a premium. His populist message was clear and everyone understood it. He stood for better health coverage, for raising minimum wage, for smaller classes and better-trained teachers, for extending unemployment benefits, for a stimulus package for small businesses, for longer vacations for state employees, for better working conditions for blue collar workers, for unionized labor, and for keeping a watchful eye on big corporations.

He had not been welcomed with paeans, but as the day wore on confidence in him grew. Amnesty was fresh on people's minds; many remembered the treatment loyalist POWs had received was humane and medical care excellent. Few blamed him for staging yet another war of northern aggression. After all, he was the President, and his paramount concern was to save the Union—the phrase their great-grandfathers and their fathers and grandfathers had heard more than two hundred years before from another president, and it was only natural it should devolve onto his successor. Besides, Jack Woods hailed from Georgia, another southern state down the road a piece; he understood the South, and he stood for the common man.

When in the early hours of the evening the exhausted but exultant President was winding up his stay in Richmond, an enthusiastic crowd gathered at the airport to see him off. He ran down the ramp of Air Force One twice shaking more hands and answering more questions, and then, as the plane was easing its way onto a runway he stood for several minutes in the doorway waving and making a victory sign. As soldiers in the crowd sprang to attention and saluted, all lungs and vocal chords broke into a deafening chant, "For He is a Jolly Good Fellow," which went on long after Air Force One disappeared from view.

The next legs of the hustings took him to Raleigh and Columbia, Atlanta and Montgomery, Jackson, and finally New Orleans. He was well received wherever he went. Several days later, bidding farewell to Louisiana and laboriously digesting rich Cajun cooking, he crossed into Texas.

/   /   /

Ever since its inception the Center for Democratic West had shown much resemblance to a freemasonic lodge where members vouch for and support one another while pursuing their diverse objectives, which in reality are common objectives dominated by a single goal—philosophical enlightenment and liberation of the human race from nefarious political, religious, or economic authority, and more broadly the strengthening and expansion of the democratic principles and practices in the country at large. In both organizations fraternal spirit is strong, and the latter had in fact been called a fraternity/sorority where members form unbreakable attachments, a leaven in the baking of the bread of democracy.

Yet in addition Center for Democratic West had always resembled a G2 Section since it nurtured cloak and dagger stratagems, intrigue, secrecy, and underhanded methods. When Huston was still in command these were necessary for survival, but after his flight and the country's return to the Constitution of 1787 they remained innocuous peculiarities, fancy figures traced on a sundial. Yet though the tenor of the center changed with the times the sustaining web of loyalties and attachments remained as strong as of old. Every loss was mourned irrespective of whether it was a section chief or a simple foot soldier who had fallen to an enemy bullet, and every assistance was extended to his or her family. It was this spirit of fraternity and solidarity that elevated the center to new ethical heights and made it a paradigm for others to follow.

In early September a mantle of sadness descended on this venerable institution. Kevin Schultz, who had been hospitalized weeks earlier, was not getting any better. Just the reverse, he was getting worse. The Cheyenne doctors and the specialists summoned from Chicago and Los Angeles could do very little to improve his condition. He was continually losing weight and was so weak he could no longer stand up. He was carried to the examination room and wherever else he wanted to go. His friends held their breath, but what infuriated them was the doctors' apparent inability to provide a diagnosis. "It's a very rare case," they kept repeating, "and much of it is fueled by the mind."

"Explain," Kevin's friends demanded.

"It is clear to us that the patient has lost the will to live. More than that, he doesn't want to go on living."

"Do you mean to tell us Kevin is killing himself by the hour?" Jose Carero shouted indignantly.

"We wouldn't go that far," the head doctor answered patiently, "but Mr. Schultz's mental condition is at the source of it all."

Another specialist was called in, this time from New York, and a succession of tense conferences was held. As a result a daring new form of therapy was prescribed, new shots administered, and Kevin's diet fortified by a variety of powerful nutrients. Concurrently, intravenous feeding was continued to generate energy in the limp and emaciated body. The doctors waited for a week to ascertain whether the new treatment had helped the patient in any way, and a battery of tests was again conducted. Alas, not even the slightest improvement had taken place in the patient's condition, and the doctors were at their wits' end. Kevin was now white as a sheet, and he resembled a comatose skeleton more than a live human being. Deep dark lines encircled his eyes, and he was too weak to speak or move a hand.

Linda visited him often, usually in the company of Helen McKintosh, Nathan's sister, and friends were always in attendance. Kevin was eager to hear what was going on in the country, and these days the news was good. From time to time his eyes would light up elatedly, and for a brief moment it was a different Kevin lying there, the lingering commitment to life and the unabated commitment to the cause shining through. He appeared to be roused hearing the president's call to the combatants on September 15 to lay down their arms, but the very next day he reverted to a nearly comatose state.

When Linda and Helen visited him on the morning of September 20 his eyes were glistening, and he looked as if he desperately wanted to say something, but he could not and lay helpless. Linda and Helen each held his hand, and Linda felt Kevin was pressing her hand lightly, ever so lightly. Then she saw blood trickling out of his nostrils and ears, and she shouted to the attendant nurse, "Get the doctors, CODE BLUE!" Then she bent over him and kissed him on the forehead. Two minutes later the room was filled to capacity with doctors, nurses, laboratory technicians, and most impressive-looking medical apparatuses. No effort was spared to keep Kevin alive, but it was a lost cause from the very start.

When a gap opened by Kevin's bed as two enormous apparatuses were being hauled away, Helen touched Linda's shoulder. "Sit by him and hold his hand. It's only minutes now." Linda held Kevin's hand in both her hands and gazed deeply into his eyes. They were live and glistening, and she noticed a faint smile forming around the mouth. She pressed his hand affectionately and saw the smile grow broader and turn almost into a grin.

Later in the day Jose Carero cornered the head doctor.

"It was a most unusual case from the very beginning," the doctor was saying, "but the end was even more unusual."

"What was the cause of death, doctor?" Jose asked. "I take it you already have this information."

"Well, yes. We know the cause, or rather the causes, of death, but they are so strange."

"How so?"

"A minute or so before the code blue signal Mr. Schultz suffered a fatal cardiac arrest. This by itself would've caused death. But simultaneously—simultaneously, mind you—his lungs stopped functioning, thus cutting off respiration. Another cause of death. And thirdly, and simultaneously again, the patient sustained a massive internal hemorrhage, excess blood emptying through the nostrils, ears, mouth, and anus. This by itself would also have caused death."

"So?"

"So, it was the simultaneous confluence of three semi-independent causes of death—heart, lungs, and bleeding—that was responsible for your friend's demise. One would've been ample, but he was subjected to all three."

"And this is unusual?"

"Highly unusual. In fact, almost unheard of."

"I see." Jose intended to go on, but the doctor interrupted.

"Let me anticipate your next question. Kevin Schultz did not commit suicide. There is absolutely no indication of any external substance being absorbed by the organism, and there is no indication of the cardiac arrest being self-induced any more than the breathing being stopped by an overt act. How could there be? I'll be able to tell you more after the autopsy, but these findings hold water."

"I see. But the state of Kevin's mind you referred to several days ago—his losing or having lost the will to live. What bearing does this have on his passing away?"

"The mind influences the body all the time and vice versa, but not to this extent. There were physical causes for the hemorrhage, for the cardiac arrest, and for the collapse of the lungs. The mind as such had very little to do with any of them. Extreme fatigue of the patient, his extreme debilitation, these are certainly factors to be considered, and as I told you I'll be able to tell you more after the autopsy and after we run another battery of tests."

"Thank you, doctor. I'll be most obliged—"

The head doctor pierced Jose with the keenest of gazes. "If your friend wished and prayed for death, whatever the reasons, it may very well be the gods answered his prayers and made damn sure there'd be no slipup. I rather fancy—and here I know I am venturing into the unknown—the gods admired his perseverance, his guts. He was their kind of guy. Who knows what'll happen to Kevin when he crosses the Styx. Like men, the gods have their soft spots."

He gave Jose another of his cryptic smiles and walked away.

/   /   /

On the evening before his hasty departure, Everett Huston was once again privileged to behold the countenance of God. This latest vision was by far the most beautiful in which he had been permitted to venerate and admire the Almighty. This time the Lord appeared to him very differently attired and commanding an entirely different historical setting. He saw before him a man in his late forties or early fifties dressed like a Victorian gentleman of means wearing a dark suit with an upturned, starched white collar from the middle of which a checkered cravat hung down onto a dark waistcoat.

His head was entirely bald with thin patches of dark hair rising above the temples, and His complexion was pallid and delicate. A thick moustache extending all the way from one end of the mouth to the other strengthened His sense of authority. Undoubtedly, he was a man of importance in business, in the government, or in the halls of academe.

A rousing memory shot through Everett's brain. Years ago, when he was still in high school, Mr. Tibbs, the English teacher, tried to interest the class in the "Art for Art's Sake" movement of which he was a devotee. He lectured at length on Théophile Gautier, Algernon Swinburne, Oscar Wilde, and others, but his favorite was no less a person than Walter Pater, essayist, critic, and novelist, lengthy portions of whose *Marius the Ephicurean* Tibbs read ecstatically to the class.

Everett remembered that in the remote time a "Walter Pater Club" had been formed in the school. The few who had joined met at Mr. Tibbs' house searching for beauty in medieval texts and Renaissance paintings, praising form in poetry above all else, and paying homage to pure art, art that was not an imitation of nature and was devoid of all moral, intellectual, social, and political considerations. The young aesthetes built an altar to beauty, which in the words of Wilde was "The symbol of all symbols," and they were experiencing aesthetic emotions on a scale unparalleled in the history of this particular high school. As for young Ev, at the mention of the word "art," or of the expression "art for art's sake" he either belched or farted, depending on which came first, and he would have preferred to pull stakes and not graduate than to join Mr. Tibbs's wimpish club.

However, the gospel of aestheticism was preached not only in the privacy of the English teacher's home but openly in the daily periods. Mr. Tibbs would bring with him to the classroom reproductions of *Yellow Book,* portraits and photographs of the principal players called to the lists, and other holy relics and mementos.

Electrified by the vision, Everett could not help but reflect on how closely the large oleograph of Walter Pater his teacher had paraded before the class years ago resembled the figure now transfixing him with a severe inquisitorial gaze—the same features, the same bald head, the same authoritative expression, and identical clothes down to the checkered cravat.

"Which was the dead spit of the other?" Everett wondered. "Or were they both one and the same person? Had the Almighty assumed the persona of an art-for-art's-sake promoter of over forty years ago, selecting an obscure high school teacher as his mouthpiece and now staging a repeat performance? Or was this the deity's first entrance upon the stage in the guise of Mr. Pater? Which was it? Or was there something entirely different in the mix?"

"I am the Lord thy God," the sonorous voice announced peremp-torily in the manner of an old-fashioned schoolmaster who command-ed obedience.

"Yes, sir," Everett replied. "I am greatly honored."

"The hour draws near when you and a handful of others will be rewarded as no son of Adam has been rewarded. You will be lifted to the celestial regions where beauty, pure beauty, reigns, and beauty will be your nectar and ambrosia." In a style of cumulative richness and sonor-ity, delicate, full of melody, and highly ornamented, the Lord gave a description of this paradise of beauty where perfection of form, bold invention freed from moral and utilitarian shackles, and a bent for the perverse and the super-refined had created a new vision of art—a vista of poems, musical compositions, canvases and pieces of sculpture, each of which was beauty in its purest and truest form.

"A score of master craftsmen have already been laboring for months in the new paradise, and you will be joining them, Everett. You've been called and you've been chosen, and presently you'll be assigned to the team where you can do most good," the Lord went on. "Have you worked in wood at all?"

"When I was a kid I collected firewood for the Atkinson Garage and Repair Shop. They needed a furnace going fourteen hours a day, and they paid me fifty cents per short ton."

"This is not what I asked, idiot!" The rebuking tone sent a shiver down Everett's spine. "Did you work with wood as a medium? Ornaments, sculpting?"

"No, Lord Almighty, I sure didn't."

"Write verse, do you? Or paint, watercolors or oil? Or maybe you compose in your spare time?"

"None of the above, Your Divine Majesty."

"That's odd." Everett was cringing under the Lord's contemptuous stare.

"I leave the selection of worthy candidates for the Paradise of Aestheticism and Decadence to my three archangels: Algernon, Oscar, and Théophile, who are the soul of expeditiousness and efficiency. Still, in any bureaucracy foul-ups are bound to happen, and it's just possible that my superb trio of assistants picked up a candidate who doesn't belong." The Lord paused and then sputtered out in the tones of a hanging judge, "One who doesn't belong!"

Everett raised his hand to be allowed to speak, but the Lord summarily dismissed his request.

"Foul-ups are bound to happen, but I always stand by the men. Their decision will not be reversed. It would be bad for morale."

"So what's going to happen now, oh Lord, my God?" Everett asked most respectfully, mustering the little courage left in him.

"It's very simple. You'll have to take some remedial courses to catch up with the others. Nothing to worry about." For a moment, Everett could swear to it, the Lord's gaze exhibited a ghost of kindliness.

"Which way does your aesthetic sensibility spur you on, my son? Toward poetry and music, or would it be toward painting and sculpture? Beauty can be found in each of these arts." At this moment there was more than a touch of kindness in the Lord's words. Of necessity, taking the measure of the situation, quick as a flash Everett made an instantaneous decision. He had to play the game or he was lost.

"It's the written word and music that attract me the most," he blurted out, pretending to be overcome by emotion. "But this in no way excludes the oil, the watercolor, and the shaping of three dimensional figures together with idealized parts of the landscape using whatever medium is appropriate. One more word . . ."

"Yes?" the Lord was in a state of suspense.

"In the search for absolute beauty we should also rivet our eyes on immortal monuments of architecture. Beauty springs from a fitting arrangement of lines, from space and proportion so employed as to create unique delight for the soul, an aesthetic alpha and omega."

"Excellent," the Lord commented with feeling. "Maybe after all Algernon, Oscar, and Théophile made the right choice, and there was no foul-up. You'll be a worthy craftsman in our heavenly creation and resurrection of beauty."

Emboldened, Everett bowed low and posed a question in the most respectful of tones. "In the previous visions you had always put great emphasis on the entire Western Amernippian nation being lifted up to heaven as a reward for its exemplary conduct. I am head of state, and you made a pledge that I and my people would ascend as Jesus Christ had once ascended. I am the leader of my people—"

As he was uttering these words the Lord pulled a scrap of paper from his coat pocket, glanced at it, and nodded. "And so you are," he shot back.

"I am the leader of my people, and I hold their welfare and their imminent salvation near and dear," Everett continued. "I am responsible to my people and a promise was made."

"What promise?!" the Lord hollered at him with fury. *"What promise?!"*

No longer caring, Everett recounted the circumstances of the previous visions in which the Almighty had appeared to him with particular stress on the last one and its exhortation to the people to repair to the famous city by the sea. "A promise was made," he asserted, "and promises are sacred."

The Lord shook his head this way and that. "You've been had, son, and I can make an educated guess who's behind it."

"Who?"

"Why, Satan, Prince of Darkness, the perennial gentleman."

"You appeared to me on all occasions as you are traditionally portrayed on canvas and in Christian lore . . ."

"Excuse me," the Lord interrupted, "I did not appear to you. I never laid eyes on you before today. It was the other guy."

"Whoever. But I was assured my people would be taken out of this valley of sorrow and lifted up on high, to heaven to dwell eternally in the presence of the Almighty. Solemn promises were made, and with all due respect I expect them to be kept. By ascension duplicating that of Jesus Christ the entire Western Amernippian nation is to be raised into heaven. The people are waiting. They've been waiting for a mighty long time. And you, Lord my God, have an obligation to see to it your orders are carried out."

"Not my orders, son, not my orders."

"Sir!"

"Listen to me, Everett, and listen with both ears."

"Right."

"Art-for-art's-sake-heaven, which is the only heaven in existence in the universe, is for the select few. It is not, and I repeat, it is *not* some sort of crazy Yankee democracy. All master craftsmen who put their talent to the test there are highly cultured, highly sensitive, refined souls who create artifacts of superlative beauty and nurture its impassioned appreciation. Pure art, which surges from the billows of aestheticism, is for the few, for the happy few and not for the masses. It is the beauty-worshipping elite that matters, less than one percent of mankind, who are destined for heaven. The masses are ignorant, common, vulgar, and in the last resort, disgusting. They belong in hell."

"I want to be with my people as they embark on the heavenly journey. I owe it to them," Everett broke out half-angrily and half-plaintively. "Promises were made."

"You were conned not once but many times. You should've been more careful."

"I feel for my people. Let my people go."

"Your people are going nowhere," the Lord's dispassionate voice pulled him back into the present moment.

"And if I jump ship, tell the art-for-art's-sake heaven to go to hell?"

"You are being closely watched, and you've been stripped of freedom of choice. You will spend eternity creating and worshipping beauty, pure breathtaking beauty. You are one of the chosen, an angel of beauty."

"And if I revolt?"

"The punishment is too terrible even to be named."

"I am not afraid," Everett gasped. "I am the ruler of Western Amernipp. I am not afraid."

The Lord pulled at his moustache. "We expect from our angels superb craftsmanship and devotion to the task. But we also expect from them a personality fully developed along aesthetic and ecstatic lines. Personality development—you've heard of it, haven't you, Everett?"

"More times than I care to remember."

"Good. This is by way of a pep talk." The Lord shifted his feet so as to face Everett directly and snapped his fingers. A sublime expression adorned his visage, and he leaned slightly forward. "To burn always with this hard, gem-like flame, to maintain this ecstasy, is success in life. . . . Not to discriminate every moment some passionate attitude in those about us, and in the very brilliancy of their gifts some tragic dividing of forces on their ways, is on this short day of frost and sun, to sleep before evening. With this sense of the splendour of our experience and of its awful brevity, gathering all we are into one desperate effort to see and touch, we shall hardly have time to make theories about the things we see and touch. What we have to do is forever curiously test new opinions and court new impressions, never acquiescing in a facile orthodoxy. Great passions may give us this quickened sense of life, ecstasy and sorrow of love, the various forms of enthusiastic activity, disinterested or otherwise, which come naturally to many of us. Only be sure it is passion—that it does yield you this fruit of quickened, multiplied consciousness. Of such wisdom, the poetic passion, the desire of beauty, the lore of art for its own sake, has most. For art comes to you proposing frankly to give nothing but the highest quality to your moments as they pass, and simply for those moments' sake."

As soon as the Lord had finished speaking, his entire body, so prominent only a few seconds before, was losing its hard distinctness, and then only a faint silhouette was visible. Unhinged and resentful, Everett shook his fist and shouted at the top of his lungs, "Lord, let my people go, let them come with me to the heavenly mansion!" But by now there was no trace of the visitor, and Everett was shouting at an empty room.

/   /   /

While Brigadiers Sherman and Bolivar were flying troops, armor, and equipment to Virginia in the greatest air-transport operation in history, a life-and-death battle was soon to be joined in Italy on the outskirts of Rome. For two weeks the forces of the republic and the Catholic Brigade had been poised on both sides of the Tiber growing in numbers and waiting for the opportune moment to spring forth. At first the Italian strategy had been to remain on the defensive and let the Vatican forces march forward, cross the Tiber, and bleed profusely in frontal attacks. Intelligence received at Italian headquarters confirmed that the brigade was spoiling for action and that its generals would stake everything on one or more powerful thrusts to rout the enemy beyond the possibility of regrouping.

As suspenseful days followed one another, however, this strategy was deemed flawed and humiliating. In parliament, angry voices accused the government of pusillanimity. The future of the Italian nation hung in the balance, and the government was content to wait—just wait until the papal fascists finished their morning or midday meal and were ready to strike. "Shame, shame!" the protesters cried in cities where marches were organized and the populace made no bones about their contempt for the government.

In a matter of days the Italian leaders came round while opposition was drafting a vote of no confidence, and the international situation was getting more and more embarrassing. Clearly a new strategy was called for, and Fabian mentality would best be relegated to the dust heap. The generals were ordered to mount an offensive, the sooner the better.

Immediately however a serious problem made its way to the top of the list, previously soft-pedaled because of the defensive planning, and now seen for the first time for what it really was. The morale in the armies of the republic was low. Ill-paid and indifferently trained, the conscripts had no stomach for fighting and no yearning for glory. Most of them were hoping to be sent home before bullets began to fly, and they held politicians accountable. The internecine conflict should have been resolved by negotiations—the notion of civil war was absurd. Someone had blundered and went on blundering. Moreover nine out of ten draftees held the papal troops in high esteem, even though many of them were cutthroats and criminals. They admired their mettle and military skill. In haste the army assigned dozens of morale officers to the troops, but they seemed to have swayed few minds.

The Italian army, numerically superior to the foe, was encamped on the right side of the Tiber, five miles north of the bank over a ten-mile stretch, and the outposts adjoining the river extended all the way from Flumencino to Magliana. The Catholic Brigade positioned on the opposite side of the Tiber wound its way from Lido di Ostia along Via Cristoforo Colombo and all the way to Via Pontica and Grande Raccordo Anulare.

Unexpectedly papal commanders received reliable information from their agents that the republican armies would attack first in great numbers, aiming at the center to break the brigade's front line. They smiled scornfully. Those raw recruits and their elders, who had seen half a year or at most a year of military service, were no match for the fascist and neo-Nazi veterans, for the terrorists and the mercenaries, and for the inflamed Catholics who had been ordered by the Almighty to build a dictatorial Catholic empire on European soil where non-Catholics would be stoned to death or burnt at the stake. "Let them come," the commanders jested with one another, "those who miraculously survive the charge will be limping back with their tails between their legs, and anyway there won't be many of them." Confidence was high in the brigade on all the echelons, confidence born of having taken every precaution, of having made provisions for every contingency, and above all of having formulated a plan that was both daring and fail-safe.

On the other side, doubt and uncertainty reared their ugly heads. Attack they must, for this was the decision handed down from the prime minister's office, but even now there was no consensus within the high command as to which sector of the brigade would be stormed, in what manner, and with what weaponry. Getting wind of this disappointing information, the president of Italy, after consulting with the prime minister, called in his old friend, the only surviving marshal in the Italian army, whose bold strokes and counterstrikes in the Middle East campaign thirty years earlier kept the enemy at bay and eventually bisected them and forced them to surrender. The president explained the situation to the marshal.

"You have some bright lads in your high command, Pietro," the marshal said. "Some of them served under me as junior officers in the Middle East. But teamwork wasn't their strong suit. Why, some of them couldn't even agree what day of the week it was. Now they are general officers. Good luck."

The president nodded. "That's why, Rodolfo, I want you to take over. You'll be named supreme commander, and you'll have the government's full support."

"I am well over the age limit, my friend. Can't you appoint a bright young brigadier or major general if that mutual adoration society is not coming up to expectation?"

"There's no one I can trust, Rodolfo. No one. And Italy is calling to us. Yes, *la patria*. I am going to beg you if I have to, but maybe it won't come to that. I am not exaggerating the danger."

"So be it. When do you want me to assume command?"

"As soon as possible."

"I'll be with the troops tomorrow morning. Have the necessary orders cut."

"Thank you, Rodolfo."

"One more thing."

"Yes?"

"I want as many pontoons assembled and shipped by any means possible, by water or on wheels, to our outposts by the Tiber, with heavy concentration at Flumencino and Magliana. Let the work start at once."

"Done."

The marshal stood up and reached for his baton. "Stay well, old friend."

"May fortune smile on you, Supreme Commander."

Change in command did not exactly raise morale of the Italian army, but it made many a private, sergeant, and officer understand better the gravity of the situation and conclude that the nation would fight come what may and whatever the cost. The aged marshal was a national hero with a brilliant military record, and his being their commander infused pride into the heart of many a private, sergeant, and officer. They were led by a man who was an icon and a legend, the best strategist and tactician in the whole of Italy, and they knew he would not let them down.

Immediately upon his arrival intensive training in close combat was instituted, and what was done with pontoons, barges, and dinghies took one's breath away. Without anyone noticing, discipline became tighter, *esprit de corps* won many converts, and this multitude of disparate individuals was at last beginning to think, breathe, and act like an army. The next three days were spent in curiously contrived maneuvers, night exercises, and small arms practice. On the afternoon of the fourth day the marshal addressed the troops and informed them that their training was proceeding satisfactorily, more night exercises being scheduled for the next three days. This day, he told them, was their R and R, advising they should retire early in view of a possible exercise in the middle of the night.

As darkness was descending on the camp, full moon became a cynosure many eyes riveted on, and it held a promise, a prospect of better things to come. Suddenly just below, it three brightly lit figures impressed themselves upon the sky, and there was no mistake as to who they were: the pillars of Risorgimento, Camillo Benso di Cavour, Giuseppe Mazzini, and Giuseppe Garibaldi. Their voices boomed to the ground, and those watching them were transformed, born anew.

"Fight for Italy, for democracy, and never forget the primacy of individual conscience over external authority!" cried the voice of Cavour.

"Remember, my brothers and sisters, that Italy has a sacred mission to lead other nations to social justice!" cried the voice of Mazzini, "Defend the sacred Italian soil for it bears a seed that will grow into the brotherhood of all men, of all human beings everywhere. *Giovane Italia.*"

"Fight against the thugs of the Vatican with the same courage my Redshirts have shown in years past fighting the enemies of motherland. Fight on and on, courage, courage, and courage again, for our cause is just." There was no mistaking this voice. It was Garibaldi's. The three exhorted the troops for several more minutes, and then just as mysteriously as they had appeared they vanished from the sky.

The news of the apparitions spread like wildfire, and when at 0330 hours the men were awakened to carry out an assault on the papal brigade they were in high mettle. Orders were executed with alacrity. The marshal had conceived the plan of a nightly assault but not from the center. Instead a quarter of a million of highly motivated troops crossed the Tiber on dozens of hastily fitted-together pontoon bridges, far outside the city limits at both ends, and in the southwest practically touching the beaches of the Tyrrhenian Sea. The two flanks, with light armor in front and infantry in trucks and on foot, converged on the dense concentration of papal forces in the center just outside Rome.

The advancing republicans mowed down the astonished and half-asleep enemy and destroyed equipment using submachine guns, heavy machine guns, flamethrowers, hand grenades, and grenade launchers. As for artillery, it had been left behind so as not to demolish buildings and, wherever possible, private property. The republican advance from both ends toward the middle was deadly, but soon the enemy rallied and tried to make a stand in three different locations before the two republican wings joined hands. It was a gallant attempt, but it came too late. The crucial element of surprise, the numerical superiority of the Italian army, and above all its newfound determination and outstanding bravery sealed the fate of the Catholic Brigade. Even so, the battle raged for more than three hours, from 0400 hours well beyond 0700 hours, and respite came only with the first light of dawn.

On the Catholic side casualties were particularly heavy: more than sixty thousand dead and seriously wounded, and on the Italian side ten thousand. When the last shot was fired the Italians held over seventy thousand prisoners, and a large POW camp was promptly established in Campagna di Roma. A handful of high-ranking brigade officers were hiding in the Vatican, and the marshal requested their surrender. It was acceded to without an incident.

In the weeks to come special military courts and other tribunals were formed to try enemy combatants. Italians who had served in the Catholic Brigade were charged with treason, but because of the extraordinary circumstances attending this ill-starred rebellion most of them received light or suspended sentences. Foreigners enlisted in the brigade were deprived of combatant rights and were treated as felons. With very few exceptions they were sentenced to twenty or more years of hard labor, and the courts did not differentiate between officers and rank and file.

Within a week after the cessation of hostilities the Vatican sent emissaries to the Italian government asking for the resumption of amicable relations between Vatican City and civil authorities. They were seeking a return to status quo ante, and to show their good will they announced that six high officials of the Roman Curia who had been active in the formation and training of the brigade were willing to surrender unconditionally to the state. The offer was accepted, and the six were placed within national criminal jurisdiction. The matter of damages that the state demanded from the Vatican dragged on for months but was finally settled to the complete satisfaction of the state.

Like a nightmare that reasserts itself again and again the Vatican's aggression against the democratically elected government and the Italian state haunted the minds of millions of Italians for years. But this nightmare was palliated by the joy that the state won and that the fascist conspiracy was foiled, exposed, and brought to its knees. Italian democracy scored an important victory, though it was touch and go for a while, and this victory energized democratic movements all over the world. Italy pointed a moral and adorned a tale. Last but not least, good triumphed over evil.

/   /   /

Unseasonably, torrents of rain, not of snow, poured down on central Wyoming in early October and were followed by scorching weather reminiscent of the summer. On a radiantly sunny day seven figures sharply silhouetted against a cloudless sky were making their way across Antelope Hills in the northwesterly direction. Their car had broken down as soon as they had crossed Sweetwater, and Les and Mary Adams, its owners, had suggested taking a shortcut across the hills to reach South Pass City on foot, where Mary's sister lived and where they would be welcome.

The others in the party were Jock Withers, at first corporal in the recent war of liberation until he was awarded a battlefield commission, the only African-American in the Virginia theater of operation so honored, recently discharged and looking for work. Julie Hoffman and Griffith Cistek, former political prisoners, freed and expecting a compensation from the government, were heading west to start a new life and put the painful memories of the New Jersey gulag behind them. Paul Ramon, an illegal immigrant from Mexico, later a decorated sergeant in the Virginia campaign, also recently discharged from the army, was settling down in his adopted country. And Susan McGinnis formerly an undercover agent for Democratic Western Amernipp, now nearly nine months pregnant, hoped to reach the hospital in Lander before birth pangs set in. She eventually planned to end up in Idaho where she had friends and an offer of employment. Starting off from Muddy Gap, Les and Mary had offered to take the five strangers in their van as far as South Pass City or Lander, whence they would proceed by Greyhound or some other means to their respective destinations. The midday sun was scorching and, wiping their foreheads, they took short breaks to regain energy.

"Just try to make it, Susan. From South Pass City you'll be driven straight to Lander," Mary tried to cheer her up. "The hospital there is top-notch, pride of the county."

"It's just a little ways now," Les joined in. "Over the next two hills, and then down you go."

"I don't think I can make it, Mary," Susan admitted, gasping for air. "The pains are starting."

"In that case, honey, we'll have to perform something close to a natural childbirth. I've assisted doctors in all kinds of ways, but never in delivery. Still there's always the first time."

"Fifty yards to the left or so there's a creek. Let's carry Susan there," Les said.

Jock, Paul, Griff, and Les carried the mother-to-be and made her comfortable on a spread out pile of blankets and coats.

"Those soapy napkins from breakfast will come in handy now," Julie exclaimed.

"Sure will," Mary assented. "Julie, look after the patient. I gotta scrub, don't you know. In the creek too, and you gotta believe me."

Julie held Susan's hand and gently stroked her body.

"It's a shame your boyfriend can't be with you now. He's the father, isn't he?"

"Bert? Yes, he's the father, and there can be no mistake about it. But, but . . . "

"Yes, Susan."

"We had one hell of a row and he walked out. Our child may never see his or her father." Then her face was contorted by pain. "I think it's coming. I can feel it."

"Yes, it's on the way," Julie leaned forward and whispered in Susan's ear. "I'm not a nurse, but I've been around hospitals. You're having twins. You're far too big for just one brat."

Susan smiled and noticed that Mary was back sitting by her side. "Let's get ready," the latter announced, her voice ringing with authority as she unfolded a sheet and two large handkerchiefs. "Are the pains regular-like, one after the other?"

"Yes?"

"Then it's coming. Julie, will you assist me?"

"Of course."

The four men were standing several yards away left to their own devices. But presently Jock's voice rang out. "Mary, anything we men can do?"

"Right. Have your canteens ready. When we need more water we'll holler. And when the actual delivery occurs, and Susan appears in all her glory, then I want you men to look the other way. You too, Les, for a man's lechery doesn't decrease with age. Just the reverse." Then she moved very close to Susan and held both her hands tight.

"Honey, I want you to push forward. Push forward as hard as you can. You'll be all right. Push forward and pray."

Susan's face brightened, and she was doing her very best. Through the film of pain her cheer rose and touched all her companions. And when she spoke her voice was resolute. "Dear God, let it be boys—boys who will grow into men and fight for a better America."

Epilogue

John Scaggs never came back to Wyn Purdue. On the first day of the battle at Medina, New York, he was mortally wounded in the chest and died two hours later at a M.A.S.H. unit. Shortly thereafter Wyn sold her house in Hempstead and moved lock stock and barrel to John's house in Cambridge, her cats reserving judgment as to the appropriateness of this wholly unexpected decision. From the outset the neighbors and passersby took due note of a large nameplate proudly announcing that this was the home of John Scaggs and Wyn Purdue, who soon became a popular figure in the neighborhood. Those who knew her slightly swore that Wyn's house was full of guests and visitors at all times because they heard a continual chatter and her voice rising in questions, explanations, admonitions. The aficionados knew better. They knew Wyn entertained few visitors but was in frequent colloquy with her cats whom she pronounced to be unusually vocal and literate.

Wyn kept the home fires burning, and John's birthday, August 18, was always celebrated in a grand style—his friends, former coworkers, and well-wishers in respectful attendance at the reception, as well as, in smaller numbers, carefully-screened faculty members and administrators. On these occasions Wyn was a stickler for protocol and horseplay was frowned on. At the appointed time glasses were raised before John's portrait hanging over the fireplace, painted in the days of his youth and showing him to the world as a jolly and handsome guy who shirked neither work nor play. Invariably John's neatly pressed sergeant's uniform was hanging on one side of the fireplace and his warrant officer's uniform on the other, and Wyn usually had a few words to say about her friend's role in the Middle Eastern campaign and the more recent war of liberation, in the course of which he had been promoted to an officer's rank.

As years went by these birthday celebrations became progressively more and more lavish, and in addition to a growing list of guests, a glee club from a local high school was invited to join in tribute to the well-remembered John Scaggs. The order of the day included also speeches and eulogies by John's old comrades-in-arms and by public figures, some of whom tried to make of it, to Wyn's intense displeasure, a political occasion.

Her proudest moment came ten years after John's death when MIT named a new building in his honor. She was surrounded by the institution's president, the mayor of Cambridge, the governor of the state, and other notables as she cut the ribbon opening the building to the general public, a posthumous recognition of her friend's faithful service to MIT over many years and his more striking services to the nation.

Linda Chadwick still lives in Cheyenne surrounded by a select circle of friends. She is always ready to help aspiring democratic activists and politicians with her knowledge of the state and her intuition, but with the passage of time her role as a resource person and advisor became more and more circumscribed. Moreover, with the return to the Constitution of 1787 at the end of 2084 the Center for Democratic West ceased to be the hub and headquarters of democratic action.

Two years after the victorious war of liberation, in the fall of 2086, Congress declared the very ordinary Cheyenne brick building with the most extraordinary history to be a national monument and a national treasure. From then on it housed archives, a library, and a large collection of mementos and artifacts of those tense and daring years when those working under its roof fought at first alone against the theocratic tyranny, and later headed the national democratic crusade. Every year visitors to the center count legion, and for the citizens of Wyoming it soon became the most important manmade site in the state, a symbol and a yardstick of their potential and willpower.

Nor was the prime resident of the old center forgotten in the euphoric years following the national recovery. In the summer of 2087, Congress enacted a law designating Nathan Chadwick's birthday,

January 25, a national holiday. Later in the same year on June 18, the anniversary of the nuclear attack on Riverton and Worland, was christened DDR, Day of Dire Remembrance, to be observed nationally in the manner appropriate to this tragic event. As before, Linda stays close to Agnes and Walden. She has not remarried.

As for the pharmacist-to-be and the future MD, on Agnes' eighteenth birthday their engagement was officially announced. Agnes soon joined Walden in Denver, where he pursued his medical studies and she enrolled in a school of pharmacy. As their professional training reached the final phases they tied the nuptial knot and several years later they were the proud parents of two bouncing boys with infinite capacity for mischief. Properly licensed and fully dedicated to their respective professions, they made a good team.

Walden's parents' affection for Agnes was as strong as ever, but of late it began to manifest itself in a bizarre manner. Myra took to referring to Agnes as "my daughter," and introduced her in that capacity to neighbors and acquaintances. Initially Walden assumed it was a loving slip or a momentary hyperbole, but when this misidentification continued mother and son crossed swords.

"Mother, please get it through your refined, upper-class, high-society skull that Agnes is my wife and not my sister. We have two children and you are a grandmother, no matter how vigorously you may deny it."

"I have nothing to say on the subject," Myra would say, and when Walden turned to his father asking him to set the record straight, Philip would either leave the room or attend to his son's request in a most perfunctory fashion.

"Mother, if you really think Agnes is your daughter, and not your daughter-in-law, you should consult someone in the profession," Walden would urge her.

"What profession is that, young man?" Myra would inquire, and Walden would tell her without mincing words. "If you are on the point of having one of your attacks of rudeness, son, one of us will have to leave the room," Myra would announce grandly. "We have tried to bring you up properly, but it is clear we have failed."

The rest of the exchange would also lead nowhere, and in the end nothing had been aired or clarified. If anything, Agnes was amused by her mother-in-law's idiosyncrasy. "I don't think she's hurting me or anybody else," she would say, and she welcomed the affection in which Myra and Philip held her. "Besides, this nonsense about my being your parents' daughter is only for their friends' consumption in Cheyenne. It doesn't affect our life here in Denver."

"No, it doesn't," Walden agreed. "But I don't want it to spread."

"Do what you think is best under the circumstances, love, but proceed gently. I rather think she needs help."

"Precisely," Agnes's husband concurred, "and the sooner she gets it the better. Who knows what else may ooze out of my mother's well-shaped head."

"Whatever you do, don't force things into a crisis. It isn't worth it. Think of Myra as a patient, not a troublesome old woman."

Walden laughed. "Easier said than done, but I promise I shall try." He held Agnes close to him, very close.

Soon after this conversation Walden sought out his father in his consulting room in Cheyenne. "Don't you think, Father, that Mother ought to receive help, psychiatric help? She hallucinates. She mistakes Agnes for her daughter, which makes our union incestuous since according to her I am married to my sister."

"Yes, I know," Philip replied. "But otherwise her behavior is perfectly normal."

"I wonder."

Philip pressed a button on his desk and spoke through the intercom.

"Terry, I shall be tied up with my son for the next half hour. Hold my calls, sexy thing that you are, and move the next appointment up by forty-five minutes."

"Yes, sir."

Philip leaned forward in his chair and cast a quizzical gaze at his son. "This conversation is overdue, Walden. I should've spoken to you earlier, months ago, and I didn't. Your mother has been under discreet psychiatric observation for six months now, by highly qualified doctors whom I trust, trust implicitly."

"And the diagnosis?" Walden shot back.

"It is unanimous. Her misreading of uncontested facts applies only to your wife. The causes are multiple and here interpretations vary. The advice I've received is to leave things as they are, and localize your mother's misidentification of your wife to a handful of people in

Cheyenne, establishing at the same time a kind of cordon sanitaire between your mother and the rest of the world, principally between your mother and your own family in Denver."

"This strikes me as very odd advice," Walden uttered the words clinically without even a trace of emotion. "Your colleagues refuse to go to the root of the problem."

Philip shook his head very slightly. "Over the years I never took you into my confidence. I didn't, but you are entitled to know the truth. I am responsible for at least some of the psychological malaise that has plagued your mother for years. I wasn't there when she needed me. I offered no support. In the course of our marriage I have been involved with other women. All these factors weighed insidiously on your mother's mind. Her present condition is to a very large extent my doing."

Walden was very still, but presently a friendly, understanding smile lit up his face. "Aren't you chivalrously accepting too much blame, Father? It looks to me that Mother had a predisposition. Besides, I imagine she reacted in kind when it came to your philandering and your offering no support."

"Yes, she did, but the culpability was not hers alone."

They went on talking for another good half-hour, and Walden could not shake off his astonishment that this conversation was taking place at all. He made a mental note: "The first and the last time."

Presently his father again leaned forward. "The bottom line is I don't want your mother to be dragged through psycho wards."

"That's understandable."

"But I am also determined that no unpleasantness due to fanciful notions of consanguinity shall be inflicted on you, your wife, and your children. This is what I promise: no matter what tall stories your mother may be telling a neighbor or a friend here on native ground in Cheyenne, when we or when she visits you in Denver all facts will be respected, and your mother will look upon Agnes, very affectionately no doubt, as her daughter-in-law. My own attitude toward Agnes is a foregone conclusion, since it is widely known that I am very fond of my daughter-in-law. Is it a deal, son?"

"It's a deal, Father, but are you sure you can deliver?"

"Oh yes, I sure can deliver. Put your fears to rest."

"I am sorry if I made your patients wait."

"Terry will explain and keep my name unblemished. She's a sexy little thing, isn't she?"

"Yes, Father."

In the 2080s and 2090s Jose Carero served two consecutive terms as governor of the state of Wyoming on the Republican ticket. Even before his second term had run its course he was asked to announce his availability as a candidate for the U.S. Senate, but he declined. He let it be known he had had enough politics to last him a lifetime, and he proposed to spend more time with his family and attend to a small business he owned. He was missed in the political arena—the man who at a critical stage had carried on Nathan Chadwick's legacy and later contributed so much to the welfare and prosperity of the state.

Siegfried La Rochelle's first two years as a farmer in Japan were marked by dismal and total failure. Apparently the wrong products had been selected, the wrong kind of seeds sowed, at the wrong time of year and with the help of the wrong fertilizers. Everything that could go wrong had gone wrong, and as if this were not enough torrential rains had wiped out what was left of the crops. Siegfried accepted these reverses philosophically, but he was told by friends and well-wishers that these biennial disasters could have been avoided had he chosen the right agricultural products and had adhered to prescribed and tested practices. It transpired subsequently that the former National Security Advisor had relied on antiquated manuals and, worse still, on agricultural precepts compiled in countries as far removed from Japan as possible in centuries past, with seventeenth-century France and the environs of Clermont-Ferrand playing a prominent role in his calculations. Siegfried regretted what he called a "not entirely satisfactory planning process" but otherwise evinced no contrition.

By this time Sayko's patience was wearing very thin, and the empress's patience even thinner. Individually and together they gave a talking-to to Siegfried to which he listened patiently, Sayko melodramatically throwing her arms high in the air and crying out, "If you won't do it for me, husband dear, do it for our children." The empress, abjuring melodrama, spoke to her son-in-law like a schoolmarm. Siegfried's brow darkened, and at first he looked painfully out of sorts. Then a change came over him, and he took the censure meted out to him to heart.

The third year of Siegfried's adventure in Japanese farming proved to be a resounding success. He had been in close touch with agricultural experts, with the officials at the ministry, and with fellow farmers in the region. The crops were even richer than anticipated, and all the *i*'s had been dotted and all the *t*'s crossed. As a farmer the German Huguenot-turned-American-and-later-Western Amernippian genius-statesman was on the road to success, and the years that followed turned an early promise into a lasting fortune.

Concurrently Siegfried was penning his memoirs, a massive work in three volumes entitled *In My Country's Service*. Published at the end of the eighties, it was soon hailed as one of the most significant political autobiographies of all times, detailing the U.S.'s rise to an unheard-of superpower eminence through its union with Japan and through its internal and foreign policy, and laying bare hundreds of diplomatic maneuvers and stratagems that made it possible.

For her part Sayko was becoming one of the leaders of Japan's financial world and a rising star on the Tokyo Stock Exchange. Still, for both parents, family carried more weight than anything else. After the wedding Sayko seemed to be breeding continually, no pauses allowed. In the first five years of their marriage she gave birth to six little monsters, each parent doting energetically on them individually and collectively, though Siegfried was occasionally rebuked by Sayko for forgetting their names. In the La Rochelle household family life took precedence over other obligations, and the two spouses saw uncannily eye-to-eye.

President Woods and then two subsequent presidents did their best to lure Siegfried La Rochelle back to public service but none scored the slightest success. "I am a family man and a farmer, and I want things to stay just like that," the eminent resident of Eastern Amernipp affirmed, and he discouraged political calls, inquiries, and requests for advice. The only exception was Timothy Hysart, who had free access to Siegfried at all times.

At the behest of the Savior of the Country Timothy Hysart filled in for the French leave-taking National Security Advisor and acquitted himself like his alter ego, which of course he was. Then, when the theocratic government collapsed like a house of cards, President Jack Woods retained the fast-talking New Englander in the same post, and when he was again elected to the presidency in November of 2084 he appointed him Secretary of State. Tim discharged his duties brilliantly, and in the years to come became a distinguished and highly respected director of Western Amernippian foreign policy, serving in this capacity in both Democratic and Republican administrations. In fact his tenure of office, which broke precedent, presaged a new practice in selecting members of the president's cabinet. To be sure, the two-party system remained unchanged and party politics played an equally important role as it had in the past, but a new trend was asserting itself: "Cabinet vacancies ought to be filled," many cried, "by men or women best qualified for the job, irrespective of party affiliation." In some instances this was easier than in others, and when the financial, commercial, or economic policy of the country did not shape its foreign policy the best brain was clearly the best candidate for Secretary of State.

On the other hand, some other departments, such as commerce or treasury, were much more dependent on and responsive to particular "philosophies," which largely determined the direction in which a given department was moving. In such situations the best brain might unfortunately belong to the wrong ilk, its intelligence quotient notwithstanding. Yet the new trend was gaining converts daily, and its muscularity had a double provenance: universities and big business. A handful of political scientists from several large universities banded themselves together into an association with a high-sounding name to put an end once and for all to party politics and realize a novel concept of government—that of manager, steward, and spokesman for all the people irrespective of party allegiances and legacies. The professors exchanged vows that under this dispensation a high government executive or the president himself would be no less than a scientist dedicated to the welfare of the entire electorate and would bear no allegiance to his or her party. Two doctrines were formulated in the academic smithies where ideals and practicalities were boldly juxtaposed and put under the microscope: the swap doctrine, whereby the cabinet of any incoming president would contain at least one-third of officers from the opposing party, this procedure being duplicated when the new president embarked on his career, thus a swap taking place every four years a third of the membership being infused from the other side of the aisle of the Cabinet making bipartisanship smoother; and the pairing doctrine whereby every congressperson and U.S. senator belonging to the party enjoying the majority in Congress would pair up with a colleague from the other party for the purpose of working together more expeditiously for the common good, party loyalties being thrown to the winds. CEOs who had formed their own association were somewhat baffled by what they called a blatant example of pseudo-scientific gamesmanship, which they also pronounced to be totally unrealistic. However, they too wanted party politics to be relegated to the trashcan and the country to be governed by captains of industry, the assumption being that they, captains of industry that is, were more concerned about the common good than the damned politicians. And so the CEOs stayed in The Alliance for Better Government though they often kept their own counsel. As years went by, the ideas of bipartisanship on a new scale, the swapping and pairing doctrines and related thoughts flickered continually without ever bursting into a mighty flame. Still the office of the Secretary of State was a constant reminder of what could be achieved in the uphill struggle, and Timothy Hysart was the darling of at least some academicians and some CEOs.

In the old days when Reverend James Hysart had been a staunch supporter of Chief Justice he had been respected and feared by the congregation. Most people had figured out he stood close to the throne, and there was pork galore flowing his way from governmental offices, which eventually percolated to the different echelons of the Church of the Holy Tabernacle. But in the summer of 2084 James Hysart turned against the Savior of the nation and soon became one of the most liberal Baptist ministers in the country. He fought against insidious forms of racial discrimination, his pro-choice stance was firm and repeatedly enunciated from the pulpit, he embraced gay rights with fervor, and he signed petitions for higher minimum wage and more comprehensive health insurance. His congregation, ninety-five percent of which was made up of African-Americans, began to love him as a father and apostle of good hope.

Hysart devoted himself to every form of social justice so far as his religious community was concerned, and he went farther afield. Without trumpeting it, he made it his business to come to the aid of those he called "the forgotten people": the incurably ill without resources to better their condition, the derelicts, those demoralized to the point of apathy, victims of drugs and alcohol, ex-jailbirds whose rehabilitation was slower than the slowest milk-train, the destitute, the underprivileged, the ones who had written off hope. No one was turned away, and the congregation loved Reverend James all the more.

Without anyone minding, the Church of the Holy Tabernacle became a hostel for the homeless, a soup kitchen, a rehab unit, a dressing station, a psycho ward, a counseling center, and the congregation loved Reverend James all the more.

In Washington D.C. secrets have very short legs, and sooner rather than later they become open secrets. Busybodies may have started the disclosures, but in no time everyone else is on the receiving end. It was common knowledge around Hysart's venerable Baptist church that relations between the minister and his two adult children, Tim and Emily, were strained. The community sided with the minister, perceiving little that could be praised in the son and daughter. "They are both stuck-up, and they have no respect for their father, our saintly minister," tongues wagged. "That Tim fella thinks he's the most important guy in all creation. If this isn't the mortal sin of pride, I ask you what else is," wagged other tongues. "And as for Emily, it is well known she's living in sin with a whitey, and a minister's daughter too. I ask you, dear, what is the world coming too?" the third chorus joined in.

Reverend James Hysart followed one good deed with another, and his fame grew. Honors and awards were conferred upon him by the Council of Churches, the International Baptist Brotherhood, by the Archbishop of Canterbury, the Pontiff of the Roman Catholic Church, the Chief Rabbi of Amernipp, and by countless religious, humanitarian, and charitable organizations. When he passed away in the summer of 2094, a well-placed journalist noted that the whole of Washington was in the funeral procession, and a good part of New York City, Boston, and Philadelphia into the bargain. Two individuals well known to the deceased did not join the ranks of distinguished and undistinguished mourners, his daughter Emily and his son Tim.

Joseph Oscar Pitkin lost his left arm to a mortar in the Virginia campaign and after the war's end decided to take a sabbatical from the rabbinate and enter politics. He served one term as a Democratic congressman from his district in Ohio and later, when an opportunity presented itself, he threw his hat into the ring campaigning for a senate seat. He won, and two productive terms as a U.S. senator followed, at the end of which he chucked politics and returned to the interpretation of the Law and other rabbinical duties, all this to the chagrin of his wife and daughters, who had easily gotten used to having an important political figure for husband and father.

Chief Rabbi Simon Hertzfeld was also in the war, for a short while on the front line, before being pulled back to headquarters where his experience as a staff officer in the Middle East conflict was greatly in demand. Witnesses later testified that upon being ordered from the front line back to headquarters Colonel Hertzfeld vented his fury in a language most unbecoming a man of the cloth, an officer, and a gentleman. He did not deny this fact; rather, he gave every appearance of being mighty proud of it. Once ensconced again in his office at the Temple, the returning warrior came to a momentous decision; from now on he wished to be addressed as Colonel Hertzfeld and not as Chief Rabbi or by an academic title. Eyebrows were raised, and comments exchanged mostly behind his back, but the colonel was adamant and those who did not observe the protocol were reprimanded.

Louise Hertzfeld, the patient and charming Louise, Simon's wife of many years, still avidly reads English classical detective novels and politely declines the hardboiled American detective stories following in the footsteps of Philip Marlowe and Sam Spade, which her grandchildren offer her as gifts. As in the past so now too, *The Scarlet Pimpernel* is still her all-time favorite, Louise and her good friend Betty Goetz continually engaging in spirited interlocutions on subjects close to their hearts.

President Woods won the election of 2084, but his margin of victory was slender and subsequent studies showed that it was the South that had put him over the top. After the election he conceived of his mission as being twofold: to make Western Amernipp again one nation after the internecine conflict and to bind up her wounds. In this he was largely successful, few regional witch hunts marring the political landscape of the country transforming herself, his repeated calls for forgiveness, toleration, and unity heeded. The appointment of the new Supreme Court was one of Woods' first priorities, and he cut a deal with the Republicans. As a sitting president he would fill five vacancies on the court and select a chief justice, the loyal opposition filling the remaining four vacancies, all nine appointees being subject to confirmation by the senate. Woods was much praised for his many efforts, but he was also constantly criticized by the Republican leadership. He was again a candidate for president in 2088, but this time he lost resoundingly to the handsome and very popular governor of a populous state.

At this point he retired from politics, returned to his native Georgia and became engrossed in numerous humanitarian projects.

Of the trio of Huston's faithful lieutenants only Homily Grister faced the high tribunal. The evidence against Phineas Léger and Ganymede Pillows was inconclusive, and reliable witnesses stepped forward crediting them with trying to dissuade Huston from committing some of his dastardly acts. Grister, who jeeringly informed the presiding judge that he was being cast in the role of the fall guy, was charged with multiple offenses, including being an accessory to the murder of Nathan Chadwick and to the murder of thousands who had perished in the nuclear attack on Riverton and Worland. The prosecution proceeded scrupulously, fully attentive to the spirit and the letter of the law, but in this exceedingly complex and elusive case the precise nature of culpability of the defendant was at times very difficult to establish. Meanwhile, the public was clamoring for swift and decisive punishment of the mass murderer, and the high tribunal inevitably took note.

In the end Grister was found guilty on all counts and sentenced to a ten-year prison term without possibility of parole, which many thought far too lenient a sentence. Be that as it may, the Grister trial was the last in a long series of criminal trials of Huston's henchmen and supporters who in their capacity of prison wardens and guards, criminal investigators, prosecutors and judges had clearly overstepped the bounds. The bloodcurdling past was laid to rest, and the country looked hopefully to the future.

Of the four crew members of Huston 84, which had carried nuclear bombs to Riverton and Worland, Glen Merrick, the pilot, and Cliff Bousson, the copilot, remained in the service. Warren Choytek, the bombardier, and Ed Kelly, the photographer, resigned their commissions and entered the private sector. Choytek joined a large commercial airline, and Kelly started his own film and photographic business, specializing in mountain scenery.

Once Huston was gone, Robbie Burger and Hershey Bar faced heartrending decisions. Whatever lure academia may have held for them at one time had evaporated, and besides too many fellow professors and administrators across the land were wise to their underhanded dealings when Huston was in power. There were blots on their escutcheons, and there would be a lot of explaining to do. Naturally the way lay open for them to relocate to an autocratically ruled country on another continent and offer their services to the head boy. But this would entail familiarizing themselves with the ins and outs of the political situation in the new country—a laborious process at the best of times. Moreover, in all those bailiwicks of absolute power, palace revolutions and other revolutions were the order of the day, and the new rulers seldom sinned on the side of compassion for the ousted ones and their followers.

After much soul-searching Burger and Bar opted to remain on native ground and attach themselves to law enforcement as informers and agents provocateurs. Their thorough knowledge of academic communities and of student life landed them in the not-so-hospitable arms of campus police and city cops, who viewed them with suspicion. In addition, ever since the collapse of Huston's regime, laws and police procedures in Western Amernipp underwent drastic changes, and nowadays word of a snitch alone amounted to very little.

The two former favorites of Chief Justice were brought down a peg or two. They investigated rowdy parties in fraternity and sorority houses, alleged offenses to public morals on and off campus, they infiltrated student organizations and had microphones planted in faculty lounges to uncover high treason hiding under an academic gown—but all these stratagems came to naught and no charges were ever leveled at anybody. Their pay was low, and they did a spot of moonlighting tailing unfaithful husbands and wives for a detective agency. They had no illusions that all their present labors were small potatoes, and there were days when they simply refused to look each other in the eye.

The bewitching memories of past glory came upon them unawares, and they bathed in them to their hearts' content. It was only the other day, they reflected, that they could be counted among the most powerful and influential public servants of the Huston regime, ferreting out the enemies of the state and sealing their fate. Surely they deserved better.

In less than a year after what had been named for posterity the Battle on the Tiber, Raoul Borgia, the pontiff of the Roman Catholic Church, took the unprecedented step of resigning, ostensibly for reasons of poor health. Insiders knew better. He retired to his native Valencia where he lived quietly, always happy to help out the local clergy with advice or a loan and remaining for the rest of his life a generous patron of the local soccer team. Considering what a big wig he had once been, the man in the street now found him modest, almost self-effacing. He grew into a valuable member of the community, and when he died in 2094 he was universally mourned. Once Borgia's resignation had been proclaimed, the election mechanism at the Vatican went into action. It was a relatively smooth run. On the third ballot a cardinal from the United Republic of Tanzania was elected to the throne of St. Peter. He was the first black pope in the history of the Roman Catholic Church.

In 2087, Prince Mikasa renounced his right to the imperial throne of Japan and embarked on a far-reaching program of architectural study, first in Eastern Amernipp and subsequently in the West. When, several years later, he was issued an architect's license he took up residence in Switzerland, a young architect full of mind-boggling ideas.

Shortly thereafter, at a reception given jointly by the Museum of Modern Art in Zürich and several art journals, he inadvertently spilled champagne on a young lady's dress, and as he was drying it off and apologizing for his clumsiness her face evoked memories of long ago. She was the daughter of the onetime Swiss ambassador to Eastern Amernipp with whose wife, an accomplished and very attractive lady with many a broken heart to her credit, the youthful prince had been at one time briefly involved. As Takahito was admiring Christina's composed countenance, the child Christina of twenty years ago—serious, self-contained and paying little attention to her mother's worldly lifestyle—flickered before his eyes, an apparition grown into a self-possessed and enticing woman. She was employed as an illustrator for several art and architectural journals and concurrently finishing her doctorate in art history, specializing in West European Baroque. It was love at first sight for both of them. They were married three months later and settled down in Zürich.

Takahito was achieving modest success as an architect and was gradually creating a style of his own. His architectural masters were all Westerners, among whom Frank Lloyd Wright occupied a place of special distinction. The grandson of the Japanese emperor learned much from the Wisconsinite of genius and lessons of Wright's "prairie" style, of low horizontal lines with strongly projected eaves, of open planning in houses and of many other innovations both in structure and aesthetics were indelibly imprinted on his own work. But to all these Takahito was adding an original feature not previously encountered in Western-style architecture. His private and public buildings invariably comprised an evocation of old animistic beliefs of Shinto religion, of spirits separable from bodies, of the *kami*, supernatural beings mostly beneficent who help humans, of objects and phenomena in nature endowed with conscious life, and of the complex interaction of the sun goddess and the supernatural order of being with the mortal order of being—all this being accomplished architecturally through the use of space, proportion, lines, eaves, arches, and through contrasts, overlappings, and blendings of the bulk and expanse. Slowly what came to be called "the Mikasa style" gained more and more followers and admirers, and Christina's loving husband was making a name for himself in the world.

For her part the loving wife found it revealing that one who had so resolutely uprooted himself nationally, religiously, and culturally, becoming for all practical purposes an assimilated Westerner, nevertheless made the traditional religious customs and rituals of Japan an important aspect of his architectural art. Takahito denied by word of mouth and in print that he was trying to build bridges between the Orient and the Occident, and usually so quick at giving tongue, he balked at the notion of explicating at length the aims of his art. This was regretted by many, yet his reputation grew.

Shortly after the November 2084 general election in Western Amernipp, Tarako Lepra made his peace with the government. He abjured violence and instructed his followers to do the same. From that point on he employed peaceful and parliamentary means only. Lepra served one term in the Eastern Amernippian Parliament, calling it the most stupefying and frustrating two years in his entire life. It was impossible to get anything done in that mutual adoration society made up, he told his associates, of "cranky old women and self-adulating pen-pushers." He was urged to run again, but his answer was "Never again!"

As he was becoming a legislator he married a fellow activist, but the union was not a happy one. Two years later the couple separated. Things were not going well for him. His grand plans had not been realized, not even in a tiny part; his socialist programs were unfulfilled, his world-shaking communal designs a dead letter. He was beginning to feel he was no more than another superfluous unnecessary human being in this irrational world, a back number. At one time the past had held the prospect of fundamental change, but it came to naught. He had been happiest when, years before, he crossed on false papers national boundaries, counseling, organizing, giving orders to stand firm or to shoot hoping that deliverance would come soon, very soon.

A Trotskyist, he fervently believed that only world revolution could make a difference and that birth of a new society, of a new world order, depended on it. But the revolution was lamentably slow in coming, and now he seriously doubted whether it was in the cards. Years before he had been convinced that his work was bringing the revolution closer and closer, if only by a day, if only by an hour, but now he saw the world locked into a greedy capitalist goosestep or into a bogus welfare state, with Marxist philosophy thrown to the winds. He was still running the Trotskyist Alliance in Tokyo, teaching part-time, and conducting workshops, but he realized he was no longer on the way to the Holy Grail. Many of his former fellow activists were dead or inactive, and his good friend Takahito had become utterly non-political. He visited the happy couple in Zürich, and the two men talked at length about old times. Alas, everything had changed.

He traveled to Western Amernipp to see for himself how the newly reborn nation was faring. He was disappointed. Linda understood his predicament and offered sympathy. So did Senator Pitkin and the fire-eating colonel, whom Joe laughingly called the Commandant of the Royal Guard and a part-time chief rabbi. Everyone he met was very polite to him, but he believed Western Amernipp and the Western world as a whole were brazenly rushing toward self-destruction. On the way back he stopped for a few days in Vienna, Prague, and Budapest and was not buoyed up by what he saw. He returned to Eastern Amernipp via the Russian Federation and caught up with his daily routine, which he was absolutely sure now was not worth a tinker's damn. He made the attempt to look on the bright side but could not muster enough strength. He was slowly withering on the vine.

The whereabouts of the eight remaining justices of the Supreme Court who had disappeared in the wake of Everett Zacharias Huston's hasty flight were never discovered. To be sure a paper or two would periodically print a story in the next several years that such-and-such former Supreme Court justice was spotted bartending in Jakarta, that such-and-such one made his livelihood as a bookie in Sydney, and still another one ran a brothel in Marakesh. But such accounts proved to be mere canards planted to beef up the papers' circulation. The eight justices had vanished into thin air.

Huston was another matter. For seven years all was silence. And then in the fall of 2091 startling reports came to light. Parties in three states, unknown to one another, observed on Sunday, October 8, shortly before ten A.M. a dirigible, a spacecraft, an enormous flying contraption, they could not be more precise, floating in the air. All three—Reverend Jonas Clifton, a clergyman in Greenwood, South Carolina, collecting his thoughts between services; Stew Hofmeister, a landscape gardener in Roanoke Rapids, North Carolina, getting ready with his family for a trip north to visit relatives; and Dolores Fouti, darling of Girlesques Inc., in Atlanta, Georgia, looking vaguely out of her kitchen window—beheld Chief Justice Huston standing aboard—there could be no mistake—smiling and waving as the enormous contraption rose higher and higher and at last disappeared from view. It was an event to remember. And in the months and years to come many a God-fearing man and woman heralded with deep emotion the good news that the one who had walked with the Lord had also flown with the Lord, and that the Lord had kept His word.